Vessel of Honor

The Negro National Anthem

Lift every voice and sing
Till earth and heaven ring,
Ring with the harmonies of Liberty;
Let our rejoicing rise
High as the listening skies,
Let it resound loud as the rolling sea.
Sing a song full of the faith that the dark past has taught us,
Sing a song full of the hope that the present has brought us,
Facing the rising sun of our new day begun
Let us march on till victory is won.

So begins the Black National Anthem, by James Weldon Johnson in 1900. Lift Every Voice is the name of the joint imprint of The Institute for Black Family Development and Moody Press, a division of the Moody Bible Institute.

Our vision is to advance the cause of Christ through publishing African-American Christians who educate, edify, and disciple Christians in the church community through quality books written for African Americans.

The Institute for Black Family Development is a national Christian organization. It offers degreed and nondegreed training nationally and internationally to established and emerging leaders from churches and Christian organizations. To learn more about The Institute for Black Family Development write us at:

The Institute for Black Family Development
15151 Faust
Detroit, Michigan 48223

Vessel of Honor

Melvin J. Cobb

© 2004 by
MELVIN J. COBB

All Scripture quotations are taken from the *New American Standard Bible®*, © Copyright The Lockman Foundation 1960, 1962, 1963, 1968, 1971, 1972, 1973, 1975, 1977, 1995. Used by permission.

Library of Congress Cataloging-in-Publication Data

Cobb, Melvin, 1969-
    Vessel of honor / by Melvin Cobb.
        p. cm.
    ISBN 0-8024-1365-X
    1. Bible. N.T. Acts—History of Biblical events—Fiction. 2. Church history
—Primitive and early church, ca. 30-600—Fiction. 3. Christianity and
other religions—African—Fiction. 4. Ethiopia--Fiction. I. Title.

PS3603.O2256V47 2004
813'.6--dc22

2003017223

1 3 5 7 9 10 8 6 4 2

Printed in the United States of America

This book is dedicated to my parents
the two people who introduced me to Jesus
and provided me with a wonderful upbringing.
Thank you very much.

Timeline of Nubian History

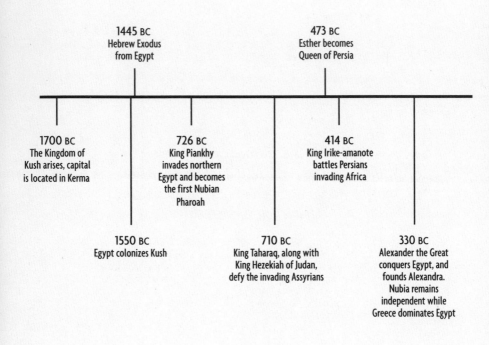

1445 BC
Hebrew Exodus
from Egypt

473 BC
Esther becomes
Queen of Persia

1700 BC
The Kingdom of
Kush arises, capital
is located in Kerma

726 BC
King Piankhy
invades northern
Egypt and becomes
the first Nubian
Pharoah

414 BC
King Irike-amanote
battles Persians
invading Africa

1550 BC
Egypt colonizes Kush

710 BC
King Taharaq, along with
King Hezekiah of Judan,
defy the invading Assyrians

330 BC
Alexander the Great
conquers Egypt, and
founds Alexandra.
Nubia remains
independent while
Greece dominates Egypt

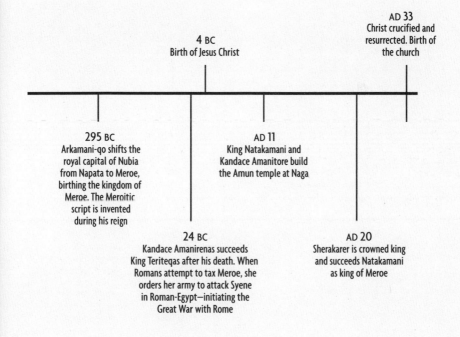

AD 33
Christ crucified and
resurrected. Birth of
the church

4 BC
Birth of Jesus Christ

295 BC
Arkamani-qo shifts the
royal capital of Nubia
from Napata to Meroe,
birthing the kingdom of
Meroe. The Meroitic
script is invented
during his reign

AD 11
King Natakamani and
Kandace Amanitore build
the Amun temple at Naga

24 BC
Kandace Amanirenas succeeds
King Teriteqas after his death. When
Romans attempt to tax Meroe, she
orders her army to attack Syene
in Roman-Egypt—initiating the
Great War with Rome

AD 20
Sherakarer is crowned king
and succeeds Natakamani
as king of Meroe

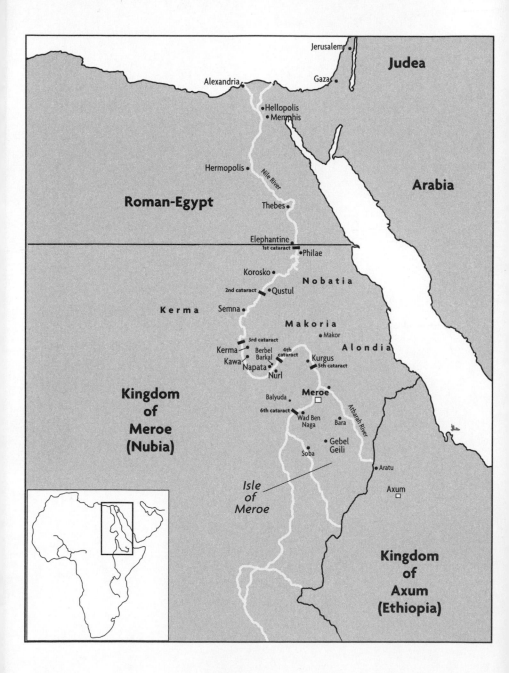

Prologue

A.D. 346

Great Ezanas*,
    Greetings in the name of the Most High God. I pray
that this epistle finds you blessed in mind, body, and
spirit. It is apparent to all of us here in Rome that the
Lord's hand is upon you. The fame and wealth that He
has lavished upon your kingdom is well-known from the
lands of Asia and Judea to as far as Spain. Indeed, the
seeds of faithfulness and perseverance that you sowed in
your youth have grown into a living legacy that shall
endure for generations to come. Your kingdom is more
than an affluent empire; it has come to be known as a
repository of Christian hope in a land that is laden with
idolatry and strife. Your obedience has altered the destiny
of Ethiopia, and it shall never be the same.

*King of the Axum Empire from A.D. 320 to A.D. 350. He is recognized as the
first king to declare Ethiopia a Christian nation.

Since retirement to private life, I have found a new peace, unrivaled by the tumultuous years that I spent in the service of the government. Aside from laboring in the ever-expanding church here in Rome, my greatest passion rests in mentoring my grandsons. I have wholeheartedly embraced the task of training them in the ways of the Lord. In addition, I have taken great pleasure in describing to them the glorious heritage possessed by our people. Though we are separated from Ethiopia by a large sea and desert, I have made a point to trace our connection to our forefathers' homeland through narratives and stories. Although we may be Romans by birth, I believe that it is imperative that we not forget the tree that sustains the branches from which we are grafted.

History. The importance of being in touch with one's history cannot be overemphasized. If a man is detached from the established record of his own people, then he faces jeopardy on two crucial fronts. First, he loses the support that a stable history lends to an individual. An accurate knowledge of the past provides one with a staunch grasp of his identity. Such an equipped man can rightly be compared to a mammoth boulder nestled upon the seashore. Though the ocean's mighty waves crash against it for a millennium, it remains steadfast, resistant to the ever-changing conditions around it.

The second potential peril is even more deadly than the first. King Solomon wrote, "People perish for a lack of knowledge." When the legacy of a culture is lost in the shadows of time, the strong possibility exists that its future will suffer the same tragic fate. An entire nation can disintegrate because it lacks proper vision of its past. We have seen such harsh lessons before in the ancient kingdoms of Israel and Egypt.

An avenue of ignorance is one of the greatest traps that the Adversary can devise. If truth is obscured, even for a short while, then a person—even an entire race of people—can fall prey to a cruel falsehood and erect their lives upon the shifting sands of a lie.

All of these elements ran uncontrollably through my spirit when I received your letter three years ago. I was more than humbled that you came to me for assistance to help you learn more about the Christian heritage that belongs to the church in Ethiopia.

Determining the approximate route in which the Christian faith advanced to your land proved to be quite a challenge. I proceeded at once to gather as much information as I could about the man who was known to be the first Ethiopian ever converted to faith in Christ. I dispatched investigators to the farthest corners of the Roman Empire in order to explore legends pertaining to this man. Over a relatively short period of time, information started to funnel in from Judea, Alexandria, Nubia, and even Arabia.

In the end, the Lord provided us with volumes of information on Sahlin Malae, the unsung father of the first African church. Recorded history dictates that he was a court official of Kandace Amanitore, a woman who ruled the old Nubian kingdom of Meroë over three centuries ago. Though he is virtually unknown today and now rests in an obscure grave in southern Egypt, he was apparently a man of great authority in his day.

As you will see, records show multifaceted views of this man. On one hand, he was a stalwart of faith and a chosen vessel hand selected by the Master Himself. But on the other hand, he was driven by the typical doubts and insecurities that haunt us all. The revelation of one's destiny can be frightening.

I have woven these narratives together out of the fabrics of historical facts, as well as oral traditions chronicled and passed down from one generation to another. I do not claim that all the stories from word of mouth are totally accurate and free from omission and/or embellishment. History is like a gem with many sides that reflect one image many different ways. Though it is valuable to all, it is not always viewed in the same light.

Above all, I have endeavored to write the truth, and truth often injures a haughty soul. Elements contained in the pages of these narratives present man's sinful nature at its worst; and this, unfortunately, is a portion of our heritage that we must behold and acknowledge.

My friend, it is my sincere hope that your interest in the history of the African church will spread among your subjects in Axum and Nubia. Since day one, I have constantly thanked the Lord for leading you to include me on this undertaking. Through it, the Holy Spirit has breathed upon me and changed my life. Though we have not laid eyes upon one another for many years, know this: I shall forever be your servant, your friend, and your brother in Christ.

In His Eternal Service,
Exekias Veridius**

**Black Roman statesman and intellectual commissioned by the church in A.D. 330 to assist the king of Ethiopia in adapting and implementing church doctrine.

Chapter 1

Sahlin Malae was plummeting into the abyss. Like a baby bird falling out of the nest, he flailed his arms desperately and prayed for a miracle that he somehow knew would not arrive in time. His stomach rolled uncontrollably and felt like a hollow gourd that was ready to be dashed to pieces on the jagged rocks below.

He opened his eyes to see the approaching floor of the Great Valley of Napata. Along with the hard stones, he saw the phantoms of his life's regrets that somehow made it down to the bottom before he did. He was able to make out each one clearly, and he rued the fact that the last images his mind projected were the twisted shadows of his own faults and shortcomings. One regret wore the sullen face of the woman that he had manipulated for many years. Another bore the image of a vizier that he had crushed only weeks before.

Unwilling to face the final reality of his degenerate state, Sahlin tilted his vision upward, toward the object of his desire.

No, it was more than an object; it was a presence for which he violently hungered. As the object grew smaller and more distant, he tried to figure out why he was not able to reach his goal—why he always fell short.

Sensing the inexorable approach of doom, he opened his mouth and voiced one last thought. "Lord God Most High, I have failed to reach You . . ."

❑   ❑   ❑

Awakening from his tormented slumber, Sahlin's eyes snapped open just in time to see the first rays of early morning sunlight pour into his room. Grateful that his body hadn't been dashed to pieces, he clenched his teeth and forced himself to exhale sharply.

Drenched in sweat, he propped himself up on one arm and tried to settle his senses. Though he knew that he was awake and the experience was no more than an overactive imagination, he still felt himself wavering between the horror of his dream and the exhaustion of his reality.

Yet, there was something more. He felt something—no, he felt someone. Instinctively, he forced his sleepy eyes to scan the room. He was convinced that his unauthorized visitor was standing next to his bed, silently waiting to reach out.

Not sure if he was yet awake from his nightmare, Sahlin stretched out his hand to grasp the visitor but found only air. Once he was certain that no one else was there, he rubbed his eyes vigorously and perused the room once more. Everything seemed in order. He felt his heartbeat finally start to slow down and resume a normal rhythm.

With his eyesight clear, he was able to distinguish the solid objects from their long shadows that were formed by the rising sun outside. As the light verified that the room was indeed empty, he felt relaxed enough to lay his head down and close his eyes again.

Today, I shall cast my eyes upon the City of David, he thought, allowing the silent words to echo deep within his soul. Images of the great city danced past his mind's eye. He and his companions lodged for the evening only a half day's journey from Jerusalem. It took him weeks to travel from the heart of Africa to the Roman province of Judea. He found it hard to believe that he was only a few hours away from completing the longest journey of his life.

Slowly, he rose from his bed and stood at the window. He peered down into the streets below and pondered the purpose of his life. At age thirty-five, he held the powerful post of chief treasurer in the queen's court, representing the fourth generation of his family to serve in such a capacity. Since before the Great Roman War, members of his family governed provinces and administered the affairs of the royal family. It was a tradition that he had been prepared his entire life to carry on.

He turned and stared at that collection of parchments responsible for his long journey. The discovery of the record that chronicled his grandfather's own search for truth and peace did far more than strike his curiosity. Most remarkable to Sahlin was the detail that his grandfather had taken to describe how and why he so fervently turned from the idols of Kush toward the God of the Falasha—the unofficial title given to the Jews who dwelt in southern Kush.

The writings continually referenced a future journey

to Judea that his grandfather intended to someday take. From everything that Sahlin could discern, the trip had to be made during or around the Passover in a specific yet undisclosed year. It almost appeared as if his grandfather was part of a prophetic mystery and was counting down to some extraordinary event. However, it was an excursion that Rahman never made. His journals tracked the numerous years that flowed past but never recorded any visits to Judea during that time.

"At least I managed to cheat death on my journey," Sahlin voiced softly, recalling the half dozen associates that warned him not to undertake the pilgrimage to Jerusalem. Nearly every soothsayer in the city of Meroë admonished him not to go, proclaiming that he would surely meet with death because of the trip.

It was late afternoon when Sahlin's party cleared the summit of the final hill that separated them from the city of Jerusalem.

"There it is," Sahlin said more to himself than to the three bodyguards that traveled with him from Meroë. His grandfather, who had been a powerful Kushite magistrate, described the great Jewish temple to him many times during his youth. As is the case with many beautiful things in life, mere words failed to capture the essence of the great building. Even from a distance, it appeared to have a soul of its own, and every other structure in the city seemed to pay homage to it.

Responding to Sahlin's muffled comment, Bakka stepped forward. Sahlin was by no means a small man; however, he was dwarfed by the robust stature of his chief guard who was almost twenty years his elder.

"I am certain that the Romans helped them to build it," Bakka said, unimpressed, cocking an eyebrow.

"Maybe so . . . but it is a beautiful building," Sahlin replied as he folded his arms and viewed the city once again.

"I hope I did not offend you, my lord. I simply miss the temples of our homeland," Bakka offered. It had been over two months since Bakka had made an offering at the Temple of Apedemack in Meroë, and he wondered how much longer the lion-god would tolerate his neglect.

The golden afternoon sunlight was accompanied by an inexorable wave of heat that affected Sahlin immediately. He responded by removing his dark gray cloak, revealing the fanciful kilt that he wore underneath.

"I understand, Bakka. I miss home as well," Sahlin admitted, momentarily contemplating the comforts of his estate in Meroë that overlooked the Nile River. However, his feelings quickly shifted as he thought about the strife that habitually invaded his home. Again, he found himself thankful that he was away from his sister, cousins, and the madness of his job.

As the wind shifted, Sahlin briefly caught the soft aroma of bread baking in a home nearby. The scent triggered similar hunger pains in all four of them.

"Look," Bakka said, gesturing towards the south. "Roman legionnaires."

Sahlin and the others turned their attention in the direction of the battalion of three dozen Roman soldiers that marched up the road. The sight of the legionnaires reminded the four Nubians that they now traveled in the conquered province of a rival empire.

As the group marched past, the appearance of the conquerors was hardly mighty or triumphant. Many of the soldiers bore expressions of exhaust and apprehension. Though they enthusiastically clutched their lances, their body language proclaimed their utter contempt for the land that they possessed and ruled by the sword.

Having once been the commander of an occupying force, it was a look that Bakka knew all too well. There was nothing desirable about living in the midst of a beaten and suppressed enemy who would rather die than live under foreign rule.

After stowing his cloak in a sack that was mounted on his horse, Sahlin glanced over at the other two bodyguards who kept a silent vigil over the passing legionnaires. The two men had hardly spoken during the journey from Meroë, letting only their hawkish eyes express their feelings. Both were career soldiers that now served in the queen's royal retinue. It was a distinction that declared their status as among the elite of the guard.

While traveling, Sahlin often wondered how the men felt about sojourning to a land that was dominated by the Roman Empire. He knew that at least one of the men was from a family that had served with great distinction in the Great War against Rome some fifty-five years earlier.

As the Romans disappeared over the hill, Bakka stepped forward and slowly shook his head. "The gods have forsaken this land."

"Even their god has been beaten and disgraced by the Romans." The scornful comment came from one of the guards.

Sahlin arched his head slightly and considered the guard's comment. He, too, had noticed the desolate veneer that coated the Judean landscape. Again, he found himself questioning the invisible hand that had driven him there. As an administrator, he was used to being in control, with the power to manipulate any circumstance that had a price tag attached to it. Yet the tumult that resided beneath his calm exterior seemed to agitate his soul more each day.

"I am sorry, my lord," the guard quickly said, noting his employer's stern countenance. "But many of the people whom we have encountered since we entered this land have been embittered and void of any sort of hope. Perhaps they have sinned against their god, and he has turned his face away from them."

The guard's pitiless words echoed in Sahlin's heart throughout their entire trek through Judea. Though many of the people they interacted with were simply resentful of the Roman occupation, some of them took out their frustration upon foreigners in general.

For the moment, Sahlin did not care. He concentrated on the gleaming temple that sparkled like a burning jewel in the heart of Jerusalem. Ready to conclude his long journey and commence his cryptic search, he started down the hill.

Chapter 2

ROMAN PROVINCE OF EGYPT

Another night went by and still sleep eluded Dikembul Nukae. Though he couldn't see it, he felt the slow movement of the sun over the distant Egyptian horizon.

Once again, he lay awake for hours as his bewildered mind wrestled with his body's growing fatigue. Throughout the night watch, he tried convincing himself the topic that provoked his consideration wasn't worth the loss of so many valuable hours of sleep. Nevertheless, the more he resisted, the more the vivid memories commandeered his thoughts.

He sighed deeply into the waning darkness and closed his eyes. As far as he was concerned, the images that ran through his mind may well have been portions of a dream that he had two months earlier. However, he knew they were real. No matter how strange they seemed to him, the memories of faces, sounds, and feelings that permeated his mind were definitely real.

Dikembul's trip to the heart of Jerusalem that morning had been uneventful. He pressed his way through the crowded streets to a stone building just outside of the temple. It was the sixth day of Sivan, fifty days after the annual barley harvest. As expected, he found himself in a sea of fellow Jewish males from throughout the known world. Like himself, they had made the journey to the Holy Land of Jerusalem in order to observe the Feast of Weeks. He doubted that very many of them had traveled as far as he had. The heart of the Kushite kingdom of Meroë was a formidable distance, to say the least.

Despite the inconvenience of having to pray in a subsidiary building outside of the great temple, Dikembul reveled in the very fact that he was there at all. He was by no means a rich man, a fact that made him that much more grateful to God for providing a way for him to make the pilgrimage. He was a simple Falasha herdsman who wanted only to obey the precepts given by Moses.

Following the directions provided by the resident priests, he climbed up a flight of stairs and entered a medium-sized meeting hall. It was large enough to hold approximately forty men, and it was already close to capacity. As he glanced around, he noticed that the crowd was fairly mixed. There were a few Egyptians and Parthinians, as well as two or three Arabs and Lybians. At the front a priest stood reverently, waiting for the newcomers to get situated so they could resume the morning period of prayer and consecration.

Dikembul settled down in the back and for a brief moment wished that he could have gotten access to the temple itself. The fact that he was a lower-class foreigner all but dashed his hopes of entering the temple on such a holy day when nearly every able-bodied man converged in the city. He closed his eyes, quieted his mind, and focused upon the goodness of the Lord. He had already presented the freewill offering that he had brought with him from Meroë. He had given the offering with a sincere heart, desiring only to please the invisible God who provided him and his daughter, Annika, with sustenance.

Among the many things that he was grateful for was the fact that he and his daughter lived quiet lives, free from the strife that often engulfed his native land. His existence as a herdsman may have been extremely unrenowned, but he had no complaints. Good friends and knowledge of the Holy One were all that he needed.

As his eyes closed, he felt a gust of wind circulate through the room of prayer. He would have thought nothing of it were it not for the fact that something brushed up against him. He opened his eyes and noted the thick veil that ran the length of the room, forming a wall beside him and partitioning this group from what appeared to be an even larger multipurpose room. Dikembul drove the distraction out of his mind and re-focused his heart on his prayers.

Within moments, the wind returned even stronger than before. This time it was accompanied with a loud, violent rumble that seemingly shook the foundations of the large room. Several men glanced around as the noise subsided and ushered in a hush. Dikembul gnawed on his lower lip as he watched the long, towering veil sway gently back and forth. Muffled voices from the other side of the veil softly invaded the room.

Dikembul couldn't make out what the voices were saying and was about to drive the noise out of his mind altogether, when he suddenly heard someone speaking in his native tongue. He frowned in bewilderment. It had been months since he had heard the dialect used in the Kushite region of Napata. Out of pure curiosity, he quietly slipped along the veil to the point where it kissed the stone wall. He opened the slit and, like a moth drawn to a flame, slowly entered the room.

The hall was a bit larger than the one where he was previously located; however, it was occupied with only about thirty men and women. Dikembul tried to filter through the unknown tongues and single out the one who had spoken in his native language. The only thing that he could discern, however, was that the people seemed to be praying. The hidden voice kept referring to the goodness and mercies of the Lord God Almighty. Finally, his eyes settled upon a burly man with a deep voice.

Dikembul watched the group pray fervently for a couple of minutes before he noticed that many men from the adjacent rooms had filtered in as well. Many of them were in total amazement as they also listened to the group of people before them worship God in the native tongues of their homelands.

A man from the region of Tiberias stepped forward and studied the group for a moment. "Behold, are not all these who are speaking Galileans?"

Dikembul, having limited knowledge of Judean geography, shook his head in bewilderment.

"What does this mean?" a Cretan asked from the back.

"They must be full of some new sweet wine!" bellowed his companion. A horde of boisterous laughs rumbled through the crowd as many of them joined the mocking.

Suddenly, the band of Galilean worshipers fell silent as one of them lifted his hand to gain everyone's attention. The tall man was powerfully built but spoke with a tone filled with meekness and strength. "Men of Judea, and all you who live in Jerusalem, let this be known to you and give heed to my words," he announced as he approached the crowd. "For these men are not drunk as you suppose, for it is only the third hour of the day.

"But this is what was spoken of through the prophet Joel, 'And it shall be in the last days,' God says, 'that I will pour *forth My Spirit upon all mankind. And your sons and daughters shall prophesy and your old men shall dream dreams...'"*

Unable to keep his heavy eyes open any longer, fatigue finally managed to overwhelm Dikembul's thoughts. As the memory slowly faded to dark, he started a dream of his own.

⚜   ⚜   ⚜

His gleaming sword pointing to the heavens, the *qeren* of Meroë stood at the head of his great army. His piercing eyes focused upon the rebellious army from the province of Nobatia that defiantly stood its ground. Only the expanse of a parched desert plain separated the two Kushite armies from the outset of another civil war.

Tension filled the air. The anticipation of death bellowed and screamed into the ear of every soldier on the arid battlefield.

Gone was love. Absent was brotherhood.

Civil war had arrived, and hatred reigned supreme.

King Sherakarer's heart was aflame with bitterness as he located the architect of the Nobatian rebellion. The fact that the vizier had once been a trusted ally incensed Sherakarer even more. Kandace Amanitore, Sherakarer's mother, had commissioned the man as vizier over Nobatia without reservations. She had been convinced that he was the perfect choice to secure Meroë's northern border with Roman Egypt.

However, this appointee's thirst and passion for power appeared to know no bounds. Within five years, the man had raised an army of eight thousand, assimilated one province, and threatened the stability of two others.

Unwilling to trust the viziers of Kerma and Makoria to

quell the rebellion, Sherakarer mobilized a portion of the grand army from the Isle of Meroë, intent upon extinguishing the flame of insurrection before it had a chance to spread any further. His force of fifteen thousand traversed north with unbelievable haste. Now the moment of reckoning was at hand.

For a brief moment, Sherakarer's mind focused upon the sacrifice that he had made to Apedemack, the Kushite god of war. According to the high priest, the great deity abhorred treason, and Apedemack's favor was with him and his army. Outwardly, Sherakarer received the blessing and proclaimed his faith in the god's power. However, in his heart of hearts, he questioned whether Apedemack, Amun, or the great goddess Isis herself could curtail the unyielding rebellion that dwelt within the hearts of men. An arm could be severed so that it could no longer lift a sword in defiance; yet how could one contend with a *spirit* of rebellion, a specter that visited one heart after another.

It appeared to Sherakarer that the only viable solution would be to replace the human heart altogether, somehow changing it so that it would no longer crave the corrupt passion and vainglory that was interlocked with the insatiable desire for power.

Yet such thoughts were too deep for Sherakarer at the moment. He drew a deep breath through his clenched teeth and relinquished the topic to the gods for debate. Today, he would simply cut out the hearts of his enemies, and there would indeed be little glory, if any, associated with his victory.

With the quick snap of his mighty arm, Sherakarer sliced through the tension in the air with his sword, triggering a lightning-fast response from his troops who thundered into action. In turn, the Nobatian troops charged forward with a defiant war cry echoing before them.

Like a furious sandstorm out of the Nobatian desert, the Kushite warriors cascaded into a ferocious cauldron of anarchy, hatred, and death.

Chapter 3

ONE YEAR LATER
A.D. 34

Thoughts of his homeland flowed through Sahlin's mind as his chariot traversed through the warm Judean desert. Earnestly desiring to be delivered from the oppressive heat, he closed his eyes and envisioned himself on a barge, sailing up the Nile. In his daydream, he could feel the cool, moist air blowing upon his face.

Though his homeland was nearly encompassed by a desert, the Nile River, which traveled through the territory for hundreds of miles, produced a temperate climate that attracted and sustained a multitude of life-forms.

The sway of the chariot on the desert road that led out of Jerusalem shook him from side to side. Curious about the time of day, he pulled open the thin veils of the carriage to see where the sun stood. Bakka, who rode alongside the chariot on horseback, glanced over at him with an inquisitive look. Sahlin acknowledged him with a slight nod, then continued to track the sun. After noting that it was approaching the ninth hour, he turned his attention back to the new parchments he had acquired from a scribe outside of the temple in Jerusalem. He already had copies of the Proverbs of Solomon and the Torah back in his home outside of Meroë. These old and worn books were Greek translations he had found among his grandfather's journals.

Sahlin found himself fondly recalling the many hours he had spent listening to his grandfather as he described his trips to Jericho, Jerusalem, and even the small town of Bethlehem. He grinned as he recalled asking him if there were any black people in Bethlehem at the time. "There were plenty there after we arrived," Rahman had replied flippantly.

During his own trip through Judea, Sahlin had made a momentary stop in the poverty-stricken town. For the most part, it was quiet and unimpressive, and he found it difficult to remember why his grandfather and so many other officials found it necessary to visit that place.

He turned his focus back on the Scriptures. As he did, the dry desert climate began to grate on his smooth, swarthy skin. He reached for a multicolored leather drinking cauldron and took a deep drink. He then doused some of the water on an embroidered towel and used it to wipe his face, alleviating some of the effects of the dry air.

As the water cooled his parched skin, he noticed that the chariot passed a lone figure walking along the side of the road. It had been hours since he noticed anyone else in the area. Perplexed, he briefly wondered what the individual was doing alone in the desert so far away from the city. Though desolate, the desert was a very dangerous place to sojourn. There was always the possibility of encountering pockets of *sacarri* that infested certain parts of the wilderness in between cities. Surely the foolish man knew that he was risking his life.

Bakka had insisted that Sahlin dress modestly while they traveled through the Judean desert. Although the road was frequented by Roman patrols, it was not wise for a traveler to draw attention to himself by enticing bold or desperate thieves with an open display of wealth. Despite the danger, Sahlin felt perfectly safe with his royal guards. No one would dare raid a carriage that was escorted by three massive Ethiopians. Their mere appearance was imposing, and their reputation as adept warriors was notorious.

Sahlin thought about Kandace Amanitore. Although she worshiped an entirely different set of gods, she didn't protest his request to visit Judea. Perhaps she perceived it to be something of a sabbatical that he had taken to temporarily withdraw from the responsibilities of overseeing her treasury. Although he had been in her service for several years without once having left her court, she didn't seem surprised when he presented his request.

"Why Judea?" he recalled her asking. "Why not Alexandria, or Adulis? Judea hardly seems like a nation to provide one with the opportunity to obtain relaxation."

"It is not relaxation I am seeking, Your Highness," he'd responded. "I will be going there to worship." Meager as they were, he usually kept his religious practices to himself and was wary of discussing his family's faith in the God of the Hebrews.

"So, you do embrace the religion of your grandfather?" the kandace had inquired, seeming only slightly surprised.

"You were aware of his religion?"

"Rahman Malae was a man of great courage and conviction," she had said, her eyes ablaze with memories of heated conversations long past. She never understood why one of the most influential men in the kingdom stood shoulder to shoulder with the lowly minority of Falasha as they prayed and made offerings to an invisible god. "He was never one to hide his views on morality. Are you also seeking the redemption of your soul?"

"I am not sure I understand, Your Highness," he had responded, looking away into the empty throne room. His eyes had fallen upon a brilliant mural of a Kushite warrior fighting a lion. The painting seemed to shimmer on the wall as a slight draft wafted through the room, hitting the torches.

"Do you wish to take this journey to worship the God of the Jews or to inquire of the Jews themselves?" the queen had asked, examining his face. In his eyes, she had seen a deep dread of the future that seemed on the verge of disturbing his usual confidence.

Amanitore had continued, "There are times when I also feel that our kingdom is on the brink of a great calamity." She often thought about how the steady march of time and the latest political problems within her kingdom were beginning to take their toll. Her vitality was being drained from her. In any case, she, too, sensed an impending catastrophe in the form of a tribal war in the province of Nobatia and Makoria. She feared that the conflict would degenerate into an all-out civil war.

"Sahlin, do you feel that the Jews possess a quality that we are lacking?" Her rhetorical question had echoed throughout the throne room.

Sahlin had searched for his words carefully. "They live as if they are destined for something great. Even the infernal Romans feel that they are destined to be masters of the world. But . . . what is *Meroë* destined for?"

Destiny. Sahlin had traveled for months to discover its meaning and perhaps even its source. He hoped to find it by earnestly worshiping the God of his fathers. He hoped that there was some Scripture that his grandfather neglected to tell him about, some ancient story that could ignite a spark of destiny that could serve as a torch for his beleaguered self-image.

What he found in Judea left him cynical of the nation as a whole. Instead of a culture bound by honor and brotherhood, the country was just as torn apart with hatred for the Roman Empire as tribes in his own nation were toward one another.

Being a royal administrator, he recognized institutionalized corruption when he saw it. The entire landscape of Jerusalem gave free rein to religious and political malignancy. The priests, who were supposed to be guardians of the truth, took advantage of the people, answering their trust and faith with deceit and corruption. The government officials were no better off. Rumors of scandals flowed out of Herod's palace as the Nile flowed out of the heart of Kush.

Political executions and private wars seemed to be the order of the day. Prior to his arrival in Jerusalem, a man rumored to be innocent of any major offense was crucified among thieves for some unknown political reason. Sahlin wondered how many more people were crushed by the corruption of the religious state.

Glancing outside his chariot, he noticed that the driver was drawing near a large body of water. The lake, flanked by palm trees that stretched toward the sky, reminded him of the lush oases frequently encountered in the great desert north of Meroë.

The chariot slowly pulled to a halt just shy of the lake. The driver of the chariot dismounted and reverently rapped the chariot's door with the end of his whip.

"Yes," Sahlin responded, sliding open the brightly colored curtains.

"We must stop to water the horses, my lord. We shouldn't be very long." Two of the massive Kushite guards dismounted their horses and led the animals over to the lake. Bakka remained at his post outside the chariot, surveying the area. They had encountered sporadic crowds of travelers on the dusty desert road earlier, but the region was fairly quiet at the moment.

Sahlin took the opportunity to focus once more on the Scripture that he was intermittently meditating on. Though he had studied the Jewish holy writings for some while, he still discovered things in them that he couldn't comprehend. His prior investigations revealed that prophecy was the central mode that God used to communicate with His people and that the Scriptures that he read were considered to be among the most sacred.

He read aloud in Greek trying to grasp the implications of the Scripture. "But He was pierced through for our transgressions, He was crushed for our iniquities; the chastening for our well-being fell upon Him." He knew that Isaiah was the author of the book he was reading; however, he wasn't sure whom the prophet was writing about. "And by His scourging we are healed."

A muscle twitched in Sahlin's jaw. *How can the suffering of one man bring healing to an entire nation?* The prophet whom Isaiah was referring to had to be a man of great power. Only those who were secure in their purpose in life could endure the treatment being described in the passage and not fight back. He thought of men of similar character in his own nation. The more powerful a person was, the more benevolent he could afford to be.

Suddenly, a gentle breeze brushed past the chariot's veils and caressed Sahlin's face, momentarily distracting him. He had been so engrossed in the Scripture he was reading that it took him several seconds to notice the young man trying to catch his attention.

"Sir," the man was saying, breathing heavily. Peering down at the young bearded man, Sahlin recognized him as the lone figure the chariot had passed on the road earlier.

Bakka slid his hand to the handle of his sword that was cloaked underneath his robe. Kushites were notorious for their ability to cut down a man by propelling a spear or sword. If the need arose, he would not miss.

"Sir," the young man called again, trying to catch his breath. "I heard you reading a passage from the book of Isaiah as you passed by me."

"Yes, what of it?" Sahlin replied coarsely.

"Do you understand what you are reading?" the man asked.

Sahlin pondered the stranger's question for a moment. Throughout his entire stay in Jerusalem, not once did anyone ask him that question. He had visited a half dozen synagogues and even worshiped at the great temple; however, not once did a priest, scribe, or even a commoner ask him if he understood the nature of his worship. Every bit of information that he obtained he had solicited.

"Well, how can I unless someone guides me?" Sahlin replied. Not fully understanding why, he invited the stranger to come and ride with him as their entourage continued south around the lake.

Bakka rode close to the chariot, giving himself a good view of its interior—as well as a good shot.

"I am Sahlin Malae, financial minister to the kandace of Meroë."

"My name is Philip," the man said, smiling warmly.

Sahlin felt as if an invisible hand gently patted his shoulder, confirming that the man who sat before him meant him no harm. Despite his initial apprehension, he felt completely at peace. "What matter of work do you perform?" he inquired, wondering what brought the man out so far into the desolate Judean desert.

"I'm a rabbi of sorts."

"Rabbi? Then you've had some formal training in the Scriptures, I gather?"

"What I know, I've learned from the greatest of all rabbis, and I am happy to share it."

Sahlin was drawn in by the invitation to learn as a shivering man to a warm fire. He leaned forward and extended the passage he had been reading to Philip. "Please tell me, of whom does the prophet Isaiah say this? Of himself or of someone else?"

Meeting Sahlin's yearning gaze, Philip knew in an instant why the Lord had set him on the forlorn desert road. In the Ethiopian's hazel eyes, he saw a hunger for something much greater than a simple explanation.

The chariot shook intermittently as the wheels struck hard stones that were embedded in the old road.

"Read the Scripture again," Philip said, gesturing to the scrolls.

Sahlin eagerly complied. "Like a lamb that is led to slaughter and like a sheep that is silent before its shearers, so He did not open His mouth."

Philip leaned back, his body swaying in unison with

the chariot's movements. He proceeded to tell the Ethiopian about the Law that was given to man by God through Moses and how no man had ever kept the sacred ordinances.

As they traveled around the curvatures of the lake, Philip described how God referred to people as being like sheep who have gone astray—destitute, with all aim and purpose in life thoroughly obscured by a sinful nature bent on greed and destruction.

The late afternoon sunlight flooded the chariot's compartment as Sahlin silently reflected on Philip's every word. He could not help but reflect upon his own life. Though he was a man of virtue outwardly, his heart had become like a cocoon of darkness that allowed him to justify his actions. He seemed every bit like a sheep that had gone away from where he needed to be.

His grandfather once told him that truth, no matter what form it took, could never be destroyed; but rather, it passed in secret from the heart of one man to another. Unfortunately, the heart of a man could be a deep dungeon, locking truth away while deception and corruption grew unchecked.

Sahlin listened intently as Philip described how God spoke through prophets and revealed how He would restore the hearts of the fathers to their children and the hearts of the children to their fathers. A lone tear streaked down his face as he heard that the sons of God would be given a mantle of praise instead of a spirit of fainting and that they would rebuild the ancient ruins and repair the desolations of many generations.

Slowly, Sahlin's heart began to fill with grief and sorrow. Even though he was taught the ways of the God of the Hebrews in his youth, he never really sought after him. Sahlin's level of corruption may not have exceeded that of the individuals that he had to govern, but he still undoubtedly fell short of the simple laws of God.

For some reason, Philip paused for a moment, filling the air with a convicting silence.

"Then, as spoken of in the Scriptures," Philip continued, "God's own Son was born of a virgin in the town of Bethlehem to save man from his sin."

Although he was staring straight at Philip, Sahlin's gaze was focused on something much deeper.

Messiah. Bethlehem.

Suddenly his mind was flooded with the missing details of why his grandfather traveled to Bethlehem so many years ago. He had been among a group of men bearing gifts for *the Christ.*

A sense of holy dread overshadowed him as Philip described the miracles performed by the child when He grew to manhood and the horrible death that He ultimately died.

Slowly, the revelation overtook him: This was the man who was crucified by the Romans shortly before he had arrived in Jerusalem a year earlier. He had seen people crucified before, and the thought of it cast a net of darkness over his already grieving heart.

Within moments, he found himself grieving for the Christ.

"But then He rose again on the third day," Philip interjected. "Just like He promised."

As Philip described how believing in Jesus and being baptized in His name would remove the reproach that all men wore upon their souls, a subtle ray of hope began to enlighten Sahlin's heart. For the first time, he saw how not only himself but his people also could be saved from the horrible tide of darkness and depravity that threatened to consume them totally.

Had it not always been peace that they were really seeking? He shook his head as he envisioned the many tribal leaders within the kingdom of Kush, each battling for his own brand of peace provided by spears and swords. They could only declare that it was achieved after they were in total control. That being the case, there would never be peace, because no one was strong enough to unite them, not even Amanitore.

This Jesus the Christ was different, however. Philip softly proclaimed that He could bring peace to the mind and the spirit of a man and change him internally.

Once again, a refreshing breeze fanned through the chariot. Along with it, new faith came to Sahlin. A faith to believe that there was a power greater than that of the political turmoil that engulfed his nation. A faith to believe that there was indeed a future and a hope. Faith to believe that there was such thing as redemption.

Philip was explaining baptism when Sahlin broke in with a question.

"And you say that baptism is an outward sign of faith in the Christ?"

"Yes, it is."

"Look! Water!" Sahlin expressed with an excitement that surprised him. "Is there anything that prevents me from being baptized right now?"

"If you believe with all your heart, you may be baptized," Philip gently replied.

"I believe," Sahlin started, trying to align his words and emotions with his newly found faith. "I believe that Jesus Christ is the Son of God."

After ordering the chariot to stop, he and Philip got

out and waded into the lake. The guards exchanged looks of bewilderment and wondered if the odd little Jew had cast some sort of spell on their chief financial minister. It was an aberrant sight to behold as the muscular Sahlin actually knelt in the water before the stranger.

"I baptize you in the name of the Father, the Son, and the Holy Spirit," Philip pronounced as he gently plunged Sahlin into the water, fully immersing him.

As he arose from the water, Sahlin was not met by the beaming rays of the sun but rather a soft breeze that was fragranced with a spirit of peace and clarity. He wiped the water from his face and turned to ask Philip if he were supposed to feel so . . . tranquil.

However, Philip was not there. He quickly looked to his right and left but saw no sign of the man who was just with him.

After wading out of the lake, he questioned his guards. "What happened to the man that was with us? Where did he go?"

The guards looked at one another, wondering if one saw something that the other did not. "We do not know, my lord," Bakka finally replied. "He was with you in the lake, and then he was gone."

Sahlin looked back toward Jerusalem and then slowly turned south, facing the direction of Africa. His steadfast gaze was met by a refreshing breeze that seemed to speak to him. Another passage from Isaiah surfaced in his mind.

"Thus says the Lord, the King of Israel and his Redeemer, the Lord of hosts: 'I am the first and I am the last, and there is no God besides Me. Who is like Me?'"

Breathless, and unable to fathom what had just transpired, Sahlin simply smiled and watched the wind move gently across the face of the lake.

Annika wasn't about to make another mistake. A slight miscalculation the night before had resulted in a rare scorching of the evening meal. At the ripe age of nineteen, she should have known better. Fortunately, she had been able to carefully cut away the burnt sections of meat without her father becoming suspicious.

Her mother, who had died nearly four years ago, had always admonished her to remain focused on the task at hand. Annika grinned sheepishly as she envisioned the warm smile that her mother must have worn as her father lavished her with praises over the meal even if it had been a little burnt.

This time she was far more alert. Gazing over the barley porridge that she had prepared for her father's breakfast, she paid special attention to the effervescent bubbles that gently exploded on the surface. Though the aroma was heavenly, she noted the rapid succession of the bubbles and poured a small amount of water into the pot. Almost instantly, the flurry of bubbles calmed down to a mellow simmer, filling the kitchen with the sweet smell of Nubian spices.

As Annika slowly stirred the contents of the pot, she tried to push away thoughts in her mind related to the fact that she had just exhausted the supply of Nubian herbs and seasoning she had purchased from the market only days before. Her upper lip curled slightly at the notion that the rations may have lasted a little longer if she hadn't had to use so much in order to cover up the mistake that she had made the previous evening.

Instinctively, she swiveled around to check on the *kizra* that was almost done. The combined aroma of the bread and porridge permeated the small house and filled her mind and heart with fond memories of their home back in the small Kushite town of Nuri. Before she knew it, she found herself unable to stave off the relentless craving for her young friends. She missed spending time with them and chatting the afternoon away as they did their chores near the Nile River. She closed her eyes and pictured the endless array of barges and small boats ferrying down the mighty river. She could even see the strong young men flirting with her and her friends as they rowed by.

Surprisingly enough, she found it difficult to believe that they would soon be back on their way to Meroë.

Home. Annika hungered for it as the dry savanna craved the winter rains—even more so perhaps. They had been away for so long and traveled through what seemed to be an endless number of towns.

In another day, they would be in the Egyptian town of Dabod. There they would stay with several relatives for another few weeks. *Another six weeks and we'll be home,* she thought as she focused again on the bubbles. Though the most difficult part of their journey, the two-week stay in Jerusalem, ended nearly a year ago, she felt as if their trip would never end.

As she thought about their pilgrimage to Judea, she couldn't help but think about the isolation she had felt there. During their stay in Jerusalem, surprisingly she had seen only eight other black women. Though she was not mistreated by any of the natives, she found it difficult to progress through the day without seeing any faces that resembled her own.

They had made the pilgrimage to devote themselves to worship and sanctification during the Feast of Weeks.

Her father deemed the journey as a once in a lifetime event. Given the tremendous sacrifices they had made in order to finance the trip, Annika was more than happy to hear it classified as such. Her father had sold a parcel of their land in order to raise the necessary funds.

All in all, she was sure that their skin color hadn't been the catalyst for the lukewarm reception that she and her father had received upon entering the province of Judea. Though she wasn't one hundred percent certain, she felt sure that their status as "outsiders" had done them a great disservice. At least that's how her father had explained it to her. Either way, she was glad to be out of that region and back among familiar dark faces.

After setting the small table, she carefully laid out the food and patiently waited for her father.

A gentle breeze drifted through an open window. She briskly rubbed her arms as the early morning air nipped at her dark skin. Knowing that it would warm up rather quickly, she resisted the urge to put on an overcoat. Though the weather was fairly nice, she was still trying to adjust to the unique climate of Egypt. Usually, the landscape was blanketed by a clammy mist in the early morning that slowly burnt off and gave way to stifling afternoons. It was totally different than their home down south.

Once they returned to Meroë, she doubted if she would ever venture more than a few miles away from the small town of Nuri again. Having fulfilled her religious duties, she would focus on satisfying the man that would be her mate and raising a family. Marriage was the one item that she continually held before the Lord while in her secluded moments of prayer.

Already several years past the customary age of marriage, Annika was often posed with the chafing question of when she would submit her name to the tribal elders in order to declare her desire to marry. Many of her peers had already paired with young men and started families, leaving her as the only spouseless individual from her small inner circle of friends. Of course, there were those in her village who whispered in the shadows and introduced malicious rumors that she felt that she was too good for any of the young suitors within the confines of Nuri. Though such talk grieved her to a degree, she chose not to dwell upon it. The simple but deep beauty that she was blessed with, coupled with her fierce family loyalty, often sparked such chatter among the older women.

Nevertheless, Annika's primary thoughts were tethered to her father's well-being. After her mother's death, it was just the two of them. Although the traditional time of mourning had long passed, everything within Annika wanted to insure that Dikembul Nukae was cared for properly—even if it meant that she had to delay starting a family of her own for a while longer.

Desiring to see if the sun had overtaken the early morning mist, Annika peered out of the window. After examining the hazy blue sky, she shifted her dark eyes and scanned the crowded street adjacent to their apartment. Though it was only the first hour of the day, she wasn't at all surprised by the number of people already in transit.

For a moment, Annika's eyes locked with those of a middle-aged man who was making his way through the growing crowd. The cold expression on his face seemed to harden even more as he stared at her and then gazed away and disappeared into the masses. She frowned pensively and bit her lower lip, praying that she would never allow her heart to become callous toward others. For a moment, she tried to imagine what it was like for visitors passing through Nuri. Because of Nuri's close proximity to Napata, the spiritual capital of the Kushite Empire, the small town seasonally saw hundreds of visitors. Annika couldn't help but wonder what sort of reception travelers to her hometown received as they passed through.

Annika was jolted out of her reflection by a gentle hand grasping her shoulder. Startled, she snapped her head around to see the smiling, bearded face of her father, somewhat amused by her apprehension.

"Don't do that," Annika sounded, dramatically throwing her hand to her chest.

"I'm sorry, my dear. I didn't mean to frighten you," Dikembul offered as he sat down at the small kitchen table to eat. He took a piece of kizra into his strong hands and tore it in half. Were it not for the scores of gray hairs laced into his black beard, he could very easily be mistaken for a younger man. To his delight, his occupation as a herdsman afforded him the opportunity to remain very active. As a result, this fifty-one-year-old body resembled that of men in their early thirties.

Annika stood still while he uttered a prayer over the food. After serving him, she turned her attention back toward the window.

"What are you looking at?" Dikembul managed to ask in between bites of food.

"There are so many people out there. In fact, there are more than there were just a short while ago," Annika replied, squinting as a beam of sunlight met her eye as the rising sun crept over the structures across the way.

"It's the first hour of the day. Many are heading toward the temple for morning sacrifice and prayer," Dikembul stated as he watched his daughter sit down in the empty chair next to him.

Just then, Annika envisioned the Temple of Isis that stood just outside of the city. Perched upon the banks of the Nile, the grand temple drew worshipers from Egypt and Meroë alike. She nodded in acknowledgment as she traced the edges of her empty bowl with her slender fingertips.

"Annika, are you feeling well?"

"Yes, of course," she replied, placing more kizra on his plate. She watched him consume the food at a faster pace than he usually ate. "Are you heading to Philae, too? You said that we would be leaving for Dabod. It's been two days now."

"I know. I'm sorry. However, there is something that has come up that I have to look into," Dikembul answered, his mind on the Jewish elders that occupied the local synagogue. The day before, he had received information from a fruit vendor that several of the elders were well versed in the Holy Scriptures—particularly those that dealt with the advent of the Messiah.

"Let me guess," Annika said. "You're going to the synagogue outside of the city?"

Dikembul raised an eyebrow at her insight.

Annika shook her head in annoyance and bewilderment. "I don't understand. Why do you keep visiting every sacred place of meeting in every city that we visit? You didn't do this on our way to Judea."

Dikembul stroked his beard and sighed gently. He knew exactly where she was heading. "Annika . . ."

"Ever since Jerusalem, you've been acting so strange," Annika stated, clearly attempting to vent some pent-up frustration. "You eat and run. You pray far more than you did before this pilgrimage, and worst yet, you won't even talk with me about it."

Dikembul quickly glanced down at the piece of bread that he held. "I'm sorry. I am simply trying to serve the Lord."

"Serving the Lord was never as complex at home," Annika muttered, unable to mask her agitation.

Dikembul put down his food and grasped his daughter's small hands. He tried to see her point. "I know that my behavior has been odd." He reached up and gently tipped her chin. "Believe me, I want to explain it to you, but I can't."

Succumbing to the urge to push for more information, Annika narrowed her eyes. "Do you think that it is something that I won't be able to understand? I may not have a formal education, but my intuition serves me well enough."

"Of that I have no doubt," Dikembul responded, leaning back in his chair. Months had passed since his experience in Jerusalem that now robbed him of his sleep. Initially, he wanted to describe the entire event to his daughter, yet decided against it. It was bad enough that he found himself struggling with the concept that the Messiah may have been revealed to the world within the past year. Potentially worse was the fact that some declared this man, Jesus, as the Son of God. The very thought seemed blasphemous. How could he lead his own daughter down a path that might very well result in her castigation? No, he first had to discover the truth.

Annika rose and strolled toward the window. "Does it have something to do with Galilee?"

Dikembul's face warmed. "What makes you ask that?"

"You were restless last night. I looked in on you and

you were muttering something about men from Galilee again."

Dikembul frowned. "Am I a child that you are looking in on me as I sleep?"

Trying to hide her frustration, Annika slowly lowered herself back into her seat. "You are no child," she declared, thrusting aside her notion to say otherwise. "I simply want you to share with me whatever it is that plagues you."

Dikembul sat motionless, convicted. Since his wife's death, he kept very little from his daughter. She was wise beyond her age and wasn't afraid to display it. "There is much that I want to tell you, but until I am absolutely certain of the facts, I simply can't explain it. Please trust me on this."

Though Annika could literally feel the quelling power of her father's words, she had to suck in a pessimistic remark that danced on the tip of her tongue.

Dikembul smiled at her. Her silent response merely confirmed to him that she was in total disagreement with his statement. Most Kushite men would have taken her silence as an insult and had her punished. Nevertheless, having somewhat of an understanding of his only child's temperament, he caressed her hands and smiled warmly. The older she became, the more intriguing her behavior was to him. He often prayed that her future mate would find her qualities just as fascinating.

Finally, Annika relented. "I think I understand what you're saying."

Dikembul stood up and leaned over to kiss her on the forehead. "I am glad that you are here with me. I really cherish the time that we have spent together thus far. I only wish that the three of us could have made this journey together."

"So do I," Annika replied softly, glancing away from her father. "Despite it all, I am sure that Mama would have enjoyed this trip."

Dikembul nodded reverently at the memory of his wife. "Yes, I believe that she would have." For a long moment, Dikembul found himself fighting off the familiar opponent of grief that accompanied even fleeting thoughts of his wife.

Discerning his brief bout with pain, Annika did little to try to dismiss the sudden influx of guilt that washed over her. "I am sorry, Papa. I didn't mean to . . ."

"Never mind, my dear," he said gently, motioning her to remain seated. "I miss home as well. We should arrive in Dabod tomorrow morning."

"Yes, Papa."

Dikembul allowed the thoughts of the mystifying Galileans to creep back into his mind. He was hopeful that someone in the synagogue might be able to enlighten him on the possibility that the Messiah may have already come in the form of the man named Jesus. He took another piece of the flatbread, then kissed her on the forehead. "Hopefully, I'll be back by the ninth hour."

"Not likely," Annika whispered as she watched him leave the room.

Chapter 4

The once defiant gates of Qustul were thrown haplessly to the side. The laughter of the once vibrant Kushite city was long been vanquished by the abrupt hush enveloping the surrounding environment. Now, only ghostly howls echoed through the dusty street proclaiming the desperation brought about by the misfortunes that accompanied civil war.

General Akinidad rode quietly alongside his regiment of troops. He surveyed the damage and desolation that humbled one of the greatest cities that sat on the banks of the Nile. His black, hardened face displayed little sympathy for the frightened inhabitants quivering behind the doors of the dilapidated sun-brick houses. Only the town's hungry children rushed out to meet the garrison of mighty soldiers that marched through.

Akinidad, neither distraught by their ragged appearance nor impressed with their display of courage, all but ignored them. His was not an errand of mercy. As far as he was concerned, their plight lay squarely in the hands of their queen, the same monarch who months ago sent her ill-adapted sons to wage war against the rebelling Nobatian tribes.

As they finally reached the heart of the city, Akinidad's nostrils flared as his eyes fell upon the administrative courtyard. The walls for the complex were overrun, the ceremonial hut trampled down, and the once proud *dufufa* scorched.

An officer inched his horse to Akinidad's side. Like the remaining complement of soldiers, he sported a gray kilt with red trim. His black breastplate was adorned with the painted molded image of a leopard. The three short gold stripes in the upper right corner of his breastplate denoted his rank of second in command. "King Sherakarer's work, no doubt," the man stated.

"They have absolutely no respect for the northern customs," Akinidad responded disdainfully. The dufufa's remains, though charred beyond recognition, refused to fall apart completely.

During his fifteen-year military career in Kerma, he had led many campaigns against neighboring foreign tribes as well as hostile Kushite clans who had designs to overthrow the existing vizier. Yet, in the many battles he engineered, he was careful not to violate the one unspoken law that every military commander abided by. Not once did he ever desecrate or plunder a Kushite temple or sacred building. To do so would affront the gods and breed hatred instead of fear in the surrounding communities. Though dufufas were administrative centerpieces, they also served as significant religious facilities that hosted important sacrifices to Amun and Osiris.

"This is a mistake that Amanitore will continue to pay for, for a very long time," Akinidad spat. Over the past year, the royal family's actions prompted him to publicly display his distaste for them. The dislike for Kandace Amanitore and her sons had already filtered down to many of his principal officers. Even a good portion of his soldiers were rumored to utter silent curses against the queen.

It took the Kerman army a week to reach the battered province of Nobatia. Every town and strip of land in the once rebellious province told the same story and bore the same scars. Throughout the journey, Akinidad forced himself to remember that they were all Kushites from the same nation. Yet, Sherakarer's firestorm through the north testified of the very opposite, underscoring the blatant fact that there had always been a distinction drawn between the Isle of Meroë and any other province north of Gebel Barkal.

Through trade and agriculture, Meroë had become a very wealthy kingdom. However, a great bulk of that wealth sat comfortably in the southern provinces of Alondia and the Isle of Meroë, leaving the northern tribes to serve as little more than buffer zones from Rome and marauding tribes from the desert.

Akinidad gripped the handle of his sheathed sword. Were it not for the fact that his elite Kerman army numbered no more than ten thousand, he most likely would have dispensed with the formalities of posturing and then sided against Sherakarer. He sarcastically mused on the two reasons that compelled him to abstain from entering the fray. First and foremost was the inept leadership of Kara, the now dead Nobatian leader and instigator of the conflict. At best, Kara was one level above the royal family in terms of competency. If there were to be a new Meroë, Kara was definitely not the man for the job.

The second factor was that of timing. Akinidad was certain that night would eventually fall upon Amanitore and her family. He predicted as well as hoped that the curtain of night would fall swiftly and hard upon the self-serving family. Time would also be the ally that would enable him to move against Carachen, the weak-minded vizier of Kerma. As the days stretched into months and years, Akinidad only found himself growing more hateful and impatient with his superior. The law implicitly declared that he report to the vizier and to the tribal council of Kerma. Yet, the entire body of men were no more than figureheads erected by the royal family. Everything within him grew weary of the masquerade that a growing number of his fellow soldiers and he donned in order to keep their positions and lives.

However, soon the time would be at hand to initiate a lasting change. Akinidad almost lost hope when Nobatia met with utter defeat. However, his hope reflourished when Vizier Carachen commissioned him with the task to survey the ravaged province. The results were better than Akinidad could have hoped for. His men had been exposed to the massive damage inflicted on the north at the hand of the royal family. Upon their return to Kerma, the word would surely spread throughout the ranks, igniting the fire he would someday use as a torch of freedom.

"Djabal, have the architects survey the remainder of the city," Akinidad ordered. "Have them place a priority on rebuilding any destroyed temples. Their efforts should start with this dufufa."

"Yes, my lord," Djabal replied crisply, already searching for the complement of designers and architects assigned to their army.

"And Djabal," Akinidad added, capturing his second in command's gaze, "make certain that you solicit the assistance of as many Nobatians as you possibly can for the reconstruction."

Djabal lifted an eyebrow. He was well aware of the orders issued by the vizier that only Kerman soldiers should perform any rebuilding activities.

Noticing Djabal's consternation, Akinidad narrowed his dark eyes at the man. "Unlike our brothers from the south, we want their gratitude, not their gall."

✹   ✹   ✹

Bakka slowly increased his hurried gait into a slow trot down the palm-littered beaten pathway. A minute but critical lapse of concentration caused him to lose track of his young target, and his anger grew by the second.

As he whisked along, his eyes peered through the brush searching for anyone with a Nubian-styled multicolored kilt. He stopped momentarily to check the position of the sun that was slowly descending into the western valley.

Several young Egyptian boys darted out of the brush, startling him. Instinctively, Bakka reached for his dagger. Surprisingly, the young boys ran past him without even glancing his way.

As he watched them scurry along the path in the general direction of the small town of Maadi, Bakka realized that his dagger was halfway out of its concealed sheath. Embarrassed, he flicked the weapon back into its place and launched a series of curses. He ran his hand across the top of his smooth, bald head and reluctantly yielded to the notion that he was indeed getting too old and was ready for retirement.

Feeling a growing sense of urgency, he cut down a narrow path that led to a tributary of the Nile. Alone next to the peaceful stream sat Sahlin. He was motionless and stoic, almost like a statue. Only the quiet rush of the water filled the air.

Relieved, Bakka slowed his pace and then stopped altogether before he reached Sahlin.

The young administrator found himself extremely quiet and resolute for the last week and a half. He hardly ate a thing and spoke even less than he did on the way to Judea. Every opportunity he got, Sahlin wandered to a secluded place and simply sat alone.

Throughout his years of service, Bakka made it a point to concern himself only with Sahlin's safety. Though the two men were on amiable terms, one would hardly know it, as they rarely spoke on a casual basis.

Bakka sensed something very different about Sahlin. From the moment that they set foot for Judea nearly a year earlier, Bakka had witnessed the slow and steady erosion of the shield of confidence that Sahlin projected to the rest of the world. Indeed, one must appear confident in a vocation such as Sahlin's. Any sign of frailty by the chief treasurer could easily result in the complete economic collapse of an entire district or even a province. It was a pressure that Sahlin managed well. In fact, he seemed to be designed to handle foibles and political maneuverings executed by *peshtes* and viziers. It was a characteristic that made him admired, feared, and even hated.

Bakka couldn't help but wonder if Sahlin's current disposition was related to his experience back in Gaza.

He couldn't erase the image of the peculiar Jew who happened to be out in the middle of nowhere, dunking the kandace's most trusted financial administrator in a lake. Bakka didn't know how, but he was certain that the man had to be some sort of seer assigned to cast an incantation upon slow-witted and unsuspecting travelers. However, Sahlin hardly fit that bill. He was a learned man of stature and influence, not some backwoods African who believed every tale spun by a radical with a silver tongue.

Just then, Sahlin looked up and glanced over at Bakka. "How long do you plan on standing there?" he asked, as if he knew how long the massive bodyguard had been observing him.

Bakka's eyes rose across the tributary and into the western sky. "It'll be dark soon. We should head back to the inn."

Though he heard the subtle assertiveness in Bakka's voice, Sahlin didn't move. Instead, he traced the water south towards its hidden point of origin around a twisting bend in the distance. "Bakka, this is part of the river that will lead us back home."

"Yes, my lord. It is."

Sahlin wrung his hands slightly as if he were processing abstract thoughts foreign to his analytical mind. "We'll pass Memphis, Thebes, Elephantine, Philae . . . Then we'll be back in Meroë. Through Nobatia, into Kerma."

Bakka slowly walked alongside of Sahlin and noticed that several rolled-up scrolls were nestled neatly by his side. He recognized the documents as the same ones that Sahlin purchased just before they departed from Jerusalem. They were the same ones that Sahlin was reading aloud when they encountered the strange Jewish rabbi.

"For some reason, you don't sound like a man who is ready to return home." Bakka's deep voice resonated through the surrounding forest of short palm trees.

Sahlin focused on the water in front of him. It was clear enough for him to see several tiny guppies scoot near the shoreline. "What makes a place home, Bakka?"

Certain that Sahlin had fallen prey to some sort of Egyptian infirmity, Bakka drew a breath and pondered how to respond to the question. Before he could answer, Sahlin spoke up once more.

"My estate is there. My work is there. Even my family." Sahlin paused for a moment to envision the host of cousins and sisters who resided in the sprawling mansion that they owned. As the eldest, he was by law the master of the house. "I own so much. But I feel as if I possess so little."

Bakka shook his head. "I'm sorry, my lord, but I don't understand what you are trying to say."

"Neither do I," Sahlin replied, rubbing his eyes.

"My lord, aren't you feeling well? Your behavior over the last week or so has been, for lack of a better term, odd."

Sahlin grinned sardonically, not even attempting to mask his frustration. "My apologies, Bakka. I cannot provide the answer for your question, as I don't know how I feel."

Sahlin wanted to say more, but an invisible hand snatched away his words. Deep in his heart, he felt a great tug-of-war being waged. Yet, he could not clearly identify the combatants. He could only describe his contrasting feelings as a struggle between the complexity of his past and the uncertainty of his future.

That was the greatest irony that gnawed painstakingly away at his soul.

His future had always been secure and never lacked definition. He had been groomed to serve as an administrator in the royal court, and as far as he was concerned, that was his destiny.

For the first time, a wave of concern covered Bakka's face. "I'm not a counselor, seer, or a prophet. However, it's quite obvious that there is something troubling you deeply. If you would like to talk about what you want . . ."

"I don't know, Bakka," Sahlin declared, rising to his feet. "I don't know how I feel, I don't know what I want, and I don't know where I am going." He turned his back and marched down the path.

Bakka stood motionless as he watched Sahlin head back towards the lodge where they were staying for the evening. Prior to their departure from Meroë, he had been charged by the kandace herself to see to Sahlin's protection.

He might have managed to safeguard Sahlin's person. However, he feared that something far more elusive had violated and captured the chief treasurer's soul.

🐞   🐞   🐞

Sahlin sat alone in the dark courtyard of the inn. The flaming yellow moon that sat high above the sleeping Egyptian town of Maadi supplied him with just enough light by which to read. Though he had to strain a bit, he continued to peruse the Hebrew Scriptures as he had every night since his encounter with Philip back in Judea. He wasn't sure why, but he felt that every answer he needed was somehow tucked away between the Greek characters.

Once again, he bypassed the evening meal in order to

devote his attention to his studies. Hours had gone by, and nearly every soul in the inn enjoyed the innate peace of mind brought about by slumber.

Sahlin's body longed for sleep. His soul would have none of it until it was satisfied. His body craved nourishment. Yet the only thing that seemed to curtail his hunger pangs was his total absorption of the scrolls that he held in his hand. He no longer even consulted his grandfather's journals but spent all of his time combing through phrases and texts in Isaiah's manuscript that had meant very little to him several weeks earlier.

There were several portions of the Scripture he no longer needed to read in order to see. Closing his eyes, he saw the words of a certain piece of text as if it had been carved upon the canvas of his heart.

Behold, My Servant, whom I uphold; My chosen one in whom My soul delights. I have put My Spirit upon Him; He will bring forth justice to the nations . . .

The words echoed through his spirit like a trumpet.

I am the Lord, I have called You in righteousness, I will also hold You by the hand and watch over You, and I will appoint You as a covenant to the people, as a light to the nations.

"To open blind eyes, to bring out prisoners from the dungeon . . ." Sahlin's voice trailed off into the darkness. He lifted his head and opened his eyes. As he did, he glimpsed a streaking star arc across the sky. Suddenly, a measure of peace settled over his heart. He closed his eyes once again and slowly lowered his head into his hands.

"Lord Messiah, I believe that You are with me," he prayed, groping with his spirit. "Why is it that You have called upon me? What is it that You desire? Make Your will known to me." As he prayed, he again sensed a titanic yet cryptic struggle between his past and his future.

Methodically, memories of his life in Meroë began to upsurge. His friendship with Paqar Harmais. His flirtatious relationships and affairs. The twelve steps that led to his office in the grand palace overlooking the sacred row of temples and marketplace in the heart of the capital city.

"I don't understand," he breathed. "I don't understand."

Like a child trying to hide, he drew his head in between his legs in an effort to hide from the prying scrutiny of an invisible set of eyes. The maneuver did not work as he felt a cold sense of displeasure nag at his heart.

"What do You want from me?" Sahlin snapped angrily. "I can give You no more than what I am."

Though he shut his eyes as tightly as he could, he could not jostle his mind away from the words recorded in the scroll. It was as if they had taken on a persona of their own and intended to chase him down.

I am the Lord, that is My name; I will not give My glory to another.

"But I don't want Your glory . . ." Sahlin voiced, on the verge of breaking down. "I just want my life."

Behold, the former things have come to pass, now I declare new things; before they spring forth, I proclaim them to you.

"Please, let me be . . ."

Unable to maintain his composure, Sahlin wept uncontrollably. Caught in between two masters, he struggled to hold on to his sanity, but even that was now in question. Soon, his tears and sweat dampened the palms of his hands while his subdued sobs carried across the dim courtyard.

Bakka stood silently behind one of the tall pillars that supported the roof. He watched in disbelief as Sahlin cried as if he were lamenting over the death of his father.

Instead of feeling ridicule or even sympathy for the

weeping man, Bakka suddenly found himself wrestling with fear. After a few moments, the dread turned into awe and ultimately a sense of reverence.

The palm trees planted in the courtyard started to sway as a gentle breeze sailed through the corridors. Bakka felt his legs grow cold and knees start to buckle as the presence of something lofty and magnificent filled the grounds.

Anxious and apprehensive, Bakka could stand there no longer. He backed away and disappeared into the shadows. Although he knew that no one else was with Sahlin, he was convinced that the chief treasurer was not alone.

Chapter 5

Egyptian cuisine had never fared well with Dikembul. However, he had to admit that it was far more preferable than the bland food that he endured while traveling throughout Judea. The meat and vegetables were far richer than dishes prepared in Nubia. Though his relatives were hospitable and did their best to accommodate him and Annika, he relished the thought that they would be on their way home within two weeks.

Despite his growing excitement, he was still aware that they had well over a month to go before their eyes would fall upon Gebel Barkal, the great flattop mountain that sat ominously across the Nile River from his home in Nuri.

Tonight, Dikembul had chosen to take Annika out to eat as opposed to taking their meal with his brother's family. Not surprisingly, Dikembul spent most of the evening regretting his daughter's selection of taverns. It was hardly the environment he liked to expose her to.

The chosen pub was crowded and noisy. The spicy aroma of seared lamb filled the lively atmosphere, as did the pungent scent of dozens of Egyptian men who funneled through the tavern. Many of them had come in directly from the field intent upon consuming as much wine as their stomachs and moneybags would afford them.

"What's the matter? Aren't you hungry?" He noticed that she had barely touched her food.

"Oh, yes. I am," she said as she stared across the room. Dikembul traced her eyes through the crowded hall to a well-dressed fat Egyptian seated with two beautiful women at his side.

"If you want, we can move over there. Perhaps he's rich and . . ."

"No, I'm not looking at him!" Annika snapped. "The lady next to him . . . she has the prettiest broach in her hair."

Dikembul grimaced as he bit into a spicy piece of meat.

"Egyptian women wear the loveliest jewelry. Someday my husband will buy me a dozen broaches like that."

"I'm certain that Akil will purchase as many as you like," Dikembul picked at his food. "He may even be an officer by the time we get back."

"You know how I feel about him, Papa."

"No, I don't. You keep avoiding the subject every time I bring him up in the conversation."

"That's precisely my point. I don't want to talk about him."

"Yes, but when we return, he will most likely want to

talk about you. Akil is a very decent man with a fine reputation, and he has chosen to wait for you." Dikembul
stroked his beard as he recalled the last time the young
soldier approached him about Annika's hand in marriage.
"I believe that he sincerely cares for you. You know that I
wouldn't just say something like that."

"Yes, but . . . I just don't know." Annika drew in her
lips and studied the carving of Osiris on the wall adjacent
to their table. Akil possessed a strong personality and was
very handsome. His profession as an elite soldier at the
prestigious fort outside of Napata gave him a status that
made him that much more desirable to nearly every
woman in the village. The one he chose to marry him
would surely travel throughout the kingdom. "I'm honored that he shows so much interest in me . . ."

"But . . ."

"But sometimes I feel that I am simply just another
challenge for him. Another obstacle to conquer."

Dikembul nodded and drew a deep breath. Immediately, he found himself fighting a losing battle against a
wave of condemnation. Ever since the death of his wife,
he had given Annika more latitude than most females her
age enjoyed. Instead of addressing the independent spirit
that she adopted due to the absence of her mother,
Dikembul encouraged it. At the time, he thought that he
was helping her through the immense period of grief.
Now, he often wondered if he had done her a great disservice. "I suppose this is all my fault," he said in a voice
barely audible above the raucous crowd.

Annika narrowed her dark eyes at him. "Father,
you've done nothing wrong."

"Yes, my dear, I have. When your mother died, I
should have . . ." Dikembul's voice trailed off as three

dark-skinned men settled down at their table. Two were clearly Egyptian while the other had Cyrenian features. It was at that time that Dikembul noticed the tavern had become even more compacted than before.

"You don't mind if we sit down here, do you?" one of them asked, as his companions already started to dig into their plates.

"Not at all," Dikembul responded, looking into his daughter's eyes. He resolved that he would finish their conversation later on that night.

For the duration of their meal, Dikembul and Annika said little to one another. Two of the three men rambled on about everything from irrigation techniques to the Roman prefect's untamed hairdo. Their conversation oscillated from their hatred of Egyptian tax gatherers to their even deeper contempt of the ones in Jerusalem. The comment caught Dikembul's attention for a moment, forcing him to silently acknowledge how much he agreed with them.

When Annika and Dikembul finished their meal, they were about to rise when one of the Egyptian men made reference to a Galilean slain by the state while they had been in Jerusalem nearly a year ago.

Dikembul leaned forward slowly. "My apologies for the distasteful interruption, but did you say Galilean?"

"Yes, friend," one of the Egyptians answered, not at all offended by Dikembul's unsolicited interjection. "We were in Jerusalem when this man from Galilee was put to death by the Roman government there. Absolute tragic case if you ask me."

Dikembul furrowed his brow. His visits to the local synagogues produced no significant fruit, as he had been unable to find out any substantial information on the group of Galileans he encountered back in Jerusalem. This was the first time he heard anyone else make mention of people from that region.

"Curious. Before we left Jerusalem, I, too, heard about this individual executed by the Romans. Then later, during the day of Pentecost, I heard a gathering of men from Galilee declaring that this man was the Messiah."

One of the Egyptians pondered Dikembul's words for a moment. "I am familiar with the concept of the Jewish Messiah. As I recall, there have been many men over the past eighty or so years claiming to be the savior of the Jewish race, each one vowing to liberate Israel from the yoke of foreign oppression."

Dikembul nodded, silently admitting that the man knew more about the subject than he did.

"Too bad that none of them ever succeeded," piped the other Egyptian. "I'd love to see Rome fall on its lazy, fat rear end."

"Please tell me, what more do you know of this man? Were you there when he was executed?" Dikembul asked, hoping for any information that would quench his curiosity. He could feel Annika's perplexed gaze drilling the side of his face.

"We were in Jerusalem doing business at the time." The words came from the Cyrenian. All eyes turned toward his direction. His dark eyes were sunk into his bearded face, giving him the appearance of a man half-awake. "Like everyone else in the city, we had no idea of the injustice that was about to take place."

"Injustice?" Dikembul questioned.

"The act perpetrated by the Roman government and the high priest office that day was a travesty." The Cyrenian's soft voice was fortified with a strong, unyielding conviction. "The Romans speak of their law being a vehicle that will bring order to a chaotic world. Yet, they refuse to judge themselves against the same measuring rod."

The large Egyptian grunted playfully. "You must forgive our companion. For some reason, Simon here believes that the man was put to death by mistake."

"No," Simon interjected before his friend could edge in another word. "It wasn't a mistake. It was an outright criminal act. Pontius Pilate knew that he was innocent of the charges brought against him. Yet, he crucified him anyway."

Simon's eyes locked with those of Dikembul. "I had just come out of a shop when the procession to the execution site marched past. Like everyone else, I was curious, and I wanted to get a look at the condemned. He was so battered that he hardly resembled a man. He was more like a walking corpse."

The table was silent. Anyone who traveled through Judea knew just how cruel the Romans could be.

"It was no surprise that he stumbled under the weight of the enormous wooden cross that he bore. Each time that he went down, I prayed that he would simply stay on the ground. But, like a beast of burden trudging through the mud, he struggled to his feet and continued to drag his cross against the paved streets of Jerusalem. The third time that he fell, a Roman soldier reached out and grabbed my tunic. He threw me forward and commanded me to help him bear the cross."

Dikembul leaned back. He tried to picture every word that Simon spoke. He could see the motley crowd that Simon spoke of—many shouting, "Crucify!" while others stood by in silent protest of yet another Roman execution of a fellow Jew.

"That cross," Simon continued gazing deeply into Dikembul's eyes, "that cross . . . It nearly broke my back. It was made out of a simple piece of wood, but for some reason, it felt like a slab of iron or something much heavier. It was as if he were helping me to carry it."

"Did the man say anything to you?" Dikembul asked.

"No. He couldn't. The Roman whips sliced through him nearly every step of the way. He never said a word during the procession. When we arrived at Golgotha, they nailed him to the cross and planted it into the ground." Simon momentarily closed his eyes. "I can still hear his flesh tearing and joints pulling from the sockets as his full weight hung on the cross."

Annika sat transfixed. Her heart raced as she pictured a bloodied man gasping for air on the execution device. Growing ever more anxious, she searched for a rationale that would provide a diversion for her analytical mind. "He had to have been a vicious criminal," she said once Simon finished.

The Cyrenian's heavy eyes focused on her. "Yes, that's exactly what I thought as I bore that cross with him. With every torturous step, I tried to envision the crime that this man must have committed to warrant such a violent execution. Murder. Rape. Betrayal. Strangely enough though, in every scenario that I placed this man in . . . my face emerged as the perpetrator. My heart devised the evil. My hand shed the blood."

The table was quiet for a long moment until the large Egyptian uttered an amused grunt. "Unfortunately, it doesn't matter what we think. Until the sun rises on the final day of that cursed empire, none of our lives matter that much."

Simon looked at his companion and then glanced

toward Dikembul and his daughter. "I believe what we think matters. Maybe not to Pilate or Caesar, but what we think about this man matters. I can't help but believe that there was something singular about him."

"Why do you say that?" asked Annika.

"Because . . . because the last words I heard him say were extremely peculiar."

Annika's eyes narrowed. "What did he say?"

"Before the Roman soldiers pushed me away, I heard him say, 'Father, forgive them, for they know not what they do.' I took it as the ramblings of a delirious man resisting the talons of death. But then . . . then he cried out, 'It is finished,' as if his death was the final piece of a great puzzle."

"Your first speculation was correct, my friend," the large Egyptian spouted. "Those were the words of a dying man urging death to finish its business. Fortunately for him, his suffering has ceased. He is dead and buried and no longer a subject of Caesar's mercurial will."

As Simon and the Egyptian launched off into a debate on Roman law, Dikembul found himself in the middle of what appeared to be an ongoing struggle between the ideologies of the two men. Thus far, everything that Simon had spoken correlated with elements of the words issued by the men from Galilee during the Day of Pentecost. "Simon, do you know anything about the followers of this man, Jesus?"

"Only that they were scattered with the wind. After this Jesus was put to death, those who followed him simply disappeared. At least, that's what I heard. The three of us actually left the city the day after the crucifixion."

"They were probably hunted down and tortured as well," blurted the Egyptian, a thin streak of wine running down the side of his mouth. "It would serve them right for turning their backs on the man."

Unable to avoid the debate, Simon shook his head. "I'm sure they had no choice in the matter." He turned to Dikembul and searched out the Ethiopian's dark eyes. "It's a shame. After the crucifixion, I made several inquiries about Jesus and his followers. Seems that he caused several commotions in the Temple marketplace by overturning tables and driving out vendors with whips. In doing so, he earned the wrath of the high priests."

"I didn't know that," Dikembul responded. The men he saw on the Day of Pentecost hardly fit the description that Simon painted. In his opinion, they were neither cowards nor rabble-rousers.

"Tell me, sir," the large Egyptian said to Dikembul, "Why are you so curious about Jewish renegades? If I'm not mistaken, you are on your way home to the land of Meroë. Seems a bit odd that you would be concerned with the lives of a few insignificant souls hundreds of miles away back in Judea of all places."

Dikembul stared at the man. For the first time since they left Judea, he asked himself the same question. *Why am I concerned about a group of men preaching what technically amounted to blasphemy to a Jew?*

It had been so long since the Day of Pentecost that the images of the Galileans were starting to fade from his mind's eye. The only thing that he could remember clearly about them was the incredible passion and zeal accompanying their words. Though their message made little sense to him, it was as if their simple words had been aimed directly at his heart. Regardless, in all of his days, Dikembul had never seen any man speak with such conviction and power.

"To be truthful, while we were in Jerusalem, I heard several men proclaiming this Jesus as if he were still alive."

"That is ridiculous," the large Egyptian spouted. "The Romans are very efficient. They kill people with the intent of them remaining dead."

Though he could find no plausible reason to debunk the Egyptian's statement, something drove Dikembul to challenge the man. "The Galileans spoke of the resurrection from the dead. They said that he arose from the grave three days after the execution."

Dikembul's statement was met by a chorus of silence. From what he could tell, the men took him seriously, for most Egyptians believed in some form of resurrection.

"That is most unlikely," said the smaller Egyptian. "They were obviously trying to deceive you."

Dikembul frowned. The thought had crossed his mind many times. "I'm not so sure. They hardly seemed like a group of liars or cowards, for that matter."

"Where were these men proclaiming these issues?" asked Simon.

"In a meeting hall just outside of the Temple."

"That was bold," Simon muttered. He wanted to ask the Ethiopian more but restrained himself.

The large Egyptian took a final gulp of his drink and slammed the cup down on the table. "If those men were followers of this Jesus, then preaching down the street from the Temple a month after their leader was executed was not an act of bravery to be commended. It was an act of suicide. Rest assured, by now, they are just as dead as this Jesus."

※   ※   ※

The last vestige of golden rays arced brilliantly over the Egyptian horizon as Annika watched the day come to a close. She never missed a sunset. Throughout their time in Judea, she always took time to watch the sun slide below the western hills. The fact that it was setting in the general direction of Nubia allowed her to connect with her friends back in Nuri. She often looked into the sky and reminded herself that they saw the same sun, admired the same moon, and counted the same stars.

In the distance, she saw her uncle and two young cousins securing the sheep for the evening. Her uncle, who was a full-blooded Nubian from the Napata region, was a strong, burly man only slightly larger than her father. His two sons were half-Egyptian and possessed a light complexion that favored their mother.

Throughout their stay, Annika often wondered if the two of them found it difficult coping with the fact that they were of mixed lineage. Egyptians and Nubians shared a racial rivalry dating back thousands of years, which was perpetuated by the myriad number of wars and skirmishes over territory and resources. She almost asked the question on several occasions. However, she always backed away. Aside from being part Nubian and part Egyptian, they were also Jewish.

Her uncle was just as devout as her father. She was certain he conveyed to them that Jehovah made no distinction between Nubians and Egyptians. It was a lesson her father reviewed with her thoroughly as they made their trek to Judea so many months ago.

He warned her that they would eventually come across fellow Jews who would not accept them because they were from Nubia. He said the best way to deal with them was to simply pray that God would open their eyes and hearts to the fact that people were different.

To say the least, Annika prayed a great deal during their trip.

Her attention was focused on her uncle and cousins making their way back to the house when her father suddenly came into her line of sight. Her head snapped back in momentary shock, prompting her to glare at him angrily.

"Why do you keep doing that?" she piped.

"I'm sorry, my dear. But I made no attempt to hide my approach," Dikembul offered, the dimming light slightly masking his smile. He perused the surrounding pasture and drank in the tranquillity that it offered. The crimson spectrum in the sky caught his eye. "You must be out here enjoying another sunset."

"Partly," Annika answered, turning toward him. "I was actually thinking about the conversation that you were having with those men earlier this evening. You never mentioned to me about anything happening at the Temple that day."

"I know," Dikembul said, lowering his head. "I didn't want to concern you with it until I had more information."

"Were you worried about proclaiming this Jesus as the Messiah?"

"For the most part, yes." Dikembul leaned against a tree stump and folded his arms. He was actually relieved to be able to voice his concerns. "Many people, even those in Meroë, are awaiting the appearance of the Messiah. The Scriptures declare that He will bring liberty, salvation, and justice to the children of Abraham."

Dikembul paused, allowing his mind to access the various reactions the men of Galilee received the day that they declared that Jesus was the Christ. "After the Galileans spoke with such conviction, many of the people, including ones I was praying with, also started to confess that Jesus was the Messiah. But then, there were many who didn't. To them, Jesus didn't fit the description of what they thought the Messiah should be."

Annika ran her finger along the ridge of her bottom lip as she did when deep in thought. "And what do you think of Jesus? Who do you say that he is?"

Dikembul focused on the last rays of light stretching up from the west. "I stayed and listened to both sides. I'm not an educated man in these matters, but I thought it through."

"What happened?"

"The longer that I stayed, the more the message made sense. The more my heart longed to hear more." He looked his daughter in the face, trying to capture her eyes in the dying sunlight. "I believe that this Jesus is the Messiah. I believe that He is the Son of God. And I believe that He has risen from the dead."

A cool breeze drifted through the pasture. Annika reacted by shivering slightly, though she wasn't certain if it were the wind or her father's startling confession that made her quiver. She was aware of the concept of the Messiah. However, her limited knowledge and the fact that she was a young woman often left her out of any conversations involving the individual prophesied to bring peace and restoration to the whole of Judaism.

"Perhaps I should have told you earlier," Dikembul confessed, noting her uncharacteristic silence. "There are many Jews who will feel differently."

"Why would they? If Jesus fulfills the prophecies from the ancient Scriptures, then . . ."

"Unfortunately, that won't matter to some." Dikembul recalled the dozens of Jews who vehemently opposed the proclamations set forth by the Galileans. "Many of the people in Judea are expecting the Messiah to appear as a great military leader who will deal with the Romans once and for all. Likewise, the Jews in our own nation envision the Messiah as one who will bring peace and justice to our land, ending the corruption and the bloody conflicts. They, too, are looking for a great warrior."

"Who else could accomplish such a feat?" Annika asked, without thinking.

"Bows and swords are probably the only items that can tame the murderous spirit in our government."

At times, Dikembul believed that only God could end the pointless fighting. Nevertheless, his experience in Jerusalem had given birth to a faith that saw through the impossibility of the situation. The last thing he sensed before departing the upper room where the Galileans preached was an undying essence of unity. There were Jews from all walks of life repenting of their sins and confessing Jesus as Lord and Christ. The image was etched in his heart, and he was sure that it would accompany him to his grave.

Noting that his brother and nephews were drawing near, Dikembul rose and took his daughter's hand. "I believe that Simon was correct. How each one of us perceives this man Jesus will be very important—one way or another."

Annika tilted her head. She curiously found herself trying to fuse together an answer for the same question she had posed to her father earlier.

Who do I say that he is?

As Dikembul's brother walked up, neither father nor

daughter spoke. They simply looked at each other and silently agreed that the conversation had run its course for the evening. Annika slipped her hand away from her father's and glanced into the darkened horizon, wondering how her newfound knowledge would affect the subsequent sunsets in her life.

Chapter 6

Alone in her throne room, the kandace of Meroë wept.

Silent tears ran down Queen Amanitore's cheeks as her soul was overcome with the dreaded sorrow that usurped the place in her heart that was once owned by her deceased sons.

Yes, the rebellion in Nobatia had been put down, but the price was far too excessive. Although nearly a year had passed, the progression of time had done little to bind the wounds that her weary spirit bore.

Not only had she lost Sherakarer, but now gone was the man who was to replace him. Ironically enough, Natakam survived the cataclysmic battle in the Nobatian desert only to succumb to an injury that he sustained that day. Though it had taken nearly a year, the infection that slowly ate away at his wound had finally run its course.

When news of her son Natakam's death first struck her ears, Amanitore ordered that three hundred bulls be sacrificed to Amun in the hopes that he would intervene and breathe life back into his broken body. Yet, her sacrifices went ignored and her prayers unanswered.

Not even the wisdom that she accumulated during her six decades of life could rationalize away the pain. With every tear, she reminded herself that life was a finite agent that eventually had to surrender itself to its cryptic master of death. It made no difference if one were a commoner tending a farm, a soldier on the battlefield, or a monarch in the palace. All would meet the same fate and all would pay the same price to the faceless avenger who stalked them relentlessly. Only the sovereign hands of the gods seemed to protect them. However, the gods were often capricious and seldom stopped to explain their actions.

As Amanitore solemnly wiped away the tears from her face, she found little solace in the fact that the gods promised an abundance of wealth and prominent positions for earthly monarchs in the afterlife. All that concerned her at the moment was the cold body of a thirty-six-year-old man that she buried the day before.

For days, she found it next to impossible to receive the definitive verdict that the gods had decreed. Could not the gods have curtailed their wrath just a bit? Was his crime so heinous that they found it necessary to end his life in such a pitiless manner?

Not even the fact that her kingdom was once again threatening to tear itself apart could separate her from her grief. The escalating feud between Kerma and Makoria only offered a transient diversion for her tortured mind.

She looked out the window to behold the vastness of her kingdom. The great temples and the soaring obelisks seemed trivial to her at this point.

Despair silently perched next to her as her grief-stricken mind came to grips with one of the most disturbing results that her Natakam's death would produce. Now that he was gone, the task of leading the kingdom would fall into the not-so-capable hands of Harmais, her youngest son. Though she loved him deeply, a majority of the time she wondered if he were truly a son of hers. Even though he tried to hide his true nature, for the most part, he was cruel, unjust, and unwilling to serve anyone other than himself.

Tears began to blur her vision of the city below. How grand Meroë had become! Since their victory over the Roman Empire, the Kushite kingdom enjoyed wealth unseen since the days of King Tarahaq. Meroë was the central corridor of trade between Rome and the Far East. Consequently, their status and power had been catapulted to heights that were never before thought possible.

Nevertheless, Amanitore knew just how shallow their wealth really was. Corruption had long since invaded the tribal councils that governed the four major provinces of Nobatia, Makoria, Alondia, and Kerma. Only her chief financial officer prevented the officials of those territories from evading taxes with impunity. Yet, in his absence, a cold rebellion had settled in. The death of her sons distracted her emotionally from administrative duties. Furthermore, she knew that someday the mighty armies that stood as sentinels over those lands would once again hurtle themselves into action against one another to capture exclusive rights to the trade routes.

Although the gods assured her that such an apocalypse would not transpire during her reign, she was often overcome with despair at the futility associated with her existence. With Natakam's death, things just didn't matter to her any longer. It didn't matter how much wealth or stability within the kingdom she produced. It didn't matter how many temples she erected for the gods. Nor did it matter that her devotion to those same gods sparked a spiritual revival throughout portions of the kingdom. In the end, all of her accomplishments would be overshadowed by the fact that a fool would now someday succeed her.

Within moments, she found herself envying her dead relatives. Her eyes drifted across the throne room and fell haplessly upon a looking glass. She paused to study her aging features. Her swarthy face was jaded and pleated— an outward expression of her tired soul.

Just then, the acute pain that plagued her physical body on a regular basis shrieked louder than her aching heart. It would not be long before her spirit would be carried across the river of death. Part of her longed for the day to be free from the torment that was called life. Though she was quickly losing her faith in the gods, she felt certain that the next world had to offer a great deal more justice than the present one did.

Shifting her eyes back into the looking glass, she silently feared that both her kingdom and family would crumble to dust long before her body would wither away in its grave.

🜚   🜚   🜚

Naytal refused to allow any unpleasant thoughts to disrupt her current state of bliss. The warm bath water caressed her body in a way that nothing else could. She sank into it up to her neck and invited the water, which was treated with a special tonic, to open her pores and invigorate her dark skin.

For the moment, she didn't mind the fact that her mother had summoned her to the palace. She hated Meroë and preferred to spend her time at Wad ben Naga with her young son, Terenkiwal. Though it was heavily fortified and situated on a hill, she loved the seclusion that the royal retreat provided. The surrounding forest gave her a sense of insulation from the rabble of the capital city only a few miles to the north.

The large bath facility was one of the amenities provided by the main royal palace in the heart of Meroë. Yes, the palace had everything one could wish for—gleaming hallways, expensive tapestries that adorned the walls of every room, scores of servants. From her childhood, Naytal had taken advantage of every benefit that being a member of the royal family had to offer.

The only drawback that constantly plagued her was the awful truth that she had to share the spoils of royal life with her siblings. Being the youngest of the four children born to Amanitore and Natakamani, she was oftentimes ignored by all. As a child, she constantly had to struggle for her parents' attention and rarely received much more than a token display of affection. Both the king and queen were far more absorbed in grooming their sons for leadership than they were in raising a family. Sherakarer was to be the future king; Natakam was to lead the armies; Harmais was to administrate the financial facet.

Nothing that Naytal did even registered with her parents—or brothers for that matter. The bridle that her parents did maintain upon her restricted her movements to the Isle of Meroë and occasionally to Napata. Even when she became pregnant with Terenkiwal, their reaction was one of indifference. Their main thoughts were always with their kingdom, their legacies, and their sons.

After King Natakamani died, the pecking order for the throne was well delineated. Fully aware that neither she nor her son would ever come close to sitting upon the throne, she set out to build and secure her own little niche in the kingdom. During her youth, she saw to her own education and relied upon her vast network of friends and associates to keep track of what was happening in the important parts of the kingdom.

Anticipating the day that one or more of her brothers would decide to use her beauty as a pawn to manipulate or appease an ambitious vizier, general, or peshte, she used her own subtle powers of conniving and manipulation to acquire exclusive rights to a little-known trade route that ran parallel with the Nile. As planned, she managed to build quite a storehouse of wealth and goods. Her clandestine plot proved to be very effective. At thirty years old, she possessed the ability to buy her way out of trouble —a luxury that could very easily become a necessity.

Naytal opened her eyes and studied the mural of Isis that was painted on the adjacent wall. The great goddess was depicted holding the sun in one hand and the moon in the other. Naytal examined every detail of the painting. Theologically, the depiction was incorrect. As powerful as Isis was, she did not have authority over the heavenly bodies. Such power was only ascribed unto the great god Amun, yet Naytal welcomed the inaccuracy. Of all the gods, Isis embodied and possessed everything that she wanted. For centuries, even the mighty men of the kingdom fell down and worshiped the beautiful goddess.

For a brief moment, Naytal saw her own face embedded in the mural. Suspended in stone, the gleeful smile worn by the painting revealed the fact that the world elevated her to a status untouched by but a select few. For centuries, the kandaces of Kush and Meroë were seen as agents of Isis and sacred vessels that carried her essence upon the earth.

Closing her eyes, Naytal allowed herself to relive the dream that dared to defy the hand of mediocrity that fate had dealt to her by mistake. She wasn't sure how, but she knew that someday Isis would intervene and demand that the fates recalculate the destiny that had been assigned to her.

Glancing back at a colorful wall that partitioned the large room into segments, Naytal wondered just how Isis planned to unfold her vision. Neither Sherakarer nor Natakam had married and produced heirs prior to their deaths. Naytal felt little positive feelings for either man. She had barely known them and perceived them to be nothing more than the two men who consumed all of her father's time. As much as she denied the existence of the feelings, she hated them for the part that they played in her exile into obscurity. Nevertheless, now that they were gone, all of her rancor focused upon her remaining brother.

The muscles in her neck tensed as she thought of Harmais. How she wished that his life had been extinguished in Nobatia along with Sherakarer's. Even though the fool was traitorous and worthless in battle, she had urged him to go. Nonetheless, his own cowardice saved his life. How wicked the fates were. In several weeks, Harmais would be coronated as the king of Meroë in Napata.

She glanced back at the partition once more. Before Harmais would be crowned as the reigning qeren, Naytal would have to endure a ceremony almost as objectionable as his coronation would most likely be. Prior to the death of his brothers, Harmais was engaged to marry one of Naytal's lifelong friends. At first, Naytal wasn't at all sure why Tshenpur had even agreed to soil herself by being joined with Harmais.

The eldest daughter of a senior vizier in Meroë, Tshenpur was lovely and more of a cosmopolitan than most of her friends. Yet, in certain ways, she was more like Naytal than she would admit. Though she said nothing, Naytal was certain that Tshenpur's engagement to Harmais was no more than a gamble to gain an influential position over the kingdom's financial quarter. If such were truly the case, then the gamble was about to pay off richly and manifest in the form of the throne.

The fates were truly tumbling over with glee as they observed the scenario.

A female servant quietly entered the room and stood pensively before the bath.

"What is it?" Naytal demanded before the servant could utter a word.

"I'm sorry to disturb you, Qar Naytal, but I have a message from the kandace for you."

Naytal resisted the urge to submerge herself completely. "What does my mother need?"

"The kandace has taken ill and wishes to inform you that she will have to delay your meeting at least another day."

Naytal's eyes rolled away from the servant in disgust. The delay meant that she would spend at least another day in Meroë. "Very well," she muttered, wishing she had brought Terenkiwal along for the journey after all. Noticing that the servant had not yet left, Naytal questioned, "Is there something more?"

"Yes, Your Highness. Lord Harmais wishes you to report to his office in the central dufufa before the end of the sixth hour."

Not wanting to display her contempt for the next king of Meroë, Naytal waited until the servant departed before she cursed him. A few days ago, she would have simply ignored him. Now she was bound to show him the one thing she felt that he truly did not deserve—respect.

Her eyes looked back at the glossy mural of Isis. For a moment, she wondered if the goddess actually existed at all. She felt betrayed by the fact that she was now nothing more than a puppet to be fondled by her brother. The prospect of being Harmais's subject turned her stomach. She silently wondered if Isis truly had any power over men. There hadn't been a strong kandace on the throne in nearly a hundred years, and she wasn't sure that Tshenpur could reverse the disturbing trend.

Within moments, she repented of her blasphemous thoughts and swore to herself that the situation would not persist. If anything, she would get Tshenpur to some-how manipulate Harmais into leaving her and Terenkiwal alone altogether.

"Please forgive me, my queen," she whispered to the pious painting. "At times my faith grows weary. But I know that you will not fail me."

Naytal could almost see the frozen image curve the corner of its lips upwards. "There is no power, no faith, no god greater than you. My life is in your hands. Do with me as you wish."

Chapter 7

The crowded thoroughfares of Philae were a welcome change for Sahlin. Their week-long trek up the Nile took them through scores of villages sitting along the life-giving river. Many of them were simple reed-and-mud huts. Others were more palatial and reminded Sahlin of his own home that was still many weeks to the south.

The day before, they passed through Philae's sister city, Elephantine. The flourishing city marked the border between the Roman province of Egypt and the great Kushite Empire of Meroë. Much like Elephantine, the streets of Philae were dusty and laden with merchants. Most of them guided mules and camels loaded with goods that would be traded in Alexandria, Jerusalem, and even Rome itself.

Part of Sahlin hated to see the massive amounts of gold, ivory, and other non-replenishable goods shipped out of Meroë. He often wondered what would eventually happen to his homeland once its resources were exhausted and the people had nothing left to barter with. Previous travels through Meroë made him well aware of the massive mining projects that plundered lush valleys and canyons, leaving them nothing more than lifeless oases in the fertile Nile valley.

As Meroë's chief financial officer, he was also well aware of the significance and status that trade with Rome brought to Meroë. After establishing numerous trade treaties with Rome after the war, Meroë had increased its wealth many times over. The prosperity and technology that flooded into Meroë from the northern empire was intoxicating to the people of Kush. In every Nubian city, one could find traces of the Roman culture steadily gaining a foothold. Bathhouses, aqueducts for irrigation, and paved roads were now becoming icons in the larger cities of Meroë.

Sahlin made his way through the crowded streets of Philae towards the Great Temple of Isis. He was nearly overjoyed to be back in a city that was under the complete jurisdiction of Meroë. In addition, for the first time in over a week, he was actually free from Bakka's watchful eye. He had somehow managed to convince the mighty guard that his services were not needed, at least for the first part of the day. In order to provide extra incentive to let him be, Sahlin shrewdly informed Bakka that he was planning to spend a significant amount of time at and around the Temple. As expected, Bakka responded by deciding to send one of the other guards to blend into the immense crowd that seemed to shroud the outside walls of the great structure.

Sahlin had seen the temple many times before but had never entered it. His Jewish training had conditioned him to forgo places that sanctioned sacrifices to idols. Nonetheless, he was still captivated by it.

Built generations ago by the Egyptians, the building was magnificent beyond imagination. The temple was a massive and colorful structure with pillars and grand colonnades that soared into the sky. Thousands of Egyptians and Nubians alike made annual pilgrimages to Philae to sacrifice to the great Queen Mother.

Sahlin stood and watched as scores of worshipers entered and departed the outer court. He marveled at how the Nubians and Egyptians tolerated each other, considering that Kush and Egypt had been both competitors and combatants throughout the centuries. The spirit of good-will was often short-lived, though. Though Philae may have been a city that promoted unity, the rate of violence between Nubians and Egyptians was extremely high in Elephantine.

Strangely enough, Sahlin couldn't help but feel a twinge of grief as he watched the people file in and out of the temple. The subtle feeling caught him by surprise and gnawed at him unremittingly. Unaccustomed to having an untamed passion run loose in his heart, he tried to contain and categorize it as he had often done with disturbing emotions. Yet, the feeling of dismay and pity only intensified. Frustrated, he turned his glance away from the scene.

His eyes fell haphazardly upon a pair of vendors. The elderly couple, who looked as if they were husband and wife, was selling doves and ravens for sacrificial purposes. As Sahlin watched the two shuffle away, exchanging money for animals to be sacrificed to the gods, his chest suddenly became heavy with an unimaginable burden. His eyes began to well with tears as he watched a young

Nubian boy holding a newly purchased offering run glee-
fully to his parents.

Sahlin shook his head vehemently. Despite the strin-
gent nature of his own religion, he had always looked
upon sacrifices to Isis, Apedemack, and the other Nubian
gods with a measure of respect. Unlike others, he felt that
a man should feel free to express his piety in whatever
form he felt necessary. True, the philosophy plowed
against the teachings of Moses and the traditional precepts of other Jewish patriarchs, but the non-Jewish facets
of Sahlin's education implored him to tolerate the earnest
beliefs and passions of other men.

Nevertheless, the tugging in his heart persisted and
almost succeeded in getting him to urge them to stop. To
prevent his making such a scene, he forced himself to
move along, hoping that a change of scenery would affect
his disposition.

As he walked along the perimeter, he marveled at the
variety of goods he found available. In fact, it was something that vividly reminded him of scenes from Judea.
Back in Jerusalem, common vendors were allowed to
conduct commerce in close proximity to great centers of
worship. While visiting the Great Temple of Jerusalem, he
had found everything from religious trinkets to livestock.

Within a few moments, Sahlin found himself in the financial center. The courtyard was teeming with booths
occupied by tax gatherers and money changers. The site
almost made Sahlin feel at home. Like a cool drink from
the Nile, he stood in the midst of the mass of humanity
and listened to people haggle and barter their way to the
best deal. A sly smile slid across his face as his ears welcomed the sounds of childhood, and for a moment, the
spirit that tormented his conscience fell silent.

Dikembul bit his tongue and tried not to swear. It was the third time that day a money changer tried to rob him.

"You must be mistaken," Dikembul breathed, glaring down at a middle-aged Egyptian financier. "I was told that currency from the Egyptian province would hold its value no matter what."

The bearded man simply looked up at Dikembul and elevated an eyebrow. "I cannot help it if you were given faulty information. The swine from northern Egypt often take advantage of travelers passing through their land, especially those entering from Judea."

"It wasn't a swine from northern Egypt that gave me the quote. It was a swine from here in Philae, before we even got to Judea . . ." Almost immediately, Dikembul regretted the words.

"No matter who it was, your problem still remains," the man said coldly as he scribbled on his ledger. "And patronizing me will get you nowhere."

Dikembul forced himself to think rationally, though the circumstances urged him to do differently. Thus far, he had wasted over two hours trying to find an honest money changer who would convert his Roman money into its equivalency in gold. Every hour he spent wading through the marketplace was an hour stolen from Annika and his journey back home.

"Are you going to accept my rate or not?" the money changer demanded. "If not, then move along. There are others with whom I need to do business."

Dikembul mulled over the man's offer. The percentage he charged was fairly large and took a considerable slice out of the budget for his return voyage. It was the exact situation that he hoped to avoid. Prior to leaving Nubia for Judea, he had verified the rate of exchange from at least three different vendors. Even after factoring in margins for possible inflation and price fluctuation, he was confident he would have enough money to finance their trip from start to finish. Now that projection was in serious peril.

"I find it extremely difficult to believe that this is the best exchange rate available in the city," Dikembul said.

The man smirked. "I didn't say that this was the best offer! I'm quite certain there are many others that can give you the rate you seek. However, I doubt very much that you have the time to search for those individuals. You did say that your journey back begins tomorrow, did you not?"

"Bright and early."

"Therefore, I suggest that you take my offer. You see, due to demand, the rate may go up at any time."

For the first time since they had arrived in Egypt, Dikembul wished that they had never stopped. He had seen the hideous face of Egyptian greed several times, but never this close. Now, he could see nothing more, and all he wanted to do was recoil in disgust.

"I doubt if the Lord approves of such practices," Dikembul said as he reached for his moneybag.

"Just remember, friend, that a percentage of your interest rate goes to support and maintain this wonderful sanctuary of worship that helps to sustain the local economy, even for the Jewish population."

"And to line the high priest's pockets," Dikembul muttered under his breath.

"Excuse me," a voice called from the side.

The bearded money changer looked up and grinned to greet the newcomer. "Ah, another Nubian."

Dikembul glanced at the man as well, with a mind to admonish the man to take whatever business he had elsewhere.

The money changer smiled invitingly. "My name is Horem. Are you in need of a currency exchange?"

"I am Sahlin Malae. Thank you for the offer, but my financial matters have already been attended to."

"That's too bad," Horem said. For some reason, the newcomer's presence agitated him. "As you can see, we are in the process of business . . . and . . ."

Sahlin smiled at the man's attempt to brush him off. "Actually, I needed a word with my Nubian brother here."

"But you just can't . . ."

Before Horem could finish, Sahlin had Dikembul's full attention. "I am sorry to interfere, but I couldn't help but overhear your conversation. I heard you say something about getting a good rate on your exchange."

"That's right," Dikembul answered, trying to identify Sahlin's Kushite accent. "Horem wants to charge me twenty-five percent."

Sahlin frowned. "That's far too much. I happen to know a man who will do it for considerably less."

The two started to walk away.

"Wait, come back!" Horem cried, trying to recapture their attention.

Within moments, Sahlin and Dikembul blended into the crowd.

"I really appreciate this," Dikembul said, grateful to be away from Horem's web.

"My pleasure. Criminals shouldn't be rewarded with the business that honest men earn. The place that I spoke of is not far."

As the two men progressed through the Temple's

outer court gate and through the streets of Jerusalem, Dikembul's curiosity got the better of him. "Which part of Meroë are you from?"

"My accent is that strong?" Sahlin smiled.

"That and the fabric of your tunic. The pattern is far too fancy to be Roman or Egyptian."

"I'll take that as a compliment. I am from the Isle of Meroë. And yourself?"

"Nuri," Dikembul answered, trying to recall if he had ever met anyone from the large strip of land outlined by three mighty rivers, thus giving rise to the analogy of an island. "I can't wait to see the sun descend behind Gebel Barkal once again."

Sahlin knew the structure he was referring to well. The great stone mountain sat in the middle of the flattened region and looked as if it were a portion of an uncompleted wall against the backdrop of the horizon. "My business takes me to Napata quite often," Sahlin replied, referring to the great city founded at the base of Gebel Barkal.

Dikembul nodded in understanding. "I own several modest herding establishments in Nuri. They prevent me from traveling as much as I would like. After this experience, I'll probably never venture out of Meroë again."

"I wish that I could say the same," Sahlin said, estimating that he probably would have to tour the whole of the kingdom at least three times and leave it at least twice within the next four years alone.

"What manner of work do you do?" Dikembul asked.

"I am employed in the queen's court." Sahlin knew that Bakka would never approve of the disclosure of such information. For some reason, he felt at total ease with the middle-aged man with whom he walked.

Dikembul decided to curtail his desire for details of

the younger man's occupation. He opted for a less revealing question. "Was your journey outside of Meroë one of business or pleasure?"

"In reality, it was neither. I am just now returning from Jerusalem where I observed the Feast of Weeks."

Dikembul's eyebrows went up. He resisted the urge to ask if Sahlin had heard of the man named Jesus. "Do you worship at the *masjid* in Meroë?"

"I've been there many times, but again, my duties to the court have kept me extremely busy."

"I see," Dikembul noted how articulate the young man was and figured that he was well educated and probably belonged to a rather important family.

Sahlin guided them down another street. "I assume that you journeyed to Jerusalem as well?"

"Yes, I was there last year with my daughter. However, we've been in Egypt with family for the last few months. It has been my lifelong ambition to worship in the Holy Land."

"Just the two of you went to Jerusalem?"

Dikembul smiled and nodded. "She's like my right arm. Besides, I couldn't afford to bring anyone else, especially with men like that out there." He pointed back in the direction of Horem.

They turned yet another corner and proceeded down a far less-crowded street. Dikembul noticed that they were in an upper-class section of the city. Scribes, tax collectors, and even a few Roman citizens patronized the shops lining the sidewalks. Everything was much cleaner and less boisterous than any section of Philae that Dikembul had been in.

Finally, they stopped in front of a small financial office.

"Here we are," Sahlin announced. "This man was recommended to me while I was in another city. I found him to be extremely fair and of good character. I have no doubt that he'll treat you with the same courtesy." That much Sahlin was certain of. His many years of dealing with financial officers helped him to develop a sixth sense about people when it came to money.

"I really appreciate this," Dikembul expressed.

"I wish you a safe journey home," Sahlin replied, shaking Dikembul's extended hand.

"Thank you. May God keep you during your trek as well." Dikembul glanced into the man's hazel eyes and saw an unspoken hunger yearning to be filled. "Perhaps our paths will cross again someday and afford me the opportunity to return this favor."

Sahlin slowly nodded and continued down the street.

🏺   🏺   🏺

Sunlight spilled over the eastern range of mountains that flanked the great valley of Qustul. The sun's rays slowly overpowered the hundreds of torches providing light for the vast military complex nestled just outside of the city. Already ahead of the new day, hundreds of Kushite soldiers marched through the valley. Some regiments worked to clear underbrush, while others funneled through the woods to patrol the province.

The refurbished dufufa stood in the heart of the city. The sacred building and its accompanying structures were more or less healed from the scars inflicted by war.

As a part of his daily routine, General Akinidad stood on the third-story balcony of the dufufa, observing his troops tend to their morning tasks. Weeks had gone by since their arrival, and he silently reveled in the accomplishments of his army. Upon the orders of Vizier Carachen, he directed his army, with the help of the local inhabitants, to rebuild the devastated landscape of Qustul.

Thus far, he had hated every moment of it. Life in the city was plagued with routine after monotonous routine. Although there were plenty of potential enemies around, there were no battles to fight or skirmishes to plan for.

The largest battle-ready army in northern Meroë had been reduced to the ignoble task of heaping up and hauling away debris. The fact that the rubble had been created by their rivals from the south only added to the humiliation.

Akinidad loathed every moment he was away from the training fields of Kerma, and he wasn't alone. Twice in the last two weeks he had to discipline soldiers who openly spoke out against the royal edict that assigned them the chore to rebuild what King Sherakarer had the pleasure to destroy. Were it not for the necessity to maintain order in the ranks, he would have promoted the offenders instead of having them flogged. Inwardly, he envied the audacity that compelled them to utter their condemnation of Carachen's decision making.

Akinidad gripped the wooden rails that lined the balcony. The entire march north from Kerma had been an exploration of his own soul. After having weeks to evaluate his life, Akinidad did not like what he saw. The patriarch of his family had groomed him to be a hardened soldier with little tolerance for mediocrity. To the few friends he had, it was plain to see that it was the pursuit of an intangible destiny which drove him to make sacrifice after sacrifice in order to rise above the rest. Instead of espousing one of the many beautiful women who flocked to him, his closest soul mate was his own ambition. Even when he felt the need to curtail his march toward greatness, his ambition crept up like a jilted lover, demanding a return to its preeminent position in his life. Above all, the tall, muscular black commander wanted it discernible to all that a man had to be prepared in order to meet his destiny.

When he was thirty-eight, the great god Apedemack had rewarded his dedication by elevating him above his peers and competitors and placing him in the right hand of a rampant if not skilled vizier. Grateful for the opportunity, Akinidad made weekly sacrifices to the lion-headed warrior god, hoping to maintain his favor.

Akinidad's hawkish eyes pierced through to every corner of the camp visible to him. Everything was much the same as it had been yesterday, and the day before that, and the day before that. Carachen had visited weeks ago to inspect the northern forts at Qustul and Kalabsha. From the vizier's point of view, the inspection had gone flawlessly. Yet to Akinidad it had been only the latest slap in the face from the reigning chief administrator. It was then that Carachen revealed his plans to have Akinidad's army rebuild the Korosko irrigation system and root out the few remaining rebels that fled deep into the western desert. Neither prospect seemed inviting to Akinidad or his troops.

Though he loathed Carachen, he was well aware that the vizier was merely an emasculated lapdog propped up by the royal court. The policies of Amanitore's administration had reduced the once proud northern province Kerma to a backwoods tribe. Over the past several years, the kandace had backed off on any further forceful expansion of the kingdom. Yes, there were always small rebellions to put down, and hordes of Blemmyes raiders to ward off; however, Amanitore had a habit of dispatching regiments from the southern army in Meroë to quell the disturbances. It was a move that Akinidad and his men despised. They quietly hated the fact that their queen chose to relegate the greatest fighting force in the kingdom to yard work.

There were times that Akinidad felt as if he were going to explode with rage because of her reluctance to use them for anything other than bridge building. Nevertheless, he kept his opinions to himself, sharing them only with Apedemack during his weekly sacrifices. Like everything else during the past season of his life, it had become part of his routine.

Devoutly religious and dedicated to the warrior-god, Akinidad had become extremely sensitive to the great deity's prompting. Though he never heard Apedemack audibly as some claimed to have, he often had dreams that he assumed originated from him. The dreams generally left great impressions on him, lingering in his psyche for days.

At the moment, he found his concentration dwelling on the vision that had visited him for the past several nights. In his dream, he saw himself soaring high into the sky, to battle Ra on behalf of Apedemack. Each time, he drove the Egyptian sun god down below the southern mountains of Kush, extinguishing his influence over the land. Afterward, he found himself shooting an arrow into the heart of the moon, only to watch it run red with blood.

Though he had no seer to interpret the dream for him, for some reason, Akinidad felt that he stood at the brink of something momentous.

As Akinidad's attention filtered down to the base of the dufufa, he noticed something out of the ordinary. A team of two unmanned chariots sat parked near the entrance. He was in the process of trying to identify the vehicles' markings when there was a knock at his door.

"Enter," he called across the room. Within moments, a sharply clad officer stood before him.

"General, couriers from Vizier Carachen have arrived with a royal decree."

Though he didn't want to, Akinidad accepted the letter from the officer and read it silently. A muscle twitched in his jaw as his eyes perused the letter in disbelief. Careful not to display any emotion, he folded the letter and placed it on his desk. "That will be all," he said, turning his back to the officer. "Tell the couriers that the vizier's orders have been received and acknowledged."

Akinidad walked out to the balcony as the man left the room. He silently pondered how to respond to Carachen's latest unacceptable decision.

A troop transfer! The fool wants me to split my forces!

Although the orders were outrageous and took him by surprise, the idea was nothing new. Nearly two years earlier, the kandace decided to erect an army that would serve as a security force between Napata and the Isle of Meroë. Despite objections from the governor of the northern provinces, her ministers started pilfering men and resources from the northern army. As anticipated by the northern army military leaders, the action incited protests among the general populace from Korosko to Kerma. Since the Roman War, the northerners felt it imperative to maintain a strong military presence in that region—a philosophy embraced by every subsequent Kushite ruler until Amanitore. Now here she was ordering a transfer of two thousand troops from Kerma to a newly formed battalion outside of Kurgus. Had she any idea of what she was doing to the security of the north? Moreover, it seemed as if Carachen were simply going to let the north go unprotected.

Akinidad dropped into his chair and stared at the transfer order. It instructed him to send part of his forces to Napata, while the other part continued the reconstruction efforts in Korosko. The letter also detailed Carachen's plans to personally assume command of the detachment to be heading south.

Resentment started to envelop Akinidad's thoughts as he glared at the letter. For the first time in days, he allowed his normally disciplined mind to dwell upon the talks of succession that had arisen at an unofficial tribal council meeting back in Kerma. Such rumors had filled the air before, only to fade listlessly into the night. Indeed, many felt that the district of Kerma should attempt to do what Nobatia did and divorce itself from the Meroë Empire.

He swore to Apedemack that if a leader worthy of his respect were to openly support succession, he would be among the first to bear arms on his behalf.

Chapter 8

"Aron, will you please slow down? I can't keep up with you!" a frantic female voice echoed down the quiet Jerusalem street.

Stalling his pace by a half step, Aron turned his head ever so slightly in order to identify the woman who begged him to stop. "I don't want to be late, Phoebe."

The young woman finally caught up with him. "You said that you would wait for me," she managed to say, clearly out of breath.

"And that's exactly what I did," Aron said as they turned a corner, the sun just starting to peek over the horizon. "You simply took too long to come out of the house. I told you last night that I would only stop briefly in front of your home and would not wait around for you to get ready."

"Yes, I know," Phoebe said, rubbing her arms briskly.

"But it's so early and cold. I still don't understand why we have to start so early in the morning."

Aron flashed her a momentary look of exasperation and then smiled. He promptly asked himself why he had agreed to take the sixteen-year-old girl along with him to help prepare the daily apportionment of food for the church widows. Though she was eager, he didn't believe that she had fully counted the cost of her commitment to help him.

"Like I told you last night, Phoebe, there's a great deal of work that needs to be done. The deacons need us to make sure that the food is divided up properly. Otherwise, some families may end up being shorted or overlooked altogether."

As he spoke, he warded off the memories of several occasions last year when the church actually ran out of food to give to needy families. He was just a new convert at the time, helping to unload several carts of grain. The thing that moved him the most was the many families that had received food and contributed sacrificially to provide for those who had none. The images moved him to tears and inspiration. He could remember many nights as a child going to bed hungry, just wishing that bread would fall out of the sky.

Generosity was only one of the many traits that attracted him to the unique body of people referred to as the "church." He recognized many of the members of the new assemblage from the synagogues in Jerusalem, many of which had hardly been the giving type at the time. In fact, some of the individuals who now volunteered their time to distribute food and help construct homes were the same vendors and businessmen notorious for overcharging foreigners and the poor. Nevertheless, there was something about the church that changed them.

Aron bit his lower lip and shook his head. He knew exactly what it was that had changed them. It was the same power that transformed his own selfish, pilfering nature. Not a day went by that he did not fondly recall the day and hour when he had heard Simon Peter preach at the colonnade of Solomon. Though he had not fully understood all of the things that Peter spoke about, one phrase ran through his mind like a tempest crossing the Sea of Galilee.

Repent therefore and return, that your sins may be wiped away . . .

At the young age of twenty-one, Aron had much to repent of. He had long lost track of how many items he had stolen from neighbors and strangers alike. As a boy, he had stolen out of necessity, but later it was strictly out of greed. His father passed away during his teen years, leaving a gaping hole in his life. Despite the loss, he managed to help support his mother and younger sisters, utilizing both legal and illegal means. He did everything from farming to running arms for individuals who hoped to someday rebel against their Roman overlords.

Aron was on his way to initiate a deal that would include him on a shipment of arms that would deliver him more money than he had ever seen as well as a sure crucifixion if he were caught. However, before he arrived at the arranged meeting place, he happened across a mass of people listening to two men declaring some sort of new message. Aron started to leave the scene but was captivated by their words and sincerity of heart.

Shortly afterward, the two men were seized by the temple guards and led away. Nevertheless, their message of repentance, restoration, and resurrection echoed throughout his spirit. The more he listened, the more he wanted to know about Jesus the Christ. Later on, he learned that the bold men were Peter and John and were leaders of a growing assembly that followed this man that was hailed to be the long-awaited Messiah. Though he was aware of predictions of the coming deliverer, Aron never gave the concept much thought. Nevertheless, he was eternally grateful that the message of the Messiah reached him before the gladius of a Roman legionnaire did.

In the past year, he had grown to care deeply about the church and all associated with it. He loved listening to the twelve men who were being referred to as the elders. He found great inspiration in their teachings and was somehow challenged to become a better man. His father, who was anything but a staunch Jew, stressed to him the importance of being a faithful man. Be it rich or poor, honest or a thief—always be reliable.

After becoming a believer in the Messiah and a regular attendee of the expanding congregation, Aron sought a function in which he could employ the one strip of advice that his father melded into him. Loading carts of grain during predawn wasn't very enticing, but it was an opportunity to be reliable—something that he desperately needed to do.

For months he showed up to volunteer his time—usually before the cart even arrived to pick up the grain. All he wanted was to be used and to be a part. Soon, he was asked to stop loading and to help unload at the various drop-off points. It wasn't long afterward that Timon, one of the head deacons appointed by the elders to administrate the food distributions to the widows in the church, recognized his faithfulness and hard work.

To his surprise, Aron was asked to help coordinate the distributions near the temple. A great number of needy families congregated at that particular site, making food distribution there difficult to organize. Nevertheless, Aron was honored and worked as hard as he could. Though he received no tangible payment, he delighted in the fact that he was occasionally called to help serve the families of the elders. He was even selected to help Timon and the other deacons serve the elders during a large meeting that drew nearly seventy other men that walked directly with Jesus.

On a more tragic occasion, he managed to meet several of the twelve elders. It had been at the burial of Stephen, one of the deacons who had been slain by the Sanhedrin. Timon was so devastated by Stephen's death that he asked Aron to perform all of his duties for a season. During that time, Aron was made responsible for tending to the family needs of four elders. His two favorite elders were Andrew and Matthew. Despite their occupied schedules, the two of them always seemed to go out of their way to give him an encouraging word and thank him for his hard work. Aron was always deeply touched by their gestures of gratitude—despite the fact that he would have performed the work even if no one ever recognized him.

Aron was also privileged to sit in on several prayer meetings that consisted of the entire twelve. Though he never uttered a word during the times of invocations, he loved to listen to the quiet zeal and composed fervency with which the elders prayed. They appeared to converse with God as if He were standing in the very room with them. Though he was aware that they in fact had walked with Jesus on an intimate level for three years, he longed to share the same familiarity that each one of them appeared to have with the risen Lord.

After each prayer meeting, Aron felt as if he had climbed a great mountain high enough to allow him to brush his hand against the clouds that hung in the sky. It was an experience that he would never forget. In fact, it triggered something so deep inside of him that he still groped for the words to describe it.

Sparse rays of sunlight warmed the crisp morning air just enough for Phoebe to loosen her scarf. She looked up at Aron who seemed to be lost in thought. She noticed that he wore nothing more than a simple tunic and coat. "I thought Ethiopians didn't like the cold," she jeered.

Aron glanced her way. "They don't. But I'm half-Jewish, remember?"

"Then you should at least wear a decent coat," Phoebe replied.

They came to the end of a deserted block and stopped. Aron kept one eye on the rising sun and another on the road, expecting the cart to arrive at any moment.

"So, have you ever been there?" Phoebe asked, trying to keep her mind off the nipping cold that plucked at her face.

"Been where?"

"Ethiopia."

"No," Aron responded curtly, trying to focus on the sounds that echoed in from a distance.

"Was it your father or mother?" Phoebe inquired.

"What?" Aron asked, starting to regret that he had brought her along.

"Who was from Ethiopia? Your father or mother?"

Aron turned toward her to check and see if she was serious. He was met by her inquisitive brown eyes. "My mother is Ethiopian. However, she was born in Caesarea. From what I understand, my grandfather migrated to Judea from somewhere in Nubia."

"Why did he come here?"

"I don't know. Why are you asking me these things?" Aron demanded, shaking his head. He was starting to get a better idea of why her father insisted that he take her with him.

"I like to get to know my friends. Besides, I've always liked your darker skin complexion."

Annoyed and sensing a trap, Aron decided not to respond to the latter part of her statement. "When my grandfather was a young man, he brought his family to Judea. I believe that he wanted to get away from the war that raged between Meroë and Rome."

"How do you feel about that?" Phoebe pressed, fully aware that she was irritating him.

Refusing to look her way, Aron's eyes darted quickly around the surrounding area. "At the moment, I wish that he would have gone back."

"I'd love to travel the world." Phoebe decided to let him off the hook. "I've heard so many stories about Egypt and Nubia. I'd do anything to go there."

"I believe those countries are that way," Aron said, pointing due south. "If you start walking now, you'll get there in about four months."

"You're so cruel, Aron. At this rate, you'll never get a wife . . ."

Aron drew a sharp, quick breath and ran his fingers through his short curly hair. "God will bring me a wife in due season. Until then, I don't think that you need to worry about it."

He glared down at her and was mortified by the

affectionate gaze beaming from her innocent eyes. "Uh . . . like I said . . . it's something that you definitely need not worry about."

"I'm not worried."

"Good," Aron breathed, wishing that the men with the cart and supplies would make haste to turn the corner. It wasn't the first time a young lady in the church embarrassed him with her eyes. He simply wasn't ready for marriage and wasn't about to let himself be enticed into family life by a set of pretty eyes.

A few silent moments inched by, and Phoebe once again found herself fending off boredom. "Would you like to travel anywhere? While you are a single man, I mean."

Aron evaluated the question before answering it. Resisting the temptation to tell a lie, he decided to be honest. "Someday, when I am much older, I wouldn't mind going to Africa, just to see the land."

"Perhaps God will grant your wish," Phoebe said, grateful that more sunlight crept steadily over the buildings in the foreground.

"I'm sure that He will," Aron said, almost as an afterthought. He had no desire to leave the church for any extended period of time. For once in his life, he felt the warm hand of unconditional love and wanted to hold it as long as he possibly could.

The soft cadence of hoofbeats bounced along the stone buildings. Aron peered down the street, relieved to see the horse-drawn cart approaching.

"Time to get to work," he said to Phoebe, handing her the ledger he had pulled from his coat. "Do you have any questions?"

"No, I remember everything that you showed me about taking inventory."

"Good. I'm sure you'll do fine."

The cart was followed by three men on foot. Aron recognized two of them as the volunteers from several evenings before. He smiled at the fact that the young men remained faithful to their word to assist with the off-loading.

To his surprise, the third individual was Timon. He greeted the other two and embraced Timon. The young men wasted no time as they started to off-load the cart. Not wanting to fall behind, Phoebe transformed herself into a well-disciplined steward and started to categorize every item the men unloaded.

Aron and Timon walked off to the side. The burly deacon was twice Aron's age and often treated Aron like a son.

"I wasn't expecting to see you here," Aron said, refusing to release the smile that he wore. "I hope there's not a problem."

"No, of course not," Timon affirmed, placing his hand upon Aron's shoulder. "I came here to speak with you. We need your help on a special project."

Timon led him to a plush business office where Aron settled down into a cushiony chair far more comfortable than the bed he slept on at home. Only curiosity prevented him from losing focus and drifting into an early morning daydream.

Aron had never been to the business district of Jerusalem before and simply couldn't help but be enamored with the phenomenal display of wealth. The walls of the room in which he and Timon sat boasted of brilliant mosaics and exquisite paintings, some of which looked as if they had been imported from Macedonia. He wasn't even sure what type of establishment they were in. The dozen or so employees in the outer offices appeared to be working on ledgers far more sophisticated than anything that he had ever handled.

Occasionally, Aron glanced at Timon. Unlike his usual talkative self, the deacon had hardly uttered a complete sentence during their walk from the distribution point.

After a few more minutes, two men entered the room from the rear door, totally catching Aron by surprise. Almost instantly, Aron recognized the bearded man as Philip, who originally worked with Timon in administrating the budget and food distributions. Aron had not seen the man since Stephen's tragic death. Philip's companion was clean-shaven and quite a bit taller. From the man's dark complexion, Aron surmised that he was a full-blooded Nubian, no more than two generations removed.

"Philip, Hiram," Timon greeted enthusiastically as he started to rise.

"Please make yourselves comfortable," the tall Nubian said, motioning Timon to remain seated.

Timon smiled warmly and allowed the two men to seat themselves. He then glanced at his young companion. "This is Aron, my friends, one of the most faithful men in the church."

Aron greeted the two men cordially, still wondering why he had been brought there.

Timon continued the introductions. "Aron, you may remember this man. We now call him Philip the Evangelist." Aron watched the three men share a mutual chuckle. "This other gentleman is Hiram, one of the most successful and generous accountants in Jerusalem."

Aron studied him for a moment. He ascertained by Hiram's body language and fine clothes that he was the owner of the establishment in which they sat. He listened to the three of them talk about Jerusalem's business climate for a few minutes until Timon finally addressed him.

"Aron, as I told you this morning, there is a very special project that we would like to present to you. Before we say anything, however, I would like to assure you that the decision to accept or decline is totally up to you. There is absolutely no pressure from us or any of the elders."

"The elders?" Aron asked, cocking an eyebrow. "What could they possibly need from me?"

Timon fought to suppress a grin. He relished that Aron was blind to the notion that he had grown to be a coveted laborer within the flourishing church. "We laughed earlier about Philip being tagged with the label of Evangelist. The fact is that he is one of the most dynamic preachers of our Lord's testimony in the church. In the past year since Stephen's death, he's been traveling throughout the countryside, proclaiming that men should repent. Scores of people have turned to Jesus."

Aron wanted to ask if this were the same man responsible for the influx of converts from the north, but decided to hold his tongue.

"Seeing so many people come to Jesus is a wonderful thing," Philip said. "It's also a pleasure to see them become part of the church family. Watching the Lord heal them physically, emotionally, and spiritually makes the discomfort of so much traveling well worth it."

Aron nodded his head in affirmation. He could still see the image of his own mother being healed from a horrific disease that ate away at the skin on her right leg. Even more miraculous, though, was that the love of God enabled her to release the sword of bitterness she had silently wielded against his father for years.

"James, the brother of our Lord, has always encouraged us to bring the new converts to the central assembly," Philip said, picking up the conversation. "It is here, among the brethren, that one can have his questions answered and faith in the Way edified."

As he listened to Philip and Timon, Aron glanced over at Hiram. The silent entrepreneur sat regally off to the side listening to every word as if Simon Peter were delivering a sermon.

"Sometimes things do not always happen that way," Timon said, almost announcing a shift in the dialogue. "Though we have several groups around the city, with plans to expand even beyond the walls of Jerusalem, we are still not able to follow up on everyone that becomes a believer in the Lord."

"Some converts have been businessmen or workers who live in Samaria, Phoenicia, or even Asia," Hiram added, breaking his silence.

Philip nodded. "That is correct. For such people, we must trust that the Holy Spirit will keep and guide them as they walk out their faith." Philip paused for a moment, allowing a hush to dominate the office. Even the colorful pictures on the wall seemed to tone down. "However, there is one foreigner I baptized a year ago who inhabits my dreams."

"Where was he from?" Aron asked, not sure what to say.

"He was from Nubia. The kingdom of Meroë to be precise." Philip shook his head as if to stave off disbelief. "Out of the hundreds of people I have met throughout this year, I can still remember his name and occupation. It's as if the Holy Spirit has etched every detail of the man into my mind."

Aron was at a loss for words, so he threw out the first thing that came to mind. "Who was he?"

"His name was Sahlin Malae, and he told me that he was the chief treasurer for the kandace of Meroë."

"Kandace?" Aron inquired, not fully understanding.

"It's the Kushite term for a queen," Hiram answered.

Philip drew a deep breath and continued. "Sahlin's image remained so strongly in my spirit for so long that I had no doubts the Lord was trying to tell me something. For months, I prayed for him on a daily basis. Finally, I took up the matter with elders as soon as I arrived back in Jerusalem.

"After hearing the story and bathing the situation in prayer, they agreed that God was speaking to us involving this man. Matthew took a particular interest."

Aron narrowed his eyes at the comment. Though he was not intimate with any of the original disciples of Christ, he was aware that Matthew was the least vocal of the Twelve. "Does that mean he'll be going to Nubia to find this man?"

"He expressed the interest," Philip admitted. "However, he eventually sided with the others and agreed that none of them should leave Judea, or Jerusalem for that matter."

"The church is only a few years old, and they're needed here," Timon added.

"Will you be going?" Aron asked Philip.

"I may be blessed with the ability to preach about Christ, but a pastor I am not. Maintaining long-term relationships has never been one of my strong points," Philip said, dropping his head. His role in relationships mirrored the fierce gales that often whipped across the Sea of Galilee—powerful yet fleeting, but always leaving a lasting impression. "I wouldn't be the right person to make the journey."

"Aron, this is the reason why we have brought you here today," Timon announced. "The elders are in agreement that someone should go to Nubia and ascertain the climate there."

"I don't understand," Aron said.

Timon nodded as he prepared his explanation. "You may already know this, but there are literally thousands of our Jewish brothers and sisters in the land of Nubia. Many of them have been there since the days of Solomon. We need someone to go there and see if they will be receptive to the gospel of Christ."

"Obviously this Sahlin was," Aron speculated.

"Yes, indeed he was," Philip echoed. "I can recall the passion that he had. But before we entertain plans of sending one of the elders there, we have to evaluate whether or not that land is ready for the gospel."

Timon noticed the concerned look growing in his young disciple's eyes and decided to cut to the quick. "Aron, we would like to ask if you would make the journey to Nubia. We already know that Sahlin Malae is in the employ of the royal court. Therefore, he should reside in or near the palace in the capital city. Hiram here has generously agreed to finance the entire journey."

Fighting to process all of the information he had received, Aron shook his head and fought back disbelief. "Why me? I am just a potter. I'm no preacher or pastor."

Timon leaned over and placed his hand on Aron's tense shoulder. "No, but you've been faithful in the small things. You've demonstrated the willingness to selflessly lay down your life for others whom you don't even know. That is a rare quality in even the most mature of men."

Aron looked into Timon's eyes and saw a confidence unscathed by his youth or lack of experience. For the briefest of moments, he almost imagined himself on an excursion down the Nile seeking the phantom of another man's dream.

Before Aron could say another word, Philip also leaned forward. "Aron, please do not give us an answer at this moment. We would like for you to take the matter up in prayer and fasting. It has to be something that you hear from the Lord Jesus yourself."

Chapter 9

Salin couldn't take his eyes away from the towering mountains that rose softly from the southern horizon. Though they were at least one hundred miles away, the magnificent structures still dominated the landscape. Above all, they testified to Sahlin that he was but a few miles away from the city of Meroë. Within hours, he would be strolling through the halls of his family mansion that sat along the banks of the great river.

The waters of the Nile were as smooth as the rolling plains they occasionally sailed past. Sahlin was grateful that they were able to complete the last leg of their voyage via barge. He had long ago grown weary of carriages and hard horsebacks. Though vast stretches of the Nile corridor were smooth and calm, there were several portions laden with rocky cataracts and waterfalls that made water passage far too treacherous and virtually impossible.

Sahlin leaned against the guardrail that ran along the

ship's bow and sighed. The tranquil rolling of the passenger barge did much to relax his state of mind. It was the first time in several days that he actually allowed himself the luxury of releasing the burden of dread that he lugged around with him. Yes, he was anxious to return to his life as an administrator in the royal court, but he was also apprehensive about the situation into which he was descending.

A week ago, when they passed through the province of Kerma, he had his first opportunity to read an official account of the Nobatian rebellion that transpired during his excursion to Judea. To his chagrin, he read the sordid details of the battle between the Kushite brothers. Although the southern army prevailed against the rebels, he was thoroughly mortified when he read that King Sherakarer had fallen in battle.

To make matters worse, he also learned through word of mouth that Natakam had also perished as a result of the campaign. Sahlin could only imagine the crushing sorrow that pressed against Amanitore's heart. He knew that she loved her sons dearly, but he was convinced that the whole of the kingdom would someday mourn them far more than she did.

He slowly shook his head as he imagined Harmais assuming a throne that was meant for his older brother. It was true that the future king was his childhood friend and current business partner, but Sahlin only trusted Harmais to a degree. Though their relationship was friendly and cordial, it was not free from the complications brought about when two ambitious individuals came together. Sahlin found himself already ruing the moment that the two would stand face-to-face. Prior to his departure, Harmais was simply a *paqar* with no ambitions or even thoughts of sitting upon the throne. Now that simple destiny had been altered, and Harmais was the most powerful man in the Nile Valley. Sahlin wondered just how much an influx of that much power had altered Harmais's character as well as their friendship. He knew that he would find out as soon as Harmais discovered that he had returned from Judea.

Sahlin's eyes fell on several smaller crafts that sailed in the opposite direction as his mind turned toward the second issue that overshadowed his return. For weeks, he pondered how his newly found faith would affect the execution of his occupation. By its very nature, honest and just men were simply not welcomed in his arena. Yet, he found a great struggle starting to grow within himself. When it came to administrating the kingdom's finances, he had learned years ago to effectively curtail his conscience in order to prevent himself from feeling remorse, pity, and regret.

However, the more he thought about his past actions of extortion, bribery, and out-and-out theft, the heavier the feeling of attrition weighed upon his spirit. During his trip home, he experienced thoughts and memories that at times nearly overwhelmed him with sorrow. Each time, he felt it necessary to fall to his knees and ask Jesus for forgiveness. In turn, whenever he did so, he felt as if an invisible hand lifted the weight from his chest and then washed him clean, removing the remorseful and soiled feeling that dogged him.

Even now, certain policies that he had initiated prior to his departure haunted him. Part of him wanted to repeal the inequitable directives that funded Harmais's clandestine war chest and a half dozen of his own private feuds. However, he tried to convince himself that any effort to do so would surely meet with failure. Unfortunately, he had involved several others in the ventures who stood to become quite wealthy—and in some cases, even wealthier than himself. Another twinge of regret seared his heart as he thought of how his actions contributed to the corruption of Kalibae, his youthful apprentice.

Kalibae started out as an unpretentious steward in Sahlin's division not long after Amanitore appointed Sahlin to his current post. At the age of sixteen, the boy was fairly naive and wanted to learn everything that he could about the kingdom's treasury system. His ambition led him to study at the Great Learning Center that sat in the heart of Meroë. Sahlin was impressed with the young man's drive and began to entrust him with tasks that were fit for experienced auditors rather than stewards. Kalibae showed uncommon initiative and creativity and quickly excelled beyond the level of his peers.

Sahlin could hardly believe that four years had already passed since he had taken the young man under his wing. During that time, he helped him to hone and develop his skills as an assertive negotiator. Quite by accident, Kalibae had grown to fulfill the role of son in Sahlin's vacuous life. The two spent hours together traveling throughout the kingdom enforcing policies and collecting tribute, taxes, and a substantial amount of coercive payoffs in the form of donations and fees. Kalibae learned the craft well enough for Sahlin to feel comfortable to leave the twenty-year-old young man in charge of the shady operations that ran through the treasury department.

Vexed by the growing compulsion to solve the riddle of his life, Sahlin closed his eyes and started to pray. Before he could utter a voiceless word, a familiar portion of Isaiah's manuscript echoed into his mind. *But you will*

be called the priests of the Lord; You will be spoken of as minis-
ters of our God. . . . Instead of your shame you will have a
double portion. . . . For I, the Lord, love justice, I hate robbery
in the burnt offering . . .

Before he could ask the Lord about the Scriptures, he sensed the presence of someone standing behind him. Opening his eyes, Sahlin leaned back to see Bakka stepping forward.

"Excuse me, my lord, the captain has announced that we will be stopping alongside the west bank once more before we reach Meroë." Bakka clutched the guardrail to steady himself. He disapproved of any type of travel by water. He even hated taking baths.

Sahlin nodded his head. "I suppose that will place our arrival home in about three hours. That isn't too bad. How are the others?"

"Anxious to see their families, of course. Though they won't admit it."

"Would you admit it?" Sahlin asked with a smile.

"No. But then again, I don't have a family." Bakka delivered the statement with as much bravado as he could. After a lifetime of military and royal service that made him moderately wealthy, the sacrifice of a family life was his one outstanding, unspoken regret. "Passion and honor are my sons, my only offspring that shall outlive my aging body."

"I understand about honor, but why passion?" Sahlin asked, noticing the silent cry of pain he heard in Bakka's baritone voice.

"You cannot have one without the other. A soldier without passion fights without purpose. A soldier without honor is nothing more than a mercenary prostituting his services out to the highest bidder. I wish to be remembered as neither."

Sahlin stroked his square jaw as he listened to the venerable warrior. He opened his mouth to say something but quickly closed it when he realized that the only words on the tip of his tongue were about his life-changing encounter with Jesus the Christ. Thus far, he had managed to successfully resist the impulse to share his story with others. However, the more time he spent in prayer, the weaker his defenses became.

"That's an interesting way of putting it," Sahlin finally managed, glancing off into the distance. It didn't take him long to realize that his life possessed neither honor nor passion in any discernible abundance. "How does one become passionate about a matter in a world that quenches hope as water quenches fire?" he asked rhetorically, looking in the general direction of Meroë.

"Passion comes from within," Bakka replied, casting his dark eyes down at the blue water, searching for the definition that once guided his life. "It's a gift from the gods, the lamp that they provide in order to give purpose and fire to our miserable existence. Without it, we accomplish nothing of substance."

Sahlin pondered the simple yet insightful statement. He had spent the majority of his life pursuing power and position, but he was passionate about nothing that his endeavors had produced. He neither enjoyed nor looked forward to the fruits of his labor. "What god is there that gives a man a purpose and direction for his life?"

Sahlin didn't hear Bakka's response. Instead, his mind was met with a passage from Isaiah that he had read many times over.

My purpose will be established, and I will accomplish all My good pleasure. . . . I have planned it, surely I will do it.

The barge coasted up to a large wooden dock. A dozen passengers disembarked from the ship with little fanfare while at least a half dozen more came aboard.

Bakka and Sahlin both remained at the guardrail, silently grappling with their thoughts.

"Bakka, you're in your fifties. What is it like not having a family?"

The question nearly toppled Bakka over the guardrail emotionally, but he maintained his poise. He started to answer but decided to restrain his words in order to insure that the words that he selected accurately reflected his feelings in a discreet fashion.

Sahlin used the brief moment of hesitation to complete an unfinished thought. "I ask this because I doubt if I'll ever have a family. At least not the type that I see those people with," he said, gesturing to a man and woman who were busy herding their five children off the dock. "I'm married to my work, as my father before me was."

Bakka glanced at the noisy family of seven as they attempted to maintain their cohesiveness in the midst of the crowded dock. The simplistic kilts they wore all but announced their status in the lower class, but their faces bore heartfelt smiles that were a rarity in the upper echelon of the Kushite caste system. He nodded his head in approval as they successfully managed their way from the small port and into the nearby forest.

"It doesn't have to be that way, my lord." Bakka masked the regret that gripped his voice. Bakka had no idea how many children he had sired throughout his fifty-plus years. He wasn't even certain as to the number of women he had been intimate with. As a soldier, he traveled to every major city in the kingdom. His uniform, rank, and stature drew more beautiful women than he could remember. Now, as he looked back upon the licentious episodes, revulsion was the only feeling intense enough to register.

"So you're saying that you would change the way that you lived your life?" Sahlin asked.

"Lived? I'm still waiting to do that, my lord. Unfortunately, there are fewer days ahead than there are behind for me."

Sahlin appreciated Bakka's uncharacteristic openness. "For the last two and a half months I've dreamt of this moment. I've dreamt of passing Gebel Barkal and seeing the lights of Napata from a hill. I dreamt of nothing but coming home. Now that I'm here, I realize more than ever that I have nothing. No family, no future."

Bakka folded his great arms and bit his lower lip. "You speak as if you are a man who is getting ready to die."

"Strange, Bakka, that almost describes precisely how I feel. I feel as if part of me has died, while another part of me has been . . . reborn."

"Reborn, my lord?"

"Yes, it's difficult to explain." Sahlin groped for words. "It's as if something inside of me is growing and getting stronger by the day. And that something is warring against who I am . . . or who I was . . . or . . . I don't know. I feel as if I'm losing my identity, losing my destiny."

Bakka sucked in a deep breath, along with the nerve to ask the question that had been burning within him for some time. "My lord, do you feel that your contrary thoughts may be related to the man we came across in the Judean desert?"

Sahlin looked as if someone had snatched a blanket

from him in the middle of a cold night. Instantly, he snapped out of his introverted mind-set. "Why do you ask?"

"You haven't been yourself ever since that day. For a time, I thought maybe that man cursed you or placed some sort of incantation upon you in order to plunder your peace."

For a moment, Sahlin lamented over the knowledge that his personal foibles had been flaunted so indiscreetly. He thought he had done a better job of masking his tormented feelings. "It wasn't a curse or spell he burdened me with. Jews do not deal in such matters. The thing that he encumbered me with was knowledge. Knowledge of my own deficiencies and incongruence. Knowledge of my offenses against a holy God. Knowledge of a man who made a sacrifice, so that I would not have to. Knowledge that that man had risen from the grave, to affirm his power."

"Perhaps the man did not speak the truth," Bakka alleged, trying to deny the force of condemnation that pressed against his own heart. "Perhaps he spoke only to trouble you."

"He spoke the truth," Sahlin acknowledged, thinking again of how the Scriptures, as well as his grandfather's journal, confirmed the man's words. "Unadulterated truth, free of malice and rancor."

"Truth from whose perspective? What may be true for his kind may not be applicable for us."

"I, too, am Jewish. His laws are my laws; his truths are my truths." Although he was well rested, Sahlin rubbed his tired eyes. "Yet, strangely enough, I don't believe that race or creed matters much to Jehovah."

"Tell that to the Romans or even those . . . Pharisees, I

believe they were," Bakka snorted, recalling the covert and sometimes blatant discrimination they encountered in Judea. "Equality in this world will come only by the sword."

Sahlin was divided. On one hand, he didn't even care to respond to the narrow view to which Bakka subscribed. Ironically, he had shared a similar worldview, only he substituted the might of the sword with the weight of the moneybag. Either way, when utilized, both alternatives left a path littered with crushed dreams and splintered families. Neither way produced a lasting peace.

Sahlin and Bakka were gently jolted as the barge's rectangular sail caught a crosswind that escorted it toward the center of the Nile.

"Bakka, what is peace?" Sahlin asked, knowing how the bodyguard would most likely answer.

"It's the unattainable product of war. The unimaginable absence of conflict."

Sahlin looked up at the thought-provoking answer. It was not at all what he expected. However, it still was not in line with the definition God had been crafting within his soul during the better part of the past year. "I have grown to believe that peace is a place. A destination that can't be bought with gold or conquered by the sword."

"A place?"

"I'm starting to believe that peace is a place where the knowledge that God is sovereign overshadows the whim of a king, or the army of a general." That much Sahlin was absolutely sure of.

Bakka silently dwelt upon his employer's translation of the term *peace* as well as the God that seemed to define it.

Though still at a distance, the city of Meroë was now in plain sight. Towering obelisks stood as signposts that declared the city's presence in the midst of the wilderness. His eyes shifted from the city to Sahlin, then back again to Meroë. Images of a sick queen lamenting over her dead sons raced through his mind.

If peace truly were a place where God was sovereign, then the God of whom Sahlin spoke of surely did not abide in Meroë.

※　　※　　※

Aron sat upon a wooden stool on the flat roof of his childhood home. Occasionally, he pretended to be the patriarch Abraham and tried to number the stars. Without fail, he found the challenge that God issued to the father of faith impossible to execute. Nonetheless, he welcomed the distraction. His weary mind was overloaded with a myriad of if-then scenarios produced by the meeting that he had with Philip and the others.

He folded his arms and leaned his head against a short wall. Tired of counting the stars, he closed his eyes and envisioned the now quiet quarter of Jerusalem in which he lived. Down below were the narrow streets that he trudged along first as a boy and now as a young man. At the moment, they were dark and secluded with only the sounds of forlorn dogs and vagabonds that shuffled through them. If one were not careful, a person wandering the streets at this time of night could very easily fall victim to rogue bandits or even worse—bands of Roman soldiers searching for dissenters and other political idealists.

Finally, Aron's mind meandered its way back to the very subject that had driven him to the rooftop in the first place. His lips moved as he issued yet another inaudible prayer to Jesus, soliciting an answer for the question that tormented his soul for the last several days. Part of him dismissed Philip's proposal as a severe miscalculation on the evangelist's behalf. There was very little doubt in Aron's mind that Philip and Timon meant well, but he was all but convinced that they had missed God. In his own mind, he simply had no business even entertaining the thought of leaving Jerusalem for the lures of a distant land.

However, part of him actually craved the long voyage to a land that no one in his family had visited in close to a century. He could hardly pronounce the word *Meroë*, but the strange name seemed to produce nothing but a cryptic peace in his heart as he thought about the people inhabiting the land.

He shook his head. No, it was more than a shadowy peace that enticed his young imagination to the great Nubian kingdom. The more he examined his heart, the more apparent the upsurging feeling became—he was proud.

Somehow, the mere thought of setting foot in a kingdom ruled by black African monarchs produced an excitement in him that he never before experienced. Thus far, he had spent his entire life in a nation dominated by a superpower from the north. It never ceased to intrigue him to think that there were nations and kingdoms in the world Rome did not have the might to suppress. Such thoughts piqued his curiosity all the more.

Within a few minutes, the temperature dropped noticeably. Aron wrapped himself in his cloak and wrestled his thoughts away from making the journey. Reality dictated his place was at home in Jerusalem with the family that depended upon him.

After rising to his feet, he leaned over the edge of the roof. He peered down both ways of the deserted thoroughfare running in front of his brick home. Like the path of his own life, he reasoned that the dim streets led to nowhere special and were condemned to digress throughout the monumental maze that was the city of Jerusalem forever.

"Lord Jesus, it is Your will that I seek. Surely this cannot be it." Even as Aron prayed for guidance, his ears were harassed by the faint clamorous sounds of pots being stowed away for the evening.

Weary of spirit and mind, he sighed in exasperation. All he wanted to do was sleep, for it was then and only then that his mind and spirit truly found a respite.

The door leading to the stairwell creaked as it turned on its hinges. Aron assumed that it was his sister, so he didn't even bother to turn around. He was surprised to hear a man call his name.

"Aron."

He pivoted to find the tall, brawny black man who had hosted the meeting with Philip several days before. "Lord Hiram, what . . ."

"I'm sorry if I disturbed you. Your mother said that you would be up here." Hiram walked across the roof and settled down upon the ledge. "She said that this is your favorite place to come and relax after a long day."

"That's one thing that it is good for," Aron admitted, amazed at how easy it was to talk with the man despite the presence that he commanded. "I like to pray up here. It makes me feel closer to the Lord. There is something about the stars."

"Yes," Hiram said, gazing down into the dark streets below. "I like to pray in a closet."

"A closet?"

"Yes. It helps me to shut everything out and focus on what the Lord would say to me."

Aron raised an inquiring eyebrow. "How does He speak to you?"

Hiram wrung his hands for a moment before speaking. "Oftentimes He uses circumstances to convey something to me. But it generally takes me a while to figure it out."

"Circumstances? I thought that maybe . . ."

"He'd use a prophet to communicate to someone who is so important to the church?" Hiram smiled as Aron stared at him blankly. "No, Aron. I'm flattered by the fact that everyone esteems me so highly, but I'm no different than anyone else. I need Jesus more than He needs me."

Aron nodded. He was impressed and inspired by the man's humbled spirit. "How is one influenced by a circumstance?"

Hiram cleared his throat and searched carefully for his answer. "I don't know if this is the same for anyone else, but for me, everything that God does involves some sort of pattern. He is predictable in what He does but unpredictable in how He does it. Does that make sense?"

Aron shook his head as he groped for comprehension.

"I'll put it like this: God is predictable in that I know what it is that He wants me to do. However, He is unpredictable in that I rarely know how He wants me to do it until I find myself in the situation that He is leading me into."

Aron knew that Hiram was a well-respected businessman throughout Jerusalem. At the moment, he felt as if the man were more an all-knowing sage from the synagogue than a magnate. "Sounds complex."

"Very much so," Hiram said shaking his head, his eyes trailing off into the darkness. "Very much so."

"What brought you here? This is a long way from your part of town," Aron said, his curiosity returning to the fore.

"I was simply wondering how you were doing. I can imagine that it must be a very difficult decision for you to make."

"It is," Aron confessed, not really wanting to discuss the topic. "I'm torn down the middle really."

"I can understand. Have you talked with your mother about it?"

Aron's eyes shot up, rolled to the side, and focused on a distant star. "Yes, I have." He chuckled sarcastically. "She feels that I should go."

"Do you value her opinion?"

"Of course I do. It's just that she doesn't understand what it means. She is so . . . optimistic. So . . ."

"So very proud of you," Hiram chimed in, using a tone of voice that was both soothing and firm. "I spoke with her for a while before I came up here. She loves you as a son, yet respects you as a man. She also believes that you should go to Meroë."

"I know," Aron calmly replied. He recalled the discussion that his mother and he had regarding the journey that would surely take him away for nearly a year. She had no problem expressing her support. "But I still don't understand. Why me? Why don't you go?"

Hiram eyed Aron like a hawk. "Circumstances."

"What?"

"Remember that I said that God speaks to me through patterns and circumstances? Every time I have tried to leave my post to dedicate more time to ministry, my firm just grew incredibly busy, demanding that I spend more time administrating it. My frustration grew until the day that I realized that I was in the will of God."

"How could you be in the will of God if you were not where you felt you needed to be in life?"

"Because '[His] ways are higher than our ways,'" Hiram voiced, quoting the words of Isaiah the prophet. "He showed me that there are two types of people in His kingdom—those who labor in the field and those who send and support the laborers. He showed me that He blessed me with such great wealth in order that I could support those who are called to go out and preach."

"But I'm not a preacher," Aron moaned, tossing his hands into the air.

"That's not for me to say. And it is not for me to question what God has called you to be. Nor would I think that it is your place to tell God what and who you are."

Hiram stood up and allowed his words to linger in the air for a while.

"Africa is so far away," Aron whispered. "And so dangerous."

"Being in the will of God is the safest place to be," Hiram said, unable to ignore the impact of his own life experience. "Aron, I want you to go."

"Why?"

"Because they are our people." Hiram paused long enough to make certain that Aron understood his connotation. "Something tells me that it is imperative they see a face that resembles their own. To let them see that the Lord Jesus stretches out His hand to all cultures . . . I just feel that generations somehow hinge upon it."

Aron was tired of wrestling with his own fate. The invisible hand he grappled against had him pinned down and showed no signs of relenting. "My mother? My sister?"

"I give you my word that they will be cared for."

Aron felt a comfort in Hiram's words that transcended the man himself. Somehow, he knew that God was issuing an irrefutable promise. "There's so much that I don't know, Hiram. Meroë, Kush, there's so much . . ."

"Don't worry. There is much to do before you leave. I have no intention of letting you go without being properly prepared." He placed his hand upon the young man's shoulder and caught the reflection of the brilliant moonlight in his deep brown eyes. "If there is one thing that I have learned, Aron, it is that we cannot outgive God. Whatever you commit to Him, He will keep and nourish it as His own."

Chapter 10

Though he had been gone for well over a year, it took Dikembul only a matter of days to adjust to life in his small hometown of Nuri. He sat quietly upon a boulder and watched his sheep graze peacefully in the distance. It was the third evening in a row that he had relieved the young men who normally tended the mass of docile creatures. His many weeks and months of travel made him long for the hush and solitude that dominated the simple task of shepherding a flock. He smiled and eagerly awaited the crimson and burnt orange colors that the fading sun would soon paint the immense sky.

He stroked his beard and bathed in the warm feeling that enveloped his heart. They were home, and life was well. The young men who oversaw his herding business had proven to be faithful stewards. They had netted him a hefty profit. He thanked God for granting him the wisdom to select the appropriate men to watch over his interests.

Dikembul traced the contour of the northwestern horizon from the soft rolling hills marking the border of his property to Gebel Barkal, the sacred mountain that sat ominously on the opposite side of the Nile. His faith in Jehovah prevented him from honoring the hosts of gods said to abide on the top of the great flat mountain. On several occasions, his Jewish companions and he had been rebuked by neighbors that esteemed the mountain as an abode of Ra. Dikembul was grateful that nothing more than idle threats and scornful looks ever migrated their way.

Nonetheless, he was pleased to see Gebel Barkal again. At this distance, he could only see the summit and not the host of temples, bazaars, and administrative structures that trimmed its base. Generally a throng of people cluttered the grounds. Many were worshipers from throughout the kingdom, while most were inhabitants of nearby Napata, the former capital of the Kushite world.

Dikembul recalled the uneventful days of his childhood spent just north of Napata. The only excitement that his friends and he could lure their way came in the form of posing as worshipers and sneaking into the small temple that was erected to Isis. When they really felt like tempting the fates, they would subtly mock the assistants to the priests by throwing cloths over the sacrificial elements left by members of the Cult of Isis. Dikembul could hardly believe that they had never been caught and flogged for their misdeeds.

"Dikembul," a familiar voice called out from behind him. "Annika said that I would find you out here."

Dikembul stood up and turned around to see one of the faces that had just flashed through his mind. "Nkosi," he responded, embracing the slender black man who was roughly the same age as himself. "I was wondering when you would show up."

"Sorry it took me so long to . . ."

"I've been back for a full week, and it took you just as long to finally come and visit us," Dikembul chided, turning his attention back toward the sheep. "You don't even have a family of your own to hide behind."

"How many times do you want me to apologize? I'm a businessman, and I have work to tend to."

Dikembul laughed. "First of all, you're a farmer, not a businessman. The last time I checked, you ate more crops than you sold."

Nkosi shook his head and grinned. "As skeptical as ever. Worshiping at the Great Temple obviously didn't impart any compassion into that cast iron heart of yours."

"No, actually it did," Dikembul replied. "However, the hot Judean sun scorched it right out. Anything that was left was stolen by the Egyptians."

The two shared a brief laugh.

"How was the stay with your brother?" Nkosi asked.

"It was good to see him. His family was just as beautiful as they were eight years ago."

"And the house? Did he ever do what I told him to do?"

"Of course not. It's the exact same size as the last time you saw it."

"What is it with Nubians who move to Egypt?" Nkosi blurted, recalling the advice he had given Dikembul's brother to expand his small home that had to accommodate six children. "They move north, and their common sense goes south."

Dikembul shrugged and waved at the two young men who fanned out into the flock of sheep to start herding them in. "I haven't been able to talk with very many people yet. How are things here?"

"Quiet, of course," Nkosi declared, gesturing to the southeast. Dikembul didn't have to look. He knew his friend was making reference to the vast royal cemetery that sat not far from the pasture. The enclosed plot of land had been used for hundreds of years, dating clear back to the days when Kerma was the seat of power for the Nubian empire.

"That's not what I meant, Nkosi. We heard about the Nobatian rebellion while we were in Sinai."

"You mean the Nobatian massacre," Nkosi said, referring to the complete rout of the Nobatian regiment by forces of the southern army.

"I heard that it was bad," Dikembul commented.

"It was, for both sides."

Dikembul nodded his head solemnly. "Where did they bury the king?"

"Just south of the altar in the middle of the cemetery. Natakam was buried in Meroë."

Dikembul acknowledged the answer with a stifled grunt. Growing up in the region, he was aware of the requirement for interment in the great royal cemetery. Although Natakam actually ruled for several months, his reign was short and unproductive. Dikembul could only imagine how Kandace Amanitore felt about separating the two brothers in death.

"What a waste," Dikembul said, thinking about the dead king. Sherakarer carried out many of the policies and civic works projects initiated by his father, making him very popular among the common people. Dikembul was sure that Natakam would have administrated much the same. "I suppose this means that the youngest brother has the throne?"

"That's right."

Dikembul cradled his staff. "Is that a good thing?"

"I don't know," Nkosi replied, trying to hide his frustration at his inability to coax more details about the new king from a scribe he knew in the Napatan administrative dufufa. "His coronation and wedding are only a few weeks from now. Looks like the two of you have returned just in time for all of the festivities."

Nkosi's statement was met by a silent cry pleading for a reprieve. Dikembul had no desire to be in the midst of the whirlwind that would descend upon the normally resigned region of Nuri. Though Meroë was the capital city, the spiritual heart of the Nile Valley empire resided in Napata. Ceremonies for royal weddings, coronations, and funerals were performed at the temple of Amun resting in the shadow of Gebel Barkal. Dikembul didn't even want to imagine the masses that would migrate from Meroë, Philae, Kerma, and Qustul in order to witness the paqar's coronation and wedding. Most of the individuals coming would be from the extreme upper class—a group that he cared very little for.

The two of them helped the younger two men usher the flock of sheep from the pasture and into an extensive fenced-in range. Dikembul swiftly examined each animal. He would have been more thorough if it were not for the deep sighs that Nkosi released every few minutes. At first, Dikembul simply ignored them. For whatever reason, he didn't at all find it burdensome to inspect his flock's condition. He knew that in order to protect an entire flock from deadly diseases, each one had to be painstakingly examined and cared for. Nkosi, on the other hand, had the patience of a hyena foraging for the scraps of a lion's kill.

After securing the herd for the evening, Dikembul and Nkosi headed back toward the main house. The fresh aroma of the seasoned lamb that Annika was preparing met and escorted them along the winding dirt path.

"I can see that Annika did not lose her touch while dwelling abroad," Nkosi said, expecting to be well fed when they reached the house.

"Actually, she burned a couple of meals, but I didn't say anything."

"Has Akil been by yet?" Nkosi asked.

"No, he hasn't."

"His regiment is probably out on maneuvers beyond Barkal. Is Annika ready?"

Dikembul considered how he might best change the subject to another topic, even though he knew that his old friend would simply shift the dialogue back until he received a satisfactory answer. "Honestly, I don't think that Annika wants to marry him."

"That doesn't matter, does it?" Nkosi chuckled. "I know that she's your only daughter, but she's still a woman. Until she learns how to manage livestock or work a farm, she is better off getting married. Most girls her age are already pregnant with their third child."

"Nkosi, we had this conversation before we left . . ."

"And it looks like we have to have it again, Dikembul." Nkosi's voice skirted between amusement and frustration. "Akil is a good young man. He's been promoted twice since the two of you left. He may not be as devout a Jew as you would prefer, but his heart is in the right place."

"Yes, I know, but I just don't think that Annika is ready to make that decision as of yet."

"It's not her decision, Dikembul; it's yours! You need to let her go. If need be, push her out."

"Do you know what you're saying?" Dikembul asked, shaking his head.

"I know exactly what I am saying. I'm telling you that she needs her own family. I'm telling you that you are clinging to her as one would to . . . a memory or a shadow. I'm telling you to let Shalonda go."

Dikembul hadn't heard his wife's name spoken in so long that he nearly flinched when Nkosi said it. Within a split second, he was filled with a longing for his deceased wife too deep for words to describe.

Even in the twilight, Nkosi could see the pain on Dikembul's face. Nonetheless, he felt the need to press on. "Dikembul, we both know what might become of Annika if something were to happen to you. You know full well that she would lose everything. Including the veil of independence that you have allowed her to live in."

Nkosi paused to let the words sink in and transform into a clear visual picture. During the silence, he knew that Dikembul's mind was filling with painful images of Annika being taken in by their nearest male relative and being forced to marry whomever that man selected. He knew that by then, Akil would be long gone to one of the major cities in the kingdom. He also knew Annika would not be able to legally retain possession of all that he labored for and built. His business ventures were modest in comparison to those of greater men. However, what he had, he wanted to pass on to his daughter's sons.

"Dikembul," Nkosi started, nudging him gently, "she's like a daughter to me too. I don't want to see those things happen to her either."

By the time he had finished speaking, they had arrived

at the house, fully surrounded by the inviting smell of the full-course meal Annika had waiting for them. Dikembul looked up at his friend's steady gaze. Since he could form no words, he simply nodded his head in agreement.

During their meal, Dikembul described their trip to Judea in full detail, except for the Day of Pentecost. Nkosi had performed the pilgrimage to Jerusalem years earlier. He wasn't at all surprised at the brutality of the Romans or the rancor of the Jews. He was simply glad that Meroë had been able to stave off the hands of the tyrannical empire.

An hour later as the two men reclined in the family room, Nkosi updated Dikembul on the latest happenings at the masjid just outside of Napata. The unpretentious temple was a decent-sized structure with about eighty or so men gathering there on a regular basis every week. All of them were looking forward to Dikembul's return. Likewise, Dikembul could hardly wait to see them again. Several of them were lifelong friends such as Nkosi.

"Tell me more about this new high priest in Napata," Dikembul said.

"You mean Khenstout? There's really not much to tell. He's not even a high priest. The only thing high about him is his attitude."

Dikembul smiled. "You said something about him threatening to take away the space that we use for the masjid?"

"Yes, but he could never do such a thing. That sort of order would have to come down from the high priest, and even then, it would be subject to the approval of the pelmes-adab. As you know, that land-use agreement goes back generations."

Dikembul was well aware of how the bravery of several

hundred Jewish Nubians earned the admiration of the greatest king that ever reigned over Kush. As a boy, he had been told the story of how King Tarahaq set out to fight against the seemingly invincible Assyrians. At the time, Kush allied itself with the Hebrew kingdom of Judah and several other nations to break the Assyrian yoke holding the land in a bloody vise grip of terror.

During one of the campaign's many critical battles, a regiment consisting almost entirely of Nubian Jews held the Assyrian army at bay just outside the valley of Kalabsha. The regiment was obliterated. However, their sacrifice provided the Nubian army the precious moments needed to mount a victorious counterattack.

When the gallantry of the Jews reached the ears of King Tarahaq, he searched for a way to honor the memory of the soldiers, as well as the God who inspired them to fight so valiantly. He ultimately issued a decree that allowed Jews and Falasha to establish tabernacles and masjids wherever there were centers of worship in Kush. Subsequently, persecution of Jewish citizens ceased almost immediately. Despite the fact that they openly denounced the worship of Ra, Osiris, and Apedemack, Jews were allowed to worship the Hebrew God whom they claimed to be preeminent over all others. Occasional clashes with the Cult of Isis notwithstanding, pockets of faithful Jews quietly thrived in the land of Kush for centuries.

"All the same, that is a very hefty statement," Dikembul said. "What drove him to make such a brazen threat?"

"First of all, he's from the region just north of Qustul. The word is that he is a very devout priest and is intolerant to any religion that threatens to unseat the traditional Egyptian gods."

"Surely he must know that is impossible. The Cult of Isis controls this region."

Nkosi took a sip of the tea that Annika had given them a short while ago to see if it had cooled. "Yes, however, there are those who believe that he simply hates Jews."

"It seems illogical that the high priest of Napata would appoint an individual who detests an entire race of people."

Nkosi shrugged. "None of the elders can figure it out. The high priest is silent on the matter. In fact, he doesn't even send representatives to our council meetings."

"You don't say," Dikembul uttered, raising an eyebrow. He had always been impressed with the high priest's display of concern for the hundreds of Jews that lived in Nuri and outside of Napata. As one of the elders, he had been one of the main liaisons between the Jewish communities and the representatives of the local governments. Though they had their differences, they had always managed to disarm conflicts and work things out. "I'll keep the matter in prayer."

Over the course of the next hour, Annika refreshed their cups with warm tea several times. She always seemed to appear right at their moment of need, only to disappear into one of the four other rooms in the cozy brick house. From time to time, Dikembul would throw additional logs into the fireplace to maintain the room's moderate warmth.

Finally, Nkosi pushed his cup away and yawned. "It's far too late. I had better get home."

"Nkosi, before you go, there is something that I must talk with you about," Dikembul announced, regretting that he hadn't the nerve to bring up the subject hours ago.

"Dikembul, can't we talk about it tomorrow?" Nkosi protested, fighting off the claw of fatigue that wanted him to remain seated.

"It's important. Perhaps more important than our very lives."

Nkosi knew his friend well enough to discern when a matter completely enveloped him. He sat up and leaned forward.

Dikembul struggled for the breath he needed to usher out the first sentence. "Nkosi, I believe that I have found the Messiah."

"The Redeemer?" Nkosi asked, not fully understanding. "You've met Him?"

Dikembul nervously rubbed the back of his hand against his bearded face. "No, not face-to-face," he replied, though he felt the contrary.

"Then you've seen Him? In Judea? Egypt?"

Dikembul shook his head methodically. "No, I have not seen Him personally. Only in my prayers."

"I don't understand." Nkosi tried to comprehend his friend's vague disclosure. What little he had heard spiked his curiosity to the point that he needed to hear more.

"There were men at the Great Temple in Jerusalem. They spoke of the One who had come to redeem men from their sins. They preached with such passion and conviction that it had to be true."

"This Redeemer, what did they say His name was?"

"They called him Jesus, the Christ."

Nkosi narrowed his eyes. "The Anointed One?" Nkosi leaned back and tapped a finger on the wooden table. He was familiar with the promise of the Messiah who would one day rise up, gather the house of Israel, and restore it as a whole. Though they were hundreds of miles both physically and culturally away from the Holy Land, they shared the same hope of restoration as their Hebrew brethren. "If you haven't met Him, or even seen Him, then how do you know that this Jesus is the Messiah? Are you taking these men at their word?"

Dikembul gnawed at his lower lip and lightly shook his head. Even as Nkosi spoke, he could still hear the burly disciple of Jesus preaching. "The things that they said were difficult to accept at first. But then . . ."

"Then what?"

"It wasn't until later, but then I recognized their words as descriptions . . . descriptions of a person whom I had read about in our masjid."

"The sacred writings?"

"Yes. The men were quoting passages from the very parchments we have that describe what the Messiah will be like when He comes." Dikembul felt a sudden burst of energy give him a lift despite the lateness of the hour. "I was skeptical at first, but then they spoke of how this man was a descendant of David. They also said many other things."

Dikembul carefully outlined the events of the day that transformed his life. Fatigue fled from Nkosi. He listened intently to a man who sounded ever more like one who had discovered the whereabouts of the family inheritance. Aside from a few grunts and requests for clarification, he uttered no words as he tried to visualize the experience that Dikembul shared. Surprisingly enough, he found it very easy to do.

"Just so that I understand you, Dikembul, this man is not dead, despite having been executed by the Romans?"

"In accordance with the Scriptures, God redeemed His soul from the power of Sheol and raised Him from the dead," Dikembul said with an excitement that surprised him. He observed Nkosi, who said nothing for a long moment. Suddenly, a hand of fear began to settle in over him. "I know that it is incredible, my friend. But when I pray to Jesus . . ."

"Pray to Him?"

"Yes," Dikembul insisted. "In accordance with the Scripture, He is the declared Son of God. Therefore, He must be entitled to receive our prayers."

Nkosi was nearly awestruck by the simplicity of Dikembul's faith. He seemed willing to take everything at face value, no matter how incredible or improbable it seemed.

"Such talk is blasphemous, Dikembul."

Dikembul's face grew stern. "It is only blasphemous if Jesus proves not to be whom He declares."

"This requires more examination."

"I intend to bring this up with the others as soon as I have the opportunity," Dikembul announced.

"I agree," Nkosi said hesitantly. He knew that some of the other elders would not receive Dikembul's testimony with open arms. A carpenter from the insignificant Judean town of Nazareth hardly described what many of them were expecting in the Messiah. "I understand your faith in the sacred writings, but how do you validate the claim of another man who is not even here?"

"That's just it, Nkosi. He is here. I see Him in the wind, and I feel Him in my heart. I don't know how, but I just know that He is here and He has changed my life."

As Nkosi responded to her father, Annika tried again to picture the face of the man whom her father had spent the evening describing. Her sleeping quarters shared a common wall with the family room, making her privy to every word the two men shared.

Sleep having departed from her hours ago, she lay in her bed and wrestled with the identity of Jesus the Christ. Like her father, she wanted to believe in something greater than the tumultuous reality that swirled around them. She too longed for the Messiah.

"Please, help me to believe," she prayed as her eyelids slowly slid shut. "Help me . . . to . . . believe . . ."

Chapter 11

Naytal, you're so spiteful!" exclaimed Tshenpur as she burst into Naytal's palace chambers. Naytal coolly whirled around to see her agitated friend signal her servant to close the door.

"I didn't know that you would be so offended by my gesture of goodwill," Naytal replied, slightly raising an eyebrow. Were it not for the fact that Tshenpur was only weeks away from becoming the next kandace, Naytal would have had her cast into the dungeon for crashing into her private room in such a disrespectful fashion.

"How could you choose to be so insensitive to my feelings?" Tshenpur demanded with one of her hands balled into a fist. Even in her exasperated disposition, she radiated with a beauty that made Naytal envious. Her light skin was smooth and flawless and shimmered in the sunlight.

"Tshenpur, the man is soon going to be your husband,"

Naytal declared, turning her attention back to the board game she played with another female friend. "Melaenis, wouldn't you be excited if your husband-to-be entered the temple where you worshiped?"

Melaenis sat and smiled quietly as Naytal shifted her pieces on the board. She had no royal blood running through her veins, nor was she even close to marrying into the fold as Tshenpur was. Thus, she simply held her peace, agreeing with Naytal in heart only.

Tshenpur marched through the spacious bedroom and up to the table where the two ladies reclined. "There are certain places where I would rather not see him intrude . . ."

Naytal grinned and slowly rolled her eyes up toward Tshenpur. "Harmais is the king of the Nile Valley. I suppose that he can intrude upon any parcel of soil that he pleases. He came to me and wanted to know where you were."

"You didn't have to tell him that I was at the Temple of Amun," Tshenpur voiced, walking toward the balcony. "He doesn't share the same respect for the gods as I do."

Naytal stroked a small wooden game piece in her hand while she considered Tshenpur's attempt at manipulating her into feeling guilty. The two women had played the game of manipulation many times throughout the decades and knew each other's moves well. Naytal had long ago convinced herself that was the primary reason why she liked Tshenpur so much. In many ways, they were more rivals than friends, and she relished the idea of having an equal to contend with since she was all but ignored by the rest of her family. Since Tshenpur was the daughter of a former grand vizier, she was considered only one step lower than Naytal in the social rankings.

Nevertheless, Tshenpur never allowed that to curtail her quest to climb even higher. She and Naytal competed for everything that two young women could contend for—attention, men, and social status.

For many years, Naytal enjoyed both the upper hand and final word in the relationship. However, her advantage was compromised when Tshenpur somehow managed to grapple her younger brother into issuing a marriage proposal. Not only would Harmais sit upon the highest throne in Africa, but Tshenpur would also ascend with him, claiming the high title of kandace.

As she had done many times over the past several weeks, Naytal flared her nostrils in a scarcely perceivable manner. In that moment, she was almost overcome by a familiar burning rage of jealousy and envy. All she wanted to do was to return to Wad ben Naga and remain there for the rest of her life. "I'm certain that the will of Isis will prevail in the matter. After all, you do love him."

Tshenpur nearly recoiled at the thought, but somehow managed to hold her composure. She wasn't about to let Naytal gloat over her misery. "I suppose you're right. The high priest of the temple tells us that we will share a long and prosperous marriage. He also declared that our reign would be noted for an accomplishment only dreamt of by our ascendants."

"And what did the great priest predict?" Naytal asked, skillfully masking her skepticism.

"That our reign would usher in unity and peace for the kingdom. And that our borders would be expanded to the gates of Herokleopolis."

Naytal suppressed her burgeoning smile at the mere suggestion that Harmais would expand the border north of all places. She was certain he wouldn't even be able to contain the marauding Nobadae tribes in the northern desert, let alone contend with the Roman Empire. "Amun is most generous to grant you such a favorable prophecy before your wedding."

Melaenis shifted her eyes between the two women. She rather enjoyed watching them spar back and forth. She had known them both well over twenty years and had grown quite used to their constant posturing. Above all, she was grateful that neither one of them ever forced her to choose sides against the other, although she knew that in a few weeks, she would have to make a choice of her own. She was certain that Naytal would have a difficult time deferring to Tshenpur once she ascended to the throne. Soon, she would have to decide which friendship would best service her and her young daughter, Jwahir.

Tshenpur pulled up a chair and observed the two as they continued their game. "I went and visited your mother this morning," she announced to Naytal.

"I haven't seen her in a couple of days. How is she?" Naytal asked, raising an eyebrow, but keeping her eyes focused on the board game.

"Her body is deteriorating, but her spirits are high."

"I may not have agreed with all of her decisions, but my mother has always been a resilient woman, to say the least. Even in the face of death, she inspires the kingdom."

Tshenpur sneered imperceptibly at Naytal's sarcastic comment. "Actually, I believe that her spirit's source is due to an outside factor."

"And what might that be?"

"Haven't you heard?" Tshenpur said, examining one of the discarded board game pieces. "The chief of the treasury has returned from his pilgrimage."

"Then the rumors are true?" Melaenis blurted like a giddy little girl. "Sahlin Malae is back?"

Tshenpur nodded her head, keeping one eye on Naytal. Though the qar's response was subdued, she could tell it vexed Naytal to know that even Melaenis was aware of something that she was not.

"How could that make anyone feel better?" Naytal spat. "That man is a criminal. He should be banished from Meroë altogether."

Tshenpur forced herself not to smile at the reaction. "Such a harsh response. You sound as if you were still upset over his rejection of your feelings toward him."

"That's a lie and you know it," Naytal declared as she rolled her eyes up at Tshenpur. "I've never had a tender thought toward that man . . . or any other Falasha for that matter." Tshenpur of all people knew that Naytal spoke nothing but the truth. The qar was disgusted with Sahlin Malae for reasons she would disclose to no one.

"I apologize, Naytal. I had forgotten your disposition toward Falashas. However, I must differ with you in regard to his reputation. Your mother has never thought of him as a criminal. Neither has Harmais." Tshenpur decided to push it to the brim. "In fact, Harmais is considering rewarding Sahlin's faithfulness in a most extravagant way."

"I have disagreed with my mother before, and I have yet to agree with Harmais. Sahlin is a Jewish embezzler and should be banished back to the hellhole from which he has just arrived."

"Those are most strong words," Tshenpur noted, immensely satisfied with the amount of disgust she was able to incite from her rival friend. "Regardless, the kandace is still enthralled with the man and loves him like a son."

"So why don't you marry him?" Naytal bellowed, unable to restrain her words.

Tshenpur simply smiled. "I believe that he's already spoken for." She glanced at Melaenis, who wore a devilish grin as if she were savoring a forbidden thought.

"Don't look at me," Melaenis said. "I believe that I would still have to compete with Imani for a sip of that fine wine."

"That's a very old flame to say the least," Tshenpur chided. "Come on, girl, you're from a noble house. You need to take what you want."

Melaenis feigned a smile and shifted her eyes back toward the board game. She had no desire to be patronized by Tshenpur.

"Come, come, Tshenpur, your remarks are distressing our friend," Naytal interjected. "It is obvious that neither one of us wants to discuss a man who is a self-serving bigot."

"I understand how you feel, Naytal. However, I think that you had better rethink the list of people that you have inscribed upon your scroll of contempt. It will only be a matter of time before many of those individuals gain the power to do more than just insult you."

For the first time, Naytal felt as if Tshenpur were actually threatening her. She glanced up to find the soon-to-be queen boldly staring her way. At that moment, Naytal became aware of the unequivocal position of inferiority that she was about to inherit. She felt every bit of the pressure that Tshenpur meant to apply and knew that it was a foreshadow of trials to come.

She silently asked Isis how much more she would have to endure before the sun rose on the day of reckoning that would bring her justice.

General Akinidad's eyes shot from one end of the conference table to the other. Accusations were projected his way like flaming arrows.

For well over three hours, the Hall of Apedemack had served as a gallery of displeasure. Embittered complaints and seething criticism collided against the hardened brick walls of the secluded midsized ceremonial chamber. The eight men gathered in the heart of the dufufa cared little that the air had grown warm and stuffy.

Through it all, Akinidad hardly had spoken a word. Then again, the men were master politicians known for their uncanny abilities to monopolize conversation. Djabal, his robust second in command, had levied more answers than he did. Nonetheless, Akinidad purposed in his heart to endure their speeches. They had arranged the meeting, and they had made the journey north to Qustul.

As Akinidad pondered the greater purpose behind the meeting, yet another scribe rose to his feet to deliver his grievances.

"I must agree with my brethren from the north. The commonwealth of Kerma is at risk with the current climate." Though the scribe spoke eloquently, beads of sweat gathered on top of his shaved head. Akinidad couldn't tell whether it was a nervous reaction or the building heat in the sealed chamber. "Vizier Carachen's decision to delay dispersion of the funds that he has received from the royal court to assist the rebuilding effort of the north is already having an adverse affect upon the Kerman economy."

"That's right!" echoed a lawyer from Kalabsha. "Many of our patrons and farmers have already migrated to

Roman Egypt! They would gladly surrender their citizenship as Nubians to line their pockets and feed their families. And what does Carachen care?"

"He cares very little," voiced an older man who had not spoken a word until then. Akinidad recognized him as Sa'ron, the *pelmes-ate* of Kerma and the highest ranking official in the room. All eyes focused upon the stirring statesman. "People do not leave a great nation simply because they are hungry. Indeed, there is food in abundance to the south. Yet, the common people are going north out of Meroë and into Egypt. Why?"

The question hung in the room like a silver moon refusing to acquiesce to the sun.

"People are departing because they no longer believe. They can no longer see the greatness of the vision that our forefathers chiseled into the stones of our monuments. Why? Is it because the monuments have crumbled to dust or have been obscured by the sands of time? No, my brothers. There is another reason. Soon the day will come when Meroë will be no more. Our borders will surely crumble, and our language will be obliterated. Our people will speak some bastardized form of Latin and Greek, and we shall lose our identity—all because the people no longer believe."

Akinidad shifted in his seat. Sa'ron's words made his ears burn with curiosity. He found himself asking whether he still believed in Meroë.

"Your words are quite vivid, Pelmes Sa'ron," Djabal started. "Are you declaring that the people have lost faith in all that is Nubian to the point that they are willing to search for something else?"

"Your question reflects your insight, Commander Djabal," Sa'ron answered, knowing full well that the question was posed on behalf of General Akinidad. "I will come right to the point. Our people are losing faith not in the gods of Meroë but in those who possess the authority delegated by the gods. I submit that the royal court has abandoned the will of Apedemack."

"Yes, yes!" cried a scribe. "Why else would Apedemack curse the royal court by allowing the death of two sons! They are leading us to ruin!"

Sa'ron held a steady gaze with Akinidad. He wasn't sure where the general stood, but he was determined to find out. "I further submit that new leadership must seize the reigns of this kingdom."

Sa'ron had to elevate his voice over the declarations of assent that buzzed through the room. "Also, this is something that must happen before the Romans violate the Treaty of Samos and ransack our land. Hear me, my brothers! If we don't act now, this event will surely happen by the time that our grandsons ascend to leadership. Our legacy to future generations will be adorned with cowardice and laced with indifference!"

With that, the venerable administrator took his seat. In the excitement of the moment, another scribe from Kerma shot to his feet, ready to brandish his endorsement of Sa'ron's proposal. Before he could finish his first sentence, Akinidad caught his attention and calmly gestured him to sit down.

The general paused and surveyed the faces of the men. Like a strong tonic, their emotions had been mixed together and agitated to the point that they all bore the same blunt and pitiless expressions. Akinidad approved of the sight.

Akinidad watched the final grains of an hourglass trickle out. Instinctively, he reset the timepiece. "Time is most fascinating. It marches on at a steady pace like a well-disciplined army. It doesn't speed up, nor does it slow down. It doesn't change. However, also like an army, it changes everything that it touches. Nothing can escape its influence."

"If we needed a lesson in the mechanics of time, General Akinidad, we would have traveled south to the Great Center of Learning," an impetuous scribe grunted.

"Yes, indeed," Akinidad replied smoothly. "But instead, you want lessons in disloyalty and treachery. I'm not the man to provide such things."

In place of dissent, silence rumbled through the chamber.

"I've been here for hours listening to you bureaucrats and administrators voice your displeasure about Vizier Carachen and even the royal court. You have laid your grievances before me as if I were a member of the Council of Ministers or even the grand vizier of Meroë."

Akinidad turned to Djabal. As if receiving an inaudible command, Djabal promptly rose and exited the room. The closing of the ironclad door reverberated through the room.

"Though I sympathize with your issues, I cannot assist you," Akinidad said.

"But, General, we were under the impression that you hated Carachen and were in staunch disapproval of the royal court's current agenda," voiced a finely robed official.

"Those are my personal views. They have nothing to do with how I respond to appointed officials and royal decrees."

"What form of meaningless double-talk is that?" the man blurted in return.

A corner of Akinidad's mouth curled up ever so slightly. "You should know. It is the same form of meaningless double-talk that your office supplied me with after the Bedja upraising three years ago."

Recalling the incident, the man scoffed impertinently.

"I am a soldier, not a politician. I am a general, not a governor. The game that I play with you today is done for your benefit." He scoured the room and noticed that more than several of the administrators were shifting nervously in their seats. "Yes, I know how important the facade of loyalty is for each and every one of you. You hide behind it as a lioness conceals herself behind the tall grass of the plains."

"And what of yourself, Akinidad?" Sa'ron interjected. "What of the facade that you must wear? If we are like lions of the plains, then you are like the hawks of the skies. We may dwell in the tall grass, but you sit upon the high branch. Because you command the loyalty of the army, you are all but untouchable . . . much like a bird in flight."

Like two warring rams with their horns locked, Akinidad and Sa'ron sat and glared stubbornly at one another . . . waiting.

"I need to hear you say it," Akinidad finally voiced, his words slow and deliberate.

Sa'ron squinted at the younger man in admiration, knowing his next sentence would alter the destiny of the northern provinces forever. "What you have heard today merely echoes the sentiment of nearly every official in the Kerman province. When Harmais takes the throne, there is a great probability that Carachen will be elevated to a prominent position in the royal court, possibly that of chief treasurer."

The glare of disbelief in Akinidad's eyes did not go unnoticed by Sa'ron. "Yes, general. It is quite possible that a man who has pillaged and disassembled the northern infrastructure could inherit a position with enough power to deprive Kerma and Nobatia of all useful financial resources. I'll leave you to imagine what would happen to the great army of Kerma if the finances to pay the soldiers dwindled and evaporated."

Akinidad already knew what would happen. The horrific vision visited him in his dreams several times a month. With no money to compensate the soldiers or to sustain their weapons and supplies, the army would weaken and eventually splinter. Troublesome nomadic tribes such as the Nobadae and Bedja would surely gain a foothold and disrupt trade. The northern provinces would suffer greatly, though the southern portion of the kingdom would most likely maintain its wealth.

"It is unlikely that Harmais would allow such a thing to happen," Akinidad said, trying to convince himself there was merit in the statement. "Surely he is aware of the ramifications of such a decision."

Sa'ron almost grinned but managed to catch himself. "Harmais is a thirty-five-year-old fool. He is a boy in the body of a man who is about to become king. His mother initiated the policy of northern diversification years ago. His brother continued it until his death. You mustn't forget why the Nobatians rebelled in the first place." Sa'ron paused to watch Akinidad's mind recount the royal court's attempt to open the northern border with Roman Egypt. Both the kandace and the qeren urged that their true future prosperity lay in increased trade with Rome and her provinces. However, there were many who disagreed—enough to initiate a full-scale rebellion. "Is there any reason to believe that he would simply abandon the policy that both his mother and brother espoused? Certain regions of Nobatia are already overmined and are sparsely populated."

Everyone in the room silently agreed with Sa'ron. Many of them could easily picture the growing number of deserted wastelands that had been produced by hundreds of generations farming and stripping the region.

"I believe that we will be fortunate to have at least five more years before he focuses totally on the south and abandons large sections of the north," said the pelmes-adab of Nobatia. "There will be no point in securing a land that has been depleted of its resources."

Sa'ron leaned back slightly and tilted his chin up.

It didn't take long for Akinidad to sense that Sa'ron would say nothing more. The general rose to his feet, the silver trim of his black tunic sparkling in the torchlight. He slowly walked across the room and stood before the ominous statue of Apedemack. His eyes climbed the hulking statue that had been fashioned with the body of a man and the head of a lion. He cryptically whispered something to the grand idol. He then turned to face the table of conspirators. "After Carachen has been killed, I want complete loyalty from each of your departments."

"You would make yourself vizier of the northern provinces? Only the king can give you such power!" a scribe rang out.

Akinidad clasped his hands behind his back, a gesture that accentuated the broadness of his strong shoulders. "I am not a paqar, a peshte, or a vizier. Your act of coming here today has labeled me a mercenary. My loyalty is not to Harmais or to you. It is to the north itself. It appears that I am its sole protector. My price for bringing stability to the region will be complete command of all northern forces."

Sa'ron gently tugged at the gray hair covering his chin. "What you ask is not impossible. However, it will attract the attention of the southern army. From what I understand, it has many fine commanders."

Akinidad smiled. "Perhaps you've misunderstood the main point, Sa'ron. Our words have power, and they have committed us to go all the way. This conspiracy will not end in Kerma or Qustul. It will culminate only in the halls of Meroë. The place where we all meet our deaths."

Chapter 12

Sahlin was pleased to find that the books were in order. He shuffled through the accounting scrolls and statements until his fingers grew weary and started to quiver. Occasionally, he flipped from one ledger to another in order to compare balances. In each case, he ended up doing the mathematical operations all over again in his mind. He grimaced several times at the revelation that his ability to quickly enumerate assets and large sums of capital had somewhat diminished.

Overall, he was more than satisfied with the job that Kalibae had done in maintaining the high standard at which he demanded that the treasury department operate. Sahlin lamented the fact that his young apprentice had been out collecting taxes when he returned from Judea and was not due back for another few days.

Forcing his mind to halt the endless calculations that ran through it, he leaned back and glanced around the room. Even after two weeks, he still found it difficult to believe that he was back in his own environment. Everything felt so familiar and comfortable. Relatively nothing had changed in his absence. The brick walls of his spacious office were still the color of brilliant pearls imported from the Egyptian seaboard. The colorful paintings of great hawks and eagles in flight hung brightly on the walls, giving the room an opulent and polished feel. Sahlin particularly enjoyed being back in his oversized chair which was lined with the cushy hide of a water buffalo.

The door to his office was slightly ajar, allowing sounds of his busy staff outside to seep in. He didn't at all mind the obtrusive noise, in fact welcomed it.

He smiled as he overheard an administrator from the province of Alondia explain to a treasury clerk why he allowed a chieftain to pay only three-quarters of his annual tribute. Normally, Sahlin would have gotten up and inserted himself in such an exchange. Though it was legal for administrators to allow tribes to pay installments on their tribute, Sahlin rarely permitted it. In the cases where he did relent, he always imposed harsh penalties and at times even threatened the tribe with economic sanctions such as exclusion from the trade market. His legalistic and pitiless manner was feared and respected throughout the provinces.

As he listened to the administrator plead his case, Sahlin grasped the arms of his chair and started to push himself up. Before he could rise, a stray thought surfaced from somewhere inside of him and gently urged him not to intervene. He attempted to shake the notion away, but it simply latched on and maintained its delicate proffer.

Slightly annoyed, he leaned back and pretended to shuffle through several ledgers that he had earlier retrieved from a safe box at his home. All the while, his ears remained fixed on the fragmented conversation that he heard through the door's narrow opening. From what he could discern, the clerk was being swayed by the administrator's pretext. Finally, the clerk relented and granted the reprieve. Everything within Sahlin wanted to march outside and impose a hefty fine upon the administrator and the tribe; however, he was bound to his chair. After several moments, he found himself strangely agreeing with the clerk's decision.

Closing the ledgers, Sahlin slowly rubbed his eyes and bit his lower lip in befuddlement. It was the third time that week that he acquiesced to a warm feeling in his chest and granted a pardon in the face of a situation that would have normally triggered his wrath.

He rose and walked over to the balcony that overlooked the immense royal courtyard. He folded his arms and leaned against the doorway. Quieting his mind, he focused on a soft patch of clouds that sat in the distant sky and listened. The words were always the same. *A bruised reed He will not break and a dimly burning wick He will not extinguish . . .*

The passage from Isaiah's scroll clung to his heart as heat did to the sun. As he had many times already, Sahlin shook his head in feeble defiance.

"Jesus, I have given You all that I can," he whispered. "I cannot afford to be merciful to all men. I must crush the reed and douse the wick." Sahlin's mind raced through the faces of the scores of administrators and scribes who made it their purpose to exploit merciful men. Mercy was not a trait that was conducive to lasting success for someone in his position. Nevertheless, his heart was again inundated by the inspired words of an ancient prophet: *He has told you, O man, what is good; and what does the Lord require of you but to do justice, to love kindness, and to walk humbly with your God?*

The prophetic question echoed louder and louder in his soul until he could hear nothing else. He sealed his eyes and fought to corral the gamut of emotions that swirled through him. "I cannot be merciful . . . Don't make me choose . . . Don't make me choose . . ." His frail voice trailed off into the wind, leaving him with the muffled sounds of a few workers in the courtyard two stories below.

An eternity passed, bringing with it a temporary stability of mind and spirit. Bringing himself back from the verge of tears, Sahlin started for his chair, even though he had no desire to work. He stared at the ledgers and books that littered his desk and wondered if his life as he once knew it was gone for good. To his consternation, the ledgers mocked him, issuing a decree that his existence was meaningless without them. His hazel eyes rolled down the columns, gathering the numbers, calculating sums with the speed of a cheetah streaking through the plains.

It was a while before Sahlin became aware of the lone figure knocking at his door. "Oh . . . yes," he said, casting the ledgers down. "Come in." As he turned around, his eyes fell upon a face he had been longing to see for over a year. "Kalibae . . ."

☸　　☸　　☸

Sahlin waited until they finished their lunch before he brought up anything pertaining to administration of the royal treasury ministry. The tavern where they dined was situated adjacent to the grand Temple of Amun in the northern section of the city of Meroë. Since they opted to take their meal early, the eatery was relatively empty.

Sahlin appreciated the quiet atmosphere for multiple reasons, one being that it gave Kalibae the opportunity to drop the facade of predominance he had grown used to wearing over the past year. The young man generally carried himself in a posture set to prove himself. It was a stance that Sahlin actually admired, even when it impeded his own authority. However, that was the exception and not the rule. Kalibae was teachable. Far more often than not, he deferred to Sahlin.

"Is Kassa happy to have you back home?" Kalibae asked.

Sahlin winced gingerly as he thought about his older sister. "I don't know if *happy* is the best word to use. She's had that mansion all to herself for close to a year. She's changed everything. She even had the audacity to embellish my study hall with tapestries from the East."

Kalibae's grin turned into a mocking laugh. "You were probably hoping that she would have remarried while you were away."

"I've uttered such a prayer several times during the last few months." Sahlin looked away for a moment. Though he wore a grin, his heart lamented that his widowed sister seemed unwilling to move on with her life and remarry. Like himself, she had no children to embrace —only a notable family heritage existed to provide her a covering.

Desiring to change the subject, Sahlin started to talk about aspects of the voyage that he had just completed. Kalibae sat fixated as his mentor described his journey to and from Judea. Although he had an inner reservation about doing so, Sahlin was careful to omit the events that transpired in the Judean desert after his departure from Jerusalem. He convinced himself that he would respond to the urge to disclose his experience in the proper time.

After he finished his narrative, Sahlin urged Kalibae to discuss the affairs of the state.

"It's probably nothing that you haven't already heard," Kalibae said. "I ran into Paqar Harmais last week while in Baiyuda."

"Baiyuda?" Sahlin echoed. "The paqar wasn't in Meroë when I arrived. I knew that he was slated to travel west, but what was he doing in Baiyuda?"

"He told me that there was a small rebellion brewing out there that needed to be addressed."

Sahlin squinted. "Unless things have changed in a year, Baiyuda's population is far too small to be a significant threat to the royal power base."

"He had a regiment of five hundred troops with him. He also said something about hunting down a renegade band of Bedja tribesmen reported to be in the region."

Sahlin found the paqar's rationale for dispatching such a large force into the midst of a vast desert odd to say the least, especially since the Bedja were known to dwell primarily in the northern desert in Nobatia. "Harmais told you this?" he asked, resisting the urge to prod for more details.

"Not exactly. He announced it during a general assembly of royal officials in the main hall of Baidu. I happened to be in the city at the time and was therefore required to attend."

"I see," Sahlin mused, filing the information away for another time. Whatever Harmais was up to, he was certain that Kalibae or anyone outside the paqar's inner circle had no idea what it was. "And you, what took you into the breath of the lion?"

Kalibae smirked at Sahlin's description of the hot Baiyudan region. "I'm sure that you'll enjoy this one. Remember two years ago when the pelmes-adab in Baiyuda attempted to falsify the trade registry during his quarterly report?"

"Vaguely."

"I'm not surprised that you can't recall offhand. He wasn't very creative in his deception. He was the fool who switched the land trading record with that of the waterway."

"Actually, I do seem to recall that. If memory serves, there was a particularly harsh famine in the region that year."

"Exactly. And the pelmes-adab thought that he could deceive us into thinking that his trading index was higher than it actually was. Remember? He somehow acquired the numbers from the pelmes-ate's report. He modified them and then sent them in expecting that he would receive the bonus for coming in over his quota."

"He almost succeeded." Sahlin tried to recall the exact outcome of the man's scheme. So many administrators attempted such ploys that he could only remember the ones involving extensive sums of currency.

"He didn't even have a chance!" Kalibae exclaimed as a servant refreshed their drinks. "Oh, I think that it was maybe one day before you figured it out by comparing the numbers to previous years. But he couldn't get past you, and you made him pay for it."

As the event came together in his mind, Sahlin began to recall every detail of the man's thwarted plan to gain additional money. With a morbid sense of glee, Kalibae recounted how Sahlin had the man flogged before his peers. To add salt to his wound, Sahlin coerced the peshte of the region to retain the man as the pelmes-adab, forcing him to live with his shame and dishonor.

What Sahlin hadn't told Kalibae during that time was the reason why the man attempted such a foolish act. Much of Baiyuda was a harsh desert with very little redeeming value. The region, its people, and even its officers were extremely poor. Even the vizier of Baiyuda earned less than a mere scribe from the Isle of Meroë. Money from Baiyuda affected Sahlin's bottom line so minutely that he was almost tempted to ignore the entire scene. Nevertheless, Sahlin had seen the man's deception as an opportunity to garner fear among other regional administrators. He didn't at all care that the pelmes-adab was simply trying to feed his family as well as the families of his employees.

"He did it again?" Sahlin slowly asked.

"Like a fool who is deaf and blind."

"How did you handle it?"

"The same way that you would have," Kalibae reported proudly.

Vexed, Sahlin found himself holding back tears as he heard Kalibae describe how the man pleaded for mercy. "I seized his property and had him thrown into prison. His sons should be arriving in Kerma any day in order to work off the debt that he amassed."

"And his wife?"

"Homeless, but who cares? It wasn't as if she didn't have any warning. You told him that if he ever transgressed again, you would take his land and have him thrown into prison. I was simply fulfilling your prophecy."

Kalibae took a long swill from his cup. He looked at Sahlin with a grin, his dark eyes like lifeless coals.

Sahlin nearly gagged at the expression in his young apprentice's face. Was this what he had molded Kalibae into—a heartless administrator whose only concern was the bottom line and meeting the quota?

"What's the matter?" Kalibae signaled for another round of drinks. "I would have had him executed, but that would have seemed a bit too harsh." He laughed, downing what was left in his cup.

Wanting to escape, Sahlin took a drink of wine and focused on the bottom of the cup instead of looking at Kalibae. Never before had he felt such a great deal of shame. The fact that his life was laden with such skeletons drove him even deeper into the pit of regret.

For the next hour, Kalibae brought him up-to-date on the treasury's strengths and weaknesses. Sahlin was thoroughly impressed with the expertise with which Kalibae had administered the kingdomwide network of tax- and tribute-gathering facilities for the past year. The young man sounded less like an apprentice and more like an executive officer.

Finally, Sahlin pulled out his moneybag and dug out several cowrie shells. However, Kalibae was much quicker than he was.

"Please, allow me," Kalibae demanded, slamming down more money than was needed to pay for their meal. "Now that you're back, I suppose that I'll have to revert back to my regular salary."

Sahlin leaned back and forced a smile. He hoped that the emotional imbalance in his soul would simply pass away with the gust of wind that rushed through the temple quarter of the city. Something deep within told him that things would only get more complex for him.

They rose and walked through the crowded square flanked by several large temples. On several occasions, council elders welcomed Sahlin back as Kalibae and he made their way back to the palace. Kalibae slowed their pace as they approached the heavily guarded entrance.

"My lord," Kalibae started as their progress slowly came to a halt. "I'm not supposed to tell you this, but I remember how much you dislike surprises."

"What is it?"

"There is a reception honoring your return planned for tomorrow evening. Word is that Paqar Harmais will be in attendance."

"I don't want any reception. If this was your idea, then . . ."

"No sir, it wasn't me. I know better than that. It was a royal decision."

"Tshenpur?"

"Since I also remember how much you hate to guess, I'll spare you. The reception was ordered by the queen."

Sahlin sighed and nodded his head. Since his return, he had tried several times to visit her, but she was far too weak to receive any callers. "I can't turn her down. Will she be attending?"

"I doubt it. She's not doing any better, from what I understand. The physicians have no idea what is causing her to wither away, but I'm sure you know that."

Sahlin said nothing in response. Something about his newfound faith urged him to remain silent when confronted with adverse circumstances. As they walked through the palace gates, he found himself musing on another one of the ancient Hebrew Scriptures.

Surely our griefs He Himself bore, and our sorrows He carried.

Sahlin could not gather why the Scriptures resonated so deeply within him, but he chose to accrue the unconditional hope that they offered him.

⁂

The warm midday sun pounded on Dikembul's back. He wiped the sweat from his brow as he positioned himself to lift another wooden beam into place. Only two more sections to go, and he would be finished refurbishing the old fence that contained his flock of sheep.

In a sense, he found the backbreaking work to be a welcome distraction. As of late, a growing anxiety held his thoughts captive. In a few days, he would stand among the other elders at the masjid and describe his experience in Jerusalem. He was still uncertain as to what their response would be when he told them his views on the Messiah. He had seen Nkosi several times since their late-night conversation. His long-time friend had yet to say anything further about the topic that consumed the entire evening.

Dikembul settled himself into a squatting position and fixed his arms around the beam. As he thrust upwards, he immediately noticed the load was far lighter than it should have been. After lowering it into place, he turned around to see the towering Akil smiling down at him.

Dikembul sighed and nodded his head. "Still sneaking up on people, Akil?"

"I thought for sure that you heard me," the strapping young man replied, dusting his hands off. Akil's smooth brown skin reflected the harsh sunlight more than absorbing it. "Welcome back to the crypt of the kingdom."

Dikembul smiled and turned back to his work. "No. I've been through Judea, Egypt, and Nobatia. Even though there is a cemetery beyond those hills, this place is far from a crypt."

"Of course." Akil flung back the dark cloak of his black-and-red militia uniform. He would never admit he was burning up. "I won't ask you a question that I am sure that you have heard at least three dozen times already," he declared, referring to their journey from Judea.

"Thank you," Dikembul said, relieved that he would not have to expound on the unforgettable trip yet again.

"I trust that you and Annika are well."

"The Lord God has smiled upon us, and we are truly blessed. And yourself, Akil? I have heard some great things about you. It appears that you have made a lasting mark upon the local militia in Napata in our absence."

Akil selected his words carefully. "*The Lord* has smiled upon me as well."

Dikembul strapped a rope around the beam and the post that it was posted upon. "A commander in the Napatan brigade. That's very impressive. You have made this small town very proud."

"I have many of you to thank for your unconditional support after my parents died."

Dikembul nodded as he recalled the tragedy that orphaned Akil as a young teenager. "To have accomplished so much by the age of twenty-three is very special. Truth be told, I'm rather surprised to see that you're still here."

"Actually, I am not. My regiment will be shipping north to Kerma after the coronation. We will be stationed there for six months."

"I see," Dikembul tried to picture Annika taking up residence in Kerma, but the vision refused to stick. "At least Kerma is a safe region. Fortunately, you're not going to Nobatia. That entire province still seemed unstable when we passed through it on the way home last month."

"Yes, I agree with you. It's hardly the place that I would like to raise a family."

Dikembul nodded sullenly and proceeded back to the task of tying down the beam. Nkosi's words rambled through his head. Heeding his friend's warning, he could see no other recourse but to stand aside. "Annika is at the river filling canisters with water."

"Perhaps she can use some help," Akil remarked as a sly smile flashed across his lightly bearded face.

"I am sure that she would appreciate it. You are a good man, Akil." Dikembul lifted his eyes only to see that Akil had already started down toward the river.

♨   ♨   ♨

Annika closed her eyes as the gentle current rushed through her toes. The chilling effect simultaneously cooled down her entire body. She had worked a good portion of the morning and felt entitled to a break from her labors.

With her eyes still shut, she tried to envision herself tending a home full of children. Though she knew that her husband would want differently, her imagination only catered to visions that displayed all girls. She longed for the opportunity to sow all of the wonder gifts that had been given her into the lives of her own children.

At times, she lamented that the vision tarried for so long. She was by no means an old woman, but she didn't want to let the opportunity pass her by. She wanted to live it to its fullest, fulfilling yet another conviction that her mother had ingrained into her.

Before she died, Annika's mother always emphasized that it wasn't enough to simply please the man that you loved. In order to be a truly good wife, a woman had to put herself in the position to complement him and, in essence, make him whole. Though Annika could not comprehend the rationale behind her mother's admonishment when she was younger, time and experience had ripened the fruit of her understanding.

As she looked upon her father after her mother's death, she saw a man seemingly broken and incomplete. It wasn't until they left for Jerusalem that she finally realized her father was no longer whole. It was at that point that her reverence for her mother was elevated to a new level. She, too, wanted to complement a man. To lift him when he was down. To push him toward something greater than himself.

"I thought that you were supposed to be working."

Annika flinched. She spun her head around to see Akil standing behind her. "Why did you do that?" she exclaimed.

"Still jumpy, I see," Akil sassed. "I don't believe that you have changed at all." He knelt next to her on one knee and examined her close up as if she were a precious stone. "I retract that statement. Your beauty has done nothing but increase since the last time I saw you."

Though Annika's eyes flashed his way, she didn't move her head. She had no desire to confirm that he had grown more handsome and stately within a year's time. There was something about Akil that made her heart pound furiously. Then again, that was an effect he had on most all of her peers as well. "What brings you out here?"

"You do, of course. I wanted to see how you were doing." His eyes perused her short curly hair and caressed her soft dark cheeks.

"I'm faring well. The Lord has been good to us," she said, resisting the swelling urge to look him in the face.

"He has been good to me as well."

"So I've heard," she expressed, starting to wring her hands. "I have heard that you have been promoted."

"That wasn't the Lord. That was simply hard work." Akil started to place his hand upon her shoulder, but then drew it back before touching her. "However, I firmly believe that it was the Lord that brought you back to me."

Annika felt enveloped by Akil's presence. His imposing demeanor was strong enough to drive most young women into a state of awe.

"You're too kind, Akil." She looked his way only to see that the running water had captured his gaze. "I thought for sure that you would have married someone else by now."

"Honestly, I didn't have the time. I've been in and out of Napata for the past nine months. Besides, it's not as if I am seeking another woman. I told you how I felt for you before you left."

"I know . . . I remember. But feelings . . . change."

"Mine have not," Akil assured. His eyes intercepted hers as she started to look away. He affectionately tipped her chin and drew her closer. Torn by her independent spirit and her mounting attraction toward him, Annika offered no resistance as he gently pressed his lips to hers. Before the kiss became passionate, Akil slowly pulled away and rose to his feet. He towered over her and allowed his eyes to convey that he was ready to do all he needed in order to make her his own.

Annika silently sat by as Akil turned around and loaded the last several canisters of water onto the mule-drawn cart. The full containers seemed more like toys to him.

"I will be in Napata until after the coronation, after which time, I will return and come to terms with Dikembul about compensation for your hand in marriage." He leaned down and brushed her cheek lightly with the tips of his fingers. "Until then . . ." He retracted his hand and smiled devilishly. He leisurely spun around and walked back up the path, his cloak fluttering behind him like a majestic veil.

Annika pulled her feet from the water and drew her knees into her chest. As she watched the man who would most likely be her destiny disappear into the forest, she suddenly felt very frigid and lifeless.

Chapter 13

The night air was warm and inviting. The untouchable stars danced around the waxing moon in accord with the music softly rising out of the palace courtyard.

The masses that lived just outside of the grand palace walls knew there was a celebration of some proportion commencing inside the royal residence. Nobody was surprised. For days, viziers, peshtes, and other high-ranking government officials filed into the city for a reason known only to the royal family.

The courtyard was lavishly decorated with flags and standards representing each province of the vast Nubian kingdom. Streamers from the Far East shimmered in the brilliant torchlight that illuminated the festive evening.

Platters of exotic food adorned every one of the twenty-five tables set up in the midst of the square. Though the drums, stringed instruments, and flutes were unseen, their lively sounds descended from all four corners of the enclosure.

Sahlin hated every moment of the attention he was receiving. He sat at the head table with Harmais, Tshenpur, and Tibo, the current grand vizier of Meroë. The stately old man wore an expression that openly suggested he also preferred to be somewhere else. Sahlin could hardly blame him.

The assembly was full of faces Sahlin recognized. Many of the people were immediate associates of his. Some were even directly accountable to him. He wondered how many of them were in appearance simply because Amanitore had issued the invitation. Though most people spoke well of him, he knew that he was not well liked throughout the upper echelon of society. His family was Jewish, immensely wealthy, and extremely powerful. Scores of administrators harbored jealousies that went back generations.

Sahlin didn't care, though. He usually enjoyed the irony behind such galas. Throughout his career, he used peshtes, scribes, and even viziers to propel him to the vaulted position he currently held. Life had drawn its definition and value from business and social status.

There was something different this time around. The food wasn't quite as rich. The music wasn't quite as loud. The laughter was shallower than usual. It felt as if he were observing the party through another man's eyes. He locked eyes with the vizier of Alondia who sat at a table adjacent to the dance floor. The man issued a warm smile and bowed his head. Though he sensed no sincerity in the act, Sahlin returned the gesture, wishing that the night would hurry to its conclusion.

Harmais gripped Sahlin's arm. "I have a surprise for you," the paqar said slyly.

"I thought this was it," Sahlin replied, not wanting any additional jolts.

"This was my mother's so-called surprise for you. I've got something far more . . . appealing than a party with a room full of men who hate you."

"Not all of them hate me," Sahlin said dryly.

"Of course they do. They hate you probably even more than they hate me. I simply strip them of their pride. You strip them of their money."

As Harmais spoke, the music smoothly transitioned into a slow and deliberate melody that summoned three extremely beautiful dancers onto the floor in front of the head table. "Ah, you'll like these. Keep your eye on the one in the middle. She's dreadfully sensual."

Sahlin watched the dancers for a moment. They twirled and twisted in agreement with the music that sped up like a lioness chasing its prey. Just as Harmais pointed out, the central dancer was openly flirtatious with her provocative moves. From the looks of her face, Sahlin judged her to be no more than sixteen or seventeen years of age.

Though Sahlin's eyes didn't want to abandon the curvy three figures that raced before him, something inside of him forced his attention to migrate elsewhere. Harmais, on the other hand, was fully engulfed with the vivacious beauties. Sahlin thought for certain that the future king would have been considerate of his soon-to-be wife in front of so many guests.

At that moment, the entire male populace in the courtyard erupted, but their applause was short-lived.

The middle dancer broke off into a solo routine designed to entice the men into a perverted frenzy.

Sahlin felt nauseated. He searched for a place to rest his weary eyes. They finally fell upon Qar Naytal, who greeted him with the scowl of a jackal. He resisted the urge to reciprocate the gesture and simply shifted his focus to the other lady seated with the qar. It took Sahlin a moment to recognize Melaenis through the generous amount of makeup she wore. However, her torrid gaze soon jolted his memory. She clearly had the look of a passionate predator stalking her prey. Not wanting to encourage her, he darted his eyes to another section of the room.

The music fired up to a furious pace once more. The young dancer spun and gyrated in compliance to the racing drums that filled the courtyard. Along with the fierce beat came memories of reckless advances that Melaenis had hurled his way prior to his departure to Judea. He didn't welcome them then, and he had no desire to become the object of her twisted fantasies once again.

The music ceased abruptly, leaving the young dancer on her knees before the head table. Her head and slender shoulders were thrown back, and she panted profusely. When the ovation that she received died down, she rose to her feet and bowed deeply before the table of honor. Ignoring the burning sweat that trickled into her eyes, she held her unblinking gaze with Paqar Harmais until he nodded his approval and signaled her to leave.

"Was this my surprise?" Sahlin leaned over and asked.

"No. That was for me," Harmais declared, feeling extremely gratified with himself. "Within the past year, that young lady has become one of the most entertaining dancers in the region."

"For obvious reasons," Sahlin chided, noting men were still commenting on the sultry performance.

"I'm sure that I can arrange a private exhibit for you, if you so desire," Harmais offered with a forthrightness that amazed himself.

"No need, Your Highness. She looked far too young for me."

"Old man," Harmais grunted. "Your surprise from me isn't as arousing, but I believe that you will find it quite . . . empowering." Harmais rose from his seat and elevated a hand to quiet the crowd. He was not a muscular man, but he dressed well enough to insinuate that he was. His voice was full, but not nearly strong enough to resonate through the courtyard.

"As I mentioned earlier, we are all gathered here tonight to welcome back and honor a man who has served this kingdom with a singular loyalty. Now that we have welcomed him with food, drink, and dance, the time has come to honor him." Harmais glanced at a servant who quickly rushed to the paqar's side and handed him a box. "Shortly, I will be married and coronated king over this vast kingdom. One of my most arduous tasks will be to select a royal court that will assist me in the wise administration of Meroë. As many of you know, members of the Malae clan have served my family in many different capacities for generations. Viziers of provinces, chief scribe, and chief of treasury, to name just a few. However, this night, I am appointing Sahlin Malae as the grand vizier of Meroë, with a voice in the kingdom second only to my own."

Sahlin was stunned. Instinctively, he stood up to receive the signet ring that Harmais revealed from the box. Never before had anyone in his family ascended so high in the royal court. He turned toward the assemblage of ministers, most of whom were on their feet lauding his great achievement. Every one of them appeared to be shocked. A few even looked a bit relieved.

Two hours later, Sahlin managed to steal away from the gala. He made his way to the broad platform that ran along the south wall. Several guards pulled watch duty along the platform, but none of them paid any attention to Sahlin. He propped himself up against an iron railing. His position was fairly high and overlooked the crowded courtyard below.

Once he was settled, he rubbed his eyes furiously. The grand vizier was one of the few positions appointed by the king that actually had to be ratified by the council of ministers. The power accompanying the post was staggering. The grand vizier oversaw the selection and appointments of the viziers that governed the provinces and served as the prime minister for the royal court.

Throughout the history of Meroë, behind every prominent king stood a forceful grand vizier. It was a general assumption that Harmais would most likely use his grand vizier as nothing short of a crutch while administrating the kingdom. Sahlin understood the enormous amount of work that awaited him along with the tremendous trial of patience he would have to endure at the hands of his king.

He stared blankly down at the crowd of people in the courtyard as he recalled the day that his father issued him a challenge that had shaped the course of his life. Like his grandfather, Sahlin's father was also immensely successful, serving a majority of his life as the peshte of the Isle of Meroë. Prior to his death, Sahlin's father had commissioned him to expand the influence of the Malae clan beyond any scope it had ever had.

Sahlin looked into the starry sky above and drank an imaginary toast to his forefathers, swearing that he would use every scrap of knowledge and skill to bring everlasting honor upon their family name.

After his pledge, he scanned the heavens for the brightest star among the cluster. Whenever he prayed to Jesus at night, he instinctively sought out the brilliant star in the eastern sky that dominated the rest. His grandfather's journals informed him that such a star had announced Jesus' birth. Though he wasn't at all certain the object he gazed upon was the same one God used to declare the arrival of the Messiah, he often used it as a reference point to fix his hope upon. Its very presence gave him comfort and reminded him that he was not alone.

"Thank You for Your favor," he whispered to the star. "I shall accomplish all that I have been destined to." As he spoke, a wave of melancholy feelings washed over him. As a result, his new title suddenly felt very small and even insignificant to a degree.

Do You disapprove after all? Sahlin asked the Lord.

He grasped at the image forming inside of his spirit. The impression was vague yet very deliberate. He closed his eyes to see a startling comparison coming into focus. Before him stood the immense mountain Gebel Barkal, mystical symbol of the Kushite kingdom. The mountain's silhouette resembled the headdress of the king. There was nothing larger, nothing stronger, nothing more desirable. Yet, as he looked again, Gebel Barkal stood in the eclipse of an ever-growing shadow that blanketed the landscape and blocked out the mountain. The shadow grew until it eventually covered him as well. Was there something or someone bigger than the mountain that could make this formation seem insignificant in comparison?

"It is far too early to go to sleep, my friend," stated an interrupting voice.

Sahlin's eyes snapped open to see Harmais standing by his side. "I didn't see you come up."

"Evidently not." Harmais perused his long-time friend for a moment and then turned his attention to the crowd below. "Since when have you become the antisocial type? It isn't like you to abandon the throng."

"You must forgive me. There is so much to do . . . so much to think about. Everything has happened so quickly."

Harmais concurred with a nod. The turn of events of the past two years astonished him more than anyone else in the kingdom. Yet, he was determined to take full advantage of the situation. "We have much to discuss, my old friend, chief of which is the appropriation of the sequestered fortune that we've amassed over the years."

Sahlin fought the urge to look behind their backs. He knew that no one but the guards could possibly hear their conversation, but caution was a companion he rarely ignored. "I checked the records. The accounts are still accruing a hefty sum of interest. Not even Kalibae is aware of their existence." Sahlin hated keeping information away from his apprentice. However, years ago he surmised that it was best not to inform Kalibae of the covert accounts that Harmais and he had erected.

"Excellent," Harmais said. "I've given it a great deal of thought, and I believe that a substantial sum of the money will be necessary to purchase the southern army."

"But as the king you already command the army."

"There is much that you have to learn," Harmais voiced, grinning. "As the king, I will command the generals who, in turn, command the loyalty of the soldiers. I don't wish to make the same errors that my mother and brother did. I intend to purchase the loyalty of the soldiers themselves."

"Why go to such an extreme measure?" Sahlin asked, already disliking the horizon of deceit that was arising before him.

"It appears that the winds of rebellion are once again gusting in the north. This time, I believe that it is starting within the province of Kerma."

"Carachen? He has always been among the most loyal to the crown. He has no reason to incite a rebellion."

"True enough. My operatives have verified that he has nothing to do with it."

"Then who? The army perhaps?"

"Not likely. The general over the Kerman forces is loyal to Carachen. His record indicates nothing less than strict compliance with royal decrees. I believe that it lies with other government officials."

"Are you certain?"

"I have summoned Carachen, his peshte, and the general of the Kerman forces to Meroë. They will arrive shortly before the coronation. I believe that I can trust these men." Harmais stroked his chin and contemplated just how far he would have to dig before he unearthed the conspirators.

"It's amazing that they would actually attempt to rebel again. I've seen firsthand the path of destruction that Sherakarer carved in the northern province."

"Sherakarer was a fool," Harmais declared. "He destroyed far more than he had to. He earned the ire of everyone north of the third cataract, and that, unfortunately, is his legacy to me."

At a loss for words, Sahlin gazed blankly across the courtyard. Part of him felt extremely elated he had not been present for the turbulence the northern rebellion stirred up. However, his ignorant bliss was often daunted by a twinge of guilt.

"It doesn't matter, though." Harmais sighed. "Once I have secured the loyalty of the southern army, through our discretionary accounts, of course, I cannot foresee anyone rising against me."

Sahlin's heart jumped in his chest as Harmais spoke. He hid the frustration that pounded furiously away at his soul. Several times during the past few months, he had experienced similar sensations. He wasn't certain why, but he perceived that it was related to a malevolent omen waiting to be fulfilled.

"What do you think of her?" Harmais asked, gesturing down to Tshenpur.

"What do you mean?"

"What sort of kandace do you believe she will make?"

Sahlin briefly eyed Tshenpur. She wore a stylish red-and-gold outfit with a matching headdress. As usual, a crowd of women flanked her. Tonight, though, Sahlin noticed that the crowd around her was larger than normal. In fact, he had to look twice in order to make out her two customary companions, Naytal and Melaenis. "She is extremely full of wit and charm . . ."

"That I already know. What about her character? Do you think her motives are pure?"

"Why are you asking me this now? She is slated to become your wife in a matter of weeks. You are just now questioning her motives?"

"I just want to make sure that she loves me."

Sahlin was nearly thrown back. "Since when do you care about love?" he exclaimed, recalling the many nights when Harmais raved about Tshenpur's physical attractiveness.

Harmais refused to hide the smile that commandeered his face. "I don't. However, love makes for a nice bridle by which to control a woman. I just want to make sure that it remains an effective means of influence over Tshenpur."

"I think she may be too wise for that, Harmais."

"Maybe so, but I have additional means of controlling her—should my masculine verve ever fail."

The two men shared the laugh, but Sahlin saw little to be gleeful about. The strategy of manipulating people at the most sacred and vulnerable levels was quickly losing its appeal to him.

"We have to get together in the next few days to discuss your new position," Harmais stated, preparing to walk away. "Before we do, I would like you to spend as much time as you can with Grand Vizier Tibo. He will be expecting you."

"I had a brief trip south planned for . . ."

"Cancel it. We have to appear to the council like we're serious. Besides, he did serve my mother well. He may be old and difficult to relate to, but there are still a few nuggets of gold that he can offer us."

"Yes, my lord," Sahlin offered as his friend grinned and strolled toward the staircase.

Sahlin remained aloft against the rail, pondering his immediate future. He had always had a good working relationship with Grand Vizier Tibo. He figured that the elder statesman would be helpful in the massive transition the government would soon undergo.

He saw Harmais enter the crowd to claim his future wife. After doing so, the two headed off into the palace.

Within a few minutes, other high-ranking officials slowly followed suit and vacated the courtyard.

Deciding that he also had had enough of his own celebration, Sahlin turned toward the staircase, intending to make a swift exit through the palace. His path was cut off by a woman clothed in a dark elegant dress that embraced her comely form. As was the current fashion among the women of Meroë, her hair was cropped low, accentuating the fanciful curls that came with the style.

"Imani," Sahlin called softly. Though the limited torchlight concealed the appearance of her eyes, Sahlin knew from experience that they were like dark brown jewels that sparkled with a rare luster.

"It's been a while, Lord Malae," she replied in a voice that commanded both adoration and respect.

"That never did sound right coming from you." Sahlin tried to recall the last time that he saw her as she walked up to him. The aroma of her perfume triggered the memory. "It's been three years since I have seen you."

"Almost four, my lord."

"Didn't you relocate to Alondia?"

"Yes, to care for my ailing sister."

"I remember now," Sahlin said, envisioning the day when the striking woman and her youthful niece moved from Meroë to Alondia.

Imani's father had been a very wealthy merchant from the easternmost region of Alondia and often traveled to Arabia to do business. Tragically, his wife and he were killed during a storm in the Great Red Sea. That left Imani with only two blood relatives, an older sister and a young niece.

"T'Sheba . . . your niece, how is she? She has to be a beautiful young lady by now."

"She's doing extremely well for herself," Imani said, nonchalantly grasping the rail. "She's one of the reasons that I am here tonight."

"You mean you didn't come to welcome me back?"

Imani's smile glowed alongside the torchlight. "Actually, I'm here at the request of Paqar Harmais. It is a business arrangement."

Sahlin cocked an eyebrow at the statement. After the death of her parents, Imani had to become very acute in the language of commerce. Ultimately, she sold off nearly all of the assets before the individuals who managed her father's holdings could raid and pilfer the businesses he left behind. In doing so, she amassed quite a fortune. It was a feat that garnered much admiration from him. "What sort of arrangement are you referring to?" he asked.

Imani hesitated for a moment. "I manage the affairs of a close family member."

"Your sister?"

Imani shook her head.

"Your niece. But what sort of . . ." Sahlin's imagination picked up where his voice left off.

"Nothing's changed. Still lightning fast, I see."

"T'Sheba . . . was one of the dancers from earlier this evening?"

"T'Sheba is *the* dancer from earlier this evening." Imani's tone betrayed the guile she tried to hide in regard to her niece's vast popularity. "Dancing always has been one of her passions. She became very good at it over the years. Too good."

"She was quite impressive," Sahlin offered, not wanting to dwell on a subject that clearly vexed his old associate.

"You're being polite, Sahlin. I saw how you looked away from her this evening."

"You noticed that?" Sahlin asked, hoping that he did not inadvertently offend her.

"You were the seat of attention tonight and a very influential man. People cannot help but notice even the small things that you do."

A late gentle breeze blew through the courtyard. The small gust brushed a fresh fragrance of Imani's perfume past Sahlin's nostrils. He responded by smiling and looking away, as if cherishing a secret reflection. "You said something similar to that the last time we saw each other."

The night air fell silent for a moment as Imani silently recapped their last encounter. At first, she looked away and smiled. As the pleasant thought revealed the intense disagreement that ended that dialogue, her face dimmed a bit. "I meant every word."

"I know you did," Sahlin admitted. The two had a relationship dating clear back to their teenage years. At times, their cordial friendship evolved into romantic episodes that were usually short-lived due to Sahlin's inability to relate on an intimate level. Even from the early days, Sahlin swiftly tossed aside Imani—or any other woman for that matter—to make room for his professional endeavors.

A small wave of shame and regret washed over Imani. Despite her lingering feelings of hurt, she didn't wish to resume the contest of wills that so often sullied their conversations. "What I mean to say is . . . congratulations on your promotion. I'm sure that it is well deserved."

"The Lord has had His way," Sahlin voiced, a slight dimple appearing in his cheek as a result of the distant grin that briefly came and went.

"And how was your journey to Judea?"

"My religion always seemed to be an obstacle for you in the past."

Imani rolled her eyes. "The God that you chose to worship was never *our* obstacle . . . It was your ambition. Your pride."

"I had a job to perform, Imani—one that I was committed to performing well. I couldn't let anything get in the way of my duty . . . not even you."

"Me," Imani breathed. She focused on a single star out of the multitude in the sky. "How about a dream? How about a life? How about some sort of destiny outside of this . . . pit of asps?" she pressed, gesturing down into the courtyard.

Sahlin's gaze trailed her slender hand below. The hundred or so guests who remained at this point were there to burn the evening away carousing and drinking. "This pit, as you call it, is my life . . . and it is my destiny to make it great again."

"As great as she was, Amanitore couldn't even do that, and she was the queen."

"She still is," Sahlin calmly protested.

"No, Sahlin. She is dying." Imani knew how much Sahlin loved the elderly kandace who for years had been like a mother to him. "I'm afraid that much of Meroë will die with her."

An eruption of emotions welled up within Sahlin. He immediately suppressed them. "No, Meroë will live on through those who believe, and I believe."

"What do you believe in, Sahlin? Paqar Harmais? Qar Naytal? The epic war of words in this city that never ceases and . . ."

"I believe in Meroë!" he barked, turning her way. "I believe in my family's mandate to serve this kingdom.

199

Most of all, I believe in myself! I will not be corrupted or shaken from those principles."

At that instance, a sudden breeze hit a nearby torch, causing the flame to abate and quickly flare back up. The brief flash illuminated Imani's face enough to enable Sahlin to see the expression of disgust she wore. Her look only served to remind him how corrupt and heartless he had become prior to his trip to Judea.

He turned back towards the courtyard and tried to hide from his thoughts amidst the music and gaiety.

"And what of your God?" Imani questioned, her eyes red with tears. "Where does He fit into your life?"

"He has His place," Sahlin answered, trying to ignore the chill that shot up his back.

"Ironic, Sahlin. I thought that the Jews abhorred idols. However, it seems that you've placed your God and everything else in your life directly behind your idol."

"And what is my idol, Imani?"

"Welcome home, Grand Vizier Malae," she called as she started to walk away. "Like I said before, nothing has changed."

Chapter 14

The congregation sat motionless, their tongues gripped with reverence for the high priest as he opened his mouth to deliver the verdict.

"Tamani, the Law of Moses is very clear on the punishment for the crime that you have committed against God, your family, and yourself," Zeruh announced. The middle-aged high priest attempted to gaze into the eyes of the young man who stood before him.

Tamani, however, rarely elevated his eyes to meet the high priest or the group of six elders that sat behind him. Instead, he concentrated upon the stone floor. Occasionally, he glanced over at the decorative ark that held the masjid's collection of sacred scrolls. The centerpiece of the collection was a copy of the Torah, purchased and brought back from Jerusalem by a wealthy Nubian Falasha at least two generations earlier.

Today, Tamani stood in the shadow of the Law and

awaited the solid wall of judgment to tumble down upon him.

"Your sins have been enumerated against you before the congregation," Zeruh said as he meticulously rolled up a scroll. "Is there anything that you wish to say before sentence is passed?"

Tamani's smooth black face flushed red with anger. He knew that they were trying to maneuver him into a stance of repentance. "What I have to say now is no different than what I've said all along," he declared in a soft yet defiant voice. "I would gladly submit to the judgment of the Law of Moses if I felt that it was relative to me."

The retort produced deflated expressions from several of the elders. However, one of elders sitting next to Dikembul found a response. "Despite your affiliation with those entrenched in the Cult of Isis, you are a Falasha. We may live among those who worship idols and practice perversion. However, we've been called by the Lord God to consecrate ourselves only unto Him."

"And thus I have done for all of my twenty-five years of life!" Tamani snapped. "I've given sacrificially. I can recite the Scriptures more accurately than most of my peers . . ."

"But what does that matter if you purpose in your mind to pollute your spirit with the ways of idolaters?" Zeruh calmly interjected. "You've chosen the path that you now walk."

"I've chosen nothing," Tamani persisted, for once looking directly at the high priest. "You cannot condemn me for being what God has created me to be."

Stunned gasps arose from the small congregation of men seated behind Tamani. "Blasphemous. He speaks blasphemy."

"I speak truth and . . . I speak from my heart. If there is anyone who is in error, it's all of you. I don't make sacrifices to Isis or Ra. Nor do I burn incense to Apedemack or any other god. I'm simply in love with a man."

The hall was silent for a long moment. Everyone was aware of his disposition but was shocked at his blatant attempt to saddle the blame for his sinful nature on God.

The high priest lowered his head and inhaled deeply. "It is clear that you have no desire to change your heart in this matter . . ."

"I cannot change what I didn't create."

"Nor can a man change that which he can tolerate," Zeruh said looking up. "For your sins of lying with a man and blaspheming the name of the Lord God, the law prescribes that you should be put to death."

Dikembul's eyes scanned the young man. He wondered if his rebellious posture was sincere or simply a veneer that hid an ocean of anxiety. In either case, surely he knew that the laws of Meroë prevented a summary execution. Outside of the royal court, only an official no lower than that of a vizier could legally order a man to be executed.

"Your judgment shall come in two phases," Zeruh said. "You shall be denied fire, water, shelter, food, and employment by every Falashan man and his family within the region of Napata. Though the laws of this land prevent us from slaying you, know one thing, young man. Although your abominable decisions have severed you from your people, your final judgment shall come from your God. There is no hope for you."

Masking his dejection, Tamani marched out of the masjid. As he did, he noticed that not one of the ten or so other men in the room even looked his way.

"Let us pause for an hour," Zeruh announced. "When we reconvene, we will hear from our brother Dikembul."

During the intermission, he was greeted by several fellow elders that lived on the northern region of Napata. The men were extremely excited to see him and were anxious to hear about his time of worship during the Feast of Pentecost in Jerusalem. Most of them had taken their own pilgrimage to Jerusalem at one point in their lives. Upon their return, each one had enthusiastically shared his experience with the other elders and finally with the general congregation.

When the meeting reconvened, several of the men who had sat in the congregation had departed, leaving half a dozen men behind Dikembul as he arose to address his fellow elders. One of the men who sat behind Dikembul was Nkosi. The two hadn't really spoken since their long conversation weeks ago. Dikembul still wasn't sure how Nkosi processed the exchange from that evening.

"My brothers," Zeruh called, lifting his hand, "today we officially welcome home one of our own."

Dikembul bowed his head respectfully as each one of them greeted him.

"Dikembul, we regret that you were here to witness the preceding event," one of the elders offered. "All the same, we are grateful to the Lord God for His mercy and faithfulness. We've heard that your daughter and you had a safe journey free of calamity and misfortune."

"The Lord was with us," Dikembul said.

Zeruh nodded his gray head. "Most of us are old men, and it's been many years since any of us have journeyed to the Temple. Please tell us about the Feast. We long to hear news from the Holy Land."

Dikembul inhaled. Somehow he managed to grin in

response to the first part of the high priest's statement. In reality, only Zeruh and one other elder had been blessed to live into their seventies. The rest of the revered body of men were no older than Dikembul himself.

For the next two hours, Dikembul described their stay in the city of Jerusalem. He meticulously painted a picture of the grand Temple constructed by King Herod. A few of the men closed their eyes and envisioned every detail that Dikembul's testimony brought to life. Zeruh was moved to tears and one other man wept openly as Dikembul purposely delivered his report as if it were a passage from the Psalms of David.

When it became apparent to Dikembul that the elders were saturated with emotion, he deliberately ended his narrative and started to sit down. Part of him was relieved he made it through without mentioning the event that disrupted his morning prayer period on Pentecost. He sighed inaudibly and promised himself that he would first visit the high priest and discuss his views about the man named Jesus.

"Thank you, Dikembul," Zeruh managed to say with a broken voice. "Your words have invited a refreshing spirit into our humble masjid."

As Dikembul turned, his heart suddenly started to race. He felt as if an invisible hand had gripped his left arm, beckoning him to remain before the broken body of leaders.

"High Priest Zeruh, I perceive that Brother Dikembul has more on his heart to share with us," Nkosi suggested from the background. He avoided Dikembul's stunned look by focusing on the stone floor. "I believe that our brother has only just begun his testimony of praise."

Like thirsty men in the desert, Zeruh and the elders looked at Dikembul expectedly.

Fear held Dikembul's tongue motionless. He opened his mouth to say the words, but his tongue clamored about, producing inaudible mutters.

"Dikembul has found the Messiah," Nkosi announced boldly as he rose to Dikembul's side.

※　　　　※　　　　※

"You may enter now, Lord Sahlin," the queen's personal nurse said, opening the large gold-plated door wide enough to reveal the elongated hallway that led to the queen's chambers. "She is very weak, but she is looking forward to seeing you."

Sahlin advanced past the servant who was only a few years younger than the aged kandace.

Light poured into the hall through the vast windows. The lazy rays slanting in from behind him caused his long shadow to meander before him. The sight of the dark figure gave him a chill. For a moment, he thought that the shadow belonged to the death angel assigned to escort the queen into eternity.

He had never been to Amanitore's personal chambers. From what he was told, she was now confined to the room, unable to arise from what was certain to be her deathbed. He found himself searching for the appropriate words but could find none that could penetrate the tumult of emotions within his soul. Queen Amanitore was the only person in the kingdom outside of his parents and grandparents that he had ever opened up to. He could not bear to think of losing the last soul that he trusted, respected, and loved.

His shadow blanketed the door. Attempting to maintain his composure, he swallowed his fear. Noticing that the door was already ajar, he gently pushed it open, permitting the shadow to inch its way in. He methodically followed the specter as it fell in the general direction of the queen's enormous bed. Sahlin gritted his teeth as his eyes fell upon the once mighty and majestic kandace.

"Sahlin," a weak voice reached out from the mass of embroidered blankets that covered the bed.

"My queen," Sahlin responded, not caring that his voice cracked slightly. He walked with a sense of urgency to the side of the bed facing a window. There she was, nestled in the blankets, only her tired face exposed to the light.

Sahlin pulled up a nearby stool and started to sit.

"The curtain," Amanitore said. "Please open it all the way. Part of it fell shut." Immediately, Sahlin rose and pulled back the curtains. The light that flooded the room revealed just how large and wide-open the queen's chambers were.

"Thank you," Amanitore said. She painstakingly positioned her body so that she could get a better view of the wilderness outside. She was amazed at how much she had not noticed before. She had always seen the lovely birds fly past, but she had never noticed the brilliant colors meticulously woven into their wings or the pleasant melodies they emitted as they streaked through the sky.

An interlude of silence passed between the two of them as they smiled at one another.

"Did you see it outside of the city?" Amanitore asked. Sahlin responded with an inquisitive look. "My pyramid. They tell me that it is finished. That it awaits me."

Sahlin drew in his lips and searched for something to say.

"They say that the walls are adorned with pictures of the victories I celebrated during my youth. They say that the shelves are lined with replicas of the monuments I built during my reign." She closed her eyes and sighed. Sahlin did not know what to make of the grin that dominated her face.

"Don't they know that the images will fade and the replicas will crumble to dust? They act as if time will have mercy upon me and spare my royal body from decay. However, a thousand years from now, I will be forgotten, forever buried underneath the mounds of history. A thousand years after that, a stranger will unearth my remains and ask, 'Who is this?'"

Sahlin resisted the urge to reach for her hand. "Time will never erase your name, my queen."

"Time . . . time used to be my enemy. When I had it in abundance, it always plotted against me. But now that it's running scarce, it has become my greatest ally. Someday, it will take the pain away."

Sahlin studied the wrinkles that creased her dark face. Many of them had not been there before he departed for Judea. He was certain at least two of them were the signatures left by her deceased sons. "Is there anything that I can do for you?" he asked.

"Water," Amanitore said, glancing over to the nightstand. Sahlin picked up the cup and brought it to her lips. She took a tiny sip and leaned back. The effort drained her of a substantial amount of energy. "I'd ask you how your family was, Sahlin, if you had one."

"Nothing's changed," Sahlin admitted, his sheepish

grin masking his guilt and regret. She had always admonished him to settle down.

"Is time your enemy or your ally, Sahlin?"

"There are days I feel that time has passed me by. That I no longer matter in its equations."

Amanitore turned her head and stared at the tiled ceiling. "Every man matters, but not every man knows it." For a moment, her eyes drifted out of focus. Her mind, though, was as sharp as a spear. "Every man must choose, Sahlin. You must choose whether or not you will make time a friend or a foe."

"What's the difference?" Sahlin asked meekly. He had never been ashamed to draw from her perpetual well of wisdom.

"If time is your friend, then you will learn to savor every moment that you spend with it. You will endeavor to embrace each day with a grateful heart and appreciate the people whom you share it with." She paused to absorb the constant abdominal pain that refused to leave her. "If you make it your enemy, you will loathe the moment that your eyes draw you out of slumber. Your disdain for your very existence will cast a shadow over every relationship, and your own soul will repulse those who love you."

Sahlin could tell she was describing the very lessons that it took her an entire lifetime to learn. She did nothing to conceal the wounds inflicted upon her tattered spirit.

"I believe I understand, my queen."

"No, Sahlin," she said, struggling to draw breath. "You must choose . . . You must forsake the past and choose."

Shaken, Sahlin rubbed his jaw and held back tears. He felt as if there were a hidden message laced with her words that was aimed directly at his heart.

"Has Harmais promoted you to grand vizier?" Amanitore asked, now turned completely away from Sahlin.

"Yes. He announced it several days ago."

Sahlin grew concerned when she did not respond to his statement. His fears were abated when he noticed her yanking at the covers.

"You've always been a voice of reason for him, Sahlin. Even when he embraced nothing but a chorus of folly, you always held up a standard. Do not be silent because he is the king. You will make him a better qeren as well as a better man."

"Your words are far too kind, my queen."

"Please, call me Amanitore," she insisted softly, her back still turned to him.

"I cannot do that."

"Then . . . call me . . . Mother, for you have been like a son to me."

Tears collected in Sahlin's dark brown eyes yet refused to spill over. "Your words reach deep into my heart," he finally managed to say.

"I've always looked upon you with such favor. Some even complained that I showed you far too much favor. It didn't matter, though. A wise man once said that favor doesn't have to be fair." She stopped to cough several times, each episode jolting her body with a sharp pain.

"Many years ago, I promised your grandfather that I would look after his family. When I appointed you as the chief of the treasury, I was merely fulfilling a promise to old Rahman. Then, I saw in you the dedication and loyalty that made him such a great man."

Sahlin rubbed his eyes in shame. "I haven't always been so loyal," he said, recalling the dark evenings that Harmais, several others, and he met to discuss how they could affect change in the kingdom. Utilizing his position, they covertly cached away storehouses of gold and other commodities that could someday be used to manipulate and cajole Sherakarer's rivals and opponents. "My loyalty has kissed its limit at times. To my shame, that limit was not as extensive as it should have been."

A soft chuckle arose from the elderly queen. "Are you saying that you have disagreed with my decisions at times? I assure you, Sahlin, that I have disagreed with many of my own decisions. My regrets outnumber the stars."

Sahlin's feelings shifted from remorse to pity. His heart ached for the woman that lay before him. He silently wondered if his final days would be racked with so great an amount of vexation.

Suddenly, a cramp of pain seized Amanitore's body, causing her to cringe sharply.

"Shall I call the physician?" Sahlin asked nervously, starting to rise.

"No," she pressed. "It's already going away." She caught her breath and tried to compose herself. Her eyes scoured the room for something to distract her from the burning pain. "Sahlin, please stay . . . stay and tell me . . . tell me . . . about your journey. Did you ever find what you were seeking? Did you ever find peace?"

Without warning, segments of Scriptures bombarded Sahlin's mind. Thus far, he had told no one about his experience in Judea. This was the first time that he felt compelled to do so. Not sure what would come out, he opened his mouth and drew a breath.

"I once thought that peace was the absence of conflict. But, while I was in Judea, I found that it was much more than that. I found a person . . . I found the Prince of Peace."

Amanitore's steady gaze met his soft words.

"I met a man who told me about the Christ—the Anointed One who would someday come and . . ."

"Deliver your people," Amanitore said, her breath coming in short waves. "The Hebrew Messiah."

"You know of Him?"

"Your grandfather spoke of this Messiah on a few occasions. He insisted that the Scriptures that he clung to foretold the future. That an extraordinary man would arise and bring deliverance. Though he possessed such a strong conviction about it, I dismissed it all as a pious fantasy."

"I thought that as well." Sahlin recalled how he had overlooked the truth behind the Scriptures that he studied for a lifetime. "But it is true. The Messiah came just as the prophets said that He would. Though He had the form of a man, He was actually the Son of God."

"You spoke with this Christ, face-to-face?"

"No, my queen, heart to heart."

Amanitore coughed violently and then drew herself together once more. She sensed that each cough pushed her closer towards the doorway to the next world. "What was this man's message? Surely He had a purpose for appearing."

"He preached that all men should repent of their sins."

"Sins?"

"Yes, He said that God wants to forgive us. All we need to do is receive the mercy that He has provided for us. He referred to God as a loving Father whose hand is continually stretched out toward us."

"And you believe these things?"

Sahlin paused to consider the magnitude of the question. As an accountant, he based his life upon solid numbers and facts. This was the first discernible time he actually tied his faith around a set of intangible beliefs and confessed it to others. "During my life, I've doubted more things than I have believed in. The unfaithfulness of men and uncertainty of circumstances only fueled my skepticism. But when I opened my heart to believe in this man, He entered and changed my life.

"It is as if His words have the power to shatter and reshape . . . to pluck up and to plant . . . to cut off and to heal. I've never met Him face-to-face, but I know that someday I will."

Amanitore's eyes drifted past Sahlin and focused on the soft blue sky that dominated the horizon. "Where is this man?"

"After He was murdered by the Romans, He arose from the grave and walked among the people of Israel, just as the Scriptures said that He would."

"He was killed?"

"Nailed to a cross as a sacrifice for our sins. After His resurrection, He assured us for all time that God's mercy will triumph over the justice that we rightly deserve."

Silence filled the room. Amanitore's eyes shifted from Sahlin to the grand sky and back several times. She wanted to be free from the pain in her body and the guilt in her soul. "Look at me, Sahlin."

As their eyes met, the large pool of tears that had formed in Sahlin's eyes spilt over and streamed down his face. She peered deep into his hazel eyes for a long moment, searching for the anguish that once riddled his soul. Instead of the yoke of hurt and fear he once wrestled with, she found the fingerprints of peace impressed all over his heart. At once, she realized that his innermost being had been handled by an entity of great compassion and love.

She also saw an additional conflict brewing within him, one that demanded payment for the new peace of mind he enjoyed. "You have a very important decision to make, my son."

Sahlin tilted his head in silent confusion.

"Someday, you will have to choose, just as you have been chosen. I pray that your convictions will not fail you."

"I don't understand anything that has happened to me," Sahlin confessed.

"You will understand it, by and by." Amanitore could feel her body going numb. She knew that more covers could not prevent her spirit from leaving her body. "Keep . . . keep . . . keep your faith. Much . . . peace will it bring."

She closed her eyes and exhaled softly. Sahlin's eyes went wide in disbelief. He slowly reached out and took her hand. It was cold and limp, but he still felt a faint pulse.

Amanitore opened her eyes and displayed a semi-disappointed look that perplexed Sahlin. "I need rest now," she said. "Thank you for the gift of your presence. May the destiny that has found you run its course un-impeded."

He rose and gazed down at her affectionately. He leaned down to kiss her hand, but at the last moment changed his angle to gently press his lips against her cold cheek.

As he walked out of the room he turned back once more and was instantly grateful that he did. The sunlight showered her bed, producing an aurora befitting her stature as the queen. He closed the door and disappeared down the long hall.

In her bed, Amanitore squinted at the sun. For the first time in her life, she knew for certain that the great ball of fire in the sky was not controlled by Isis, Horus, or Ra. She pushed aside everything that she had spent a lifetime learning about the Egyptian and Nubian gods. Not one of them offered her peace. Not one of them promised her salvation. Not one of them had proven that they could overcome death.

Knowing her remaining breaths were in short supply, she drew the one that she somehow knew would undo the knots of regret and sorrow encumbering her heart. A tranquil blanket of peace and assuredness slowly enveloped her as she closed her eyes and tried to envision the faceless being that beckoned unto her weary spirit.

"I . . . believe . . ."

Chapter 15

A hot gust of dry air blasted across Akinidad's back as he arose from his prayer. He loved high places. From atop the great dufufa that stood ominously in the midst of the city, he could see for miles.

Another gust of hot air assaulted him. This time, he turned into it. Sweat began to bathe his face and saturate his dark tunic. Soon it rolled down his hardened face like the goat blood that ran down the sides of the sacrificial stones in front of him.

Though he had made the sacrifice two days earlier, the altar was still caked with dried blood. He made the offering to Ra as a gesture of gratitude for bringing him back to his home city. He was thankful for the influx of destiny that his expedition to Qustul had garnered. There wasn't a day that he did not think about the words spoken by the governing officials of the major northern provinces. He felt as if he had been hand selected by the gods to fulfill the great destiny that belonged exclusively to the black tribes of Nubia.

Like a vivid but elusive dream, Akinidad could see the greatness the kingdom of Nubia once wielded. Hundreds of years ago, they once ruled from the southern tip of the Isle of Meroë to the mouth of the Nile River that drained into the Great Sea. For nearly a century, even the once mighty Egypt belonged to Nubia. On more than a few occasions, Akinidad had beseeched the gods to allow him a mere glimpse of the vicious battles that allowed the great Nubian kings to swallow up Thebes, Memphis, and Luxor.

Akinidad was sure that the mighty Nubian army would again storm north into Egypt and reclaim its place in the eyes of the gods. He envisioned a battle that would drive out the Romans, a heartless race of people to whom the cowardly royal court of Meroë kowtowed. Akinidad begged not only Ra but also Apedemack and even Osiris to grant him the honor to lead and even die in the first attack. He was certain it would be a death that would surely grant him immortality.

The thought of engaging the white invaders from the north dropped him again to his knees to resume his prayerful watch. Even if it took the sacrifice of a thousand oxen, he was determined to see his dream cross over to reality. Before he could move, though, Djabal joined him on the apex of the great dufufa.

"General Akinidad, I respond to your summons, my lord," Djabal reported, adding a crisp bow.

"Djabal, I apologize for calling you on your day of relief. However, the matter is most urgent."

Seeming not in the least inconvenienced, Djabal stood at attention, his eyes trained on his general.

Akinidad inspected Djabal's disposition and was

pleased. "There has been an unforeseen development which may alter our plans in regard to Vizier Carachen," Akinidad wiped his own face with a towel. Though he had been in prayer, his body felt more like it had just completed a rigorous workout session in the parched desert. "Paqar Harmais has summoned the vizier, the peshte, and myself to the capital city."

Djabal's eyes narrowed slightly.

"I'm not clear why he has chosen to do so, but I have come to view it as a possible opportunity." Akinidad examined his understudy for a moment. Djabal was a seasoned veteran who had accompanied him on many expeditions. The stocky young warrior had covered Akinidad's flank during many battles. He had proven to be a sagacious warrior as well as a dedicated subordinate.

The only thing that Akinidad questioned was Djabal's depth of humanity. Like many of the officers under his authority, Djabal was a man of great honor, and Akinidad knew that he would follow orders that sent him lurching into the depths of hell. However, he was not certain that Djabal could rationalize the paradox of honor and dishonor that would surely be produced by the conspiracy developing around them.

"Djabal, I've yet to ask what your opinion is of the deed that must be done."

Djabal remained at attention as he quickly formulated a response. "I apologize, my lord. Soldiers do not have the luxury of questioning their orders . . ."

"Yes, I understand that. However, no orders have been issued. The deed that we have committed ourselves to was born from the union of desperation and necessity. There will be those who will question the honor associated with our actions. Are you prepared for what lies ahead?"

Djabal hesitated for a moment before his lips parted to issue his thoughts. However, Akinidad cut him off.

"I see that you have your doubts about our mission. Djabal, we have served the kandace for many years. But, what I do now, I do for Meroë." Akinidad paused in mid-thought. For the first time that day, the sun's blazing rays irritated him. "I'm motivated by a vision entrusted to me by the gods, not by the scornful disdain possessed by a handful of disenchanted administrators. The army will follow me because they believe in me."

Djabal held his silence and trained his disciplined mind on the task before them. He had already drawn his own conclusions regarding their plot to eliminate Carachen and was convinced it was the prudent thing to do. However, Akinidad's subtle assertion that their path would only widen and stretch deeper into the pit of transgression concerned him. It was almost as if he were drawing a parallel between their "mission" and a stampede of buffaloes that careened out of control.

Akinidad stepped up to Djabal's face. "You will not accompany me to Meroë. In my absence, you will retain control of the army. In you, they will see me."

Resisting the urge to protest, Djabal held his tongue.

"I'm giving you a direct order," Akinidad announced ominously as his piercing gaze anchored into Djabal's soul. "I'll be gone for several weeks. Don't allow the army to be split apart. It must remain intact for what is to come."

"I understand, my lord."

"If another royal messenger arrives with dispatch orders, kill him, and don't heed the orders. After we meet with the paqar, we are scheduled to proceed to Napata for the coronation. Carachen will not survive long after that."

Holding his general's unholy gaze, Djabal nodded. For the first time, he sensed the magnitude of the task with which the gods had commissioned them. His heart raced at the thought of the glory they were destined to attain. Yet, his excitement was overshadowed by the very cloud of dread that he had observed over Akinidad's head. He was certain their glory would come with an expensive price tag.

※　　※　　※

"You're working far too hard!" Dikembul insisted as Annika scurried past him with two large bowls full of fruit. Before he could command her to sit down and rest, she set the food down on a table off to the side in their living room. The colored assortment of fresh fruit brought a refreshing accent to the spread of dates, nuts, and slices of lamb.

Without saying a word, Annika hustled back into the kitchen, only to return a moment later with two large pitchers of fresh juice that she had spent a good portion of the morning coaxing from a hoard of mangoes. She set the pitchers on both sides of the table and stepped back. Finally, a thin smile showed her approval. The red-and-black tablecloth that her mother had fashioned years ago made the food appear even more inviting.

"I told you that you didn't have to make a habit out of this. It is simply too much work for one person," Dikembul said, not knowing how to deal with the guilt that the lovely assortment of food produced in him.

It was the fourth time in three weeks his daughter had prepared the minifeast to welcome the men who accompanied Nkosi to Dikembul's home. Early on, Dikembul had made it clear to Annika that they were there strictly for study purposes and that she was not required to prepare an entire spread. Nevertheless, the pride that her mother instilled in her always seemed to override his admonishments to her. Even when the number of men gathering to study the Scriptures topped a half dozen, Annika took it upon herself to serve them.

Dikembul wasn't sure how many to expect tonight. Nkosi seemed to bring at least two new people every time they gathered. The gatherings initially started as a period that Nkosi and he used to comb through the Scriptures in search of additional knowledge about the Messiah. Eventually, several elders from the masjid started to attend. Though not thrilled at first, Dikembul's excitement grew every time they appeared at his door. Though they had been soft-spoken and even stoic in the masjid, they appeared to be completely energized whenever they conferred with Dikembul and Nkosi about the Christ. Surprisingly, they always had something to contribute to the discussions. It was as if each one of them had a small piece of a larger puzzle that only came into focus when they shared their insight with one another.

Her job complete for the moment, Annika kissed her father on the cheek and then disappeared into another part of the house. Dikembul was certain that she would reappear if anyone even hinted that he needed something.

After retrieving the sacred scrolls from a secured storage compartment in his room, Dikembul carefully laid them out on a large table. One of the elders had brought over his personal collection of scrolls and insisted that Dikembul retain them for future study sessions.

Dikembul reclined on a couch and offered a prayer of

thanksgiving to the Lord for the favorable response his testimony had received from the elders of the masjid. He closed his eyes and recalled how his apprehensions and uncertainty had been chased away back in the masjid three weeks earlier.

⁂ ⁂ ⁂

Dikembul had spoken so much that his throat felt irritated and raw. A silent hush darkened the masjid as the men pondered Dikembul's story in context of what they knew of the Scriptures.

Dikembul glanced back at Nkosi and wondered how long it would take before they both were expelled from the august gathering. Part of him was irate at his friend for initiating the dialogue. However, it wasn't the first time that Nkosi had done something like that to him. Many times throughout their childhood and well into their adult life, Nkosi had successfully managed to maneuver him into situations that were less than ideal.

Finally, Zeruh's hard voice crashed through the silence.

"The search for the Messiah predates the recorded history of our masjid here in Napata. The expectation for such a person predates even recorded time in all of Africa." He paused, forcing Dikembul to raise his eyes. "Many have claimed to be the Anointed One from the Lord God. Yet, none of them ever met the requirements prescribed by the sacred Scriptures. I would like to believe that this man named Jesus is the Anointed One. However, my age and experience urge me to resist the thought."

Dikembul's heart sank in the mire of uncertainty and

disappointment. The other elders would surely follow the lead of the high priest. "Yes, but what of the prophecies that have been fulfilled through this man's life? His death and . . . resurrection. They were all foretold."

"Dikembul, how quickly you forget the attributes of the land in which we dwell," Zeruh interjected. "Stories of resurrected gods and heroes dominate the beliefs throughout Nubia and Egypt. Have you forgotten the tale spun of Osiris?"

"Yes, I'm aware of the legends and myths, but . . ."

"Dikembul, it would be different if you were an eyewitness," Zeruh declared in an even voice. "If you had met this man, witnessed His miraculous resurrection. Yet, you were not even able to speak with those who followed Him. I've prayed that before I close my eyes forever, I would see the day of the Anointed One, that I would hear of the reports of Israel's liberation. But that does not seem likely now."

Dikembul's heart sank. He wanted to flee from the gathering. He willed his feet to remain still and ignored the mounting pressure from an unseen force that railed against the precious faith residing in his heart.

"Dikembul," the high priest resumed, appearing as if he were ready to end the session, "you are a faithful man and well respected throughout the community. However, you are asking us to believe in this Jesus without proof. You are . . ."

"Zeruh," one of the elders called, "Zeruh, what Dikembul is asking us to do is to have faith. Sadly enough, I believe that is something many of us have forgotten how to use."

Dikembul recognized the man as Hosea, the only elder as old as Zeruh, who rivaled him in wisdom and insight.

"Hosea, there is a difference between faith and wishful thinking," Zeruh countered.

"Yes, but what is faith but the ground of things aspired for? The confirmation of the hopes in a man's heart." Many of the men in the room perceived that Hosea was simply picking up the baton in a contest that Zeruh and he had begun years earlier. "We cannot dismiss the things that we have heard, especially since . . ."

"Then you're saying that you believe it all without proof? That you're willing to go on blind faith?"

"No, Zeruh. However, we cannot dismiss the things that we have heard, especially since we have not heard all of the facts that are available to us."

"My point exactly," Zeruh stressed, placing both of his palms down against the table in front of him. "Now I think that . . ."

"Dikembul," Hosea called, knowing that he was the only man in the room with enough stature to get away with cutting off the high priest. "Dikembul, how old was this man?"

"I don't know, sir," Dikembul's mind fumbled about trying to recall that detail. "I wasn't told His approximate age. But judging from His disciples, He may have been between thirty and forty."

Hosea leaned back and nodded his head slowly. "It would have been about thirty or thirty-five years ago."

"What are you referring to?" Zeruh asked.

Closing his eyes, Hosea fell silent for a long moment. As if lost in a distant memory faded into a dream, he drew a deep breath. "Your proof, my old friend. You were there when they departed."

"As usual, I do not follow you, Hosea."

"Surely you remember our first trip to Jerusalem? On our return voyage, we came through Egypt."

Zeruh nodded halfheartedly, dredging up the long-buried memory.

"As we were passing through, we spent a few days in a small town near the ancient city of Heliopolis."

"I remember now. That was the city that Joseph ruled Egypt from centuries ago. But there was something else that day . . . something else that happened when we arrived . . . a funeral."

"Close, old man." Hosea smiled. He looked towards Dikembul. "We were young men with our families at the time. We were concerned because of a great commotion taking place in part of the town. Once we secured lodging for the evening, Zeruh, several others, and I went out to find the cause of the disturbance. Do you remember what we found at the scene?" he asked the old high priest.

"The little boy," Zeruh uttered. "He was waving farewell." A hush fell over the room as the two aged spiritual fathers recounted an event long passed. "They acted as if they were losing a prince or king. They all loved that child."

"Indeed," Hosea said. "The child was accompanied by his mother and father. When we asked who they were, no one would say. They only told us that they were heading back home to Bethlehem—where the child was born two years earlier. We were told that they had fled to Egypt to escape Herod's merciless decree to slaughter male children under a certain age."

"Yes, it was horrible." Zeruh cringed at the dreadful tales that he recalled hearing during their trip to Jerusalem that year.

"Another prophecy," Dikembul breathed. However, Hosea heard him loud and clear.

"Yes, my young friend. Though no one would confirm it that day, it was intimated that the child in some way fulfilled several messianic prophecies. And we witnessed Him fulfilling yet another one."

"When Israel was a youth I loved him, and out of Egypt I called My son," Nkosi recited. Dikembul turned to see his close friend once again standing by his side.

"Is that Scripture? Where is it from?" asked one of the men in the audience.

Nkosi looked back at the man and then turned towards the elders. "From the prophet . . . from the prophet Hosea. Written over 750 years ago."

"I see that you are an excellent student of the Scriptures." Brandishing the warm smile of an old man, Hosea complimented Nkosi. "My father always liked Hosea. He too hoped to see the day of the Anointed One. He was a man of faith."

❄   ❄   ❄

A man of faith . . .

Dikembul opened his eyes to find himself back in his living room. He somehow felt that the very attribute of the word *faith* was destined to shape and mold the remaining path of his life.

Because of the dialogue between Zeruh and Hosea, the elders agreed to commission a body of men to thoroughly review the Scriptures. They were to search for references to the Messiah—how He was to be presented, how He was to live, how He was to die. Most important, though, they were to glean from the Scriptures what ramifications His life would have upon the masses of humanity, especially those who chose to believe in Him.

Though Dikembul was not surprised when Hosea appointed him to lead the commission, he was a bit taken back by the response he received from his fellow countrymen. Initially, it was just Nkosi and he trudging through the Scriptures seeking clues. However, more and more men from the masjid expressed interest and generously offered their time and research skills to help unravel the mystery hidden for generations.

Sadly, in the three weeks since their decree, Zeruh had passed away, and Hosea lay on what appeared to be his deathbed.

In a sense, the dialogue between the two men about the nature of faith continued through the remaining elders. However, it was clear to all that faith possessed two irrefutable characteristics—it thrived on truth and it grew at a staggering rate.

Chapter 16

These maps contain the current deployment patterns of the southern army," old Tibo announced, brandishing a half dozen charts from a black-and-red sack. He carefully rested the documents on top of Sahlin's immaculate desk. "Now you have all the information you need in order to fulfill the duties of your new position."

Sahlin sucked in his bottom lip as he filtered through the contents of one, two, and then finally three of the charts.

"The charts are updated on a weekly basis," Tibo added, careful to note the subtle hints of Sahlin's befuddlement.

"There is something here that I don't completely understand, Vizier Tibo," Sahlin muttered as he studied the last scroll. "The information in these documents contradicts the military reports outlined to the council of ministers two days ago. We were informed by the peshte of Meroë that the southern army was encamped outside of Bara. According to these, the regiments are west of Shagudud."

"The reports issued to the council were correct, as are the documents that you have before you."

"Are you telling me that there are two southern armies?"

Unlike many of his aged associates, Tibo refused to wear a beard. Wrinkles and other fingerprints of time marred his clean-shaven face. The old man often displayed his feelings across the tablet of his face, usually scowling at subordinates instead of talking to them.

In all of his years of service, Sahlin had never seen the man smile, until today.

"I have told you a great deal over the past few weeks, young Sahlin. Now I must give you the final chapter of the lesson." The old man moved across the spacious office, pausing momentarily to study an exquisite wooden carving of a cow. "Egyptian."

"The vizier of Nobatia gave it to me several years ago," Sahlin confirmed.

"What do you know about it?"

Sahlin fought to suppress the sneer of aggravation that struggled just beneath his calm countenance. Tibo was a master at maneuvering around an issue while concealing an opinion. "It represents Hathor, the Egyptian goddess of love, dance, and alcohol."

Tibo nodded and moved away from the carving, his hands clasped behind his back. The old man walked with a slight limp that made him appear to shuffle along the carpeted floor. He stopped to examine another piece of Egyptian art on a shelf. "You are intelligent, and you learn quickly, Sahlin. You will need all of your insights to execute the requirements of your position."

"Vizier Tibo, I still don't understand the . . ." Sahlin's voice trailed off as he observed the old man transfixed by the piece of art, which was nothing more than a decorated vase.

"Beware of gifts, Sahlin. They often carry a double message and reveal the true intentions of the men who bear them." Tibo approached Sahlin and cornered him with a gaze that blazed with the conviction forged only through the foundry of age. "Hathor may be the goddess of love, but in Thebes she was also the goddess of the dead."

Sahlin's right eye twitched ever so slightly as a chill ran along his spine. Though Tibo had been his mentor for several weeks, this was the first time the old man actually incited a twinge of fear inside of him.

Tibo slowly reclined in a chair. "I have tutored you in every detail of the grand vizier's post except for one. The council was apprehensive about acquainting you with the facts that I am about to share. I wasn't sure if they were going to approve it at first, but I have informed them that you are a man who can be trusted."

Gripped with intrigue and frustration, Sahlin sat down and awaited the old man's narration as if it were a slow river barge emerging from fog.

"It is the grand vizier's responsibility to assure that the king's council of ministers is manned by those who are loyal to the crown."

Sahlin nodded a tad. He recalled the discourse in which Tibo described how the grand vizier assembles and maintains the most crucial body of governing men in the kingdom. Made up of administrators from throughout Meroë, the council of ministers was integral to the organization of the central government. Nearly all viziers entertained aspirations of serving on the king's council. Every man who sought power and influence understood that the Great Round House of Meroë was the central hub from which the kingdom was administered. To be one of the elite sixteen men who sat in deliberation and contrived the lesser laws that the king delegated to them was the pinnacle of a man's career.

In addition to the council, the grand vizier also had great sway over the military. Sahlin was still unclear about the degree of influence and how much he was expected to be involved with the generals. He had made it clear to Harmais weeks ago that he was absolutely void of military training and was apprehensive about accepting any responsibility over the army.

"You will find your task to be even more difficult than the one given to me," Tibo was saying. "There are members of the council who didn't like Amanitore or Sherakarer. These men also loathe the fact that Harmais is to become king."

Sahlin shook his head. "It doesn't matter what they think. And why did you allow these individuals to remain on the council? They, above all, should be in complete agreement with the royal edicts . . ."

"You were an excellent financial administrator, Sahlin. But you have much to learn about functioning in a purely political environment."

"The king's word is law. There should be no need for political maneuvering in Meroë." As the words left his mouth, Sahlin realized how naive he had been. For once, he saw just how many assumptions he operated under.

"The king may rule, but it is up to the men beneath him to execute those orders. A kingdom is built upon the loyalty of the subjects. If that loyalty ever wavers, then the king may as well travel upon quicksand."

"So, you're insinuating that it is the council that drives the grand vizier and ultimately the king?"

"To a degree, but the council can only do so if it has the power." Tibo glanced down at the charts on the desk. "There is a sad truth that you must know, Sahlin. Amanitore and her son were disliked not only by the council, but by large sections of the armies. Their policies were extremely unpopular."

"I was aware of that . . ."

"Yes, but you weren't aware of Amanitore's plans to cede a portion of Nobatia to the Roman Empire," Tibo disclosed, noting the bewildered look on Sahlin's face. "She was fixated on opening up a greater trading market with the Romans. A noble idea but extremely foolish given the sensitive disposition of the northern tribes. Many of them felt disenfranchised after the war with Rome decades ago. I urged Amanitore and Sherakarer to abandon such pretense. But they did not. With every step that they took, they lost the support of the council until . . ."

"Until what?" Sahlin breathed.

"Until the rebellion in the north. There were those in the council who had enough and saw the rebellion as an opportunity provided by Apedemack himself." Tibo glared at the charts once again. "There is a division of the southern army that is strictly loyal to the council. They will obey the word of the grand vizier before they obey the command of the king."

"What?"

"The Bebel Geilian division is an elite part of the southern army that consists of no fewer than twenty-three hundred officers and soldiers. I had to coax them into traveling with Sherakarer to Nobatia."

"I've never heard of a military base in Geili," Sahlin said, flicking his thumb on and off the edge of the desk. "There have been no requisitions or financial statements that would even come close to substantiating that kind of operation. How could they be supported . . ."

"Without the knowledge of the queen's chief financial minister?" Tibo chaffed, turning his gray head like a wise old owl. "You did know, my young administrator. You were among the greatest supporters of the cause. Every time you issued discretionary funds to the grand vizier. Every account that has been set up to support the small southern provinces bordering Ethiopia's mountainous region. Haven't you ever been to Soba or Shaikina or Dukima?"

A blank stare draped Sahlin's face. It took him a moment, but he finally recalled the tiny provinces that lay on the southernmost tip of the Isle of Meroë.

"Evidently, you have not. And rightly so, for they do not exist," Tibo reported.

"The viziers and peshtes . . ."

"Are actually members of an advisory council that serve the Geilian regiment. As you know, the regions don't pay taxes due to the tribute exemption policy instituted for certain provinces less populous than others."

Speechless, Sahlin pondered the ironic twist that came hand in hand with the revelation. For years, he had siphoned off vast portions of wealth at the behest of Paqar Harmais. The fact that he had been used by the council of ministers to perform a similar deed almost did not surprise him.

"The kandace was unaware of this?" Sahlin asked, briefly wishing that he were back in Judea.

"Amanitore had no knowledge at all. Only when she finally crosses the river into the abode of the dead will she find out the truth."

Sahlin steeled himself for whatever was about to come his way.

"Have you read the accounts of Sherakarer's victory in the Nobatian desert?" Tibo inquired.

"No, I have not. I've only heard of what happened there."

"Then there is much more that you haven't heard." Tibo paused to make sure that he had Sahlin's full attention. "As I mentioned before, I had to order the Geilian regiment to go to Nobatia with the king. Sherakarer didn't want them at first, but I managed to talk him into taking them."

"I don't understand. If they didn't want to go and if he did not want them to come, then . . ."

Tibo cut Sahlin off by raising a hand. "I made the arrangement because I knew that Sherakarer was not secure and needed the protection."

"He had his contingent of guards," Sahlin interjected, referring to the four hundred troops that escorted the king into battle.

"As I said before, there were many who didn't like Sherakarer. I didn't believe that any of them would actually plot against him."

Sahlin's chest rose with air. "Are you saying that he was murdered during that battle?"

"Most likely by members of his own guard."

"That's impossible!"

"Read the accounts provided by the guards. They

reported that he was at the head of the army during the initial charge."

"That much I've heard," Sahlin said. "But that simply means he was struck down by the rebels early in the battle."

"At first sight, yes. But, the commander of the Geilian forces informed me that Sherakarer stormed the battlefield with approximately three hundred members of his own guard after the second wave was sent in."

"How does this commander know this if he was fighting in the battle?"

"Because he was not in the battle. None of the two thousand Geilian men that drew up in formation that day were allowed on the actual battlefield. According to the commander, the captain of Sherakarer's guard managed to convince him that the Geilian regiment should be held in back." Tibo scoffed at the thought. "The most elite force of the southern army held in reserve. Foolishness."

"Suppose that this is the case. Why murder Sherakarer? Were they trying to send a message to Amanitore?"

"No, I believe that they were sending it to Harmais," Tibo declared, his hard dark eyes burrowing through Sahlin.

"But Natakam . . ." Sahlin started to say in a perplexed tone.

"There is strong reason to believe that Natakam didn't die from a wound but rather from a slow-acting poison that prevented his injury from healing. I believe that he was murdered and that the perpetrators want Harmais on the throne."

"Why?" Sahlin asked slowly.

"He is younger, more arrogant, and far more foolish than his brothers. He is just the kind of king that can easily be manipulated into launching an attack against the Romans in Egypt."

"What? There is no need to fight Rome again. We have everything that we need. We do not pay them tribute, and we stand with them as equals."

"And I agree with you." Tibo nodded. "But many in the military feel the opposite. Many want to reclaim Egypt and take back that which was once ours. They feel that power, passion, and glory are the sentiments upon which our society has been built."

Sahlin stood and walked over to the window. "That was hundreds of years ago. Such thinking is irrelevant and counterproductive."

"No one ever said that the first priority of a soldier was to be productive. However, when you consider what the Romans have done and what they have stolen . . ."

Not wishing to debate the alleged merits or vices of the Roman Empire, Sahlin raised his hands to cease the current line of discussion. His eyes burned with fury, accusations, and disbelief as he fought the images of betrayal that commandeered his imagination. The only words to surface through the hideous vortex in his mind formed a simple question.

"What does this all mean, Tibo?"

"The very fact that I am telling you these things denotes that you have met with the council's approval. There are a few who are concerned about your Jewish heritage, but that is of little consequence."

"The council's approval? That's the second time you've said something like that. What does their approval have to do with anything?"

"Harmais is the last of the royal line. If anything were to happen to him, it would fall to the council of ministers and the grand vizier to select an individual to present to the priests for coronation."

Again, Sahlin's imagination ran past his ability to speak. Instinctively, he slowly turned away, as if he were trying to hide from a predator in the jungle.

"You hail from a great family, Sahlin." Tibo continued to position himself to leave the office. "The council is looking to you to display the same type of leadership that your forefathers had in times of crisis."

"You speak as if you already have an inclination of things that are to come," Sahlin muttered, not at all sure what to think of the information provided by the proud old man.

"The equation is simple. If Harmais proceeds down the path of his brother and mother, then you may very well end up selecting the next qeren of Meroë."

"Surely there is something that we can do? Warn him, post guards . . ."

"Such efforts would be useless. He has inherited a legacy of unparalleled animosity among the most powerful bodies in the kingdom—and he knows it."

To his disdain, Sahlin nodded in agreement. He recalled Harmais's words that night at the banquet and wondered just how much the man knew about the undercurrent against him.

"Where do you stand, Tibo?"

"Where the gods demand me to stand. With Meroë. I am an old man. However, I seek only the greater good of the kingdom." He opened the door and turned to leave. "Where does your God have you stand?"

With that, Tibo made a swift exit, leaving his words to echo throughout the room. The door turned quietly upon its hinges until it shut with a soft thud.

The room suddenly felt excessively crowded with thoughts and speculations. Sahlin went over to the window if for nothing more than to escape the oppression that weighed him down and choked off his air supply. "Lord Jesus, where should I stand?" he whispered. Torn between his loyalty towards Amanitore, her last surviving son, and the rest of the power brokers in the kingdom, he found it difficult to resist the specter of dread encroaching upon his faith.

A brief rap at the door snapped Sahlin out of the prison of his mind. He issued an acute order to enter the room, not at all surprised to find Kalibae file dutifully into the office. The young man flashed a smile as he went about his business, shuffling through financial documents stored in cedar chests along the contour of Sahlin's office.

Glancing outside, Sahlin became aware that the once clear blue sky had now become dark with ominous gray clouds. Without warning, a thunderous storm rolled in from the east, drenching the landscape with a furious rainfall. In many ways, the day paralleled his own life. Things started out fairly clear. However, within an hour, even the very meaning of life had become ambiguous and uncertain.

"I'm glad that old fool is gone," Kalibae mused aloud as he collected his final set of files. "Whenever he shows up, nothing but bad things follow him."

"What?" Sahlin whispered, barely paying attention to Kalibae's words.

"Take this storm, for example. It was a perfectly clear day not three hours ago. As soon as old Tibo got here, the gods started to moan, and the heavens started to cry."

"You don't know what you're talking about," Sahlin retorted as he tried to rub the gloom out of his eyes.

Kalibae paused for a moment and treated himself to a scant laugh. "I certainly do. Didn't you hear about his wife? Oh, that's right! You were gone when it happened. It was a scandalous disaster. You see, there was this woman in his . . ."

"That's enough, Kalibae!" Sahlin roared. "You're babbling as a child! Until the coronation, Tibo is still the grand vizier, and you will treat him with the honor and respect that is due his position."

"Yes, my lord," Kalibae managed in a subdued tone as if he had been slapped.

"I want it clear that such disrespectful outbursts will not be tolerated in my presence." Sahlin could feel the heat emanating from the young man's brow, but he didn't care. "Furthermore, I expect and demand the utmost decorum from the individual who is slated to succeed me as the chief treasurer."

For the first time, Kalibae's eyes dropped down in shame. In that instance, Sahlin felt a spear of guilt jab into his own heart.

"I am sorry, my lord," Kalibae remarked, still taken back by Sahlin's reaction. "In the past, you've always found such stories amusing. I simply thought . . ."

"Things change, Kalibae," Sahlin voiced, his stern tone returning. "Whether we like it or not, we must change as well."

The attention of both men was drawn to the door as a young man sharply clad in a black-and-white tunic appeared in the doorway. Kalibae recognized him as one of the palace's messengers.

"I'm sorry to interrupt you, Lord Malae," the young

man said, slightly out of breath. "Your presence has been requested at the palace, with all haste."

Sahlin picked up a small ledger he had been working on earlier that day and started towards the door. Though his anger with Kalibae had all but subsided, he still shot the young man an annoyed look as he marched past.

As Sahlin's cloak fluttered past the door, Kalibae's dark eyes rolled upwards and a muscle twitched in his jaw. By the time Sahlin had left the building, Kalibae had uttered several curses in contempt against his mentor.

🐚   🐚   🐚

It was quite possibly the only time that Naytal could recall seeing a glimpse of their father in Harmais. He stood tall and erect, his broad shoulders flung back like the protracted wings of a proud eagle. As she approached him, she silently admired his manly features from a distance, knowing that she would only encounter the countenance of a fool when they met face-to-face.

She stopped for a moment and lamented over the fact that even the weight of the crown would fail to mold him into something other than the embodiment of a small boy at play. Love and affection were rare elements in their family, and she had very little of either for any of her brothers. At the very least, she respected Sherakarer and Natakam simply because they were men who demanded as much. However, Harmais possessed neither the bravery of a warrior nor the cunning of a thief. She found it all too easy to treat him as one would a common beggar.

"How long do you plan on standing there?" Harmais said without turning to greet her. "She was your mother as well."

Naytal forced herself to step up next to him. As she did, Amanitore's lifeless body came into full view. The kandace rested peacefully on top of the fancy blankets that covered her bed. Most of her body was draped by a silky purple sheet that glistened in the sunlight. Though her hands were covered by the sheet, Naytal could tell that her mother's arms were crossed at her chest in the traditional style of a monarch who has passed on into the next world.

As she studied Amanitore's face, Naytal noted that the signs of constant struggle against the invisible talons of death were gone. She also sensed that her mother's face had a cryptic aura of peace. The phenomena puzzled Naytal and even vexed her somewhat. She had been so used to seeing her mother rage against one thing or another. To see the kandace at peace was a sight that she was not prepared for.

"She finally rests with her sons," Naytal said softly.

"May their reunion in the afterlife be filled with the affection that evaded their lives here on earth," Harmais expressed solemnly.

Surprised by the depth of his statement, Naytal refrained from making any sort of comment. She appreciated the moment of piety and respect that Amanitore deserved for simply bringing the two of them into the world.

"Now it begins," Harmais stated, adjusting the gold bracelet on his left wrist. "My mission in life becomes clearer every day. It has fallen upon me to restore greatness to this kingdom."

Her sentiments shifting like a tempest, Naytal glared at him through the corner of her eye. Yet, she knew that she had to show restraint. "For your legacy to eclipse hers, Ra will have to smile upon you from now until the sunset of your life."

"That he will do, and much more, I'm certain. His favor has rained down upon me like a flood. I shall repay him with sacrifices and temples unrivaled in the history of Meroë and Kush."

Naytal rolled her eyes and said nothing. The gesture did not go unnoticed.

"My lovely wife-to-be tells me that you are considering not making the journey to Napata for the coronation and wedding ceremony."

Naytal's nostrils flared as she drew in a breath. She hated having to explain herself to her brother. "I mentioned to Tshenpur and Melaenis a few days ago that I may have to return to Wad ben Naga to tend to my son. I received a message that he has a slight fever."

"Really, sister, a slight fever shouldn't hamper Terenkiwal that much," Harmais pronounced. "If he is ever to become a man worth anything, you must allow him to persevere through difficult times without the aid of his mother."

"And didn't our mother baby you?" Naytal retorted, holding back as much rancor as she could. "I have vivid memories of you clinging to her skirts at the sight of a hyena on a leash."

"Of course you do." A slight smile coated his lips. "I was only offering some manly advice."

Naytal successfully managed to hold back a retort and decided to withdraw from the scene altogether.

"One thing before you leave," Harmais said. "Well, actually two things. Initially, I didn't care if you missed the coronation. However, Tshenpur felt that for you to do so at such a time as this would not be proper."

"Proper?"

"Yes. And after giving it some thought, I'm inclined to agree with her. Therefore, I am ordering you to attend the ceremony and coronation."

"But . . ."

"Whether I like it or not, you are my last surviving sibling. That being the case, we must be mindful of the image that we project to the tribes and provinces."

"But my son . . ."

"Is not my problem. Your king has given you a command, and you will obey it." The room filled with an antagonizing silence as he paused.

A lump formed in Naytal's throat. Her tongue refused to form the words that Harmais awaited. Finally, her tired will relented. "Yes, my lord." She turned to depart, but his words accosted her once again.

"One last thing, Naytal," Harmais called as he turned to leave the chambers as well. "You will make arrangements to vacate the palace at Wad ben Naga. Tshenpur is the kandace now, and she has other plans for the structure."

"Wad ben Naga has been my home since . . ."

"The past no longer matters, my sister. The world has changed. You may feel free to live anywhere in the Isle of Meroë. However, I must insist that you do not leave the confines and protection of the rivers."

Naytal couldn't breathe. Anger and despair flooded her heart all at once. "Was this something that the lady Tshenpur suggested?"

"Not at all, it was my idea," he said leaning down into her face. "I wanted to make certain that you witness the transformation I intend to take this kingdom through. I want you to see it from the beginning until your bitter end. Every contrary prophecy that you've uttered against me will haunt and consume you until you are a crippled old woman clinging to your sanity."

Wanting to spit in his face, Naytal drew in a breath. However, like that jackal that she knew him to be, her brother withdrew before she could deliver an epithet of her contempt for his wife and him.

Incensed, Naytal flung her head around and focused on her mother's still form. At the moment, she envied Amanitore's blissful ignorance of the pitiful tragedy playing out around her. Tears welled up in Naytal's eyes, yet she refused to allow them to spill. She had no intention of letting the world know that she had been wounded.

Slowly, Naytal moved towards the doorway. Her path was abruptly impeded by Sahlin Malae, who nearly ran into her as he rushed in. The two slowly pivoted like two predators feeling one another out.

Though Sahlin could feel her hate, surprisingly enough, he wanted only to express his sympathy for her loss. "Naytal, I . . ."

"I want nothing from you, Sahlin. I especially have no need for your pity."

As she stormed past him, Sahlin called, "Naytal . . ." She stopped and swiftly turned around to face him. "I know that this is a difficult time, but I've been wanting to speak with you. There are some things on my mind . . ."

"No, Sahlin. The day that you conspired with Harmais to convince my father that I was not worthy to hold the position of vizier over Alondia was the day that I swore a vow never to let you block my path again." Sahlin dropped his eyes briefly as she berated him for the eight-year-old offense. "To his discredit, my father believed your lies. Your deceit even influenced my mother, and she never entrusted me with an administrative post. Instead, I've had to watch my fool brothers advance beyond me because of your treachery."

"Naytal, let me explain . . ."

"Explain what? You poisoned my family against me. Someday, you will pay for it."

"Naytal, King Natakamani asked me to assess you as a leader, and I gave him my opinion."

"You filled his ears with guile about me," she retorted, coming close to slapping him.

"No. He asked me if I thought you would be a fair and impartial administrator." Sahlin felt a chill as he gazed down into her dark eyes. They were beautiful but bottomless with hate. "I expressed my concern that you would show favoritism towards those to whom you were in debt."

"Again, lies! You knew nothing about my financial accounts . . ."

"Perhaps not yours, but at the time I was also employed by several of the individuals who were expecting large settlements from you. I simply thought that the king should know if one of his potential administrators had a sword of debt hanging over her head."

"You had no right . . ."

"I knew those men that you were indebted to, Naytal. They would have blackmailed you and riddled your administration with scandals. None of which would have reflected well on King Natakamani." Sahlin's heart started to race with anger towards the qar as he recalled the corrupt road she had started down several years ago. "From what I recall hearing, a few of them did call in a few favors at your expense."

Naytal's eyes seared with fury and embarrassment.

Sahlin stepped close enough to her to see the pools of tears form in her eyes. "I thought that you would have been a corrupt administrator then, and I still believe so now."

Naytal's face was so dark with malice that it almost frightened Sahlin. "I don't care if you are the grand vizier or the servant who polishes the sandals on the feet of Osiris. You will pay for your disrespectful slander. I swear it."

Sahlin said nothing as he watched her storm away down the hall. He composed himself and turned towards the queen's bedchambers.

The silence in the room was a painful reminder that he had come to bid farewell to a cherished friend. Gathering his thoughts, he walked over to Amanitore's bedside and kneeled. Surprisingly, not one despairing feeling was present in the room. In fact, the chamber felt completely void of the residue that the dreadful sting of death always seemed to produce.

Sahlin looked longingly into her lifeless face. Instead of wrinkles and creases of pain etched into her skin, a blanket of peace shrouded her entire face. At that moment, his heart quickened. His soul somehow knew that this was not a good-bye but rather a temporary resignation that would last only a few years and a lifetime at best. He nodded his head as tears of joy coursed down his face.

Chapter 17

The scores of gold-and-red streamers lining the streets of Napata gently waved westward as a stiff breeze rushed through the crowded city. Every thoroughfare that led to the massive temple complex settled at the base of Gebel Barkal was decorated with standards and flags bearing the image of the Kushite pantheon.

Dikembul tried to imagine how many man hours had gone into adorning the city for the upcoming coronation. As a young boy, he often dreamed of scaling the walls of Napata's brick buildings to mount flags to honor the king and queen as they made their way to the temples at the great mountain. Most people in the kingdom went an entire lifetime without glimpsing a single member of the royal family. Living near the spiritual nerve center of the Kushite kingdom guaranteed the city's citizens at least three opportunities to see the reigning monarchs.

It was the third hour of the day. Nkosi and he had just

departed from the masjid. The two men decided to make a rare visit to the administrative square to observe the preparations for the majestic ceremonies that were less than a week away. Most of the streets of Napata were dirt roads; however, the city's administrative plaza section as well as the temple complex possessed paved avenues. The brightly painted promenades accented the great sacred and magisterial structures that lined them.

"If someone would have gone through this much trouble for me, maybe I would have gotten married," Nkosi said, watching a pair of workers hoist up yet another banner across the busy street.

"There's always your funeral," Dikembul said. Almost immediately, he regretted the comment.

Two days earlier, the news of Kandace Amanitore's death reverberated through Napata and the surrounding regions. In a matter of days, a royal funeral procession would press through the streets. Dikembul wondered if the outpouring of grief for the kandace would rival the grief expressed over her husband's death a decade earlier.

The report of Amanitore's death was met with a mixed reaction that manifested in heated debates over her legacy. The exchange was particularly great in the masjid as members either praised or vilified Amanitore based on her policies towards Meroë's considerable population of Falasha. Dikembul, though, kept his feelings sequestered, hoping only that the administration of Meroë would fall into capable hands.

The rays of the sun became more pronounced as the breeze died down. The two men sought refuge under one of the few remaining trees in the plaza area. They rested on a bench and watched the people crowd by. Many of them were priests, lawyers, and scribes. Dikembul figured that the province viziers and peshtes would probably be arriving within the next three days.

"I love coming here," Nkosi confessed, a slight grin cutting across his face.

"I don't see why," Dikembul retorted. "This place represents the center of idolatry for the entire kingdom. Not to mention the corrupt officials that paddle in and out of here like crocodiles through the Nile."

"After all these years, you still don't understand. If any change is to take place in Meroë, it's going to start right here. Barkal casts a shadow over the entire empire."

Nkosi's brown eyes swept over the crowded landscape scanning for men dressed in stately black and gold tunics. He knew from many business associates that the officials who wore the blue and gold cloaks were scribes for the local government.

On rare occasions, Nkosi's trade brought him to the grand bazaar adjacent to the temple complex. Whenever he knew that he would be in the vicinity, he dressed in his finest kilt and entered the great meeting hall to sit and listen to the scribes argue various issues affecting the region. Ever since he was a young man, he dreamt of standing and debating with the mighty orators. In his grandest dreams, he saw himself giving a grand discourse before the royal council of ministers. Yet, it was an exploit that his reduced status would forever keep in check. Outside of the training available to him through the masjid, no one in his family had ever received an official education. Despite the ever-present pains of reality, he leaned back and smiled, relishing the unspoken dream that he cherished deep within in his heart.

"Someday, this will all be gone," Dikembul remarked. "The temples, the people . . . all of it."

"Perhaps. Five hundred to six hundred years maybe."

"I believe that it may be sooner than you think," Dikembul said, images of the half-buried ancient Egyptian cities that he passed through on the way home from Judea moving through his mind. "No kingdom lasts forever. Just think about the Scriptures that we went over a few days ago."

"The ones describing the different kingdoms that would arise over time," Nkosi answered.

"Yes, only I still believe that they have already come and gone . . . except for the last one."

"I heard a bit of the minor debate that you had with Udezae about that matter." Nkosi regretted he hadn't the presence of mind to insert himself in the controversy that raged on that evening. As of late, the research sessions of the sacred Scriptures tended to evolve into arguments that pitted elder against elder. "I know that the Scriptures are literally a collection of prophecies, but . . ."

"But what? Think about it. The imagery recorded by Daniel was quite clear. Babylon. Persia. Greece." Dikembul drew heavily from the knowledge of the world that he gained from his travels outside of the Nile Valley as he went on. "I am convinced that the last kingdom he was referring to has to be none other than Rome."

Nkosi grinned and shook his head vehemently. "If that's the case, then you truly have more insight than Udezae. . . who happens to be our historian now that Hosea has died. According to some of the others, you almost made a fool out of him." Nkosi chuckled softly. Dikembul had as much education as he did, and here he was debating Udezae, a learned sage trained in the city of Elephantine.

"I didn't mean to do that." Dikembul sighed heavily.

"It's just that some of our own people are so shortsighted. Many of the truths we have pored over in this short period seem so self-evident that one would have to be blind to miss them. I really believe that there is much more to the Messiah than what we've read."

"Dikembul, that may well be the case. In fact, I agree with you. However, you're going to have to be patient with many of the others. People have been waiting for the Messiah for generations, during which time their anxiety grew as well as their expectations. Not everyone is expecting the same manner of man."

Dikembul started to respond, but then caught his words just as they were about to leave his mouth. He had never been an impulsive man jumping to conclusions before examining all of the facts. In regard to the Anointed One, an invisible hand compelled his heart toward a specific direction, and his mind had been made up. He found it nearly impossible to disregard the strong impressions that illuminated his soul every time he sat down to muse on the collection of Scriptures.

"I'm convinced, Nkosi. I'm convinced that there is something greater coming. Greater than a vizier or qeren. Greater than an army. I believe that the Messiah will cast a shadow over these temples and pyramids and that someday soon all of this will be abandoned for the truth that He brings with Him."

"The words that you speak will cause many divisions among even our own people," Nkosi warned, thinking about the fault lines that had already formed within the masjid. At least half of the elders were prepared to accept Jesus as the Christ based on the Scriptures alone. The other portion that included Udezae balked at the notion that a lowly commoner from an impoverished region of

Judea could possibly be the One who would restore the Jewish state and exalt Jehovah above all other gods.

Dikembul straightened up and tiredly rubbed the back of his neck. "I understand, my old friend. I just feel that choices will have to be made. Either Jesus is the Messiah, or He's not. People are going to have to choose one way or the other."

"I feel the same way, but that's such a narrow . . ."

Nkosi's words were cut off by a commotion stirring through the plaza.

"No! Please, no!" cried a middle-aged woman.

The crowd parted enough for Dikembul and Nkosi to see a contingent of four temple guards prodding on what appeared to be a teenage boy. The youth's hands were bound, and he stumbled forward wearily, struggling to keep pace with the guards. Every few steps, he turned his head to catch a quick glance of the woman who trailed the party of guards.

"Please, my lord," the woman pleaded, tears of desperation streaming down her ashen cheeks. "Don't take my son! He's all that I have left! Have mercy, have mercy!"

As the woman's cries rose up beyond the clamor of the rabble, a sharp pain arrested Dikembul's heart, and he stood to his feet. Nkosi was jolted by the sensation as well and rose to his full height. The sudden burst of sorrow in his eyes turned into bitter anguish as he caught a clear view of the person the woman was petitioning. "Khenstout," Nkosi whispered.

Dikembul studied the man as thoroughly as he could. He was tall and bald and was neatly clad in yellow-and-red robes that denoted him as a priest in the Temple of Apedemack. Like the deity he served, Khenstout's hawkish demeanor was void of any trace of sympathy or humanity.

The woman continued to trail the group of men while passersby offered her little more than quick, pitiless glances before moving on. With one last burst of energy, the woman ran in front of the small procession and fell to her knees.

"Please, Lord Khenstout, I beg of you. If you take my boy away, how will I live? He's all that I have left."

As if annoyed by an insect, Khenstout's eyes rolled down towards the groveling woman. For the first time, he noticed how tattered her kilt was. "He is no longer your son. He is now part of the down payment for the debt that your deceased husband owes to this temple."

"But how will I live?"

"That is not my concern. If I felt that you were worth anything, I would sell you into slavery to pay off the debt as well."

With that, Khenstout ordered a guard to shove the forlorn woman out of the way. As they disappeared into the temple, the woman's sobs were soon enveloped by the throng of people that shuffled past her.

Nkosi's eyes burned in a cauldron of shame and rage. He had heard about Khenstout's cruel manners but had never witnessed his behavior before. More than a few elders in the masjid complained about the blatant disregard the priest wantonly displayed for anything Jewish.

Another moment went by before Nkosi noticed that Dikembul had left his side and had proceeded into the crowd. Confused, Nkosi squinted, looking for his friend. He watched him emerge from the masses with an arm around the woman.

As the two approached, Nkosi bit his lower lip and searched for something to say. A heavy feeling dominated his heart and prompted him to turn away in shame. His feet, though, defied his wish and instead drove him toward Dikembul and the woman.

Chapter 18

I hate them," Naytal grumbled to Melaenis as they walked through a deserted stretch of the royal palace. "I hate them with all of my heart."

Melaenis nodded her head slightly. She was careful to be mindful of any bystanders who might possibly overhear Naytal's disgruntled tone. Although the halls were empty, voices carried far and, at times, even through stone walls.

"Harmais can't even rule a herd of swine, let alone the kingdom," she continued, not even attempting to lower her voice. "And Tshenpur, may the gods curse her."

"I still cannot believe that she was that callous with you," Melaenis said in a subdued voice.

"Not only with me, but with my son! She actually sent a slave to tell us which parts of the palace we no longer had access to." Naytal shook her head furiously. "It's bad enough that we have been banned from Wad ben Naga.

Now we have to endure such indifferent treatment from two fools I watched grow up. I detest them, Melaenis. Absolutely detest them. Harmais is even toying with the idea of having me marry the vizier of Alondia."

"Why?" Melaenis exclaimed.

"Most likely to secure their loyalty, and by the gods, I don't want to marry that man! Not only is he an idiot, but he is fat, and his skin is far too light."

"What are you going to do?" Melaenis asked, not really expecting a rational answer. For weeks she had served as Naytal's therapist and listened to the painful stories of mistrust and betrayal that the qar related to her.

"Pray," Naytal replied.

Melaenis raised an eyebrow. Although Naytal's answer was laced with skepticism, she still detected a strand of hope intertwined with the gloomy report. "I am certain that Isis will answer your supplications."

"You don't believe that!" Naytal laughed with a tone that surprised Melaenis.

"But you do?"

"I have to," Naytal answered, all mirth draining from her lovely dark face. "I have to believe that there is some purpose behind all of this, or I'll go insane. I have to believe that even now, Isis is finding a measure of humor in watching Harmais patch together an administration for the kingdom. I also have to believe that she is devising a day of reckoning for that treacherous Tshenpur. I have to believe . . ."

The raw hate that exuded from Naytal subtly pressed Melaenis away from the qar. Even Naytal's gold dress seemed to be dulled by her disposition.

"I'm sorry that there isn't much that I can do to help,"

Melaenis said, actually hoping to stay out of the struggle she watched ripen between Naytal and Tshenpur.

"Your faithfulness will be rewarded someday, I promise."

They turned a corner and were struck by a blast of afternoon sunlight pouring in through several large windows. As their eyes quickly recovered from the shock, they noticed that the hallway was lined with palace guards, signifying that Harmais was likely somewhere secluded in one of the chambers adjacent to the hall.

Naytal was about to utter a disdainful remark when she noticed that at least a third of the uniformed men were not palace guards at all. The men wore black kilts with leather-molded breastplates. She was unfamiliar with the insignia that the body armor bore. She flashed a look at Melaenis, who shrugged in return.

The two women stopped in front of a large door that led to a conference room. Naytal walked up to one of the soldiers. She was about to inquire which province he was from when the large door flung open. Her eyes narrowed sharply as Harmais strolled through the doorway. He was followed by two men she had never seen before.

"Sister," Harmais called, gesturing her to step closer. "What a pleasant surprise."

Naytal forced herself to bow her head. Instead of looking Harmais in the eyes, she looked past him into the large conference room from which he emerged.

"Men, this is Qar Naytal, my last living relative," Harmais announced, stepping aside. "Naytal, this is Carachen, the vizier of Kerma. And this distinguished soldier with him is General Akinidad."

"Welcome to Meroë," she greeted, glancing at them ever so briefly.

Carachen smiled down at her. "You are lovelier than the king described."

Naytal responded with a slight bow, yet kept her eyes focused on the ground.

"My lady," Akinidad said as he walked past her.

In a courtly gesture, Naytal glanced up at the general. Immediately, she was taken by his striking facial features. His square jaw was covered by a light beard that gave him a rough, yet lordly visage. His most prominent feature was his beaming gaze that seemed to bore through her. Naytal found herself unable and unwilling to withdraw from the enticing stare.

🐢   🐢   🐢

"Holy, Holy, Holy is the Lord of Hosts, the whole earth is full of His glory." . . .

Then I said, "Woe is me, for I am ruined! Because I am a man of unclean lips, and I live among a people of unclean lips; for my eyes have seen the King, the Lord of hosts.

A stiff breeze swept from the surface of the Nile and billowed against Sahlin as he quietly sat on the edge of an old wooden pier. The strong gust was hardly enough to drive out the old Scriptures from his mind. Repeatedly, the ancient words resonated throughout his head but more so throughout his heart.

Then I heard the voice of the Lord, saying, "Whom shall I send, and who will go for Us?" Then I said, "Here I am. Send me!"

Like he had when he was a boy, he drew his legs into his chest and buried his face in his knees. Though he wanted nothing more than to escape from the ancient voices haunting him, he admitted to himself that there was definitely something alluring about these particular Scriptures. He felt as if he were being invited to a repast held especially for him. He somehow sensed that the invitation would continue to find its way to the door of his heart until he finally accepted.

"Haven't I already accepted the one invitation that counted?" A sigh of exasperation seeped through his lips. "What more do You want of me, Lord?"

He closed his eyes, trying to entice an answer to come forth.

Whom shall I send, and who will go for Us?

"Go where?" Sahlin said to the shadows. "My life is bound to the royal family. I can only go where my king sends me."

A hazy vision began to take shape. Though they started out as specks, the shapes soon started to resemble people. Young, old, Egyptian, Nubian, and even Arabian men slowly paraded past his field of sight. Some were warriors and noblemen, but most appeared to be commoners and slaves.

Whom shall I send, and who will go for Us?

"You cannot send me. Like my fathers, my path is set."

There was silence.

A chill rushed through Sahlin's body. For the longest moment, he held his eyes shut because he felt as if something very lofty and immense stood before him. He stretched out with his feelings to probe it. It was wider than the Nile and broader than the expansive blue heavens. Sahlin felt so insignificant that he almost stopped breathing.

"I cannot go. My task is here," Sahlin finally managed to say. He opened his eyes, not sure what he was expecting to see. The water flowed by at a swift pace, and he could see barges floating by in the distance. He leaned his head back against the post that supported his body.

"I have no choice," he softly stated for no apparent reason.

Suddenly, his heart was gripped by the last words that Kandace Amanitore had uttered to him before she died. "You will have to choose."

For the first time that afternoon, the shadows of the ancient Scriptures abandoned his mind. Due to the stifling pace of the events happening in his life, he hardly had time to dwell on the vast void that Amanitore's death produced inside of him. The absence of her presence wasted no time in draining his emotions. He closed his eyes again, this time sorrowfully, and invited some other thought to canvass his mind.

Instantly, Tibo and the council of ministers crowded out every other concern from his thoughts. Sahlin shook his head disdainfully at the arrival of the new train of thought that commandeered his attention. "Amanitore, my choices outnumber the stars, yet they all lead to the same result."

His soft remark was unexpectedly met by another Scripture. This one hailed not from Isaiah but from the old proverbs that his grandfather used to recite to him. *There is a way which seems right to a man, but its end is the way of death.*

"Death," Sahlin said. "The end is death."

Sahlin cleared his mind to focus only on his breathing. Within moments, he dozed off, his face bathing in the golden rays of the sun as it prepared to set into the western horizon.

"It's been a while since I've been out here," a voice

spoke, rousing Sahlin from his stupor. His eyes slowly rolled right and were greeted by Imani's warm smile.

"I always did like this spot," she said, drinking in the luscious scenery provided by the river and surrounding region. "I am surprised that this old pier is still standing. It has to be what . . . twenty-five, thirty years old?"

Sahlin stared at her for a moment. As usual, her colorful outfit complemented her smooth dark skin and accentuated her natural beauty. Like a gracious flower, she seemed to fit perfectly into the scenery.

"Thirty-one years," Sahlin answered. "My father had it built when I was a baby. I loved coming out here." Memories of fishing and hunting excursions poured into Sahlin's heart. Despite his adult life, he was grateful that his childhood recollections were pure and innocent. He looked past Imani back towards the large parcel of land his family had controlled for more than two centuries. He could think of no more beautiful place in all of Meroë.

Imani leaned against one of the waist-high posts.

"What brings you out here?" Sahlin asked. "I thought that you returned to Alondia with your niece weeks ago."

"No, we actually never left the region." Sahlin could tell by the way she rubbed her arms that she wrestled with an unwanted thought. "More business."

"I'm surprised that Bakka let you this close," Sahlin said, watching the water sweep past. He knew that his chief bodyguard wasn't very far away. He was probably posted behind a tree just off the beaten pathway. "But then again, he always did like you."

Imani smiled briefly as she thought of the gruff old warrior who always had a surly remark at hand for anyone who crossed him. "We were preparing to leave when we received word about the kandace. I just wanted to come and say that I'm sorry for your loss."

"Thank you," Sahlin replied softly, his eyes still cast over the river. "It is a loss for all of us . . . the whole kingdom."

"Yes, but I know that she meant a great deal to you. Saying good-bye to a woman who was like a mother to you is not an easy thing to do."

Sahlin sighed heavily.

Imani's eyes slowly rolled away from him. She knew that her sympathetic stare would only drive him deeper into his emotional cove, and that was not her desire. She wanted him to divulge feelings and to share notions.

The silence of the moment made Sahlin fidget. "Will you be going to Napata for the ceremonies?"

"To be honest, I have had my fill of ceremonies and festivals. All I want to do is go home."

"I can't blame you for that," Sahlin muttered as he picked at a small sliver of wood that protruded from the pier. "Imani, there's something that I've been wanting to tell you since . . . since that night in the palace." He sucked in a deep breath and grimaced ever so slightly. "I'm . . . I'm . . ."

"You're sorry for the way that you treated me?"

Sahlin's hazel eyes darted her way. "Yes."

The lone word hung in the air. She did a brief examination of her heart and quickly determined that she did not care to exert the emotional effort to scale the great barrier Sahlin so often retreated behind.

Sahlin looked up at her and drew in his bottom lip. The silence drove him through an additional round of fidgeting. His fingertips danced along his knees like quails skirting across the sand. He briskly searched for a thought to replace the ones that Imani's presence evoked.

"Have you ever seen the Great Round House in which the council of ministers convene?" Sahlin finally managed to ask. "It's the largest of its kind in Meroë. It is . . ."

His words were curtailed by a skeptical chuckle from Imani. "I came out here to talk with you. I want to know how you feel. I don't care about the Great Round House, the council of ministers, Harmais. I want to talk about you."

"I don't," Sahlin retorted. "I don't want to talk about me, and I don't want . . ." Without warning, his words trailed off leaving only a blank stare gazing at Imani's sandaled feet.

His eyes finally glared up at her, brimming with a confused defiance.

"Sahlin, what is it?"

Sahlin's lips moved, but nothing came forth. He squinted and tried again. "It's so strange. When I was in Judea, I met someone. We spoke . . . and . . . I can still hear his voice as if he were here in front of me."

"Who was he?"

"He was . . . He was . . ." Frustrated, Sahlin gritted his teeth and sneered at himself for almost telling her about the experience that managed to set his whole world askew. He pressed his lips together and turned his head.

Instinctively, Imani emotionally withdrew from the conversation. Experience had trained her how to read his face to prevent herself from being bruised by the backlash that usually accompanied any attempt of his to open up.

"Nothing," he said to the wind. "It was nothing."

Imani wanted to reach out, but stopped short. She was tired and wanted to go home. Yet, something floated to the surface of her heart. "How long can a man live with unfinished business, Sahlin?"

"I have no unfinished business. I know who I am and what I am supposed to do."

"It sounds as if you are trying to convince yourself of that."

"I don't need your input or your sympathy, Imani."

Imani's dark eyes suddenly burned with angry tears. She somehow managed to keep them from spilling over. "You're wrong, Sahlin. While you may not need me, you do have unfinished business to tend to. The day will come when it will demand your attention, and you won't be able to shut it out like some annoying scribe who wants an appointment."

She turned and gracefully stormed from the pier, warm tears now streaming freely down her cheeks.

"Imani, thank you for your . . . compassion," Sahlin called, unable to avoid the awkwardness of the moment.

Though she stopped briefly, Imani didn't bother to look back. She increased her gait and headed down a path that led in the opposite direction of the Malae mansion.

Sahlin was sickened with himself. His disgust finally gave way to regret and self-pity. "I know what I'm doing," he whispered.

His turbulent thoughts were overshadowed by a constant, still voice that seemed to echo through the waning afternoon air.

Whom shall I send, and who will go for Us?

Chapter 19

Tens of thousands lined the streets of Napata just to catch a fleeting glimpse of the royal court. Rich, poor, nobleman, commoner, craftsman, nomad—all gathered together in a throng of humanity to pay homage to the new rulers of the great kingdom of Meroë.

Arrayed in imperial black armor with black-and-red cloaks streaming behind them, the royal guard marched down the main thoroughfare of Napata, leading a magisterial procession that seemed to be showered in gold. The ground that they traversed was shrouded with petals of exotic flowers cast down by the immense crowd that flanked both sides of the street.

On the heels of the three hundred fifty stout warriors sauntered several rows of priests dressed in fine linen ephods. The first three rows strutted silently forward, seemingly oblivious to the masses around them. However, the final tier of priests bellowed thunderous praises and blessings to Amun, thanking him for the gift of a great king to reign over them. Their proclamations incited heartfelt cries from the multitudes.

Like a moving wall, a team of three elephants emerged behind the priests. The colossal animals were adorned with black-and-gold tapestries and were tethered to a massive transport that towered high above the crowd. The structure resembled that of a pyramid on wheels. On one side, it bore a portrait of Harmais gazing into infinity, while the opposite side depicted Tshenpur suckling an infant. An illustration of the sun god Ra dominated the rear of the massive mobile monument.

In an alcove on the face of the pyramid sat Harmais and Tshenpur. Both sat stoically as the crowds hurled praises and adoration their way. On occasion, Tshenpur glanced towards her husband and came short of revealing how close she was to succumbing to the fear that welled up inside of her. To her surprise, each time she managed to draw a degree of strength from the marginal grin that skirted across his face. Nonetheless, she knew better. Harmais had not spoken a word since they had said their vows an hour or so earlier. Something told her that his tongue was gripped by the overwhelming awe of the moment and not her sheer beauty.

Scores of honored officials rode in chariots that trailed behind the great pyramid. The procession of figureheads was led by the council of ministers and the grand vizier. Sahlin had never been in front of so many people before in his life. At the very least, he was extremely grateful that most all of the attention fell squarely upon the newly wed king and queen.

The assemblage finally made its way out of Napata to the temple complex at the base of Gebel Barkal. The crowd had been sectioned off by the retinue of temple guards to allow the royal party to halt in front of the grand Temple of Amun. The hundreds who could see unleashed a great roar as Harmais and Tshenpur disembarked the transport and entered the temple to complete the final phase of their installation as qeren and kandace.

Along with the council of ministers, Sahlin watched the two disappear into the temple with a select group of priests. Though the crowd noise was deafening, it was still not enough to drown out the resounding echoes of Tibo's warnings.

Just over an hour later, the royal couple emerged from the temple and was hoisted onto a great platform. The massive crowd had not decreased. A priest addressed the congregation and presented the newly installed qeren and kandace. Harmais stepped forward, wearing the silver crown that once sat upon the head of his older brother.

The crowd erupted into a fury and chanted something that Harmais could not clearly make out. After a moment, he reached back for the hand of his wife. She took it coyly and stepped to his side, marveling at the sight of the awesome multitude congregated before them. Her head was adorned with the shimmering tiara that announced her ascension to the highest position that a woman could hold in the kingdom.

Down below, Sahlin could not help but be taken back emotionally. His throat was gripped with excitement for his childhood friend. He shook his head and smiled as he watched Harmais thrust his scepter towards the sun in a gesture to honor Ra. In that moment, his heart skipped several beats. He dropped his eyes from the platform and bit his lower lip pensively. Convinced that the sudden flash of anxiety and dread had been brought on by a momentarily lapse of self-discipline, he quickly asked the Lord for forgiveness. Respecting the beliefs of others while always maintaining a distance between himself and their object of worship was one of the greatest quandaries for a Jew to avoid in an idolatrous society.

Somehow Sahlin sensed that this feeling was different. He almost felt as if he were being warned by the same omniscient presence that cryptically beckoned unto him. He slowly glanced around at the group of royal ministers that stood with him. Immediately, his eyes fell upon two men who were not cheering or applauding but were focused upon him. A muscle twitched in his jaw as he held their gaze while the thunderous salute to Harmais rumbled on. One of the men turned to the other and uttered something in his ear. Both nodded and then turned their attention to the new king and queen on the platform.

🜨   🜨   🜨

Though his military persona was repulsed by the environment, General Akinidad forced himself to endure the grand reception for the newly wed king and queen. The massive room was decorated with more gold than he had seen in a lifetime. He felt as if his senses were under siege as the tingling aroma of seared meat collided with varying scents of perfumes and delicacies that he had never smelled before.

Preferring the murky trenches of a battlefield, Akinidad stood alone in a far corner of the great hall. While there, he consumed what had to have been his third chalice of *tej*.

Grateful that the formalities had long since passed, he convinced himself that he had fulfilled his duties and stayed long enough. He plotted a course through the crowd and started out of the hall. On his way out, he scraped past Carachen and several other officials from Kerma who seemed to be intent on enjoying every moment that they could of the festive gala.

As Akinidad reached the exit, he turned around to survey the room of men and women that he despised so much. Unimpressed with their fine linen cloaks and glittering jewelry, he paused long enough only to conjure up a curse that he thought worthy of their status. Before he could utter a word, a soft yet domineering voice captured his attention.

"Leaving so soon, General?"

Akinidad rotated to meet the gaze of Qar Naytal. "I'm sorry, your highness, but it has been a very long day, and I have had my share of the festivities."

"No need to apologize, General. The feeling is mutual."

Though Akinidad nodded politely, Naytal's apparel for the evening did not escape his notice. She wore a long, elegant white shawl that cleverly covered up portions of her form-fitting purple dress.

"May I have the honor of escorting you to your carriage?" asked Akinidad.

"The pleasure would be mine, General."

🦂　　🦂　　🦂

No longer able to maintain his mock smile or feign interest in the occasion, Sahlin searched for a way to escape from the reception. Every time that he started to leave, a vizier, peshte, or scribe managed to corner him. The customary greetings generally degenerated into political conversations that always seemed to end up describing the plight of their individual regions. Sahlin, used to discussing financial matters as opposed to politics, found it difficult to do anything more than nod his head and ask, "Really?"

At the moment, it was the vizier from Alondia who held him at bay. Sahlin had already spent at least ten minutes listening to the man drone on about irrigation systems and feuding clans staking claims over wadis and dry riverbeds.

Sahlin could see the doorway that led to freedom. He caught a glimpse of Qar Naytal leaving the hall with someone who appeared to be a high-ranking military official. For a moment, he was actually jealous of Naytal. The fact that she was painfully sour and relatively unimportant made her a less desirable target for those who wished to ingratiate themselves with the royal court.

Just as the vizier was finishing up his list, Sahlin saw a way out. As fortune had it, Kalibae and a small retinue of associates were starting to make their way to the exit.

"Kalibae," Sahlin called, trying to distance himself from the people already in pursuit. As soon as he reached Kalibae, he grabbed him by the arm and attempted to blend in with his associates. Together, they pressed through the crowd.

"My lord Sahlin, where are we going?" Kalibae asked.

"Out of this hall," Sahlin replied. The awkward squint in Kalibae's eyes told him that the young man had consumed a fair portion of the honey wine.

"Wonderful reception," Kalibae delivered, gesturing to a beautiful young lady to his side. "I'm going to like being an official administrator."

"Believe me, it has its shortcomings," Sahlin said, discreetly waving the young lady back.

"That's what you say. You've been to a hundred of these things. I was too young to attend Sherakarer's wedding and coronation."

"Trust me, they are all the same. Everybody wants something from you."

Sahlin led Kalibae outside of the temple into the chilly night air. Kalibae's companions followed, but at a distance.

"Are you heading to the inn now?" Sahlin asked.

"No. Actually, we're just stepping outside for some air. I heard that the king has provided some after-hours entertainment. I'm hoping that it's that dancer from Meroë —you know the one."

"Yes, I know who you're speaking about," Sahlin voiced, momentarily averting his eyes from Kalibae's gleeful visage. "Kalibae . . ."

"But that's not all. I also heard that the king is going to have . . ."

"Kalibae, we have business to take care of tomorrow. I need to have you alert."

The youth's expression slowly faded to disappointment. "Business? Who's going to be working tomorrow? Everyone of any importance is here tonight celebrating the king's coronation."

The indifference in Kalibae's tone prompted Sahlin to raise an eyebrow. "You've had too much to drink, Kalibae. I told you earlier this evening that we have a meeting with the chief financial officer of the Napata temple complex."

"But I thought that you said it was going to be an informal discussion, tying up loose ends and the like."

"Yes, I said that. But that doesn't give you the freedom to show up unable to concentrate because you had too much entertainment the night before, even if it was at the king's coronation banquet."

Kalibae started to fidget as the conviction set in. Sahlin had never been that stern with him before in similar situations.

Noting Kalibae's apparent mood swing, Sahlin decided to show no quarter.

"Kalibae, if you are going to receive the council's confirmation to fill my former position, you are going to have to show a greater level of maturity."

Kalibae looked up with puzzlement in his eyes. "Confirmation? But I . . ."

"You thought that it was a given because you've worked with me for so many years?"

"Well, I thought . . ."

"No, it doesn't work that way." Sahlin placed his hand upon Kalibae's shoulder and immediately felt the tension in his body. "I have given this a great deal of thought and have decided that you will have to go through the full confirmation process as anyone else would. You will be awarded the position because you are the best qualified, not because of whom you know."

The cold, unexpected dose of reality shook Kalibae out of his semi-intoxicated bliss. For the first time that evening, he looked up at Sahlin Malae not as his mentor but as the Grand Vizier of Meroë.

"Yes, my lord. You're right." He glanced back towards his friends. "I'll head toward the inn right now. And I'll meet you in the morning in the plaza quad."

"Very good. Get some rest. I have a feeling that it might be a long day tomorrow." Sahlin disappeared into the sparse crowd gathered at the bottom of the stairs.

Akinidad and Naytal strolled leisurely through the enormous temple that housed the reception hall. The walls were adorned with colorful carvings of Amun either receiving worship or slaying his enemies. Akinidad found it difficult to study the murals and walk with Naytal at the same time.

"So, what did you think of the ceremonies today?" Naytal asked.

"They were . . . impressive. I've never seen anything like them before. I suppose that it was the opposite for you, though."

"Not really. In the past, I have generally managed to excuse myself from such affairs. I find them haughty and extraneous."

"Really," Akinidad responded, lifting an eyebrow. "Far be it from me to judge, Your Highness, but that sounds rather ironic coming from a member of the royal family. I would think that . . ."

"That we all relish the attention lavished upon us by the masses? That we all long to hear our names bellowed from the summit of Gebel Barkal?"

The light beard that covered Akinidad's face stretched as he smiled at the aggravated tone of her voice. "Actually, I was going say that I think you would want to do all that you could to support your brother during this time of transition."

Naytal's soft giggle echoed through the temple. "There is much that you have to learn, General Akinidad. I can see that you are a complete stranger to the dealings of Meroë and the royal court."

"That would be an accurate assumption. And please,

call me Akinidad." He paused for a moment until she nodded in compliance. "To be honest with you, I would feel much more at home in the training fields of Kerma than the place that we just left." For the first time in weeks, Akinidad admitted to himself that he was indeed a bit homesick.

"I love my family," Naytal lied, "but before my mother died, I spent most of my time in Wad ben Naga with my son."

"You have a son?"

"That surprises you?"

"You don't look as if you have had a child."

"Thank you," Naytal smiled, happy that her skin was dark enough to hide any traces of a blush. "He is the love of my life. Do you have a family?"

"In the traditional sense, no. My only family is my army."

"*Your* army?"

"We have lived and fought together for so long that it's difficult to think of them as anything other than family. They are like my brothers and my sons."

"It sounds as if they are truly committed to you."

"No, Your Highness. They are committed to Meroë. They merely follow my lead."

"And a great leader you must be to command their respect in such a fashion."

Akinidad clasped his hands behind his back as they approached the entrance to the temple. "Great leaders do not command respect, Your Highness. They earn it."

"And how do they do that?" Naytal asked, walking up to the carriage that waited to take her to the royal family's lodging complex.

Akinidad held out his hand to assist her as she

stepped into the carriage. "They do it by becoming whatever their followers need them to become. A leader's sacrifice can become an extremely powerful motivational tool."

"Motivational tool?" Naytal echoed. "That sounds more like a manipulative device."

"All leadership techniques employ some form of manipulation, Your Highness," Akinidad replied, his eyes gleaming in the dim torchlight.

"Are you saying that people expect to be manipulated, General?"

"Soldiers want strong leadership. I don't know about common people . . . or family members, for that matter."

Naytal grinned at the images that danced through her mind because of his statement. "Sometimes family members are the easiest people to manipulate."

"Perhaps so, but I've noticed a strange law established by the gods. What people give out, they always seem to receive in like."

"That's an extremely perceptive observation, Akinidad. I look forward to speaking with you again sometime. Oh, and you may call me Naytal."

Akinidad smiled as he bowed while Naytal signaled the driver to depart. He found himself staring at the back of the carriage as it disappeared into the dark blanket of night.

🐢　　🐢　　🐢

Seven towering torches beamed brightly along the face of the resort where Sahlin was staying. A small crowd of royal officials conversed in the quad just in front of the building under the surveillance of several soldiers from the Napatan garrison.

The inn was only a short jaunt from the Napatan royal palace—a convenience that Sahlin was extremely grateful for at the moment. He rubbed his arms through his thick cloak to counteract the nippy night air. As he approached the inn, he still found it difficult to believe that he had somehow convinced Bakka that he was in no need of a bodyguard for the evening. He suspected that his loyal bodyguard kept a watchful eye on his moves even through the blanket of darkness anyway.

Sahlin recognized a few of the administrators standing around talking but had no interest in joining in the conversation. He lowered his head and increased his gait. He was almost up the stairs when he heard his name.

"Lord Malae," the female voice called.

Against his better judgment, Sahlin slowed down and looked toward the direction of the voice. His facial expression tensed as Melaenis stepped from the shadows.

"How long have you been waiting here?" Sahlin asked, trying to avoid making direct eye contact with her.

"Not long at all," she replied, stepping close enough for her perfume to caress his smooth face. "I'm staying here as well."

"I didn't know that."

"How could you have known?" She laughed. "You're such a busy man." Her red lips glistened in the bright torchlight as she smiled. The cosmetics that she wore accented her dark complexion perfectly. "You are the Grand Vizier of Meroë now. How proud your father would have been of you!"

"Yes," Sahlin replied, peering through the lobby's entrance.

"I know for certain that I am very proud of you." The warmth of Melaenis's voice enticed Sahlin's eyes back her way. "You have accomplished all that you said you would and then some, just as I knew that you would."

Sahlin barely refrained from flinching as she gently stroked his arm. He commanded his heart to stop fluttering as her touch enticed a cascade of long-suppressed memories.

"As usual, your words are most charming, Melaenis. I trust that your daughter is doing well."

"Oh, she's fine. Headstrong and beautiful, but fine nonetheless."

"Just like her mother."

"Headstrong or fine?"

Sahlin smiled at her crafty play on words. Her sheer wit had been one of the things that had drawn him to her years before. "I can see that you haven't changed much," he said, leading them into the lobby.

"Nor have you. But I'm eager to see how your new responsibilities will alter your priorities in life."

Sahlin lowered his head as a strange sensation fell over him. He felt compelled to tell her about his experience in Judea. However, he pressed his lips together, determined not to utter a word about the subject. "There have been a few changes in my life," he finally managed to say.

Melaenis's soft chuckle was seductive as well as flippant. "I'd like to believe that, Sahlin, but somehow . . . I simply cannot see it." She took one of his hands and started to caress it. "Besides, I don't think that I ever want you to change. You are too good the way you are."

She reached up, drew his head down, and pressed her lips passionately on his. The kiss between the two of them lingered for a long moment.

Though surprised, Sahlin did not draw away. Rather, he found himself pulling her closer. As he embraced her, memories of their past encounters streamed through his soul. Feeling increasingly like a small animal caught in the mighty jaws of a leopard, he closed his eyes and summoned the will to resist.

Sensing his apprehension, Melaenis drew back slightly. "See, Sahlin, I haven't changed. No woman will ever love you like I have—not even Imani." She tried to reel him in for another kiss but was met with resistance.

"Why do you mention her?" Sahlin asked, searching for a way to escape from Melaenis's web before her beauty totally engulfed him as it had so many times before.

"Your sister told me that Imani paid a visit to your mansion a few weeks ago. She said that the two of you were alone down by the river. I thought maybe Imani might be trying to rekindle something that has been extinguished for a very long time."

"I don't approve of being spied upon. Imani was simply being kind and expressing her condolences."

"What does it matter?" Melaenis quietly declared, fondling his earlobes. "Come with me tonight, and I will express something much more desirable to you."

She started to pull him along through a corridor. A cold chill volleyed down Sahlin's back and quickly gripped his conscience. He took several steps along the stone walkway before he slowed and stopped.

"What's wrong?" she asked, seemingly anxious to get to her stateroom.

"No, Melaenis, I've changed . . . or something has changed me."

She rubbed against his arm. "What is it? Another woman? I'll make you forget Imani or whoever she is once and for all. Come with me, Sahlin. It's been far too long."

Once again, the scent of her perfume alone almost compelled him to go with her.

Then, something happened.

As he gazed at her, little by little, her face began to change. Hard wrinkles and creases commandeered her once smooth face. Her eyes, which a moment before had been soft and inviting, were suddenly fiendish and glowed with an eerie red effervescence. Sahlin's jaw dropped as he saw what looked like a streak of blood trickle down the corner of Melaenis's mouth, now full of sharp fangs.

"What's wrong?" Melaenis pressed, nearly obsessed with the desire to get him through the doorway to her room.

Sahlin drew a deep breath as he listened to her. The once sweet and enticing voice now rumbled with the scratchy reverberation of a hollow gourd.

"Sahlin . . ."

"No," he said, shaking his head. He looked at her again only to see the beastly aberration gnashing its fangs at him.

"Sahlin . . ."

"No," he grunted, backing up. He shut his eyes once more, then snapped them back open.

Suddenly, Melaenis's comely figure and beautiful face replaced the devilish ghoul.

Sahlin rubbed his eyes and continued to retreat. "I am sorry, Melaenis, but I have changed. I'm . . . I'm . . ." He spun around and trudged through the lobby.

Jilted, Melaenis traced the contour of her lower lip with her forefinger. "Next time, Grand Vizier Malae. Next time."

Chapter 20

Annika loved history. The temples and dufufas of Napata never ceased to amaze her. She lagged behind her father and his companions as they made their way through the great temple complex of central Napata enroute to the financial district.

Ever since the day that her father taught her how to read, Annika perused every stele, pyramid, and monument that she came about in order to soak up the rich legacy of the land in which she lived. During moments alone at home, she often closed her eyes and wondered what it must have been like to live in the period of the old kingdom when Kerma was the capital of the Nubian empire. Like an eagle in flight, she let her mind drift back five hundred, seven hundred, and even one thousand years into the past. Based upon many of the accounts that she had read during their sojourn in the northern provinces, Meroë once stretched all the way to the great sea known to the Egyptians as the Mediterranean.

She stopped in front of a temple, rather modest compared to the worship center built to honor Apedemack that was across the street. As she read the inscriptions carved into the cornerstone she noted that the paint at the base of the stone was fading and chipping off. In place of the flakes, she could see different shades of older paint jobs that had probably been caked on centuries ago. She squinted at the inscriptions as she attempted to find something indicating the date of the temple's construction.

"Annika!" Dikembul called over the noisy crowd. She looked up, embarrassed to see her father and the others waiting for her. She sheepishly hurried over to them, careful to avoid her father's gaze. "Stay close. There are all kinds of people here."

"Yes, sir," she replied.

The plaza was still embellished with the streamers and banners from the coronation ceremonies that had taken place the day before. Annika silently bemoaned that her father had opted not to bear with the crowds and attend the ceremonies for the qeren and kandace. Yesterday was probably as close as she would ever come to even catching a glimpse of the royal couple.

"Nkosi, I will be very surprised if these men are even open," Dikembul complained.

"Come on, Dikembul, they're businessmen. Look at this crowd. Of course they're open for business. They've probably already swindled a thousand people since yesterday."

"Are you sure that we can trust them?" Dikembul questioned, wondering what his friend was leading them into.

"I didn't say a word about trusting them. I just said that they could probably supply us with the thing that we're searching for."

Dikembul nodded sullenly and glanced back at Kenechi and Lamahl. The two men had been studying the Scriptures with Nkosi, several others, and him for over a month. He turned back to Nkosi and shook his head. "Are you sure these Nubian traders you're taking us to may be in possession of actual copies of books written by Moses? It seems pretty far-fetched that they would have such rare documents."

"And I agree with you," Nkosi assured him as they passed a couple of blind men who sat at the base of the Temple of Apedemack begging for alms. "And I didn't say that they had full copies of these books. In fact, I'm certain that they only have bits and pieces of one or two of them."

"That's not what you said earlier," Dikembul groaned.

"Well, that's what I meant." Nkosi couldn't keep himself from smiling, even though it wasn't really funny. Like his companions, he was anxious to obtain additional Scriptures that might provide them with more information on the Messiah. "From what I understand, these men came across a huge sum of artifacts and literary works from a synagogue the Romans had plundered about fifteen years ago."

"I don't know, Nkosi. Peddling Scriptures? These men can't even be Jewish. I don't think that . . ." Dikembul's words stammered to an end as he looked around for his daughter. "Where is Annika?"

"Not again," Nkosi grumbled.

The four men stopped and scanned the plaza for Dikembul's wayward daughter.

Kenechi pointed towards the Temple of Apedemack. "She's back there."

At last, Annika found an inscription that mentioned the date of dedication for the grand temple she stood in front of. Her attention was focused squarely upon a large, black stone tablet that appeared to be centuries old. She shut out the noisy commotion behind her and traced the carved message with the tip of her forefinger.

She didn't even hear the second time that the harsh, surly order was issued.

"I said out of the way, woman!"

Annika spun around to see a temple guard bearing down upon her. Her eyes went wide as the huge man brought up his arm and prepared to hurtle her to the side with a backhand. Too afraid to move, she cringed like a terrified gazelle.

"No!" yelled Dikembul, lunging to place himself between Annika and the guard. Not a moment later did Nkosi, Kenechi, and Lamahl rush behind Dikembul to shield Annika.

Surprised, the guard drew back and snarled.

"There's no reason to strike this girl," Nkosi declared.

"She is blocking our path," the guard said, amazed that he was even bothering to explain himself to the commoner.

"She was just reading this tablet," Nkosi said with a boldness that not even he recognized. "She's not bothering anybody."

The guard responded by grasping the ivory handle of his sheathed sword.

"Wait," Dikembul said, before the guard's weapon was fully revealed. "We don't want any trouble. We'll move along."

"Too late for that, peasant," rumbled a heartless voice from the background. Dikembul tilted his head as a man revealed himself from behind the guard. The man was dressed in the traditional fine black-and-red ephod worn by the priesthood of Napata.

"Khenstout," Nkosi whispered.

"My lord, we are just passing through," Dikembul said. His stomach tightened as three additional temple guards appeared from out of nowhere.

The hardened expression on Khenstout's dark face more than conveyed the message of his displeasure. His square jaw and chiseled chin gave him more the look of an angry statue than a man. "Unfortunately, you have already polluted this sacred place. The stench of your presence will linger long after you are gone."

"We have as much right as anyone else to walk through this plaza," Kenechi interjected.

Khenstout's eyes rolled Kenechi's way, then meticulously scanned the entire group. "Where I'm from, the peasants knew where their place was . . . living in mud huts in the jungle with baboons . . . and Jews. There is no place for you in a great center of worship."

"Were it not for the fact that we were tax-paying herdsmen with business in this city, we would not even step foot in this den of idols," Kenechi shot back, levying a scornful look at Khenstout. "You priests are corrupt and arrogant. Someday you will pay for the suffering you have caused."

"You dare blaspheme in the shadow of the great temple?" Khenstout barked, his thick eyebrows furrowing between his dark eyes. "For that alone I should have you arrested."

The temple guards unsheathed their weapons and started to move in.

"Wait!" Dikembul cried. "This is unlawful."

"Your sin against the great god Apedemack is the only lawless act here," Khenstout replied.

"We are Jewish. Your law does not apply to us," Nkosi announced. "No matter what you think or how you feel about those who embrace the Jewish faith, you cannot have us arrested for not conforming to your religious standards."

Khenstout walked up to Nkosi to examine him more closely. "Falashas? I'm familiar with your type. You people are all alike. Rebellious . . . refusing to pay the portion of tax to support the temples. Your codes and rites are subversive to our way of life. However, that is going to change."

"Unless you have the ear of the qeren or the Council of Ministers in Meroë, that will be a very difficult task to accomplish," Nkosi spouted. "Jews have been allowed to congregate and worship in Napata for centuries. And unless you can . . ."

Nkosi's words were abruptly stunted when Khenstout resentfully turned his back on him. The priest walked over to one of the guards and muttered something to him that produced a mischievous grin on his face.

"We'll be going now," Nkosi declared, intent on walking off.

"Not quite," Khenstout snapped. "There is still the matter of the damage that the girl caused to the tablet."

"What do you mean?" Dikembul questioned. "She didn't even touch the . . ."

All five of them turned around in time to see one of the temple guards stroll away from the tablet that Annika had been examining only a few minutes before. In his wake, they noticed that a wooden marker previously attached to the large tablet had been hacked off, leaving jagged splinters in its place.

"What the . . ." Nkosi croaked, barely able to contain his mounting rage. "You can't . . ."

"I can't do what?" Khenstout bellowed, stepping back into Nkosi's face. "You people may have the right to be here, but you do not have the right to deface temple property."

Dikembul stepped in between Khenstout and Nkosi. "My daughter did not touch the tablet. We are all witnesses to that."

"Your word doesn't matter against ours," Khenstout said, looking towards his guards.

"I saw her do it," one of them said.

"So did I," declared another.

"She's very strong for such a slight creature."

"We've had enough of this," Nkosi fired. "We are leaving."

"I don't think so," Khenstout said, motioning to the guards, who quickly flanked the five commoners. "You will not be going anywhere for a few days. Or at the very least until you have appeared before the magistrate to answer for the crime of defacing an important temple marker. I must warn you, vandalizing portions of sacred temples is a very serious offense punishable by the loss of a limb . . . or two."

Annika shrieked and then nestled into her father's chest. Hardened and uncaring, the temple guards harried them along through the plaza to the main administrative dufufa.

* * *

289

The first thing that Sahlin did as he and Kalibae stepped forth from the dufufa was draw a deep breath of fresh air. The stale atmosphere in the administrative facility left him with a slight headache. No doubt impressed by Sahlin's new title, the chief financial officer had insisted on showing them the renovations done to the dufufa's conference center. What started out as a one-hour visit was painstakingly transformed into a two-hour tour of the temple's nerve center.

Though he found a portion of it interesting, Sahlin found it difficult to remain engaged with the administrator's courteous trek through the refurbished building. The whole time, his mind drifted between thoughts of the long journey home, meeting with Tibo's men, and the sorrowful fact that he had not prayed in three days.

Despite how much his life had changed within the last few months, it was the latter of the three that surprisingly dominated Sahlin's thinking. He felt a tangible presence whenever he prayed to Jesus. It was a feeling that was both soft and stern, enticing him in and prodding him on. It was a feeling that he longed to experience yet loathed to endure.

"That went well," Kalibae was saying as they started down the stone stairs towards the streets. "It's too bad that I'll only have to come here twice a year. I really like what they are doing to the place."

Regardless of what his personal religious beliefs were, Sahlin had to admit that the efforts to beautify the Napatan worship complex were deserving of praise. The current high priest had petitioned Amanitore for years for the capital necessary to rebuild many of the temples slowly withering away. Sahlin could clearly recall the apprehension he felt the day he signed the warrant that released the money for the massive project. At the time, he was more concerned that the priest would abuse and misappropriate the money.

Kandace Amanitore had been adamant about giving the project priority over several building efforts in the capital city itself. Though newly appointed by the queen, Sahlin saw it as his duty to support the establishment of her legacy. He did all he could to expedite the proposal's trek through the kingdom's ever-increasing bureaucracy. At the time, he didn't think much about the fact that the ultimate ends of his actions propagated the worship of idols and did absolutely nothing to bring people closer to Jehovah.

Looking back on it, he saw himself for what he really was, a man-pleasing administrator blindly driven by his own ambition. The only opinions he esteemed were those belonging to peshtes, scribes, and viziers who could assist him in his quest to bring honor to his family name. Today, as he was escorted through the dufufa and the adjoining temple dedicated to Isis, his stomach turned like a weed cascading freely through the desert. The murals commemorating Egyptian gods along with the newly installed marble altars stood as glimmering testaments to the unspoken portion of his legacy.

Sahlin shuddered. How many other monuments would stand for a thousand years with the aid of his self-serving ambitions? As Kalibae and he walked along the dufufa's perimeter, he quietly tallied the number of temples in the adjacent plaza that somehow bore his fingerprints. The steady stream of people filing in and out of the buildings made him cringe with melancholy and regret. Deep in his heart, he wondered if the Messiah could truly forgive him for forsaking his heritage and endorsing a path that led so many people to the doorstep of a false god. He wondered if there was anything he could do to rectify the situation.

"My lord," Kalibae was calling. "My lord? What's the matter? You look upset."

Sahlin's eyes darted from the temple complex across the street to the young man. It was then he realized that he hadn't heard a word Kalibae had uttered. "I'm sorry, Kalibae. My mind was stuck on something that I saw inside the conference room."

"Of course," Kalibae said, turning his head to hide the faint grimace of aversion that flashed across his face. "The conference room . . . The conference room . . . No . . ."

Kalibae stopped and patted himself down in a semi-frantic search. "My notes. I forgot my notes in the conference room."

Sahlin smiled. Apparently he wasn't the only one who was being distracted as of late. "Go ahead. I'll be right over there, next to the north entrance of the dufufa." He watched as Kalibae darted through the crowd and back into the administrative building.

Sahlin meandered his way through the ever-growing mob of people in search for a quiet section in front of the dufufa. After finding a respite near the north entrance, he sat down on a stone bench. He closed his eyes to try and clear his thoughts.

"I thought that I told you not to do such things."

Sahlin opened his eyes slowly to see Bakka's hulking figure glaring down at him. At that moment, he remembered one of Bakka's primary rules.

"Never close your eyes like that in public," Bakka was saying. "You cannot be aware of your surroundings if you . . ."

"Cannot see them," Sahlin muttered. "I'm sorry. All of a sudden, I'm very tired." Sahlin rose to his feet and tried to shake off the onrush of midday fatigue.

"What did the boy forget this time?" Bakka asked, peering around for Kalibae.

"Meeting notes."

Bakka smiled to himself and nodded. "What are your plans now?"

"As soon as Kalibae returns, I'm going to let him go. I have a meeting with Tibo this afternoon."

Bakka folded his stout arms and grunted. "Are you sure that's a wise thing to do here in Napata? You know what he wants."

"Yes, but I am the grand vizier. I can't just ignore him and two members of the Council of Ministers."

"From what you said the other night, their intentions may not be pure."

Sahlin's left eye twitched as he wondered if he had revealed too much to his trusted bodyguard. He started to respond when a company of temple guards ushered a band of commoners towards the dufufa's entrance.

The administrative dufufa's finish shimmered in Khenstout's eyes like a sparkling jewel bathed in the sun's golden rays. He loved drawing near to the nerve center of Napata and thanked Osiris every time he laid eyes upon it. The great building served as a signpost that reminded him of the image once shared with him by the gods. In his divinely inspired vision, he saw himself ascending to the position of high priest over Napata. As if set aloft upon the wings of Ra, his ascension would be swift and inexorable. Though it was improbable, he felt predestined to lead the priesthood into a new era of communion with the gods.

Despite his grandiose dreams, the only thing that Khenstout was leading at the moment was a band of rebellious Jews to the dungeon. He was determined to make them pay for their insolence with at least a few weeks, if not more, of their worthless lives.

As they came upon the entrance of the dufufa, Khenstout brought the group to a halt. "Keep them here for the moment," he said to a guard. "I will get the attendant who is responsible for their processing."

The guards commanded Dikembul and the others to line up against the wall and to wait silently. Nkosi and Dikembul exchanged helpless glances and stoically obeyed their orders. The only sound emerging from the group was Annika's subdued sobs.

"Poor devils," Bakka said to Sahlin as he watched the woman and four men line up against the wall adjacent to the bench that Sahlin had been sitting on. Despite Napata's pomp and grandeur, both of them had witnessed firsthand how treacherous the temple officials could be to commoners and lower-class citizens.

"Where is that boy?" Bakka groaned, resuming his search for Kalibae. The young woman's sobs grated against him like a stonecutter's chisel. "Let's wait for him inside." He turned back towards Sahlin only to find that his employer had walked over to the forlorn captives.

Sahlin walked along the group and examined them one by one. The intricate design on his fine linen tunic and cloak suggested to them that he was a man of some stature. Each one lowered his eyes as he passed by, with the exception of Nkosi.

Sahlin stopped at the woman. "Why are you crying?" he asked softly.

Annika drew in her lips and stifled her sobs, but tears

still streamed down her dark face. Each track that careened along her cheeks produced waves of sorrow and compassion in Sahlin's heart. One of the men slid his arm around her shoulder and drew her close. The simple act appeared to have comforted the young woman greatly as she stole a quick glance at Sahlin.

Sahlin's eye drifted into the man's stern face. Without warning, Sahlin was struck by a strong sense of recognition as their eyes met.

"Do I know you?" Sahlin probed his memory for a name and place.

Dikembul squinted. He was positive that he had seen the man before. A slight smile breezed across his face as the recollection fell into place.

"In Philae, my lord. You escorted me to an honest money changer that day."

"I remember," Sahlin said, nodding his head. "Philae . . ."

"Dikembul Nukae, my lord."

"Yes," Sahlin mused. "This is your daughter?"

"Yes, my lord," Dikembul replied, rubbing her arm. Annika hesitantly looked up at Sahlin and boldly made eye contact with him.

"I am Sahlin Malae."

Bakka moved up behind Sahlin as the temple guards started to approach.

Sahlin paid no mind to the advancing guards. "Dikembul, why are you in custody?"

"A priest claims that we defaced a temple marker," Dikembul replied, watching two of the guards take up position behind Sahlin and his companion. "We did no such thing, of course."

"Yes, the accusations are false," Nkosi implied. "Those guards damaged the marker and blamed it on this girl."

Sahlin raised an eyebrow. He glanced back at the two guards who were smiling perversely as they gripped the handles of their swords.

"Where is this priest?" Sahlin asked.

"What does it matter to you?" growled one of the guards. "Both of you move along before you end up in the dungeon along with them."

"Did any one of you see her damage the marker?" Sahlin demanded.

"Again, that's no concern of yours. Now leave, before someone has to carry you away."

"I don't intend to go anywhere until you have answered my question," Sahlin pressed in a commanding voice.

"They won't answer because they are the ones guilty of damaging the marker. The cowards," Kenechi snorted. His outburst was met by a fist hurtled into his face. His head snapped back into the stone building, and he sank to his knees. Lamahl reached down to catch him, but one of the other guards violently shoved him back against the wall.

"Animals!" Nkosi bellowed angrily.

"Halt!" Sahlin commanded as the men started to reach for Nkosi. Something in Sahlin's voice arrested them as they abruptly stopped their advance. "You are temple guards, not butchers. You have no right to treat these men this way."

"It is you who are mistaken," Khenstout declared from the rear. An official dressed in a black-and-green kilt accompanied him. "It is they who do not have any rights. Nor do you have any authority to interfere with temple business."

"And you must be the priest responsible for this," Sahlin voiced, not at all impressed by Khenstout's intimidating demeanor.

"I am Khenstout, the chief priest of the Temple of Ra. And whoever you are, I want you to understand that you will be prosecuted for your lack of discretion." He motioned the guards to take Sahlin and Bakka.

Sahlin defiantly stood his ground and stroked his chin with his right hand. The official with Khenstout saw the gesture and gasped.

"I don't know what province you are from," Khenstout hissed at Sahlin. "But it will be many months before you see it again."

"My lord Khenstout, I don't believe that would be wise," the official stammered, trying to be discreet.

"What do you mean?" Khenstout questioned, highly annoyed.

"He means that you are trying to arrest the grand vizier of Meroë, you fool," Kalibae proclaimed as he walked up to Sahlin's side. "I'd love to see you explain that to the vizier of the city."

Khenstout glanced at the official from the dufufa, who nodded in compliance. He gestured towards the royal signet ring on Sahlin's right index finger. Immediately, Khenstout's heart sank, and his mouth went dry. "Forgive me, my lord," he finally managed to say, hoping that it was all just a bad dream.

"Release these people," Sahlin commanded.

Even as the temple guards started to back off, Khenstout found the voice to protest. "But, my lord, these people have insulted the gods. They are filthy Jews who have defaced this holy ground with their presence. Like all other Jews, they bring nothing but misfortune and famine and are accursed of the gods."

Sahlin fixed his gaze at Khenstout like a pointed dagger. "I am Jewish."

The hush that fell over the small crowd was deafening. Khenstout squirmed in his ephod that was already slightly damp from a nervous sweat. "Forgive me, my lord. I didn't mean to offend."

"But you did offend," Sahlin asserted, his eyes glowing with an intimidating scowl. "You have offended me, and you have offended these people. How do you propose to make it up to them?"

"My lord?"

"As with any culture, we Jews are very sensitive about our devotional life. I've chosen to forgive you for your transgression, but how do you propose to procure theirs?"

Burning with frustrated embarrassment, Khenstout lowered his eyes to the ground. "I . . . I . . . ." He looked over to Dikembul and the others, doing his best to mask his intense hatred. "I apologize for any insult . . . You are free to go."

Before the five of them took a step, Khenstout offered a nominal bow to Sahlin and quickly led his men into the dufufa.

"The grand vizier?" Dikembul stated, staring at Sahlin.

"It was a rather recent promotion." Sahlin smiled. He traced the path that Khenstout took into the building and sighed. "There are far too many men like that in this kingdom."

"But there aren't enough men like you," Annika said. "Thank you so much for your kindness." Her soft expression of gratitude prompted a small deluge of appreciation from the other three men. Dikembul took the moment to introduce his companions to Sahlin.

"It is good to know that someone in our government has a heart for the common people," Nkosi said, offering his hand. A warm feeling flushed over Sahlin as he grasped and shook it.

Bakka moved over to Kenechi and examined the bleeding bruise at the base of his head. "You'd better have a physician bandage this. I believe there is one just outside of the plaza."

"No," Sahlin interjected. "The wound looks far too serious. There is a physician inside of the dufufa. Kalibae, take them in . . ."

"What?" Kalibae croaked. "They are commoners. They cannot . . ."

"You heard me, Kalibae. This man is injured. Take them in."

"My lord, we know where the physician outside of the plaza is," Kenechi said, rising to his feet. Lamahl grasped his arm and steadied him.

Sahlin drew a deep breath to protest. "There is no reason . . ."

"My lord," Dikembul started, "we are from this area, and we know it well. The physician is actually not far from the trading post we were heading to. It's probably best this way."

Sahlin blinked several times as if he had been woken up from a dream. "You're probably right. I am sorry that we continue to meet under such circumstances."

"I guess that is two favors I now owe you." Dikembul shook his hand and then led Annika and the others into the crowded temple plaza.

"Unfortunate," Bakka was saying, analyzing the entire scene. "That priest was way out of . . ."

"What's wrong with you, Bakka?" Kalibae spewed. "Since when are we in the business of meddling with priests and assisting pitiful commoners?"

"Isn't that the responsibility of public servants, Kalibae?" Sahlin snapped at his former apprentice.

"If it is, it's a responsibility that we have never bothered to embrace before, *my lord.*"

"Things change, young man," Sahlin replied, surprised at how in control he was over his anger despite Kalibae's spiteful tone. "I regret that I wasn't more of a model of compassion and civility to you."

Not sure of how he should respond, Kalibae stood at bay, trying to comprehend the mounting contradictions Sahlin had revealed during the last several months. He wasn't at all sure of what brought on the changes and at this point didn't care.

"When did you say you were planning on returning to Meroë?" Sahlin asked Kalibae.

"In three days. There are some temples and other places that I wanted to visit."

"I see," Sahlin muttered. "I want you to leave tomorrow."

"Tomorrow? But . . ."

"I understand your desire to explore the city. However, there are several urgent matters that I need you to tend to back in the capital."

Kalibae defiantly acquiesced and bowed his head. "Yes, my lord."

Sahlin was hurt by the young man's response but refused to reveal it. "I have several more meetings that I must attend. Hopefully, I will start on my journey to the capital the day after tomorrow."

Chapter 21

The sun hung directly overhead and assaulted General Akinidad's retinue of soldiers with a singular intent. Akinidad enjoyed the kiss of the sun's stinging rays. He was used to being in places far more arid than Napata and craved a return to the climate he had been away from for the better part of a month. He hid the broad smile that dominated his face as he contemplated the impending journey back to Kerma. He inspected the faces of his men as they mounted their horses and saw the same eagerness to commence the long trek north.

Vizier Carachen's carriage was fully loaded and was already under way. A convoy of four other chariots fell in line with it as they headed out of Napata. Carachen had chosen to take the desert road to Kerma instead of the waterway via the Nile. It was a decision that actually pleased Akinidad, for it would make his maneuver that much easier.

The general examined his men once more. He was satisfied that each one was prepared to consummate the deed. Each one of them was his disciple, molded and crafted in his very image. All of them were committed to toppling the very regime that was born not two days earlier. All of them endured the grotesque and lavish galas that celebrated the inauguration of Qeren Harmais's rule over Meroë. They were prepared to die in order to alter the path of the great kingdom—if only for a generation.

Akinidad clenched his teeth and forced the notion of mercy and peace out of his soul. When the time came, and the gods assured him that it would, he would not hesitate to kill the king, the queen, the grand vizier, and the entire Council of Ministers in order to execute vengeance against the southern provinces. Their part in the travesties perpetrated against Nobatia and the other northern provinces had to be rewarded in similar fashion. He mounted his steed and prepared to give the order to move out.

"General Akinidad," a feminine but firm voice called out. Akinidad turned to see Naytal standing in the sun, her golden necklaces and bracelets shimmering like torches.

"Qar Naytal, this is a very pleasant surprise," Akinidad said with a fragile smile invading his stern facade. A slight wave of his hand sent his soldiers down the road after Carachen's carriage. "What brings you out here?"

"I heard that you were leaving, and I wanted to bid you farewell."

"I am honored."

The two gazed at one another for a long, silent moment.

With each passing second, Akinidad found his defenses waning under her lovely smile.

Finally, Naytal broke the connection and traced the path taken by the soldiers. "I've never been to Kerma. They tell me that it is a beautiful city this time of year."

"Kerma is a lovely region year round, my lady. However, should you ever choose to visit it, your presence will only enhance the climate." Akinidad tightened his grip on the horse's reigns as if he were trying to steady himself.

"Is that an invitation, General?"

Akinidad was stunned. He jabbed at his horse with his leg as he tried to extricate himself from the spell that Naytal cast upon him. He looked back at the convoy of carriages and chariots as they shrank in the distance. Almost immediately, his aim and objective returned to the forefront of his thoughts. However, he couldn't ignore the emotions welling up inside of him.

"I would be most honored to host a visit from the royal qar," he said. Part of him cringed as the words proceeded past his lips, but something deep inside of him urged him on. "In fact, if it pleases the qar, let her come in seven weeks."

"Why in seven weeks?" Naytal inquired, admiring the way the general's hands firmly grasped the reigns.

"My schedule is completely engaged with military affairs."

"I may be a female, but military issues have never confused me."

"That's not at all what I meant to imply, my lady."

Naytal shrugged it off, deciding not to pursue the matter any further. Inwardly, she scoffed at the fact that she would have to petition Tshenpur for the permission to travel to the north.

"Of course, you didn't," she said, finally starting to feel the sun's relentless rays through her loose-fitting red dress. "Isis willing, I shall someday pay you a visit and explore the beauty of Kerma for myself."

Atop the horse, Akinidad bowed his head reverently. Naytal beamed a deep smile at him as he turned his horse and trotted away.

❋ ❋ ❋

The Great Round House of Napata was dim and vacant. Sahlin quietly walked into the center of the great room and stared up at the hundred or so empty seats that encompassed him in a semicircle. The seats were organized in graduated rows and could easily give the individual who stood in Sahlin's spot an inferiority complex. Sahlin knew better. Most men who took the center dais were generally great orators who commanded the respect, admiration, and even fear of the tribal elders that generally filled the stands.

Every time Sahlin tried to imagine himself delivering a speech, he sneered and shook his head. At times, the strange destiny that elevated him to the post of grand vizier resembled the objectionable crescendo of a cruel joke. Yes, he possessed the greatest post ever held by a member of his clan, but the knowledge that accompanied the position drove a stake through his heart on a daily basis. Even at that moment, he dreaded the appearance of Tibo and the men who were coming with him.

Restless, Sahlin slowly paced the length of the dais. There was so much to dwell upon that he found it nearly impossible to quiet his spirit and focus on any one subject.

"Why am I so vexed?" he whispered, peering around the dim meeting hall. "Great Lord, why is it that I have no peace?" Indeed, peace was the one thing that evaded him the most. Ironically, the one commodity he enjoyed in abundance at one point was now nowhere to be found. His experience in the Judean desert so long ago had given him a taste of the delicious fruit. His craving for it now accentuated its dwindling presence in his life. "Lord, where have You gone?"

The opening and closing of a door echoed through the empty hall. Three long shadows struck the stage on which Sahlin was standing.

Sahlin knew who they were immediately.

"This way, Sahlin," Tibo said, without stepping on to the dais. "We can talk in here."

Sahlin followed the men into a marginal-sized conference room concealed underneath the graduating row of seats. As he entered the room, he shuffled down several steps and was amazed at how deceptively large the room was. Most of the room had been burrowed out of the ground and was ventilated by an ingenious system of air ducts that managed to keep the air fresh despite the torches.

Tibo closed the door and joined the three men at the conference table in the center of the room. "Lord Sahlin, this is Makal and Rogo. They are both members of the council."

"Ministers," Sahlin greeted them thoughtfully. Neither man wore the traditional black, red, and gold robe long sported by members of the Council of Ministers. From their weathered looks, Sahlin deduced that both men were in their midfifties. It took him a while, but he finally placed the two men as the same ones who were eye-balling him during the coronation ceremony.

Tibo seated himself next to Sahlin, who sat across the table from the two ministers. "Finally, here we are."

"Sahlin Malae," Makal started, "we've been looking forward to this meeting for quite a while. We've heard so much about you."

"What exactly have you heard?"

"That you are unlike the current generation of young administrators," Rogo said. "Sources say that you share a deep love for Meroë, just like your father and grandfather."

"Yes," Makal continued, "the house of Malae has a long, distinguished history and has served the kingdom well for generations."

"Your words are kind, if not well chosen," Sahlin responded.

Makal smiled and leaned back in his chair. "They are both. As the grand vizier, it is a language that you will learn to master."

"Indeed," Sahlin voiced, his left eye twitching acutely. "How may I help you men?" The two ministers glanced at one another.

"We hail from the southern region of the Isle of Meroë," Rogo announced.

"I've heard." Sahlin peered at Tibo from the corner of his eye.

"Though we are from the south, we represent several other elders in the council," Rogo said. "We have come to a consensus that you are a man who can be trusted."

"Though I appreciate and am honored by such a statement coming from esteemed members of the council, I'm at a loss of its need to be recognized."

Makal leaned forward and wiped away all pretense

from his face. "Let us get straight to the point then. We're here to inform you that a decision has already been made."

Without warning, Sahlin's pulse started to quicken. "Decision on what?"

"Lord Tibo has informed us of what you have been privy to at this point," Makal said, his expression sharp. "There is much more that you do not know."

Sahlin dejectedly shook his head in disbelief. "This is . . ."

"An object lesson in the politics of Meroë, my young vizier." Makal's words sliced into Sahlin's heart like a newly forged sword still smoldering from the furnace. "Tibo has told you that there is an elite regiment of soldiers from Geili at your disposal. However, we didn't allow him to tell you that the troops have already been mobilized. Even now they have taken up position in the southern hill country outside of Wad ben Naga."

"What?" Sahlin breathed, placing his hands menacingly upon the table. "You have no authority to mobilize any portion of the army . . ."

"True," replied Makal. "But you do. And, since we control you . . ."

"You don't control me . . ."

"Yes, we do," Makal answered, his voice overlapped by a maniacal shadow. "The Council of Ministers has always controlled the grand vizier, as well as the royal family."

Rogo grinned and shook his head flippantly. "That the royal family is granted the divine right to rule by the gods is a misconception. The council selects the rulership of Meroë, the legion of Gebel Geili that enforces the council's desire. Before a royal lineage is established, it must first be approved by the elders who sit upon the governing body. This has been the system for over five hundred years."

"This cannot be true," Sahlin uttered in disbelief.

"They speak the truth, Sahlin," Tibo offered, recalling the shocking day his eyes were opened by the elder who held the post of grand vizier before him.

"So, you mean to say that Harmais is aware of this?"

"He is," Makal replied. "As were his brothers, mother, father, and forefathers. He understands exactly who holds the key to his power."

"Actually, Sahlin, that is the central reason we wanted to meet with you today," Rogo declared. "Normally, it is the outgoing grand vizier who informs the incoming one of the true hierarchy in the government. Keeping matters covert in such a fashion brings legitimacy to the throne and keeps tribal skirmishes to a minimum."

"What makes you break with tradition this time around?" Sahlin questioned coldly.

"Getting back to the reason that we called you here," Makal emitted over Sahlin's voice, "while it is true that Harmais is aware of the arrangement, it is also true that he disapproves of it. This doesn't really matter, because we don't approve of him. However, he somehow believes that he has a choice in the matter."

"That is why he has personally been purchasing the loyalty of the soldiers in the Isle of Meroë and Alondia," Rogo chimed in. "It appears he believes that he can raise a force that will defeat the Geilian regiment. Such an endeavor is a foolish one. He has limited support here in the south, and his family is very unpopular in the north."

Sahlin glared at the two men.

"The council thought that Sherakarer or Natakam would be popular enough to win back the people," Rogo continued. "Unfortunately, all they did was alienate them. Now that a new wave of trouble brews in the north, we've decided to make a change. Harmais must go."

"He's the king. You just can't command him to step down," Sahlin protested. Harmais may not have been a prime royal administrator, but he was still a friend.

"That is correct," Makal said. "If at all possible, we would like to remove him without any bloodshed. The best way for that to happen would be for him to abandon the throne. We are hoping that the mere threat of an opposing army outside the gates of Meroë is enough to force him to step down. We would like for you to encourage him to do so."

"You want me to tell the king to leave his own throne?"

"No," Makal said in a tone laced with an arrogant annoyance. "We want you to speak with him as a friend. We want you to convince him to take his wife and leave Meroë. He may yet salvage a shred of dignity if it looks like he is being chased out by a powerful ruler."

"And when he is gone?"

"We will install a new king and royal lineage," Rogo declared. "Unfortunately, Amanitore did much to undermine the stability of the current line. Her disagreeable policies toward the northern provinces have all but ruined the credibility of future rulers from her clan. Sherakarer had it difficult, but Harmais will find it impossible to govern effectively."

"Yes," Makal muttered with contempt oozing from his lips. "She was as stupid as she was absentminded . . ."

"Watch your tongue," Sahlin hissed, fighting the urge to spring across the table and strangle the minister.

"Ah, yes. I had forgotten that you, like many others,

had an affinity toward her," Makal gruffed. "Completely illogical."

"What do you know of logic?" Sahlin shot. "From what I've seen, you men are the ones behaving irrationally and with no honor. Why not discuss this matter in the open where Harmais can at least defend himself? But no, you would stab him in the back."

Makal laughed for a moment, though Rogo and Tibo did not share his humorous outburst. "There is much for you to learn. This kingdom was not founded upon honor. Therefore, honor and loyalty will not sustain it. Nonetheless, your disposition is admirable."

Ready to retreat from their presence, Sahlin demanded, "What do you want from me?"

"Tell him," Makal commanded, his words directed at no one in particular.

Tibo answered the call. "There are two things that we need you to do, Sahlin. First, we need you to urge Harmais to step down and leave Meroë. If he doesn't do that, we need you to oppose him openly on a matter of national security."

"What?"

"Prior to their deaths, Amanitore and Sherakarer were in the process of negotiating with representatives from Roman Egypt. Allegedly they were planning on ceding a portion of Nobatia over to the Romans in order to secure trade routes." Tibo paused for a moment and watched Sahlin digest the revelation. "That served as a catalyst for the Nobatian rebellion."

"In short, Sahlin," Makal started, "if Harmais refuses to leave his post, then you must challenge him in open court and charge him with conspiracy to break up the kingdom. Such an accusation will erode whatever sympathetic support he has and force him out."

"If it doesn't get him killed first," Rogo added.

Sahlin surveyed the room in utter disgust. A cold, sick feeling flushed over him as he made eye contact with Makal. "Since you already have *control* over me, I suppose that you want me to assume the throne afterward?"

Makal instantly noticed his sarcasm and matched it in kind. "Your name is on a short list. However, the throne will most likely fall to Tibo."

Rage, fear, and confusion collided inside of Sahlin all at once. He felt like vomiting as he watched Makal gloat with a twisted smile that rivaled the one worn by the god Apis. "If I refuse to cooperate?"

"The fact that your house is highly esteemed will make our response to such a foolish choice very difficult," Makal answered. "It will force the council to denounce you and condemn you along with Harmais."

"On what charges?"

"What does it matter? You were appointed by Amanitore and have been best friends with Harmais for years. To simply imply that you were a part of Amanitore's scheme to ransom off a portion of Meroë to Rome will raise more than enough eyebrows. If you're not careful, someone may try and kill you along with Harmais."

Sahlin sat motionless and unable to speak. Part of him wanted to run away from the room, Napata, and Meroë altogether. Another part of him wanted to throttle Makal. In him, Sahlin saw the man he was destined to become had it not been for . . .

"Please keep in mind, Sahlin, that scenario doesn't have to happen. It is your choice," Rogo stressed.

"My choice," Sahlin voiced, staring past Rogo to a burning torch. *Choose you this day whom ye will serve,* a still voice whispered in his spirit.

"That is correct," Makal voiced. "And we need a decision, right now."

Chapter 22

Traffic along the Nile waterway was busy as ever. The wind propelled barges and boats of every size along the river's surface while smaller one-man canoes struggled against the brisk current. Though a never-ending series of stiff breezes swept across the river, the late afternoon sun bathed the entire region with a warm golden glow.

Leaning against a rail on the upper deck, Dikembul and Nkosi watched silently as the barge that transported them from Napata to Nuri slowly made its way across the Nile. The lower deck of the boat was crowded and noisy. Most of the people were returning from the coronation in Napata to their homelands. Though neither of them expressed it verbally, both Dikembul and Nkosi begged for the day that the visitors were gone and normalcy returned to the region.

Throughout the trip, Dikembul occasionally looked back to check on Annika. She somehow managed to find a quiet corner of the upper deck and was fast asleep despite the ruckus that swelled from below.

"Is she still asleep?" Nkosi asked.

"Incredibly, yes, she is."

"I envy her. I wish that I could just curl up, shut out the entire world, and simply drift away like that." Nkosi turned and cast his attention to the approaching landmass. "I'm actually surprised that she can sleep at all after everything that happened today."

"It doesn't get any easier for her. I received word from Akil a few days ago. He will be returning to Nuri in a couple of weeks."

Nkosi folded his arms and sighed. He knew how difficult the next period would be on both Dikembul and Annika. "It's for the best, my friend. We both know that."

Instead of focusing on his daughter's imminent departure, Dikembul forced himself to think about the day's near-horrific events. Although he was incensed at their treatment at the hands of Khenstout and the temple guards, he was grateful that they were on their way home as opposed to the dungeon. "I hope that Lamahl and Kenechi were able to track down those traders that you brought us out here to see."

Nkosi raised an eyebrow at the statement. "You make it sound as if all of this were my fault."

"I didn't mean it that way, Nkosi. It's just getting to be increasingly dangerous to go to the temple plaza. There's so much prejudice."

"Prejudice? It's outright corruption!" Nkosi trumpeted, his eyes red with anger. "The temples exact taxes from us. They take our produce and our money and still treat us like dirt. Men like Khenstout should be put on trial.

Just because we are Jewish doesn't make us any less human. We can't trust anyone in the government."

"I'm not sure about that," Dikembul countered. "I think that Sahlin Malae is a decent man."

"Who would have thought it? A Jewish grand vizier!" Nkosi cried. "I'll never forget the look on Khenstout's face!"

The two men shared the memory as well as the laugh.

A soft breeze sailed past Dikembul's face and unexpectedly brought with it an intriguing thought. "Nkosi, are we still Jews?"

"What?"

"I mean in the traditional sense." Dikembul looked up at his old friend. "Do you think that discovering the Messiah changes the essence of who we are?"

Nkosi rubbed his chin and pondered the question. "I don't think so," he finally answered. "The Scriptures that we have studied describe the Messiah as One who observes the traditional customs. I don't think that anything has changed."

Dikembul's mind rattled through the myriad of messianic Scriptures they had pored over the last several months. Though he could not recall anything that directly contradicted Nkosi's assessment, something prevented him from totally agreeing with it. He had already seen a rift form between those in the masjid and the increasing number of men who joined Nkosi and him during the messianic study sessions. A majority of the elders in the masjid were staunch traditionalists and felt uncomfortable with granting the Messiah issue more attention than they felt it merited. Many of them simply were not willing to declare that the Messiah had come unless official word had first come from Jerusalem. On several occasions they published their feelings to the congregation in an effort to discourage the growing messianic movement within their small region.

Despite Dikembul's strong objections, several of the people who attended the sessions had stopped attending the masjid altogether. They favored the idea of starting a new assemblage dedicated to unraveling the mysteries of the Messiah. Not surprisingly, Nkosi was head of the list, speaking out with a boldness and singular conviction that Dikembul had never seen in him before.

"That's the thing that I've been trying to tell the elders," Nkosi was saying. "Just because we believe that the Messiah has been revealed doesn't mean that we no longer hold fast to the truths that Moses and the prophets gave to the world."

"Do you really believe that, Nkosi?"

"Of course I do. Why do you ask?"

"It is just a feeling that I have." Dikembul paused as the barge softly collided with the shoreline. Almost immediately, people started to disembark and fan out toward the town of Nuri. "I know that the Scriptures declare that God is the same and He never changes . . ."

"But . . ."

Dikembul's eyes quickly darted back at Annika who had been aroused from her sleep by the barge's abrupt collision with the land. "But I feel that there is something . . . something new that has been introduced. Something that once was hidden, but now has been revealed. The more that we study, the more convinced I become that the world as we knew it has changed and will never be the same."

⬧   ⬧   ⬧

Imani leaned against the wall and stared aimlessly out of the window. Her attention was captured by everything from a hawk soaring high in the cloudless sky to a black beetle perched on the wooden window frame. A soft melody arose from the courtyard below, partially soothing her vexed spirit.

She wanted to return home. She longed for the familiar land of Alondia that featured a contrasting terrain of rolling hills and wide-open plains with only a small neighboring tribe in the immediate area. More often than not, she envied the small tribe of herdsmen. True, they lived in huts made of brick and mud, but their lives were extremely simplistic and seemingly void of the chaos that constantly enveloped her. Some days she spent hours standing on the deck of her family mansion overlooking the sleeping plains of Naga, just watching a group from the tribe warden their flocks of goats.

Imani shifted and studied the painting of Isis on the adjacent wall. The inn that she had occupied during her stay in Napata was far more lavish than her dwellings back in Alondia. However, that was totally by choice. She was wealthy enough to purchase the very inn where she was staying if she so desired. At times, she went to the temple near her home and vehemently queried Isis, demanding to know why she had been cursed with such beauty and wealth. The silent answer was always the same.

As a younger woman, she dreamt of having a large family of her own that she could nurture with a bounty of love. The gods had mercilessly set her affections upon a man who was indifferent towards the expression of true love. Throughout her twenties, she stubbornly defied the counsel of a priestess of Isis and was determined to breathe life into Sahlin's inert heart. For years, their relationship rose and set like the sun. However, the past several years had seen little more than a chilly darkness with no sight of dawn on the horizon.

Now in her midthirties, she wrestled more with depression and regret. Instead of warding them off, she found herself clinging to them as if they were imaginary companions from her childhood come to life. Where the garden of her heart was once full of optimism and hope, it was now overrun by the thorns and weeds. The only fruit that a man would ever pluck from the branch of her heart would be raw and bitter.

The door swung open suddenly.

"T'Sheba, I told you to always knock before you enter my room," Imani declared, not even bothering to look at the young woman who was adorned in a black-and-orange outfit with a matching headdress.

"I knew that you weren't asleep or anything like that," the teenager replied.

"That's not the point," Imani snapped, already disillusioned with the conversation that was yet to start. "There is so much that you need to learn."

"So you've mentioned before," T'Sheba blurted as she flopped onto a cushioned sofa. "Isn't there anything else that goes through your mind?"

Imani glared at the girl and then turned back toward the window, hoping to catch a breeze. "Are you packed?"

"Yes, I am, but I still don't see why we can't stay a few more days. The king has given us an open invitation and . . ."

"The king is gone."

"Yes, he is, but I wasn't finished. The vizier of the city would like us to stay and perform one more time. I told him . . ."

"You told him what?"

T'Sheba raised a defiant eyebrow. "I told him that I would have to speak with you about it, and that you would most likely decline the gracious offer."

"Good," Imani said, glad that T'Sheba did not circumvent her authority as she had done several other times during the past year. "You girls have danced enough during the past week."

"All in the service of our king," T'Sheba gloated.

Imani shook her head disdainfully. "No going out this evening. We leave at dawn's first light."

T'Sheba groaned and rolled her eyes. "I don't understand you. Here we are in one of the greatest cities in the kingdom, and all you can think about is leaving. You've spent most of this entire time here in your room as though you're hiding from the public. It's as if you don't even appreciate the opportunities placed before us."

"I thought that you understood, T'Sheba. This was a business trip, not a vacation."

"For you maybe, but definitely not for me."

"I don't like your tone," Imani warned. "We've made more than enough money. It's time to go."

"I'm sorry if you don't agree with how I feel," T'Sheba lied. She briefly admired the elegant white shawl that ran down the back of Imani's purple dress. "I think that it's only fair that I tell you the others and I have been talking about changing the nature of our relationship with you again."

"We've been through that discussion before as well. The others can do what they want, but your rights belong to me as long as you are underage."

"That won't be for very much longer."

"Indeed," Imani breathed, wishing that the futile talk

was over. "And like I've said before, as soon as the sun rises on that day, you will be a very wealthy young lady, free to do whatever it is that your immature heart desires." She turned around ominously just long enough to capture T'Sheba's waning insubordinate stare. "But until then, you will obey me and abide by the rules that I've established."

With one stroke, T'Sheba pushed herself up from the sofa. She pressed the creases out of her dress and offered a feigned smile to Imani. "As you say. There is one more matter that we need to discuss."

Only half listening to T'Sheba, her eyes probed the skies for a sign from Horus that the long, dreary day was nearing its conclusion. She followed two doves sprinting freely in the air, one pursuing the other like a passionate, determined lover. The two birds finally nestled together in a tree planted in the inn's courtyard.

Her eyes turned to the ground and perused the flowers decorating the yard's perimeter. Her heart suddenly started to flutter as Sahlin Malae entered the area. He was accompanied by his ever-present bodyguard, Bakka. Instantly, her heart was assailed by both spite and guilt. Strangely enough, guilt won over and dominated her thoughts. At their last encounter next to the river, she had told him that she would not be attending the ceremonies —knowing that she would.

"Him again," T'Sheba hissed, suddenly standing next to Imani at the window. "Despicable man. Scandalous to the core. How did he ever become the grand vizier?"

"Fate," Imani murmured. "Simple fate."

Chapter 23

The warm rays of the late morning sun drove back the heavy fog that blanketed the fields of Kawa. The retreating mist revealed the burgeoning war machine congregating below. At the heart of the encampment of tents sat the five modest brick buildings that comprised the borough of Kawa. Once a small trading outpost outside of Kerma, the depot had undergone a transformation into the command center for the southern regiment of the Kerman army.

Mounted upon his dark horse, General Akinidad slowly rode past regiment after regiment of his growing army. Through one violent act of necessity nearly a month earlier, his forces had nearly doubled. Today, Peshte Sa'ron would be delivering even more troops to his doorstep.

The soldiers stood crisp and erect as their general perused their weapons, their armor, and their hearts. Row after row, their dark faces were as flint ready to strike against the hardened essence of the royal cadre in the south. Akinidad masked his pride with a subtle scowl that camouflaged his face as well as his emotions.

Somewhere above the deserting fog, a piercing shrill descended from the heavens. Akinidad recognized the cry as it echoed through the still sky. In solemn reverence, he took his eyes from the soldiers to the only other power that he deemed worthy of his attention. The mist dissipated just in time for him to see a red hawk mount an invisible gust of wind and soar out of sight.

Great Horus! You bless me with your presence! Behold what I have built for your glory! May divine wisdom guide our spears to the hearts of our enemies. I give you praise! When I reach the gates of Meroë, I shall offer sacrifices unrivaled to you and the great god Apedemack!

The thundering sound of horses interrupted Akinidad's prayer. The group, which included Peshte Sa'ron and other government officials from the north, was led by Commander Djabal, Akinidad's dutiful lieutenant. As they came to a halt, Akinidad noticed that a few of the individuals wore wary expressions that he was only used to seeing on the faces of old women.

"General Akinidad, Ra has smiled upon you," greeted one of the administrators. Akinidad almost grinned at the raw fear laced in with the man's words.

"The gods have smiled upon us all," Akinidad replied.

"You more than the rest, it appears," Sa'ron added. The old man somehow managed to retain his stately visage despite the long ride from Kerma by horseback. "As we agreed, the remaining complement of soldiers will arrive within several hours. You are the sole commander of all northern forces for as long as the gods see fit to keep you in command."

Akinidad's fiery eyes glared at Sa'ron. He hated administrators, especially ones who were audacious while in extremely vulnerable positions. "We have much to discuss. My tent is this way."

Unlike other commanding officers, Akinidad refused to lodge in one of the permanent structures. He threw open the flap of his large tent and marched directly to a map. Sa'ron and two others followed him in.

Akinidad mumbled to himself as he studied the map. Sa'ron watched him shuffle through the charts for a moment and then walked over to him. "You fulfilled your bargain when you killed Carachen, and we have fulfilled ours and delivered to you the armies of Nobatia. Now, calm our nerves and let us know what your plans are."

"Is that why you came here?" Akinidad asked, his eyes looking up at Sa'ron.

"I think that we deserve to know. After all, Harmais will come after us."

Akinidad squinted sharply at Sa'ron. "You speak more like a child than a peshte."

"Perhaps. But like a child, I'm looking forward to my future."

"You really are a coward." Akinidad laughed. "I once told you—all of you—that Carachen's death would trigger a war. The young king is a fool, and his grand vizier is spineless. It is prudent for us to go on the offensive rather than sit and wait."

Sa'ron nervously cleared his throat. "I understood what you said that day, but . . ."

"You didn't believe that action would have to be taken so swiftly?"

Not accustomed to being cut off in midsentence, Sa'ron's eyes twitched in annoyance. "I thought that you were speaking figuratively. However, you are preparing as if you are actually going to attack Meroë."

"I am," Akinidad announced coldly. "I intend to march eighteen thousand soldiers into the heart of the capital and tear down the palace stone by stone. Furthermore, I will execute every member of the royal court and all who serve them."

Sa'ron folded his arms and leaned against one of the posts that supported the tent. "So, you have gone from soldier to butcher."

"No less than you have gone from idealist to conspirator. I have rid you of Carachen, and I intend to rid you of Harmais. I fail to see the problem with that."

"The problem is simple," Sa'ron growled. "You may have eighteen thousand troops, but the southern armies consist of well over thrity-five thousand. You will march those men to their deaths!"

"I will march them to honor . . ."

"There is no honor! There is only Meroë! If you do this, you will be committing suicide." Sa'ron was stunned to see Akinidad's expressionless eyes slither up at him. "Also, if you remove those soldiers from the region, you are opening the door to the Bedja and the nomads from the deserts to plunder the northern tribes and provinces at will."

"You administrators truly amaze me! You talk of change but refuse to pay the price that is attached to it. Your battlefields are dim hallways and dark alleys. You have no idea of what true honor consists of."

"Oh, I disagree with that, Akinidad! I know what honor is. The question is, do you?" For once, Sa'ron saw a spark of interest beam in Akinidad's dark eyes. "I may be a conspiring administrator, but I understand the concept of honor. Why did I involve you? Because I thought that it would prolong the life of Meroë. I shouldn't have to tell you that a soldier's honor is tied to the country that he serves. If you take the armies south to a sure defeat, not only will you have exposed our northern borders to nomads, but also to the Roman Empire. Is that the legacy you want?"

Akinidad was silent for a moment as Sa'ron's words paraded through his mind. The more thought that he gave it, the more feasible the scenario became. "So, I am to do nothing?"

"No. No, Harmais and his family must be dealt with. The gods demand it. However, there has to be another way, a way that wouldn't destroy all that we have been working for."

"There is a wisdom to your words, old man," Akinidad said. "The risks that you speak of are great, perhaps even too great. I shall give your words greater consideration."

      🜨   🜨   🜨

"It's true. From what I have heard, Udezae is ready to forbid further studies of the messianic prophecies that attest Jesus of Nazareth is the Christ," Lamahl was saying in the midst of Dikembul's family room.

Nkosi and Kenechi sat stoically as they digested the unfavorable but not totally unexpected report. Dikembul was propped against a wall, his attention drifting out of the open window next to his shoulder.

"After so many months . . . I can't believe that they

would just abandon all of the work that we've put in. All of the . . . revelations that we have come across," Kenechi remarked. "It doesn't seem right."

"We shouldn't fool ourselves," Nkosi declared. "Udezae's decision has nothing to do with a quest for truth. It is a purely political move. Ever since he was appointed as high priest, he's made it clear that he doesn't want to deal with any subject that might be perceived as divisive."

"But who is he to overrule the Holy Scriptures?" said Lamahl. "If the Messiah has come, then He has come. No one priest can capture truth and dispense it at will."

"But he can," Nkosi persisted, his anger starting to brew as he thought of the temple priests in Napata. "He already has most of the elders believing that what we are doing is detrimental to all Falasha in the region. He doesn't care about truth, worship, or even Jehovah for that matter."

"Those are strong words, Nkosi," Dikembul said, looking out of the window.

"Maybe. However, they are true. At some point, someone is going to have to stand up and confront him. If you ask me, he's not much different from the men who had the Christ executed. The San . . . San . . ."

"Sanhedrin," Dikembul enunciated. He listened to Nkosi rant on for a moment and then looked back out the window. Though he chose his words carefully, Dikembul wholeheartedly agreed with Nkosi's assessment of their new high priest. He prayed that they would not be pulled into a divisive battle over the messianic Scriptures; nevertheless, as the rich heritage of their forefathers attested, truth had to reign.

As Nkosi, Lamahl, and Kenechi sought solutions for

problems that had not quite yet materialized, Dikembul's eyes looked down the road, just beyond the fence he had repaired weeks earlier. There stood Annika and Akil discussing their future.

Though Dikembul could not hear a word that they spoke, their body language reverberated through the surrounding forest. Dikembul wrung his moist hands as Annika took a step back and shook her head. As her lips moved, Akil, dressed in his stately militia uniform, begrudgingly hoisted his hands upon his hips and barked at her.

"If that is Udezae's attitude, I think that we should break away from the masjid altogether," Lamahl was replying to Nkosi. "I know at least a half dozen families from Sanam that would support us."

"I know several there as well," Nkosi said. "Most of the men who have attended the study forums are also in favor of starting a messianic masjid. Wouldn't you say, Dikembul?"

"They've all expressed support at one time or another," Dikembul responded, his eyes not withdrawing from the silent drama unfolding down the road. Akil was hovering over Annika, who had her back turned to him. She appeared to mutter something that compelled Akil to grab her by the shoulder and spin her around. He waggled his finger in her face and then waited for a response.

Dikembul fought the urge to leave the house and march down the road in her defense. Everything within him wanted to intercede, but he managed to hold his emotions in check. Annika was a grown woman betrothed to Akil. The two of them would have to work things out on their own.

"I think you're right," Nkosi was saying to Lamahl. "It

will take more than words to start and maintain a masjid. It will take money, organization . . ."

"And most of all, power," Kenechi added. "More power than any one of us have. Not only would we have to contest with Udezae, but we would also have to deal with temple priests like Khenstout. We are so far down on the political food chain that we wouldn't have a prayer in that environment."

"A prayer is all we have," Nkosi said, sneering at the circumstances sprouting before them like weeds.

"A prayer is all we need." Dikembul's voice was tranquil and assuring. "If God is leading us to take such a drastic step, then He will provide a way for us to do so." He turned to face the three men. "I believe that the Scriptures are clear about one thing. Before a man can be true with God, he must first be true to himself. If God has called us to break away and teach about the Messiah, then we have to be true to ourselves and at least try."

"Yes," Lamahl echoed. "We have to at least try."

Dikembul glanced back out the window to find Akil and Annika. To his surprise, the two had vanished, leaving only the wooden fence in plain view. He sighed and prayed that they were able to settle their differences.

Later that afternoon, Dikembul sat alone in his home. He pondered everything from the condition of his flock to the first serious discussion that they entertained about breaking away from the masjid. At first glance, he thought it was a horrible idea that would meet with a disgraceful end. Nevertheless, each passing day produced a reassuring feeling that it was the right thing to do.

The front door opened, and Annika slowly walked in. Dikembul rushed to her side. He immediately noticed that her eyes were red and heavy with tears.

"I saw Akil and you hours ago. What happened?" His question was met with a subdued sob she barely managed to choke down.

"Annika, I know that it's none of my business, but what did he say?"

Like a wayward arrow, her eyes darted around the room until they landed squarely upon Dikembul. "It's not what he told me. It's what I told him." With the look of a mother who had just lost her son, she settled down on a couch and stared at a wall. "I just can't believe that I did it . . ."

"Annika, what is it?"

"He comes from an honorable house, he's very handsome and extremely hardworking . . . Every one of my friends kept expressing how much they wanted to be in my place. Now . . ." Fat tears rolled down her cheeks and onto her father's hand. "There must be something wrong with me! There must be!" She collapsed into Dikembul's embrace and wept.

Not knowing what to do or say, Dikembul simply held her as he did when she was a child. He rubbed her arm gently and prayed for the right words to soothe her soul. At least a dozen scenarios explaining her distraught frame of mind flooded his head—each one of them finding Akil guilty of an unforgivable infraction. His anger swelled with each passing moment.

"I'm sorry, Annika; this was my fault."

She shook her head and dried her eyes, only to have more tears blur her vision. "No, it was me. I told him that I didn't want to marry him."

"What? But, my dear, we were clear on that," he said, recalling the day that she agreed to the terms of the wedding contract as described by their tribal customs.

"Yes, I know . . . but I didn't want to live a lie. I don't have any feelings towards him."

"But, Annika . . ."

"Oh, Papa, I know that it is wrong. I know that it goes against our ways, but I want what Mama and you had. I want to be in love with the man I marry."

"Love?" Dikembul rubbed the bristly black-and-gray whiskers on his face. "What your mother and I had was special. But you must know that we started out the same way Akil and you have. There was no real courtship to our relationship at all. I selected her and made the arrangement with her father, and she became my wife. The Lord then shortly blessed our home with love."

"That's because Mama and you were meant for each other. I don't feel that for Akil."

"Annika, feelings can be both a blessing and a curse, but most of all they change. They are as unpredictable as the wind . . . especially when you're young."

Unable to maintain eye contact with her father's logic, Annika lowered her head and prepared for another storm. "Papa, I had a dream."

"A dream," Dikembul echoed, his tone growing a bit stiffer.

"One night, I prayed to the Messiah to show me the man whom I would marry."

Dikembul flashed her a puzzled look. He had known for some while that she had embraced Jesus of Nazareth as the Christ with a strong and sincere heart, but he had no idea if her convictions actually stood in league with his own. He decided to listen.

"Papa, I know that it must sound strange, but after I prayed, an image of a man came into my heart. It was like his face was branded into my heart with a hot iron."

"Who is this man? Is he here in Nuri?"

"I don't know. I don't know his name. I can't even describe how he looks . . . I just know that I'll recognize him when we meet."

Part of Dikembul wanted to embrace her vision and accept it as truth. Customs and traditions aside, he wanted his daughter to be happy. However, he also knew that happiness was a fleeting emotion. It temporarily satisfied the soul but never filled one's belly or put a roof over one's head.

"Annika, I understand your feelings, but you must understand that . . ."

"Papa, I don't want to be a burden or a shame to you." She choked back the sobs that bubbled within her. "If you wish it, I'll marry him."

Dikembul almost kissed her for the gift that she presented to him. Her offer was enticing. It gave him the authority to end the controversy he had created once and for all.

He was about to make the decision for her when something that he said earlier that day silently revisited him.

Before a man can be true with God, he must first be true to himself.

His own words dangled before him like the stars hanging in the black of night. As if they were guided projectiles, they attacked him from every side, each syllable hitting him with all the force of a spear hurled by a mighty warrior. Suddenly, his heart was filled with shame and conviction. He wanted to make the whole situation disappear, but he couldn't. Racked with confusion, he embraced his daughter once more and pondered how he should respond.

Chapter 24

Cool, refreshing water rushed past Harmais's face, ears, and torso as he propelled himself beneath the surface of his enormous indoor pool. With a mighty lunge, he forced himself to the bottom, intent on staying there as long as he could. He found the smooth floor and slowly pulled himself along with his fingertips.

He loved the simple cover and priceless silence that the depths provided. Underwater, there were no scribes, viziers, or peshtes badgering him to make a decree for this or that. Tshenpur, Naytal, and the Council of Ministers were nowhere to be found. Besides the fizzing and popping of tiny air bubbles, the only discernible sound was that of his own slowing heartbeat. Truly, this was his personal domain, one that was void of the nagging demands and annoying ruckus occupying the great throne room.

In time, the air in his chest forced Harmais to the surface. He reluctantly emerged into his forlorn reality and immediately regretted it. As soon as the water cleared from his face, he opened his eyes to see the scantly clad statue of Isis greeting him with outstretched arms. He uttered a curse at the deity and took a deep breath to retreat back into his watery refuge.

He ignored the fading echo of his name as it was washed away by the water that engulfed him.

Sahlin paced along the pool's edge waiting for Harmais to return. Though annoyed, he was actually impressed at how long the king could remain submerged.

When Harmais resurfaced, his eyes were focused directly upon his grand vizier. "Come on in. There's nothing like a cool swim after a long, hot day."

"No, thank you. I haven't the time." Sahlin's tone was grave and deep. "And neither have you, my lord."

"I have plenty of time," Harmais pushed himself away from Sahlin's general direction. He gracefully glided across the water's surface until he got to the opposite side. "It is I who determines the registry of affairs for this kingdom."

He dipped his head back underwater. A moment later he reappeared at Sahlin's feet.

"The Council of Ministers would disagree with you."

"They are fools." Harmais climbed out of the pool and donned an awaiting towel from a stone bench. "Weak fools."

Sahlin could smell the wine upon the man's breath and grimaced with the shame that Harmais lacked. "They may be fools, but they are definitely not weak."

"All they do is talk," Harmais spat, mopping his head and face.

"You should listen to them more."

"I read their reports."

"That's not good enough. You are the king. It would be appropriate for you to be present at a few of their meetings."

Harmais shook his fist. "I don't need a lecture on what is appropriate . . ."

"Then, let's talk about what is prudent. In the month since our return from Napata, you've concealed yourself from everyone, even me. You took an ill-advised trip east without even talking with me . . ."

"How could the trip have been ill-advised if I didn't seek your advice beforehand?" Harmais's mocking laugh revealed his lack of sobriety.

Sahlin's left eye twitched uncontrollably as he watched Harmais clothe himself in a fine purple robe. "You lost sorely needed support during your absence."

"I don't think so." Harmais smiled as he filled his cup with another round of honey wine. As soon as he finished it, he repeated the act two more times.

Sahlin cringed as he watched the man drive himself towards a drunken oblivion. He had hoped that Harmais would have acted more sensibly, but his worst fears were coming to pass. At the moment, the only thing that Sahlin could hear were the ominous warnings issued by Makal weeks earlier. He had hoped to speak with Harmais much earlier, but the king's unscheduled excursion ended that possibility.

"You're asking yourself why I'm doing this, aren't you?" Harmais inquired, downing yet another drink.

Sahlin looked away in anguish and disgust. "Harmais, the Council of Ministers . . ."

"Yes, yes, I know. I've been waiting for us to have this conversation." Sahlin was surprised to see a sober glare shine from Harmais's empty eyes. "I know what you're here to talk about."

Sahlin looked confused. "Then, why have you gone out of your way to avoid me and the subject?"

"Because there is nothing that anyone can do about it." Harmais chuckled. He continued to snigger as he started to refill his cup. Before one drop could leave the bottle, Sahlin grasped his arm and guided the container down. Harmais offered no resistance as he continued to laugh.

"Won't you let me drink to the cursed memory of my mother? The great Kandace Amanitore!" Harmais waited for the echo to fade as it bounced through the pool area. With a twisted look of spite, he turned to a speechless Sahlin. "Think me a fool to be ridiculed? Oh no. I am more like the beggar to be pitied. I am no king; I was hardly even a paqar. The Council wants me dead. They want to select a new leader. Such is their right, but they will have to fight for it."

"Harmais, listen to me. The Council has an army . . ."

"Yes, yes, the regiment at Gebel Geili. I also understand that you control it." He slapped Sahlin's shoulder and flashed a mocking grin. "Sahlin, the great military general of Nubia! That is just as ridiculous as me being a king!"

"You already know about the Council's intentions?"

"Of course. Why else do you think that I selected you as the grand vizier? I knew you would never attack me. I knew that you, above all, believed in my mother's sick vision of the future—of us walking together with Egyptians and Romans, embracing Greek thought, enlightening our culture and poisoning our minds. Yes, my friend, it made about as much sense to appoint you as grand vizier as it did for the gods to ordain my birth."

Harmais grabbed the near-empty bottle of wine and flung it across the pool. The bottle hit the statue of Isis and shattered. "A curse on you!" he hurled at the emotionless stone idol. "A curse on you!"

After composing himself, Harmais turned around to face his old friend. "Where do you stand, Sahlin?"

"I stand with you." As the words came out of his mouth, Sahlin felt a knot develop deep within his abdomen. He took a deep breath to counteract the discomfort, but it cryptically remained.

"I never doubted it. Besides, we are both fools."

"What are you going to do?" Sahlin asked softly, figuring that the two of them would eventually meet the same fate at the hands of the Council. Harmais's red eyes rolled up at him.

"I'm going to fight them."

"Fight? How? The Geilian army is the strongest regiment in the south. You are unpopular among the remaining southern generals. And the northern armies . . ."

"Shhh!" Harmais hissed. "Can you hear that? The gods are laughing! Apedemack is in love with me. He told me last night in a dream. He promised me that I would have a glorious battle and triumph."

"Harmais, I don't understand . . ."

"I bought them! During my journey east, I purchased every southern regiment outside of the Geilian contingent. They may hate my lineage, but they love my gold."

"How can you be sure that they will not betray you?"

"I'm quite certain that they will not. Apedemack assured me of that. He told me that the one who will betray me does not wear a uniform."

Sahlin's puzzled look became defensive.

"No, my friend. You're a man of honor, not a back-stabber." He sat down on the hard bench and sighed. He dropped his head into his hands. "The one who will betray me lurks in the darkness and is concealed by the gods. A curse on the gods . . . a curse on mankind . . . and a curse on me . . ."

A heaviness filled the room. The weight of the oppressive spirit prompted Sahlin to turn towards the exit. But he looked down upon Harmais languishing in the mire of self-pity and hate and took a step toward him. Instead of seeing the king of Meroë, Sahlin saw himself during the long days when he sought out peace and purpose in life during his trip to Jerusalem. Then, a new feeling rose from within him that compelled him to sit down next to Harmais.

"It's something that you cannot buy," Sahlin said, staring down into the water. Harmais briefly glanced his way, as if Sahlin had somehow read his mind. "When I found that I couldn't inherit it, I tried to buy it. When I found that its price was too excessive, I searched for it. When I couldn't find it, it strangely enough found me."

"Peace is elusive. Not even the gods can capture it."

Sahlin drew in his lips and found himself praying for the words to speak. "The Christ."

"What?"

"He is the One anointed by God to set men free."

"Which God?"

"The Lord God Jehovah."

"Ah, yes. I forgot that your family embraced that flawed Jewish credence. One God—absurd."

"My one God has brought me peace. Your many

have brought you and the entire kingdom nothing but torment."

Harmais offered a halfhearted laugh. "And you suggest that switching my allegiance to your God would improve my plight as well as the condition of the kingdom?"

"No," Sahlin replied, searching for an answer that he wasn't sure existed. "But it would give you hope. A hope that someday you would not be ruled by the fear of death and driven by the lust of your eyes."

"I am not afraid to die."

"No, Harmais. Not only are you afraid to die, but you are afraid to live. You've always been afraid to live. That fear has driven you into a drunken stupor so many times that you crave it. You yearn not for wine or its intoxicating effect but rather for the shelter that it provides you from the reality of who you are."

Harmais's forehead glistened with a cold sweat. "And who am I?"

Compassion forced Sahlin's lips. "Only God—the Christ—can tell you that. Just as He did for me."

Harmais swallowed hard. He tried to measure Sahlin's words against the depths of his own heart. Oddly, they were more than enough to fill the void that he had spent a lifetime inundating with wine. Slowly, a realization washed over his face. "Where is your God and His Christ that I might inquire of Him? Must I go to Jerusalem to see His image?"

Sahlin was at a total loss. His eyes skimmed the room until the words finally came to him. "He does not dwell in a temple. He is everywhere. But you will know where He is when He speaks to you."

Harmais wasn't certain if he had consumed far too much wine or less than he thought he did, but he suddenly felt altogether sober. For the first time that evening, he gazed directly into Sahlin's hazel eyes and noted a profound difference. Perplexed that he hadn't noticed it before, he sensed that the bitterness and tumult Sahlin used to conceal were completely absent. All he could see now was an intense peace that openly ruled his spirit. It was something that Harmais had never before witnessed in a man. He wondered why.

"If He has no temple, and there are no images of Him, then how does one speak to your God?"

"We pray . . . like this."

❈   ❈   ❈

Qar Naytal's silent scream rattled the beautifully painted stone walls around her. She drew long, deep breaths through her nose and attempted to keep her lips pressed together in an effort to keep from cursing the very gods that she adored.

More than a minute had passed by since Tshenpur stormed out of the room leaving her standing alone in the receiving room, the site of the latest skirmish in their perpetual clash of wills. The battle left Naytal's pride and self-esteem bloodied and bruised. Were it not for the fact that she had a son to groom, she would have petitioned the gods to end her life that very evening.

Finally, she diverted enough energy from her intense anger to her feet and left the room. Strolling aimlessly through the palace's outer hallways, Naytal happened upon her personal servant who bowed reverently as the qar passed by.

"Go at once to Melaenis's home and tell her to come to

my room immediately." The young girl bowed once more, then scurried out of the great palace.

After receiving the message, Melaenis made her way through the palace to Naytal's quarters as soon as she could. She rapped on the door several times and waited for one of Naytal's servants to open the door. Each time, she was met with an eerie silence until she finally decided to open the door herself.

Several candles dimly lit the room, causing the shadows to dance loosely against the walls. Melaenis heard Naytal long before she could identify her.

"I've been sitting here waiting for her to answer me."

"Naytal?"

"I don't understand. Why is it that she has ordained for me to endure such pain?"

Melaenis moved past the room's furnishings that separated her from Naytal. As she approached, the qar rose to her feet and started to pace back and forth in front of one of the candles.

"Could it be that Isis is testing me, Melaenis? Could it be that she is preparing me for something so grand that she must tear me down and supplant even my very soul?"

"What happened?" Melaenis asked, finding it very difficult to make out Naytal's face in the dim light.

"Tshenpur and I were actually friends. You remember. How could it have come to this? What demon has possessed her to treat me in such a fashion?" True that Tshenpur and she had always competed for influence, popularity, and men, but there was also a level of respect that the two held for one another that neither one seemed willing to breach.

"She was gloating over her victory in successfully arranging for me to be married off to a fool peshte in

Baiyuda. My son was right there in front of us. She looked at him and said that the peshte in Baiyuda would tame me and show him how to be a real man. He protested. When she commanded him to be silent, he refused. Then, she slapped him."

Melaenis gasped as her imagination escorted her through the narration.

"I grabbed Tshenpur's arm and pulled her away from Terenkiwal. She threw a fit as if she were a mad cow, and then slapped me . . . Slapped me!" Naytal stopped pacing and turned towards Melaenis. "I wanted to kill her right there! I was about to, but . . . but . . ."

Naytal didn't have to finish in order for Melaenis to figure out what happened next. She watched the qar sag into a sofa. "Common sense can be a cruel taskmaster," Melaenis said softly.

"It was a curse for me today. Once I realized what I had done, I begged for her forgiveness. I assaulted a queen of Meroë."

"She may be a ruler, but she is not a queen, Naytal."

"She commanded my son and the others to leave the room. Afterward, she commanded that I go to Napata and make the appropriate sacrifices to atone for my sin. When I return, I am to repent to her publicly. She even threatened to convince Harmais to rescind the commitment to the peshte and to have me marry a second-rate scribe here in Meroë."

"What are you going to do?"

"What she wants," Naytal answered, her tone plagued with defeat and shame. "I'm going to take my son and go north—perhaps even leave Meroë altogether."

Melaenis shook her head in disbelief. "But you can't do that. You can't just run away from her."

"She is the kandace now. In time, when she's finished toying with me, she will simply give the order to have me or my son impaled. I can't let that happen."

"She wouldn't do that."

Naytal watched the shadows flutter against the wall like black ghosts worshiping the lord of the underworld. "If I were in her position, I would do it with no delay. Terenkiwal is a potential heir to the throne and therefore a threat. Yes, I would kill us both while I had the chance."

Though it made her shudder, Melaenis could not deny the fiendish logic that supported Naytal's reasoning. "Where will you go?"

"First, to Napata, to make it appear as if we're obeying her command. Then, we'll go to Kerma and ultimately Egypt."

Melaenis could taste the bitterness that seasoned Naytal's answer. She, above all, understood the qar's disdain for retreating from a fight. "We are friends, Naytal. Where you go, I go."

"No," Naytal asserted, almost too fast. "I appreciate your loyalty, my old friend, but . . . this is a journey for my son and me. Hopefully, Isis will allow you and me to renew our friendship in a more sanitary environment."

Chapter 25

Your daughter's behavior is intolerable! I demand that you speak with her," Akil barked at Dikembul. More than a few eyes glanced their way as the two men stood just outside of the shopping district of Nuri. "You must make her understand that she is in direct violation of . . ."

"Akil, I've already spoken with her."

"And?"

Dikembul waited for a small crowd of people on their way to the market to finish passing by before he continued. "This isn't an easy matter, Akil."

"I don't see why not. An arrangement has already been made. You have already agreed to my dowry and have blessed the union. This is a very simple matter to decide."

"I respect you a great deal. The things that you have managed to accomplish are exemplary. It would be an honor to have you as a son-in-law. However, there is one question that I have to ask you."

"What is that?"

"All of the arrangements have been made according to the customs, but . . ."

"But what?"

"Do you love Annika?"

Dumbfounded and irritated, Akil fumbled for a response. "Love her? She's very beautiful and will make a fine wife."

"Yes, but how do you feel for her?"

"I like her, and I have chosen her. She should be honored."

"But do you love her?" Dikembul pressed.

"What . . . what do you mean, and why does it matter?" The muscles in Akil's thick neck bulged as his patience wore thin.

"Have you ever been in love before?" Dikembul's question was met with a hawkish glare riddled with confusion and bewilderment. "When your parents died, I often wondered if you had anyone in your life to help you understand such feelings. You were always so aloof and distant."

Akil's expression softened a bit as he pondered the older man's words. "While I appreciate the compassion that you demonstrated to me back then, I fail to see your point at the moment."

"I guess that my point is this, Akil. It is difficult to give someone else love when you have never really been the recipient of it."

"What do you mean? Everybody loves me. And if they don't, to blazes with them!"

Dikembul raised his hands defensively and shook his head. "That's not what I mean. Do you remember my wife? I loved her. I was committed to taking care of her and providing for her. I didn't just want her. I wanted for her."

"With all due respect, Dikembul, how you managed your household was and still is your business. I appreciate your concern for my feelings, but this has nothing to do with Annika and the agreement that we had solidified for well over a year."

Sensing defeat at the hands of Akil's emotion barrier, Dikembul prepared to make his final pitch. "Annika has expectations. She saw the relationship that I had with her mother, and she longs for that. She wants what her mother, had—a love affair." Dikembul slowly looked away as if he could hear his wife's sweet voice reminding him of the many years that they had spent together.

"Why are we even having this discussion?" Akil asked. "I like her, and that should be enough. Someday, I will grow to love her as she loves me. She's just confused right now."

"No, she's not confused," Dikembul stated. "She doesn't love you, Akil."

"What?"

"She respects you and honors your accomplishments, but she does not love you. Nor does she want to be married to you."

Akil tossed aside the disclosure as a warrior would deflect an oncoming spear with his shield. However, he could not hide the wound his eyes clearly betrayed. "Like I said, she is confused. Love, affection. What does it matter? We have an arrangement."

Dikembul pressed his lips together and tilted his head up slowly. "No. The arrangement is off."

"What? You can't do that."

"I'm sorry, Akil. I love my daughter, and I want her to be happy. I want to give her what her mother had—someone who would love and cherish her. I cannot command you to do such things and make her happy, but I can at the very least avoid forcing her into a situation that will make her miserable."

A thundercloud of rage slowly eclipsed the hurt in Akil's dark eyes. Soon, his entire visage was overcome with passion and fury. "How dare you!"

"I'm sorry, Akil. I don't mean to insult you. In fact, this is my fault . . ."

"That is the only statement of yours that I am in complete agreement with. It is clear to me that both your daughter and you are out to make a mockery of our traditions."

"Akil," Dikembul called, reaching for the young man's arm.

"Don't touch me! Now I understand what they've been saying about you. At first, I couldn't believe it, but now I see."

"What are you talking about?"

"Reports have been made to the temple prefect about a rogue bunch of Jews who are causing a commotion among those in the masjid. Your name has surfaced. At first, I couldn't believe it, but now . . ."

"Akil, who has been making such claims?"

"What does it matter?" Akil spat, backing away. "Their claims must be true, because your daughter and you have persisted in mocking the rule of law." He turned and started to storm away.

"Akil, wait. Let's sit and talk," Dikembul offered, trying to defuse the young man's mounting ire.

Akil slowed his gait for a curt moment. "No, Dikembul! You will pay for what you have done. You have insulted me and have mocked our customs. I will see to it myself that you and your daughter are held accountable for your actions!"

⚜   ⚜   ⚜

Therefore thus says the Lord God, "Behold, I am laying in Zion a stone, a tested stone, a costly cornerstone for the foundation, firmly placed. He who believes in it will not be disturbed."

Sahlin paced through his study hall like a caged leopard as he read the Scripture from the loosely bound book that he fashioned from the papyrus that bore the works of the prophet Isaiah. No matter how many times he read it, Isaiah's ancient prophecy never failed to leap from the page and engage something deep within his soul. Every time he allowed his mind to be immersed in the pages of the book, certain passages mysteriously inspired him to the point of rejuvenation. No matter what his mood or disposition was beforehand, he always experienced a sense of deep renewal after devoting himself to Jehovah's recorded words.

In fact, there were times that he purposely blocked out one or two hours from his demanding schedule in order to pursue the peace offered by the divinely inspired texts. It was a practice that he found himself repeating several times a week. There seemed to be no other place in the kingdom, indeed the world, that offered him sanctuary from the tumultuous malignant duties that accompanied his post.

He lowered the Scriptures and thought about the Council's ominous unspoken ultimatum to Harmais. The blood rushed from his head as he recalled the reckless response that the king intended to hand to the very body of men that held the key to his power. Sahlin's knees grew feeble as he imagined the unspeakable carnage that would no doubt be produced when the two sides finally collided.

He walked on to the adjacent balcony of his study where his eyes were met with a breathtaking view of the Nile. His mansion was stationed high enough on the slope of a mountaintop so that he could see the mighty river gently twist behind a patch of soft, rolling hills.

At the moment, he forgot about the Scriptures and disengaged himself from the life-changing encounter with the Christ. He even managed to detach his mind from the menacing specter of a civil war that would surely result in his own death. Instead, the view of the eternal river leisurely flowing past reminded him of how much he loved Meroë. It was a land that would forever possess his heart—no matter what power tried to rend it away. He believed in it and, like his fathers, wanted it to prosper. Nevertheless, it seemed intent upon consuming itself and all those who loved her.

With the exception of his grandfather, most of his immediate ancestors were interred in a field just a short walk from the mansion. Someday he too would rest there among the men who gave their lives in the service of the great Nubian kingdom. He couldn't help but imagine that he was destined to join them in the grave in a relatively short period. He saw no reprieve on the horizon that offered even a glimmer of hope that his nation would survive.

Though he thought it selfish, he wondered how history would remember him. Now, only he, the king, and the Council of Ministers knew how impotent his position truly was. Though it had the grand appearance of an embellished chalice, in reality it was merely a hollow gourd with no substance.

No matter which angle Sahlin examined the situation from, he saw the inevitable ruin of his life. The only question now was how much family honor he could salvage from the wreckage.

A dark depression took him by the hand and nudged him towards the path of self-destruction. If there were any honor to be obtained, it would come only under the guise of suicide—a rite available to noblemen who admitted that they had been outwitted by the gods. In his desk was a dagger that had been passed down through his family for hundreds of years. Though it was old, the blade was far from dull and sharp enough to . . .

As he lingered on the unpleasant but seductive notion, his thoughts were invaded by words from the book that he still clutched in his hand. *He who believes . . . will not be disturbed.*

Sahlin held the book tighter and shook his head. *He who believes in it will not be disturbed.* An intense feeling in the pit of his stomach nearly drove him to his knees. He felt as if he were being torn apart—caught in the midst of a great struggle between two awesome and invisible forces. The image that came to his mind was that of a lion and hyena squabbling over a fresh kill.

"I believe," he whispered. At that moment, a mighty roar from the lion sent the scavenging hyena fleeing in the opposite direction. His very soul shuddered.

Then, there was peace.

"I believe," he said once more. A gentle breeze sailed across the balcony and brushed against his face. It brought a refreshment to his soul that made his faith stand tall and erect. He opened his eyes just in time to see the wind disappear into the trees below.

"Christ, why am I tormented so? Your ways are unknowable. Please allow me to sleep with my fathers. Please, forget me. Release me, and forget me."

Can a woman forget her nursing child and have no compassion on the son of her womb? Even these may forget, but I will not forget you. Behold, I have inscribed you on the palms of My hands.

Sahlin dropped the book and examined the moist palms of his own hands. For an instant, he saw mangled, bloodied wounds at the base of his wrists. The sight seared his conscience, and he began to weep uncontrollably.

"Forget me, forget me." Though his moans rose softly up to heaven, Sahlin somehow knew that he would never partake of the fruit of his requests. He knew that he would never be forgotten by the One to whom he prayed.

🔹   🔹   🔹

Imani wanted desperately to be somewhere else.

In a futile attempt to distract herself from the cold discomfort that enveloped her, she darted her eyes from one end of the office to the other to find anything of interest. She shook her head in absolute disdain, convinced that she hated her surroundings just as much as she hated her condition. Never mind that the stone walls possessed an extremely fine finish and produced a glossy reflection that brightened the room. Nor did it matter that the crown molding running along the perimeter consisted of what appeared to be pure gold. The impressive life-size statues of male models caught her eyes for a moment, but the distraction was short-lived.

"Just relax," the physician said. "The examination is almost completed."

Imani closed her eyes and tried to picture herself at the parlor adjacent to the bathhouse receiving a massage. However, the physician's hands, which were cold and aggressive in their probing, made it clear that she was not receiving a rubdown but a critical examination that would reveal her future.

As she lay unmoving on her back, she found it ironic that the pain had chosen this moment to temporarily withdraw itself. The only discomfort that she felt was produced by the firm pokes and jabs levied by one of the royal family's attending physicians. She felt extremely fortunate and thanked Isis that she had the means and the favor to receive treatment from the finest medical staff in Meroë. In the span of six months, she had been to many other physicians in different provinces. She only prayed that the prognosis would be different this time around.

Finally, the husky physician concluded his probe of her lower extremities. "One moment," he said. He walked across the office to a shelf laden with scrolls.

Imani watched him shuffle through the carefully cataloged scrolls until he arrived at one in particular. She had seen the same scenario at least half a dozen times before and wondered how long he would brood over what she assumed to be the description of the disease that vexed her insides and caused her to bleed.

Like a moving statue, he rolled up the scroll and reshelved it. Imani pretended to focus her attention elsewhere as he walked over to her.

"Please, Lady Imani, you may sit up." The moment

that she did, a sharp pain jolted through the left side of her body. She absorbed the shock and met the physician's gaze straight on.

"As I mentioned to you before, I'm not one to disguise or shroud a serious condition. Here's where you are."

Chapter 26

With every fiber of his being, Akinidad prayed for a miracle. He was determined to assault Apedemack's throne with sacrifices to validate his petitions for divine intervention. He paced through the jungle, fully expecting the half-lion, half-man god of war to meet him at any moment.

Though they were at least half a mile to the south, sounds of his expanding army dominated the countryside. In just over six weeks since he had been named general over the forces of both Nobatia and Kerma, his army had inflated to close to twenty thousand troops with more disillusioned men filtering into the ranks every day. Though he hated to admit it, he had to give credit to Kandace Amanitore and her foolish sons for his good fortune. As fate would have it, he was merely the recipient of years of reckless policies and a brutal civil war that ostracized nearly every citizen of Meroë who resided in the northern provinces.

Akinidad paused and leaned against a tree. He collected his thoughts and fought to find a fatal flaw in Sa'ron's argument opposing a direct military assault against the Isle of Meroë. In his mind, all he had to do was kill the king and the grand vizier. Afterward, the Council of Ministers would have no choice but to confirm him or whomever he selected as the new qeren.

Akinidad sneered. What did he care if the northern borders were left unprotected? Nomadic desert tribes had always been a concern, but they had never been able to mount or maintain the type of offensive that was necessary to disrupt the major trading artery that sustained the kingdom.

The general also scoffed at Sa'ron's notion that Meroë would be torn apart and cease to exist. As in nature's daily poetic drama, the strong would survive. Akinidad was certain that his army was the most potent and passionate and—above all else—favored by the gods. Were it not for Apedemack's invisible hand holding him back, he would drive his legions south and rightfully derail the current monarchy and its ineffectual administration.

The sound of crunching palm leaves and snapping twigs drew Akinidad's attention to the rear. He turned in time to see one of his officers brush aside a large fern to clear his path.

"General, I'm sorry to disturb you, but a visitor has arrived for you."

"At the camp?"

"No, sir. She is at the dufufa in Kerma."

☙ ☙ ☙

Terenkiwal buzzed from one corner to the other of the receiving room. He had been in many dufufas before, but none that had such a staunch militaristic aura about it. The room was filled with archaic objects of war, such as arrows, leather shields, and old iron swords.

Naytal stood by the window and waited. Though she was exhausted from the three-day journey, she found herself wrestling with an anxiety that she hadn't confronted in years. Her heart quickened as she heard footsteps marching up the hall.

There was a brief knock at the door. Then, it ceremoniously opened.

"Qar Naytal, you bless us with your presence," Akinidad greeted. He stepped into the room, followed closely by Djabal. "What brings you up here so far from the Isle?"

"I'm simply responding to your invitation. Surely you remember."

Akinidad's smile camouflaged his race to recall the issuance of such an ill-advised invitation. "Ah, yes. After the coronation." He flashed a look at Djabal who appeared to relax ever so slightly. "So, I trust that you are simply escaping from the bustle of the palace back in Meroë."

"To say that would be true."

"The king and queen are well?" Akinidad asked, hoping for a baleful report.

"Yes, indeed they are."

"This must be your son?"

"Yes," Naytal answered, motioning the boy to her side. "Terenkiwal, this is General Akinidad."

The boy perused Akinidad's dark leather breastplate and ivory-handled sword. "How large is your army?"

"Large enough to protect the kingdom's northern border from the Roman Empire." Akinidad smiled.

"You must have over fifty thousand men!" Terenkiwal yelped.

"No, my son. The general's army is no larger than seven thousand men, from what I understand. He is the commander of the Kerman forces."

Terenkiwal glanced up at the general, who gave him a quick wink. "Have you secured lodging yet?" Akinidad asked Naytal.

"Yes, we have, thank you. However, we have not yet seen the vizier, or any other high-ranking governmental official, for that matter."

"Please, let me be the first to apologize for the subpar greeting that you received. I'm sure that the appropriate officials will make their way to you as soon as they are alerted to your presence."

"You are quite right." Naytal chuckled. "We are here unannounced. In fact, I would like to avoid anything that resembles a royal reception or dinner."

"I understand, Your Highness," Djabal answered, bowing slightly. "I will pass the word along."

"Djabal, before you do so, why don't you escort Paqar Terenkiwal to the armory here in the dufufa. Perhaps he would like to inspect the cache of spears and catapults that we have."

Terenkiwal quickly looked up for his mother's approval. Naytal nodded and watched the two leave the room.

"You have a fine son. I didn't realize that he would be so tall for his age."

Naytal smiled. "Actually, though he is my son, he is not a paqar. Only the son of a kandace is considered a paqar. Terenkiwal will never be in line to sit on the throne."

"That bothers you?"

"Every mother wants the best for her son. I am no different."

Akinidad nodded respectfully. "If it is any consolation, my mother was instrumental in molding me into the man I am today. She saw a potential in me that no one else could, not even my father. She refused to let me settle for anything other than the vision that filled her heart."

"I see," Naytal said. She turned toward the window and exhaled sharply. She wasn't used to being alone in a room with a man whose presence dominated the scene and shoved her own aside. "This is so strange. If the vizier is not available, then the peshte should come and greet a member of the royal family . . ."

"You are absolutely right. Again, I offer my apologies for the awkward situation. However, if you are up to it, please allow me to give you a brief tour of the administrative center."

Naytal had been nearly completely drained from her long excursion, but something about Akinidad's persona charged her with a renewed excitement that she hadn't felt in ages. "Very well, General. I am up to it indeed."

※　　　※　　　※

A crisp blue sky was the first thing that came into Sahlin's sight. He made his way down the stairs from the complex that housed the baths used by governmental officials and other noblemen. As usual, the streets of Meroë were congested with a sea of humanity—most of which was headed to or from the great bazaar adjacent to the city.

Unlike his weary soul, Sahlin's body felt at total ease, a by-product from the two hours that he had just spent in the baths. Both his face and head were shaven clean, and his skin was smooth and soft as a result of the mixture of Eastern oils used by the bath attendants.

He progressed down the street, purposely avoiding eye contact with the people. He didn't want to betray that he was aware of an impending strife that would likely envelop the beautiful city and drench its streets with blood.

He watched the masses flow past him.

Insanity! If they only knew what was coming.

He was almost moved to tears as he saw a family of five fight to remain together as it maneuvered through the crowd. The blissful expressions on their faces declared that they had no knowledge of the treachery at work behind the walls of the administrative dufufa.

Father, mother, son, daughter, daughter. They joined hands to form a singular cord of love and trust. He envied them. He envied the ignorance that went hand in hand with their innocence. Most of all, he envied that none of them was alone.

As if to avoid frightful scenes from a bad dream, Sahlin turned his head and sped up his pace. His eyes wandered aimlessly through the faceless crowd until he came upon a familiar one that for an instant blew away the dark cloud overshadowing his deepest thoughts.

"Imani." He elevated his voice over the crowd. She paused and gave him a warm but cautious smile.

"Where are you heading?" he asked before thinking.

"To that wonderful bathhouse."

"I just came from there," he said, stepping out of the way of two and then three more passersby.

In the moment that she held his awkward gaze, at least six people obstructed her view. She thought about asking a question but decided against it. "Enjoy the day, Sahlin."

"Imani," Sahlin called after her as she started to walk away, "I'll walk with you."

When they arrived at the bathhouse's base, Imani stopped short and started to look around.

Sahlin fought off the desire to ask her whom she was expecting. "Do you know if they are scheduling to build one of these in Alondia?" he asked, regarding the great stone bathhouse.

Imani threw him a quick, uneasy look. "There's already one there. It's not as fancy as this one is, though."

"I can't imagine being in a city without one. This one may not be as elaborate as those in Roman Egypt, but it still has . . ." Sahlin's voice trailed off when he realized that Imani wasn't even listening to him. She was still peering around for her mysterious friend.

"Imani," he called and waited until she turned his way. "Imani, I feel bad about the last time that we spoke. By the river, I mean."

She laughed, her beautiful mouth forming a sarcastic grin. "Are you still trying to apologize to me, Sahlin Malae?"

"Yes . . . yes, I am. I offended you."

"There's no need." She shrugged. "You said what was on your heart. I can at least appreciate your honesty."

"Sometimes being honest isn't very prudent."

Imani was taken back by his humble tone of voice.

"Perhaps not. But most of the time, it is very considerate and . . . preferable."

In an instant, Sahlin recalled the many times that he was neither wise nor considerate when it came to her. Before he knew it, he was waist-deep in regret and conviction. Before he could respond, Imani turned and greeted someone else.

"There you are. I was starting to wonder if the two of you had gotten lost." Two teenage girls strolled up to Imani and innocently batted their eyes. Sahlin recognized them as two of the three who had performed at the banquet held in his honor.

The two girls were engrossed in a conversation of their own and had to be reminded by Imani to greet Sahlin. "T'Sheba, Ma'laa, please pay your respect to the grand vizier."

The girls responded and turned his way. Ma'laa greeted him with a deep bow and an even deeper flirtatious gaze. However, T'Sheba offered a slight nod, rolling her eyes away from his general vicinity. Imani was relieved that Sahlin hadn't noticed the disrespectful gesture. She made a mental note to scold T'Sheba for her lack of discretion.

"Enjoy your time in there," Sahlin said. The two scurried up the stairs and into the complex.

"Your niece is altogether lovely, Imani."

"Maybe so, but she has her moments."

"Let me guess—boy problems?"

"I wish. It's more like man problems. She acts so grown-up."

"That's probably because she is. She has to be what, sixteen, seventeen years old?"

"Seventeen in another month." Imani sighed, suppressing a sharp jolt of pain from her midsection.

"What is it?" Sahlin asked.

"Back spasms. Must be my old age."

"Or the teenage niece. What does her fa—"

"Grand Vizier Malae," called a young man clad in a robe worn by dufufa messengers. "Elder Makal respectfully requests your immediate attendance in an urgent meeting that convenes within the hour."

Fully aware he had just received what amounted to a polite order from a ruthless man, Sahlin nodded in acknowledgment.

"I have to go anyway," Imani said, chancing a glance into Sahlin's face. "But, if you ever have the time, there is something very important that I have to speak with you about."

"Whenever you like." He gave a brief smile then departed with the messenger.

❦   ❦   ❦

Naytal's legs were burning, and she was completely out of breath. "How much farther, Akinidad?"

"Not much farther."

"You said that an hour ago."

"Come now. It hasn't been that long."

"It feels longer." She grunted to herself. As frustrated as she was, her body ached all over and left no room for anger. Besides, she had only herself to blame for her current predicament. What started out to be a tour of the Kerman administrative complex had slowly evolved into a tour of the city and surrounding regions. Akinidad had been nothing but a gracious and considerate host, at times imploring her to rest. She constantly declined his offers and *commanded* him to show her more.

At her request, he showed her the almost five-hundred-year-old wall that provided protection for the city of Kerma. Their journey continued on horseback to the hilly outer tract of the area just east of the city.

When they reached a peaceful section of rolling hill, they abandoned their horses and started on foot. Naytal spent most of her time following Akinidad, who she reasoned had to be in excellent shape.

"Kerma is a lovely region," Naytal huffed, "but why is it that we have to continue to climb this hill?"

"The sight that I wish to show you is best seen at the apex of this hill."

Naytal nodded and pushed on, doing her best to conceal her fatigue. She abated her mounting irritation by imagining the valley's picturesque view that had to lie on the other side of the hill.

When she finally reached the top, she instinctively looked back on the path that they had taken. The slope actually didn't appear to be as steep as it felt.

"I was debating whether or not to bring you up here. But the gods impressed upon me that it was the appropriate thing to do."

"This does provide one with an excellent view of the city," she replied, noting how the city's dufufa bathed in the late afternoon sun like a swan. "It almost looks like . . ."

"No. Look this way."

Naytal turned his way. Immediately, her eyes drifted past him and into the vast valley below, where the bulk of his army rested. The camp seemed to stretch out into eternity. "Those are your men?"

Akinidad nodded like a proud grandfather.

"There are so many of them."

"Twenty thousand, give or take a few hundred."

Naytal smiled and nodded coyly. Though instinct alerted her to be cautious, she was reluctant to raise her guard. "Very impressive. However, I don't recall hearing my brother ordering such a high concentration of troops in this region."

"He did not. I did."

"Were you carrying out the vizier's orders?"

"Carachen gave no such orders, because he has been dead for well over a month."

A chill of fear crept through Naytal's body that strangely enough excited her.

"I am curious. Is it customary for the qeren's sister to be informed of troop placement?"

Naytal slowly turned her back on him and studied the massive Nubian war machine that lined the horizon. "Such is not the custom. But I make it a point to be aware of such things. I have sources that help keep me abreast of standard military protocol—to a degree."

"I see," he answered, grasping the handle of his sheathed sword.

"Since I have no idea what your intentions are, I'm going to be bold. Why did you bring me up here?"

"Look at me," he commanded. When she complied, the first thing that she noticed was the fire in his brown eyes. "I brought you up here to see the angry future. Down below are men who are convinced that your family's reign over the kingdom is ready to come to a conclusion. The vizier and his administration did not share that view. Therefore, they have all paid the price. The force that you see consists of the combined armies of Kerma, Nobatia, and several other tribes."

"I don't understand," Naytal said.

"Do not feign ignorance. You have already demonstrated

365

that you are not the type of woman to go without knowledge." He closed the gap between the two of them. "Our past conversations suggest that you possess a great deal of awareness. What I would like to know is just how aware are you?"

Somehow, Naytal knew that her life depended upon how she responded to the cryptic question. She held his searing gaze without flinching, all the while beseeching Isis for the proper answer.

Akinidad's hand inched back up to the handle of his sword.

"Surely you must know that any plan to invade the Isle of Meroë would never work. The southern armies are far too strong."

"Those are things that I already know."

"Do you really? Then, why have you amassed such a force? It is clear that you intend to attack."

"What do you know of my intentions?" he snapped, drawing even closer to her. "Your family has never understood the needs or wants of the northern provinces. They would sell us all off as slaves to Rome in order to fill the treasury. But now I believe that it's time for you to understand that our needs will become known, and we will take what we want."

With that, he slid his arm up her back and forcefully drew her head up to his lips. He kissed her savagely as his fingers massaged the back of her head. Unaccustomed to being overpowered, Naytal resisted momentarily. Her struggle was short-lived as she gradually succumbed to his powerful magnetism. She drew him closer and clung to his muscular frame.

Akinidad withdrew from the kiss and waited for her to speak.

"I have more love for death than I do for my brother or his wife," she breathed, gazing deep into his eyes. "However, you'll never defeat the south unless you first kill them, the grand vizier, and . . . the Council of Ministers."

"The Council?"

"They are the true power of Meroë. A family does not reign unless it bears the Council's seal. Although he is appointed by the king, the selection of the grand vizier must first be confirmed by the Council."

Akinidad stared at her blankly. "By what authority does the Council enforce its resolve?"

"There is a very strong division of the southern army that is primarily loyal to the Council." She read the perplexed look in his dark eyes. "Though very few know it, this is the way that the rulers of Meroë have been selected since the days of Tarahaq."

Akinidad released her and then gazed at his army. A flock of vultures off in the distance caught his eye. No doubt they were circling a dead or wounded animal.

"You are part of a family that has betrayed the trust of the northern provinces. When you arrived in Kerma, I was certain that I was going to have to kill you."

"Since I still breathe, what has changed your mind?"

"Your son . . . and your lips."

"My words . . . or my passion?"

The smile Akinidad offered was genuine and devious.

"As I said, I have no love for my brother. He fills me with loathing. But he is merely a figurehead. Any attack that you mount would have to be aimed at all three levels of government. That is, of course, if change is what you are truly after."

Akinidad grunted and looked away. As he did, Naytal

breathed a minute sigh of relief, sensing that the threat to her life had abated for the moment.

She looked back down the hill towards Kerma. Suddenly, a colorful flower captured her gaze. She stooped down to examine the lovely purple-and-yellow blossom. It resembled the type of flowers Tshenpur, Melaenis, and she used to receive from young men who once courted them years ago. However, she knew better.

"This is mandradi," she said, fondling the inviting flower.

Akinidad did not respond.

"This is extremely poisonous. So poisonous that . . ." Her mind zipped through a dozen different scenarios in the fraction of an instant. A divinely inspired thought entered her mind.

She stood up and walked over to the brooding general. "Akinidad, I believe that I know a way to supplant King Harmais and Grand Vizier Sahlin without a military campaign."

🐞　　🐞　　🐞

Sahlin stormed through the halls of Meroë's central administrative dufufa.

Bakka could hardly keep up with him. "My lord, is there a problem?" Sahlin stopped, frustration etched all over his face. It was a look that Bakka had grown accustomed to seeing after Sahlin had been with Makal and Rogo and other members of the Council.

"They are sending me to Napata for five weeks!"

"Napata?"

"They said that Harmais actually approved of the prolonged mission. They are up to something." Sahlin glared down the hallway. "I'm going to find out what it is."

Like an unrelenting shadow, Bakka followed Sahlin as he marched through the city to the palatial quarter. Sahlin ordered Bakka to remain in the hall as he entered Harmais's personal chambers.

"That look on your face must mean that the Council has given you your orders to venture to Napata," Harmais announced, remaining out of Sahlin's sight.

"What's going on, Harmais? They said that you approved of it."

"They thought of it. I merely suggested that you stay the five weeks to assist the new vizier in organizing his administrative team. The temples in Napata are an important source of revenue. Your financial expertise will greatly aid in the . . ."

"That's enough, Harmais! Why are you sending me away?"

Harmais appeared from behind a marble support column. "Simple, my old friend. One of us has to live."

Sahlin shook his head in dismay. "What are you . . ."

"One of us has to live, and I figure that it should be the one who loves Meroë the most."

The two men stared at one another.

"Are you going to attack your own kingdom?" Sahlin asked.

"Of course not. However, I am taking a trip." Harmais pointed toward a rather large duffel on his bed. "I need a small vacation. When you return, I'll make sure that you receive one as well." Harmais smiled and walked over to his dresser. He rifled through a small chest of gold rings and diamond studs.

"Harmais, I don't . . ."

"You know, I prayed to Him again last night. The Christ, that is. In fact, I've prayed to Him every night since you told me about Him next to the pool. Remember?"

Sahlin nodded blankly.

"It's odd," Harmais continued; "I don't feel anything when I pray to Him. I guess that I'm so used to making sacrifices that it's difficult for me to simply talk to a god the way that you described. Do you ever . . . feel anything . . . when you pray?"

Bewildered more by Harmais's disposition than his words, Sahlin tilted his head and blinked. "Yes, I do."

"Peculiar. Perhaps in time, I shall as well. Enjoy your trip, my old friend. May the peace that the Christ has given you sustain your soul."

Chapter 27

Naytal! I expected you to be gone for more than just two weeks!" Melaenis bellowed at the sight of the qar. "I gathered from our last conversation that you were leaving for good."

The two women strolled through a garden park outside of the royal cemetery. The flowers were in full bloom despite the gray sky. They walked until they came up to a stone bench with markings that honored the god Horus.

"It's strange how the gods communicate with us," Naytal was saying as they sat down. "At times, it's as if they are simply ignoring us—mocking our prayers and making sport of our pain. But I've learned something, Melaenis."

"What is that?"

"That nothing just happens. I had almost given up hope . . . No, I had given up hope. I was fully prepared to follow the Nile to Egypt, never to return."

Naytal went silent for a while, roasting Melaenis in curiosity. "Obviously, something changed your mind."

Naytal's dark eyes were blunt and forceful even in the overcast daylight. "I had my doubts that Isis loved me. I had been jilted so many times. In my lowest moment, she gave me a vision."

Melaenis slowly leaned forward.

"I saw a lion bathing in its own blood. Then, I saw a hawk descend from the heavens and consume it."

"I don't understand," Melaenis said softly.

"Neither did I. But, then I saw a leopard snared in a trap. It struggled and struggled until that same hawk again plunged out of the sky and devoured it. It did the same thing to a pack of hyenas."

"A bird of prey slaughtering predators? What do you believe Isis was trying to tell you?"

Naytal gently placed her hand on Melaenis's thigh. "That's the strange thing. I knew exactly what she was telling me. It all happened in an instant, but I knew exactly who those creatures represented."

"Who?"

"I know who they represent, and I know what it is I must do." She stood up and analyzed the steep pyramids that rose up before them in the short distance. "As a small girl and even into adulthood, I never believed I would be buried in there."

Melaenis followed Naytal's eyes. They focused on the midst of the cemetery that served as the final resting-place for the kings and queens of Meroë. Dozens of pyramids and funerary temples dominated the landscape.

"What did Isis show you?"

Naytal appeared to be in a trance. "When they weren't ignoring me, they were mocking me. Now . . . I am the only one left."

Not being able to make out what Naytal was mumbling, Melaenis rose to her feet. "Naytal . . ."

"Melaenis, I will need your help."

"Anything, you know that."

Naytal produced a small pouch from the bag that she was carrying. "How is Jwahir?"

"She's fine."

"You haven't abandoned your dream of her learning to prepare the fanciest delicacies and dishes, have you?"

"No."

"Then, you still have her serve in the royal kitchen at least twice a week?"

"Yes. Yes, I do."

"When does she serve next?

"Tonight."

"Good," Naytal whispered. "Very good."

♜   ♜   ♜

"It has to be over here."

Sahlin took a few steps and surveyed the vast burial ground that lay before him. For the most part, many of the graves were clearly discernible. A great deal of them were designated by chiseled boulders that served as headstones. Though he had not been to the Nuri cemetery in well over ten years, the rouged terrain was starting to look familiar to him.

Bakka quietly followed the grand vizier through the old graveyard. Even if it were only for a day, he was glad to be out of Napata. He actually found trailing Sahlin through an ancient royal cemetery in search of a relative preferable to meandering through the streets of the religious center.

Sahlin's pace sped up as one particular headstone caught his attention. He stooped down to read the inscription, only to sigh and swear under his breath. He looked into the sky towards the sun and determined that his time was growing short. If he intended to make it back across the river to Napata before sundown, he would have to vacate the old cemetery within the hour.

His hopes began to sag as he entertained the thought that he might never locate his grandfather's final resting place. He had been in Napata attending meetings for nearly two weeks. This was the first and maybe only time that he would have a chance to visit Rahman Malae's graveside.

Bakka noted the intense look of disappointment on his employer's face and slowly walked beside him. Just as he started to speak, Sahlin dashed away. He watched him kneel down next to a moderate-sized stone planted next to a tree.

"This is it," Sahlin whispered. He ran his fingertips along the contours of the inscriptions, chipping out the dirt and sediment that had built up over the last twenty years.

Bakka moved reverently behind him and softly read the words. "Even though I walk through the valley of the shadow of death, I fear no evil, for You are with me. . . . You prepare a table for me in the presence of my enemies. . . . Goodness and lovingkindness will follow me. . . . I will dwell in the house of the Lord forever."

Sahlin lowered his head and allowed his thoughts to roam freely through his collected memories of his grandfather. "He was such a man of conviction. Such a man of honor."

"Such men belong buried among the kings," Bakka said. Though he had never met the legendary Rahman Malae, the reverence attached to his name was more tangible than a towering pyramid.

Hearing his words, Sahlin looked around the silent, dry graveyard. His grandfather had been one of the last nonroyal individuals interred there.

"Those words on the stone—where are they from?" Bakka asked. "They do not sound familiar."

"They are a portion of something called a psalm."

"A psalm?"

"Something similar to a song of worship or praise. A way that a person expresses his feelings to the Lord."

Bakka clasped his hands behind his back. "Is it similar to the chants uttered by the priests in the Temple of Amun?"

"Yes . . . no . . . no, not at all. According to the holy writings, the Lord God cares for His people and provides for them. In return, they . . . we give Him praise and worship Him as the One true God."

"Your grandfather was a very special man. You wanted to make him proud."

"He was more than special." Sahlin stared down at the dirt covering Rahman's remains. "He . . . he was a man of faith and hope. He was able to give that to others. I just didn't understand at the time."

"Understand what?"

Sahlin rose to his full height, yet kept his head bowed. "I didn't understand what it was he was trying to give. I couldn't comprehend the hope that he clung to with such conviction. He kept writing and talking about the Messiah. His faith was so strong."

"You share his faith . . . about this Messiah?"

Sahlin acknowledged the question with a slight nod. "Every day that goes by, I grow to understand the Messiah's mission more."

"Mission?"

"The purpose behind His death on the cross. But more importantly, the miracle of His resurrection from the dead."

Bakka nudged a stone around with his foot as he pondered Sahlin's statement. As Sahlin's personal bodyguard, he had overheard many things; however, the talk of death and resurrection prompted him to believe that he must have missed something. "My lord, you mean to say that this Jewish Messiah is as powerful as Osiris?"

"Osiris is but an idol, the fertile idea of a man now dead for thousands of years," Sahlin stated in a blunt yet respectful manner.

"The same could be said of the Jewish God, my lord."

"It could be said, but it wouldn't be true." At that moment, Sahlin's heart filled with words that seemed to cascade from an invisible waterfall. "The Messiah is more than a myth carved upon the stones of time. He is a promise that was whispered into the hearts of countless thousands since the beginning of time. Men like my grandfather waited. They hoped and prayed that they would see the day that the Messiah would come and fulfill the promise."

Bakka's heart grew heavy, weighed down by an inexplicable guilt that intensified as Sahlin spoke. "What is . . . this promise?"

At first, Sahlin squinted, not exactly sure what Bakka was asking. Then, like the rising of the sun, the words came to him. "To bind up the brokenhearted, to set the captives free."

"Free from what?"

"Darkness, despair." Sahlin's lip quivered as his voice faded. "From the dark evil that lurks in the heart of all men."

The words, though soft and meek, nearly drove Bakka back against the large stone grave marker behind him. They brought with them images of every hardened and brutal act that he had ever committed. His customary stern facade hid the frightened little boy that he had become.

Neither one of them said much after leaving the cemetery's confines. Both men fought desperately to maintain the image of total emotional stability but failed. Each sensed the inherent weaknesses of the other yet silently agreed not to address them.

A crowd of locals heading in the opposite direction marched past them. Bakka asked one of them if they had just made their way up from the port. When the local confirmed his speculation, Bakka turned to Sahlin with apprehension starting to fill his eyes.

"It looks like we may have missed our ride back across the river."

"Surely there has to be another boat making the trip," Sahlin replied.

"According to them, the last one just departed. They said that the captains don't like to cross in the dark."

It was just the situation that Sahlin was hoping to avoid. Though he was in no great rush to return to the idolatrous environment of Napata, he had very little desire to commence a search for lodging in rural Nuri. "Let's continue down to the port anyway. There's bound to be something down there that can take us back across."

They continued down the beaten dirt path that

wound past a series of huts and mud-brick houses. The sun was nearly gone, and not a soul walked their way from the port's direction.

Eventually, Sahlin embraced the inevitable and started looking for a person to inquire about lodging. For a while, no one was in sight until a man and woman walked their way from another path that fed into theirs.

"Sir, do you know if there are any boats departing to Napata this evening?" Sahlin asked after greeting the two.

"I'm sorry, but the only boats departing at this time are owned by fishermen."

"Do you think they would be interested in taking us across? We can pay them beyond the normal rates," Sahlin added, straining to see the man's face in the dying twilight.

"I don't know whether or not they would be interested, but I can't necessarily speak for them," the man replied. The woman at his side whispered something in his ear and rubbed her arms fervently. "Yes, of course," the man replied.

"Thank you for your assistance," Sahlin said, already pondering their limited options.

"The ferries will resume at the crack of dawn. Your best option is to find lodging for the evening. Do you have a place to stay?"

"No, we don't. Can you recommend a place?"

The man started to point up the road but drew back his finger. "You can lodge with us for the evening. Our home isn't that large but we welcome you nonetheless." The woman whispered in his ear once again. "It will be fine," he assured her. "It's the least we can do for a man who saved our lives a while back."

"Who are you, sir?" Sahlin asked.

"I'm not surprised that you don't recognize us, especially since the sun is going down. Besides, you must meet so many people. It is I, Dikembul, and my daughter, Annika. We would be honored to have you spend the night with us. Our home is right down this road."

🐞   🐞   🐞

"This will not stop the bleeding, but it will at least ease the discomfort," the physician informed Imani. She accepted the pouch of medicinal herbs and examined it. The dry leaves gave off a pulpy scent that made her squirm.

"Ingest the herbs by mixing them with fruit or even a drink," he ordered.

The medicine's objectionable odor prompted Imani to consider a third option. "Last time we met you mentioned that a certain combination of herbs might successfully cure the condition altogether."

The physician's ever-sullen expression only seemed to harden. "Your condition is very rare," he said, recalling the lumps that he felt on Imani's otherwise flat abdomen. "I have only seen it twice before in my twenty years as a physician. Both cases ended in fatality. I'm sorry if I misled you into believing the medicine that I described had any serious possibility of curing you."

Imani's heart fluttered as she imagined embracing the cold specter of death that slithered closer to her every week. "No, it's not your fault. I suppose that I heard what I wanted to hear."

The physician shook his head slowly. "I'll never blame a person for having hope. Perhaps the gods will . . ."

A knock at the door sounded through the examination room. Before the physician could answer, the door

379

cracked open just enough for a man to deliver an urgent message.

"Physician, come quickly! The king has fallen ill!"

🐞   🐞   🐞

Bakka reclined on the couch and rubbed his stomach sluggishly. "That was the best meal that I've had in two weeks! How did you make it so quickly?"

Annika glanced his way and smiled but didn't answer.

"I must agree," Sahlin added, pushing himself from the table. "This was excellent. The lamb meat literally fell from the bone. How did you manage to make it so tender in such a short amount of time?"

"The meat has been soaking in a special blend of spices," Annika answered as she scurried around clearing the table.

"By the gods, she knew that we were coming," Bakka blurted.

Annika shook her head. "No. I actually have a dozen portions of lamb marinating in the spices since this morning. I'm preparing it for a feast tomorrow evening."

Sahlin glanced across the table to Dikembul with a look of concern. "Dikembul, we don't want to impose."

"You won't be, my friend," Dikembul assured. "Besides, I wish that it actually were a feast."

"With a dozen portions of lamb, what else would it be?" Bakka commented, struggling to his feet. "Oh! I've eaten too much. I need some air." Sahlin raised an eyebrow in amazement as his overstuffed bodyguard quickly left the house, leaving him alone with two almost complete strangers.

"My daughter insists on making a large meal for the

men who come over and do research with me once a week."

"Research? What is it that you study?"

Dikembul deflected the spear of wariness that the question produced. "At least four times a month, a dozen or so members of our masjid gather together to study portions of the Torah."

"Really?" Sahlin said, perking up. "Any subject in particular?"

"Messianic prophecies. Anything that deals with the signs of His coming."

Sahlin's stomach started to tighten. "Have you come to any conclusions?"

"We have, but they have not been endorsed by the elders of the masjid. Therefore, we cannot proclaim it as truth among the congregation."

"I understand." Sahlin briefly thought about the parcels of truth that his allegiance to one faction or another prevented him from distributing to those whom it would benefit. "If I might ask, what have your conclusions led you to believe about the Messiah?"

Dikembul fiddled with the fruit that his daughter had placed before him. "Based on the studies of the Scriptures, we believe that God has revealed the Messiah in the person of a man named Jesus from a town called Nazareth in Judea."

Sahlin leaned back. To his surprise, he was on the verge of tears. "Jesus."

Dikembul glanced away. "We debated and debated, but that's who the Scriptures led us to. Many find it hard to believe that some obscure man from forlorn Judea could be the long-awaited Messiah, but truth doesn't care about public opinion."

"No," Sahlin breathed as he watched a portion of his life come into focus. "I don't suppose that it does."

"To be honest, the entire matter has caused a split in the masjid. It's gotten bigger than I ever thought it would." The twinge of regret laced in Dikembul's words did not go unnoticed.

"You can't blame yourself for people wanting to have something to place their hope in. Place truth in front of people, and they will eventually be lured in by the refreshing odor that it produces. If Jesus is the Messiah, then people will be drawn to Him despite what the elders of the masjid or the temple priests say."

A comforting silence filled the room that caused both men to relax. Each one of them focused on a different object in the house, only occasionally glancing at one another.

Then, their eyes met and locked.

"You've heard of Jesus?" Dikembul questioned.

"Before we ran into you this evening, we were in the royal cemetery. My grandfather is buried there." Sahlin paused to reflect for a moment. "He was one of those who waited with great expectation for the Messiah. In fact, he died waiting, hoping, and believing that the Messiah would come and bring some form of salvation to the world. He tried to tell me . . . he tried to . . . impart it to me. But I just didn't understand it at the time."

Dikembul nodded instinctively, thinking about the men from Galilee who spurred him in His search for truth. "God is a master at providing voices that point us into a certain direction. He is wise. He knows that those voices will eventually lead us to Him."

"For me, it was a voice in the desert. One lonely voice that somehow opened my ears to the chorus that my grandfather sang to me as a boy." A single tear ran down Sahlin's cheek. It was soon followed by three others, but Sahlin didn't care. "I believe as well, Dikembul. I believe Jesus from Nazareth is the Messiah and perhaps much more. Much more."

"So do I," Dikembul whispered boldly.

Connected by an awesome sense of providence, the two men silently wept together. Both men pondered their personal experiences that led them to the revelation of the Christ and expressed their gratitude to God for the benevolent moment.

"My life," Sahlin started, still shuffling through his thoughts. "I feel as if my life is just starting, as if I've been born again. Everything that I've done, everything that I've accomplished . . . it all seems so . . . vain." The image of the parched ground that covered his grandfather's bones haunted him. "My grandfather . . . I feel as if . . . I feel as if I have started the journey that he only dreamt about. A journey that will . . . a journey . . ."

Sahlin rose and walked into the living room. Two large wooden masks decorating one wall caught his attention. The masks were similar in style and color yet bore differing expressions. He was amazed at how much of himself he saw in the lifeless, unfulfilled decorations. How many masks had he worn in his lifetime? Two? Three? Seven? How many lives had he lived to earn and maintain the masks that he wore?

"A chosen vessel," Dikembul said, suddenly standing behind Sahlin.

"A what?"

"When a master potter creates an exceptional piece of work, he takes his time and crafts it more carefully than he would the others. After he completes it, he places it in a drawer or locks it away in a closet. Sometimes, it can remain there for years. Eventually, an individual enters the store with a specific need in mind, wanting the very best. Knowing that the potter keeps his best work hidden, that person will ask for a chosen vessel."

Though it was Dikembul speaking, Sahlin heard his grandfather's voice completing a sermon that he started over twenty years before.

"The potter will then select the appropriate vessel from his hidden locker and take it to the counter. Once there, he turns the vessel upside down and inscribes his name upon it, acknowledging that he created and selected that particular vessel, and that it is ready to be placed into service."

"You believe that I've been selected and set aside for something?"

Dikembul's humble smile warmed Sahlin's heart. "It appears that you already know that. What you must determine now is what sort of vessel you will be."

Sahlin narrowed his eyes, trying to comprehend.

Dikembul walked back into the kitchen and stood next to two large clay jars. "In any house, there is a vessel of honor that contains clean and pure water. There is usually also a vessel used to hold the wastewater like this vessel here. It contains the leftover fragments from tonight's meal. It is the vessel of dishonor. I will take it out and discard its contents sometime tonight."

Sahlin stepped into the small kitchen and studied the large containers. He could smell the stench that arose from the vessel of dishonor as Dikembul removed its lid.

"God has given you a great position and has chosen you to abide in a great house. You must choose which vessel to be—one of honor or of dishonor."

Chapter 28

Harmais was dead.

An eerie calm swirled through the chambers that held the king's lifeless body. Tshenpur stood at the foot of her husband's corpse choking back burning tears of frustration, fear, and rage. Harmais had been dead for two days, but she wasn't at all surprised by the lack of grief she displayed. Her mind was far too absorbed with the various administrative duties that had fallen into her lap.

She gazed into Harmais's lifeless face and envied the strange peace that seemed etched upon it. She was puzzled. More than any time that she had known him, he finally appeared to be at rest. Life had filled him with a devious hate that death had somehow detached.

Several servants finished the final touches to the embellished bedspread that draped his body. In keeping with custom, his body would lie in state for two more weeks before being entombed. Sadly, she doubted that her husband's funeral would garner a great deal of fanfare similar to his mother's or his brothers' funerals. At the end of the day, she knew that Harmais's reign would simply be a brief footnote doomed to be forgotten rather quickly in the registry of the great kings of Nubia.

She cursed under her breath as she had done for the last two days. "How dare you leave me!"

Her indignation quickly turned towards the gods. It was accompanied by a demand for answers that she knew she would not receive.

Although she tried to hide it, she was racked with anxiety. She knew that her front would crumble completely if Sahlin Malae did not hurry up and return to the capital. The day that Harmais died, she dispatched a messenger to Napata where the grand vizier had been sent on an inconsequential extended mission. She could only pray that Sahlin had received and read the urgent message that morning and was at that moment racing back to Meroë. Above all, she would need his assistance to articulate her authority as kandace.

The two servants looked up and bowed deeply. Tshenpur noticed the gesture and quickly ascertained that it was not for her.

"Leave us," commanded a voice from the shadows.

When the two had departed, Tshenpur shook her head in disdain. "I was wondering when you would slither in, Naytal. I was hoping that it would be a time when I wasn't present."

"He was my brother, Tshenpur. Thus, I had a greater reason to hate him."

"How dare you speak in such a manner!" Tshenpur turned around to see that Qar Naytal was not alone. "Who are these men?"

"That isn't important at the moment," Naytal remarked as she walked over and studied her brother's remains. "About as much of a man in death as he was in life, wouldn't you say?"

"I would say that you are out of line and that you are not welcomed." Tshenpur clenched Naytal's shoulder abruptly. "Leave."

"No."

Anger gripped Tshenpur. "Very well, Naytal. You have asked for and deserved the penalty that you will receive."

"What penalty is that?" Naytal slapped the queen's hand away from her person. "I find it hard to believe that we were once friends, Tshenpur. Do you remember that?"

Tshenpur stood silently by. She was shocked by the qar's blatant insolence.

"Do you remember when we were girls, maybe thirteen or fourteen years old? My father once told us about the importance of loyalty and remaining true to your friends no matter what."

"From what I recall, he also mentioned that friendship was always subservient to allegiance," Tshenpur sneered, preparing to walk out.

"You remembered. I'm most impressed. Too bad you never put it into practice. Now you are the one who must pay the penalty."

Tshenpur rolled her eyes and started to march toward the door. Before she could take two steps, one of the men stepped out of the shadows and blocked her path. The man wore a black-and-red kilt and body armor. She knew instantly that he had to be a soldier but wasn't familiar with the insignia on his black leather breastplate. "Out of the way," she commanded.

The man did not move.

"Out of the way! Your queen has given you an order; now move!"

The man simply glared down at her like a bird of prey ready to devour a field mouse.

"Like myself, Commander Djabal no longer recognizes you as the queen of Meroë," Naytal announced. She waited to see Tshenpur's stunned eyes well up with fury and hate before she continued. "I trust that it's clear to you that you will not be leaving this room alive."

From a pouch, Naytal produced a small vial of liquid and placed it at the foot of Harmais's bed.

Tshenpur's eyes zoomed from Naytal to the vial and then back. She spun back around to the soldiers. "It's clear that you men are members of the army. You are bound by the laws of the gods to obey the royal family. As the kandace, I command you . . ."

"Tshenpur, they are members of the northern army. If you had any knowledge, you would realize that northerners hate you as much as they hated Harmais, Sherakarer, or Amanitore."

Tshenpur moved away from Djabal. "What makes you any different? You are of royal descent."

"True. But, I have made certain promises. When I am kandace, the northern province shall receive their due consideration."

Tshenpur could smell the odor of her doom. "You killed Harmais?"

"The credit for that goes to a poisonous plant. I merely provided him with it in a form that granted him a quite painful end." Naytal followed Tshenpur's eyes down toward the vial. "It took Harmais a couple of days to die. However, the liquid form of the poison acts much faster than the leaves. You should be dead within half an hour."

"I have no intention of swallowing anything! I'll have you impaled first."

"Very well. I'll give you a choice. You can consume the contents of that vial, or you can be hacked to pieces by the vengeful sword of a northern soldier."

Tshenpur stood austere and silent. If she weren't so frightened, she would have admired the web that Naytal successfully managed to spin. "How will you explain this?"

"Very simple. The queen was distraught at the death of her husband, so she ended her own life in order to be with him for all eternity."

Tshenpur closed her eyes and sighed. Before she knew it, she was wrapped head to toe in a cold shroud of death that slowly constricted her breathing. She craved to live. Then again, she wanted to die. She hungered for vengeance. Yet, she felt like surrendering. She yearned for mercy. However, she wanted nothing more than to curse Naytal into eternity.

Despite it all, she simply wanted to escape. With tears streaming down her eyes, she reached for the vial and brought the kiss of death to her lips.

Chapter 29

The streets of Napata were just as compacted and rowdy as Bakka had left them. What started out to be a half-day trip to the cemetery had evolved into a two-day excursion to Nuri. He was rather disappointed that Sahlin still had business to tend to in the raucous city.

Sahlin pushed through the crowd toward the administrative dufufa. The sight of the gold-and-red structure made Bakka recoil as the mere thought of entering the presence of the baleful priests and governmental ministers crept into his mind. At the last moment, Sahlin veered to the left and led them to a booth that was laden with myriad fruits and vegetables.

After purchasing a small sack of dried dates, they slowly approached the dufufa. They stopped just short of the northern entrance and settled down on a stone bench. Sahlin offered a few dates to Bakka, then ate some himself.

"What am I doing here?" Sahlin whispered.

"My lord?"

"What am I doing here?" Sahlin repeated, gesturing at the grand building behind them. "There has to be more to life than this. Wealth, influence. It doesn't mean anything."

"You've worked very hard to obtain your position, my lord."

"And that is all that I have obtained? Position . . . status? What more is there?"

Bakka crunched a seed with his teeth and ground up the remains. "You have brought honor to your family name."

"My family name was already honorable. I've simply lived off the legacies from my forefathers. The man lying in that cemetery was far more honorable than I. He offered people hope and tried to convey that to others— most of all, his family."

Sahlin's mind fluttered through a catalog of images that showed his grandfather gathering the family and leading them in prayer to the great invisible God. "I've cheated myself, Bakka. I have status and position, but I don't have a family. I have no one to pass down the things that I have learned. I am a failure."

"It wasn't your fault."

"Yes, it was!" Sahlin nodded in compliance with the overwhelming sense of grief that washed over him. "I'm almost forty years old. I don't have a son. I don't have a daughter. I've cheated myself. I've cheated those who loved me . . . Imani."

"I've said it before, my lord. It's not too late for you to . . ."

"I know, but . . . but I have lost something that I will never get back . . . Time, Bakka. I've lost time." Sahlin stared at the towering statue of Apedemack that stood guard over the temple plaza. "Those faithful to Jehovah are supposed to abhor idols. I fashioned one in the back of my mind and paid homage to it every day for nearly twenty years. I was so foolish."

"With all due respect, my lord, it's not my place to say, but it's difficult to understand what you want. You have worked and accomplished more than any man I know. Yet, you debase your achievements as if they were trifle items from a cheap vendor. How can your God give you what you want if you keep changing your mind?"

Sahlin's eyes zoomed at Bakka like Nobatian arrows falling upon desert marauders. There were two instances that he could recall clearly being double-minded—the period of time after his return from Judea and, more recently, now. "Bakka, I feel as if I am caught in between two worlds. Being the grand vizier, bearer of my family's honor and . . . something else . . . I don't know what it is . . . but it *calls* me."

Bakka's eyes were full of a mixture of bewilderment and envy. "You spent many hours alone in the pasture with that man Dikembul, my lord. Perhaps this is all a result of something that he said to you."

Sahlin thought fondly of the time that he spent with Dikembul mending fences and tending sheep. There was something about the simple lifestyle that relaxed his mind and comforted his heart. He felt closer to God. "We talked about many things. Family, faith, love, loss . . . what things we wish to leave behind."

"Leave behind?"

"After death," Sahlin shrugged. He recalled the hours they spent next to an irrigation stream that branched off from the Nile. "As it turns out, the only thing of value that we leave behind is truth. The truth that we pass down from one heart to another." He sighed heavily. "That's why my fathers were so much wealthier than I will ever be. They died passing down truth. I'll probably die passing down nothing more than money and the vices that accompany it." Sahlin couldn't help but picture young Kalibae, his personal disciple of corruption.

Bakka's large mouth sat partially open. "All I have to pass down is a sword. However, it's covered with blood. How can I clean it?"

For the first time, Sahlin heard the hollow pain resonating in Bakka's deep voice. It resounded with regret, sorrow, and fear. He wanted to reach out and touch the wounds that afflicted the man who was sworn to protect him. If truth were the only thing worth passing down, he would offer the only trace of truth that seemed to bring him any amount of peace.

"Bakka, we also talked a great deal about the Messiah. We . . ."

"Grand Vizier Malae!" called out a frantic voice. Sahlin looked up to see a young man clad in a stately kilt. The man also bore the token of the royal household.

Sahlin rose to meet the man who extended a scroll that had been sealed with wax and bore the royal signet.

"An urgent message from the kandace, my lord." Sahlin took the scroll and broke the seal.

"I've been searching for you for a day, my lord. But no one knew where . . ."

Sahlin read the short message and exhaled. It was a long moment before he was able to force air back into his lungs. "Bakka, we must leave immediately. Harmais is dead."

❧   ❧   ❧

Akinidad's arm slipped stealthily around Naytal's waist. He drew her ever closer even as she continued to drone on about the various committees and scribes she needed to meet with. He kissed softly at her neck and even managed to distract her on several occasions.

"Akinidad, we don't have time for this . . . right now." She had the will power to pull away but lacked the strength. She melted in his arms and enjoyed the pleasure that his touch provided.

"Shall I make an appointment?" he asked between kisses.

"Yesss . . . No!" Finally, she pried herself free of his grip. She walked over to the other side of the empty throne room to compose herself.

Akinidad lowered himself into a chair and stalked her with his eyes. "There appears to be a great deal on your mind, my lovely qar."

Naytal stood next to a window and stared down into the courtyard. "There is much to do."

"Speeches to give, appointments to keep, promises to break. A kingdom to build."

"First, I have to make sure that it doesn't split," she replied, rubbing a small gold medallion that her father had given her years ago. "As soon as I'm confirmed as queen, I will have to find some way to unite the kingdom."

"How about a war on Rome?"

"What?"

"Any aggression against the Romans in Egypt would garner you the immediate support of at least the northern tribes and provinces."

Naytal smile wryly and shook her head. "All you think about is war and battle."

"Why not? Kings are simply remembered while great generals and warriors are commemorated. Legacies are forged from the raw materials produced in courageous battles." Akinidad's voice carried across the throne room. "The greatest monuments are hewn from the greatest conquests."

Naytal turned and studied the awesome warrior. Even at peace, he was an intimidating specimen that embodied the essence of conflict under control. She rolled her eyes from his direction and refused to give in to his seductive persona for the moment. "You have a limited frame of mind, Akinidad. At times, I honestly believe that you enjoy war and destruction."

"No more than you enjoy murder."

"Enjoy?" she snapped, spinning back toward the window.

"I saw the expression on your face as Tshenpur took her pained last gasps of air. You had the look of a lioness enjoying the warm flesh of a fresh kill . . . one that she had been stalking for a very long time."

Naytal clasped her hands behind her back pensively. "Tshenpur was evil," she said. An image of the dead kandace writhing on the floor in death's merciless clutches danced through her mind. "She was evil, and the gods demanded that she be removed."

"If that's what the gods told you, then so be it. For a while, I thought it was simply pure hate that motivated you to kill your own brother and his wife, not divine inspiration."

"Don't mock me, Akinidad. Isis favors me. She trusts that I will faithfully accomplish her will."

"My apologies," Akinidad offered. He walked over to a table and poured two cups of wine. "Come, let us drink to Isis's will as well as the execution of another one of her enemies."

Naytal accepted the cup suspiciously. "What do you mean?"

"Yesterday I dispatched a team of men to intercept and kill the grand vizier. I apologize that you will not be able to see him die." Akinidad raised an eyebrow at Naytal's unhinged countenance. "Is there a problem? I thought that you would be pleased."

"Why did you do that?"

"I've listened for weeks about how much you loathe that man."

Naytal placed her cup on a table and went back to the window. "I need him alive, Akinidad."

"What? What for?"

"You just don't understand," she said, in such utter disbelief that she found herself hoping breath was still in Sahlin Malae's body. "He's still the grand vizier. I need him to confirm me as the queen."

"What do you need him to do that for? You are the last surviving member of the royal family."

"Yes, but it doesn't work that way in this situation. My brother bought off the southern armies to support him against the army from Gebel Geili that is controlled by the Council of Ministers. When the final phase of our plan is completed, we will need the grand vizier to influence both armies to stand down and cast their support behind me." Naytal gritted her teeth behind her closed lips. "Without Sahlin Malae, those two armies will clash and destroy themselves."

"That's not too bad of a prospect," Akinidad said. "If that happens soon enough, there won't be much of a southern army left to resist my forces when they arrive."

"What did you say?"

"Seventy-five percent of my men should be advancing past Napata by now."

"Akinidad, what have you done?"

"A general is not a general without his army. I wanted them here for insurance."

"Insurance," Naytal took her cup and sipped at the red wine swirling within it. "I fear the only thing you have insured is a devastating war that will decimate Meroë."

☗   ☗   ☗

Commander Djabal was on the hunt. For nearly a full day, a regiment of twenty-five men and he had prowled through the roads and beaten pathways between Napata and Meroë in search of the grand vizier. His orders from General Akinidad were clear and simple, and he intended to carry them out.

Like a thunderstorm rising from the mountains, the small army of men rumbled down into a canyon in search of their unsuspecting quarry. Operatives in Napata informed Djabal that the grand vizier had departed for Meroë in great haste. The stout warrior calculated that he would find Sahlin Malae somewhere in the lush canyon below. Only two hours before, an advanced scout confirmed his calculations, having spotted the grand vizier and his lone bodyguard watering their horses at a nearby well.

"There's a clearing around that ridge, sir," the advance scout shouted to Djabal as they thundered through the canyon. "They can't be too far ahead of us. We should be able to track them down shortly!"

The soldiers pressed on, trampling bushes and shrubbery in their wake. As they started to round the corner into the clearing, Djabal thought only about reporting to General Akinidad that the mission had been completed and that the grand vizier was dead.

The soldiers roared around the ridge and into the clearing, ready to advance at attack speed.

"What!" Djabal exclaimed, not believing his eyes.

"How can this be?" the scout hollered, nearly choking on his words.

Djabal slowed his company of men down until they came to an ungainly stop. "This is impossible," he muttered in disbelief. "Impossible . . ."

Chapter 30

Shadows fell eastward, and the heat of the day started to abate as the sun began its slow descent into Nuri's western frontier. From atop a hill, Dikembul sat and watched over his sheep that grazed in the valley below. The air was quiet and still, carrying only the mellow sounds of the herd below.

Dikembul loved his perch on the hill. The high place was a sanctuary that allowed him to view life from an elevated perspective. He often retreated there to pray and to seek the face of the Lord. The serenity of the surroundings brought a peace to his soul that he grew to cherish more every time he visited there. Instead of wrestling with the major issues that pressed for his attention, he simply closed his eyes and prayed for wisdom.

Among his flock of sheep stood the young man who ran his business during the time that he spent in Judea and Egypt. Dikembul was extremely proud of the young man, who was slightly younger than Annika. In fact, he was proud of all the young men he employed. He looked at each one of them as if they were sons he could pour all of his experience and knowledge into.

Dikembul caught a glimpse of another man approaching from the east. The man's muscular build and slight limp immediately told Dikembul that it was Nkosi. He sat quietly as his friend hiked up the hill.

"Daydreaming again?" Nkosi asked, slightly out of breath. Dikembul smiled and then focused back on the young man and flock of sheep.

"What brings you here so early? We don't meet for another three hours."

Nkosi took a seat alongside Dikembul. "I know. I was hoping to catch you alone before the others arrived."

"What's on your mind?"

Nkosi leaned over and picked up a stick. He then produced a dagger and started to carve the stick with leisurely swipes. "I heard that you had some rather important house guests for a couple of days."

"Just a couple of men who needed shelter," Dikembul replied.

"Oh, yes, certainly. One of them just happened to be the grand vizier of the kingdom. He's what? Second? Third? Fourth in command?"

"Third."

"Right. Now, how did the third most powerful individual in this kingdom end up sleeping under your roof?"

Dikembul shrugged. "Like I told you, they need shelter for the evening. I was only being hospitable as God commands us to be."

"Annika said that he was the same man who saved our hides in Napata a while back."

"That's right."

"She also said that he was an outstanding person."

Dikembul's eyes rolled toward his old friend, smothered with suspicion. "And?"

"And she also said something else about him . . . something very extraordinary."

"Go ahead."

"She said that he is a believer in the Messiah and that he embraces Jesus as God's chosen Christ."

"He does."

"Dikembul! This is incredible news! Why are you acting this way? Why didn't you tell me?"

"First, I knew that Annika would. Second, Sahlin really opened his heart to me during his time here. It wouldn't be right to discuss it. Besides, I'm certain that there are many others who believe as we do."

"Very well, I agree with you. But we at least have to tell the others when they arrive tonight. I believe that it will really encourage them to know that even members in the highest positions of government believe that Jesus is the Messiah."

Dikembul shook his head pensively. "I don't know. I don't believe that it is right to exploit the fact that the grand vizier shares our views about the Messiah."

"But he does. That will convince others to do so as well. Can't you see . . ."

"Yes, I see, and I don't like it," Dikembul snapped. He composed himself and nervously rubbed his hands together. "Can't you see, Nkosi? You, I, the others, even Sahlin . . . we all came to faith in Jesus because of some nugget of truth that God enabled us to see. We weren't manipulated, tricked, or pressed into doing it. It just

happened, like someone lighting a lamp in a dark room
. . . It allowed us to see better."

Nkosi folded his arms and leaned back. As he pondered Dikembul's words, he discovered a newfound appreciation for the deep well of wisdom his friend possessed. "I see your point. However, I still think that we should mention it to the others tonight, especially in light of what we are planning to do in a couple of days."

Nkosi's words reminded Dikembul of one of the issues that had been pressing on his heart. After weeks of prayer and fasting, Nkosi and he felt led by God to officially break away from the commune of Jews that gathered in Napata. Nearly three dozen people stood behind them and were ready to follow their lead.

Even if it were just Nkosi, Annika, and himself, Dikembul was determined to leave the masjid. The new high priest, Udezae, had already proven to be a closed-minded man who shunned anything that went contrary to his interpretations of the Scriptures. Dikembul had seen enough and was ready for a change.

"This is going to take a great amount of courage," Dikembul said.

"Courage flows from conviction."

Dikembul glanced at Nkosi and smiled. "And conviction anchored in faith is immovable. You've become quite a philosopher."

"Runs in the family."

After they laughed, Nkosi's expression turned grave.

"Dikembul, I was in Napata a couple of days ago, and I ran into Akil. I asked him how things were going with Annika and him, and he . . . he was outraged."

Dikembul drew a sharp breath as Nkosi dredged up yet

another pressing issue. "I told him that Annika didn't want to marry him and . . . I wasn't going to force her into it."

Nkosi nodded forebodingly. "You reneged on a promise . . ."

"How can I promise that which does not belong to me?"

"Dikembul, we've been through this before . . ."

"And we can go through it again. I will not make my daughter live a loveless life with a man who sees her as a possession to be had instead of a woman to be loved."

"Dikembul, that is commendable, but . . . but making an enemy out of Akil isn't wise."

"I don't view Akil as an enemy."

"That doesn't matter. You can hope that he judges you by your intentions, but the fact is that he will judge you by your actions. And you know that."

Dikembul sucked in his lips and growled silently. He knew that Nkosi's words were truthful and most likely prophetic. Akil was on a track to becoming a commander in the elite Napatan guard and could make life difficult if he so chose. Nevertheless, Dikembul put his faith in God. He hoped that the young man would act neither rashly nor impulsively.

"I understand, Nkosi. I understand."

⚜ ⚜ ⚜

The many colorful portraits and ornaments that hung on the walls of Minister Makal's office rattled as Sahlin slammed the door shut to announce his arrival.

Makal had seen murder in a man's eyes before. However, this time he actually flinched with fear when Sahlin stormed into his office. Though his aggressive posture didn't portray it, the grand vizier looked tired and almost haggard.

Makal rose from his seat and feigned a courteous gesture while Tibo and Rogo remained seated. None of them were happy to see Sahlin.

Sahlin glared at the trio of men with a loathing that made each one of them shiver as if a freezing gust of wind slapped them in the face.

"It wasn't our work," Makal declared before Sahlin could unload.

"Both of them!" Sahlin growled. News of the queen's demise met his ears just outside of the city gates. "Dead!"

"It wasn't our work!" Makal pressed, surprised that he was actually defending himself. "Besides, the physicians say that Harmais died of natural causes."

"That's far too convenient! You wanted Harmais dead," Sahlin barked as he inched closer to the group of men. "You wanted nothing more."

"No, Sahlin," Rogo interjected. "We wanted him removed, not dead."

"What better way to *remove him* than to kill him? Are you going to kill me too?" Unable to control his rage, he reached for Makal and slammed him against the wall. The force was enough to cause a weighty black iron mask to crash to the ground.

"Sahlin, stop this," Tibo ordered. "Think about the law. There is no profit for us in murdering Harmais and his wife. None at all. In fact, their deaths complicate matters."

Something about the old man's worn voice coaxed Sahlin's angry hands from Makal's tunic and robes. "What does the law matter? There is no Nubian honor left to speak of."

"The law still matters a great deal," Rogo responded.

"Had Harmais stepped down or been forced to abdicate the throne, we would have been able to select the next ruler. However, because both the king and queen died so abruptly, rulership is transferred directly to the last surviving member of the royal family."

Sahlin felt nauseated. "Naytal."

"The moment that Tshenpur died, Naytal became the kandace," Rogo continued.

Sahlin rubbed his eyes. He wished that he were back in Egypt or even Judea. "Just like that? She's not fit for rulership . . ."

"And we wholeheartedly agree," Makal chimed. "Naytal's ascent to the throne would be an absolute travesty. A downgrade from Harmais if you ask me . . ."

"No one has asked you anything," Sahlin shot.

"Watch your tongue, grand vizier. You still answer to us."

"Makal, I could kill you right now!" With fire in his eyes, Sahlin started to move towards the minister.

"Sahlin, enough of this!" Tibo called. "Due to the current situation, Naytal has even less support than her brother did. In fact, she has basically no support in the Council."

Rogo nodded grimly. "I'm surprised that she hasn't already come to us, especially in light of the developments over the past two days."

"What developments?"

"Haven't you heard?" Makal asked in a sarcastic tone. "There is an army from the north advancing toward the Isle of Meroë."

Sahlin blinked wildly as if he had been slapped. "What army? From which province?"

"All of them, we believe," Tibo said. "This is a full-scale rebellion."

"Rebellion? Who is the leader?"

"We don't know. There have been no demands, no proclamations or dictums."

Sahlin couldn't believe the words coming out of Tibo's mouth. "What is being done about this?"

"It is Naytal's problem," Rogo announced. "She is the kandace. However, the real question is, what do you intend to do, Sahlin?"

"Me?"

"Yes, you are the grand vizier. We control the Geilian forces, but . . . we doubt very seriously if the southern regiments will support Naytal unless . . ."

Sahlin's stomach turned uneasily. "No . . . no, I can't do that."

Tibo nodded in vexation. "Harmais somehow managed to purchase the loyalty of all southern forces. And now, they need a leader."

"I'm not a military commander . . ."

"We don't need you to be," Makal announced. "We simply need you to encourage the southern generals to support the Council. That should eliminate any threat Naytal could possibly pose to us."

"And why would they listen to me?"

"They are military men. They understand the chain of command. Besides, they know that Harmais trusted you implicitly. There is every reason to believe that they will do the same."

Although it sickened him, something about Makal's reasoning made sense to Sahlin. He surveyed the room of men who hid their desperation with an incredible amount of skill. "What makes you men think that I won't take those armies and march against you . . . just like Harmais wanted to do?"

The challenge was met with Makal's sardonic laughter. "I knew that he would suggest it! Sahlin, you are more like us than you choose to believe."

Before Sahlin could retort, Tibo stepped in. "Sahlin, you could very well do such a thing. But we believe . . . I believe you possess the same love for Meroë that your grandfather had. Acting on such an impulse is not in your character."

Sahlin clasped his hands behind his back and tried to formulate a response worthy of Rahman Malae.

A stiff silence filled the office.

"We will take your silence as a note of compliance," Makal said.

Rogo raised his hand to silence his colleague. "We're not as arrogant as Makal would convey, Sahlin. We would like to know where you stand."

"Is it still your intention to install Tibo as the new king?"

"Indeed, it is," Rogo answered in a hopeful tone. "Tibo comes from an honorable house and has a long, distinguished history of service to the kingdom."

Sahlin could taste the bitterness of the morsel that had been portioned out to him. He hated his option but managed to convince himself that he could live with the proposed outcome. Yet, one thing bothered him. "I know that there is evidence that Tshenpur consumed a vial of poison on her own volition, but who found her body?"

"One of Naytal's servants," Rogo said.

Sahlin folded his arms and grunted. "Odd. I never thought she loved Harmais that much . . ."

"Come again?"

Sahlin's head snapped up as he realized that he was thinking aloud. "Oh . . . nothing. I was just . . . thinking about . . ." He started to march for the door but turned back to address the men once more. "Meroë may not endure much longer, but it is greater than any one of us. For that purpose, I'm willing to make a sacrifice for her."

"Where are you going?" Tibo questioned.

"I have to speak with someone."

      🏵   🏵   🏵

Akinidad's controlled fury burned through Djabal's leather breastplate. "This is unlike you, Djabal. Normally, when I ask you to do something, the end results are guaranteed. Now, why is the grand vizier still alive?"

The commander's black face blushed with shame. He still couldn't believe that the grand vizier had outmaneuvered him. "I cannot explain it, my lord."

"Don't tell me what you can't do, Commander. Answer my question."

He stood erect and made eye contact with Akinidad's demanding gaze. "My scouts told me that he was traveling with a lone bodyguard. However, the report was inaccurate."

"Go on."

"I had over twenty men with me, more than enough to accomplish the mission. However, when we caught up with him, he was actually being escorted by over two hundred men on horseback. I can only surmise that he somehow found out we were trailing him."

Akinidad squinted at the commander acutely. "Were they from the southern army?"

"They had to have been, my lord."

"Strange, I would have known if that many soldiers had departed for Napata to escort him back." Akinidad was about to dismiss the entire episode until he noted the look in Djabal's eyes. "Is there something more, Commander?"

Djabal's lips tightened into a thin line as he arranged the words floating through his mind. "I'm not sure where they were from, General. To escape detection, we veered off and lost contact with them for a few hours. Later on, I checked with the hidden sentry that we have outside of the city. He reported that he saw the grand vizier and his bodyguard approach the city. But, they were alone. There was no sign at all of the company of soldiers that we saw."

"They simply doubled back or circumvented the city," Akinidad replied, his mind already exploring a totally different topic.

"They couldn't have. We would have seen them. We weren't that far behind them, General. I asked around, and no one even saw them."

Akinidad's nostrils flared as he studied Djabal. "So this regiment just disappeared?" Djabal averted his eyes from Akinidad's uncaring gaze. "It doesn't matter. It appears that we need the grand vizier alive for the time being. Later on, I will kill him myself."

※   ※   ※

Naytal smiled as she sat and admired her hands. The bright shade of red covering her fingernails glistened almost as much as the golden bracelets adorning her slender wrists. The exotic perfume that tickled her nostrils came from the same bottle that she had given Tshenpur as a wedding present months earlier.

She silently recited a poem that lauded Isis for her grace and favor. Just as she had foreseen in her vision, all of her most vindictive enemies were now dead, save one. Now that last one stood before her.

"You must be overcome with grief for your brother and childhood friend, Naytal," Sahlin voiced in a low tone.

"I have done nothing but grieve these past few years. My father, my mother, my two eldest brothers. Now Harmais and . . . dear, sweet Tshenpur." She purposely diverted her cold eyes from Sahlin's gaze. "I shall see to it that their funeral is a spectacle worthy of their opulent lives."

"I'm sure that they would appreciate such a noble gesture." Sahlin wanted to weep at her cold, sorrowless heart. Her very persona made him feel queasy.

"Is there anything that I can help you with during this time of tragedy, Sahlin?"

"No, I just needed to verify something," he said, starting to turn away. "I will tend to the business of the state while you are in mourning. But you must know that there is an army from the north advancing. I don't know what their intentions are."

"I'm aware of them." She stood up, displaying her lovely red-and-gold dress. "However, it appears that my time of mourning has to be relatively short due to the circumstances. I know that we've never gotten along, Sahlin, but you've served my family well. Your service has been appreciated."

"Most kind of you to say."

"You must understand, though, that as an incoming kandace, I will most likely appoint my own grand vizier."

"The thought had crossed my mind."

"You must understand that it is not a reflection upon your administrative skills. You have served my family well, and by the laws of Horus, I am bound to repay you in kind."

"No repayment is necessary. I only want the kingdom to prosper."

Naytal slid gracefully across the floor up to Sahlin. "Of that, I have no doubt. And . . . I would like to offer you the opportunity to fulfill that desire."

Sahlin didn't care if his eyes betrayed just how much he wanted to squeeze the life from her body. "How may I be of service?"

The door opened, and a lone figure slipped in. The man's attire announced that he was a high-ranking soldier. The man graciously kept his distance and remained just beyond earshot from the couple. Naytal didn't seem to mind that they were no longer alone.

"You may or may not be aware of the law stating that I am now the ruler of Meroë in the wake of Harmais and Tshenpur's untimely deaths. It's a strange twist of fate, but one that I will have to live with."

Sahlin's eye twitched. He suddenly felt murky and unclean, as if he were talking with the devil himself. "What do you want from me?"

"True, the law states that I am the kandace, but there are those who would contend with that. Those individuals need to be convinced. I would like your final act as grand vizier to be my confirmation as queen over this land."

"Confirmation? Why do you need that from me? If the law gives you the power to be queen, then act upon the law. There is no need for someone to confirm something that you can easily take . . . Your *Highness*."

A dark cloud of resentment settled in over Naytal's head. Nonetheless, she remained in total control. It was an accomplishment that Sahlin noticed.

"If there is any legitimacy at all to your claim to the throne, then you have no need for me. But, that's not the case, is it, Your *Royal Highness?*"

A twinge of hurt flickered through Naytal's dark eyes. Compelled by a loathing deeper than the Sea of Hades, she pulled out a dagger of her own. "Perhaps you are right. However, I cannot help but believe that it's what my mother would have wanted."

A muscle in Sahlin's jaw twitched as he clenched his teeth in disgust. He threw her a scowl and turned his back. As he stepped from the room, he sucked in a deep breath of fresh air and prayed for the strength to execute the task that had to be done next.

Chapter 31

The streets of Meroë were uncharacteristically silent and still for a late afternoon. It was a peculiarity that ruffled Bakka. He took long strides to keep up with Sahlin, who hastened from the palace to the Great Round House where members of the Council of Ministers convened.

When they arrived at the Great Round House, they circled its immense perimeter until they came to an opening that led to the chambers housing the council members' offices. They hurried through the entrance and made their way through the dimly lit maze to Minister Rogo's office.

"Something's not right," Bakka voiced.

"I know," Sahlin replied. He had been away from Naytal's presence for nearly half an hour, but he still felt cold and defiled as a result of their meeting. Worse yet, the entire city seemed to be blanketed by a dark veil. It was nothing that he could see or even describe. He just knew that an unseen force was manipulating the very environment that existed before him.

As they reached Rogo's office, Bakka took up a sentry position at the door. There were other guards there as well, but he chose to say nothing to them.

Sahlin was immediately shocked at the scene that met his eyes when he opened the door.

"Grand Vizier Malae, we were just discussing you," Minister Rogo said. He courtly gestured to two powerfully built soldiers who sat in front of his desk. "This is General Kota and General Pot'non. They represent two of the four southern armies in the Isle of Meroë."

The men snapped to their feet and granted Sahlin the salute that his position as grand vizier demanded. Sahlin nodded and then turned his eyes towards Rogo for an explanation.

Sahlin's glare made Rogo visibly uncomfortable. "After Harmais's death, we felt it necessary to open up a dialogue with the commanding officers of the southern armies."

"You neglected to tell me."

"You left Makal's office rather abruptly."

Sahlin looked away and shook his head. He dismissed their blatant subterfuge and prepared to deliver a devastating blow. "I believe that the king and his wife were slain."

"Sahlin, we made it clear that . . ."

"I understood that clearly enough," Sahlin snapped. He noticed the look of relief that zipped across Rogo's face. There was no way that the minister wanted two generals from rival forces to have even an inkling that they could have killed the king. "I just came from Naytal's chambers. As you predicted, she wants me to confirm her as kandace."

"Confirmation? She's smarter than we gave her credit for."

"Yes, but she wasn't alone. There was a high-ranking general there as well."

Rogo glanced at General Pot'non.

"To our knowledge the other two southern generals are overseeing the buildup along the Atbarah river."

The term *buildup* stabbed Sahlin in the side. He forced himself to ignore the fact that a massive campaign appeared to already be in the works. "No. This man was from the north."

"The north?" Rogo fired.

"He wore a gold bracelet possessed only by viziers in Kerma."

"You know this for a fact?" General Pot'non asked. "There are many high-ranking soldiers in the palace."

"I saw the inscription on the bracelet. It is a northern custom to wear it midway up the left arm. It is a sign of rulership in Kerma. This man may be the one responsible for the uprisings in that region."

Rogo rose to his feet and swore like an Egyptian barge captain. "This changes everything."

"Of course, it does!" Sahlin exclaimed. "If this man is linked with the advancing northern army, then it stands to reason that Naytal murdered Harmais and Tshenpur with the full support of the northern provinces."

"Then, our worst fears have come to pass," Rogo sighed. "Above all, we feared most that a third party would emerge and validate her claim to the throne. We were hoping to have the situation under control before something like that could happen."

Sahlin elevated a skeptical eyebrow. "Well, Minister

Rogo, there are tens of thousands of soldiers approaching who probably would like to endorse her reign."

"How could this have happened?" Rogo asked rhetorically.

"How it happened doesn't matter," General Kota announced in a deep, confident voice. "How it will end is my only concern. In light of the grand vizier's information, it is apparent to us that Naytal has acted treacherously. We will never support her. Furthermore, I suggest that we lay aside any of our differences and combine our forces to snuff out the rebellious conspirators from the north."

Rogo hesitantly nodded. "I would have to agree. The Geilian forces will march with you . . . if the grand vizier gives the official order."

Sahlin inhaled methodically and then held his breath even longer. Never in any of his wildest dreams had he imagined issuing the order that would in all probability tear the kingdom apart and fling it into oblivion. It was a fate that would come too soon for Meroë. However, blood had been drawn, and honor had to be satisfied.

"We go to war."

🛡   🛡   🛡

The halls of the Malae mansion were long and cold. The sun had settled behind the hills, leaving the diminished light from small lamps to illuminate the immense home.

Imani didn't need the sun or a lamp in order to find her way through Sahlin's home. Years ago, when Sahlin and she were on better terms, she practically lived there. It didn't surprise her to see Sahlin had done very little in terms of embellishing his portion of the home. A few of the paintings were new, but many of the statues planted along the hallway and in the corners of the large living room had been frozen in those very positions since Sahlin was a young boy.

Imani sat down on a cushioned sofa and rubbed her aching side. At times, she was successful in prodding the agonizing pain away. This time, however, it only intensified.

The sound of footsteps echoing down the dim hall caught her attention. She peered in their general direction and shrugged when Kassa came into full view.

"Imani, are you certain Sahlin is back in Meroë? Like I said before, he hasn't been by here yet."

Imani ran her fingertips along the edge of a cushion. She had been there for nearly an hour waiting for him. "No, several people have told me that he was in the capital this afternoon."

"If you say so. I suppose he has to come home sometime. Can I have one of the servants bring you something to eat? Or another drink perhaps?"

"No, thank you. I suppose that I should . . ."

Her words were cut short by the sound of the front door opening and closing abruptly. The sound of leather-bound sandals beating against the ground marched their way.

"Sahlin," Kassa called to her brother who streaked through the room oblivious to the two women. "You have a lovely guest here."

Sahlin turned around but continued to walk backwards. "Imani . . . I . . . I don't have time." He spun around and hurried into another hallway.

"I'm sorry," Kassa sighed. "You know he'll never

change." She turned to Imani only to see that she was already stalking him down the hall.

Sahlin burst into his study and rifled through a closet. He emerged with a long black box. He retrieved a small key from a container on the shelf and painstakingly worked open the lock.

The first thing that Imani noticed when she entered the room was the thick layer of sweat that covered Sahlin's shaven head. His near-frantic movements declared that something was dreadfully wrong.

"Sahlin, I've been waiting for you."

He continued to pick at the old lock, swearing under his breath. "Not now, Imani. I really don't have the time."

"There is something very serious that we have to discuss."

"Serious? Nothing is more serious than what I have to do! If only you could have understood that years ago." The key slipped out of his sweaty fingers and bounced around several times on the floor. He pounded the table with his fist before retrieving the wayward key.

"I understood it all too well. You were so selfish and arrogant . . ."

"Everything that I did was for someone else," Sahlin snapped, looking up at her.

"Nothing that you did was for anyone else! It was always for Sahlin! Sahlin's family honor! Sahlin's career! Sahlin's . . ."

"Imani, shut up! Harmais and Tshenpur were murdered. While you stand there and cry about how you felt that you were neglected fifteen years ago, there is a hostile army from the north preparing to march on the capital. By this time next week, there may not be a Meroë!"

Imani grimaced as her side was jolted by a searing

pain from within. She opened her mouth to respond to him, but the spasm snatched away her words.

A click popped through the silent room, and Sahlin flung open the box. Moments later, Sahlin revealed a sheathed sword with a gold and ivory handle. He partially drew out the shiny blade and stole a glance at himself in the reflection.

"My great-uncle used this sword in the war against the Semnans and later on against the Romans. He was the greatest warrior in our family history . . . the only warrior."

He walked over to the balcony and took a moment to gaze up at the stars. In a short while, he would be on his way to join up with Makal, Rogo, Tibo, and the two southern army generals. From that point on, his life would experience yet another unlikely transformation.

"You see, Imani, I could never be the things that you wanted me to be . . . a husband . . . a father." His voice revealed an innuendo of regret that stopped at Imani's feet. "My life is linked to this kingdom. As prestigious or as pitiful as it may seem, I'll never be anything more . . . or less."

"You will be that which you choose to be. Good or bad. Honorable or dishonorable."

For a moment, Sahlin found himself back in Dikembul's kitchen examining the contents of the vessel of dishonor. He closed his eyes as the remembered foul odor invaded his nostrils. He wondered just how much he had let himself become defiled that day alone. "I have to go." He moved sluggishly towards the door. "I'm sorry, Imani. Go home to your niece. Go back to Alondia, while you still can."

"Sahlin, I'm dying."

He stopped in his tracks but didn't turn around.

"One other thing. T'Sheba is not my niece, she is my daughter . . . and yours as well."

Sahlin slowly twisted around without taking a breath. "Why . . ."

"Didn't I tell you? I tried. A hundred thousand times I tried. But you made it clear that you didn't want a family. Do you remember what you said that one time in particular?"

Sahlin didn't need her to verbalize it. The infamous scene had been rehearsed in the back of his mind at least once a week for the last fifteen years. It was the cruelest that he could ever remember being with anyone—even a vicious enemy.

"I was pregnant with her at the time. I had just found out. I was going to tell you. Before I could say anything . . . your words, Sahlin . . . they nearly killed me. But, I kept loving you. I kept hoping that you would . . ." She turned her head in anguish and confronted a pain in her heart that was far more agonizing than the one in her side.

Sahlin remained speechless, his verbal assault bombarding his conscience.

"You said that a whore was of more value to you than I was."

"I was a child, Imani . . ."

"You called me a leech, a parasite that needed to be burnt away."

"Imani . . ."

"I did what you wanted me to do. I moved away . . . far away. I went to Alondia and birthed my children."

"Children?"

Imani rubbed her arms as if to offer herself a comforting hug. "I gave birth to twins . . . a girl and a boy."

"A boy . . ." Sahlin breathed, staring aimlessly at the ground.

Silent tears streaked down Imani's cheeks. "He was stillborn . . . but he was so beautiful. He was so . . ." She dropped her head and began to sob uncontrollably. Sahlin rushed to her side and caught her as she started to collapse. She crumbled in his arms and continued weep. "I wish that you could have seen him."

Sahlin was totally numb. He was barely aware of his own breathing as he simply held her.

"But T'Sheba . . . T'Sheba was strong and healthy. Even as a baby, she was strong willed."

"Does she know who I am?" Sahlin asked, his voice cracking with emotion.

Imani slowly drew away and searched his face. "Yes, she knows exactly who you are. She's known since the day that Amanitore appointed you as the chief treasurer. She also knew that you had no desire to be involved with her life."

"Why did you tell her that?" Sahlin demanded.

"I didn't, Sahlin. You did. It was your mandate—you didn't want a family, remember? I had no intentions of subjecting her to such cruelty. I prayed to the gods that you would change. You never did . . . you never did."

He let her go. Images of T'Sheba twirling around and carousing with the men during his banquet soared through his head. Worse yet, the faceless body of a son whom he would never know haunted him. The load of regret that had been heaped upon his back was finally starting to break it.

He looked deep into Imani's eyes and recalled her initial revelation. "You said that you were dying."

"There is some sort of growth that is causing me to bleed. The physicians can do nothing about it. They say all that I have left is a few months, maybe a year at best. I don't even believe that it is that long. That's why I finally had to tell you about T'Sheba. I can only hope that someday the two of you can make things right."

Sahlin lowered his head and walked over to the table. There lay the scrolls that had been the object of his studies for over a year. He yearned for the sense of security and peace that he felt when musing upon the Scriptures. He affectionately traced the contour of the bound group of parchments that made up his grandfather's journal.

"Imani, there is so much that I have to apologize for. My only fear now is that I will never have the opportunity to do it. If I could go back in time and talk to that young fool who was so cruel to you, I would. I would tell him that the life he wants is a corrupt and lonely one. I would tell him that he is destined to become a bitter, unaccompanied man who dwells behind a facade of success and a family name made great by men far more valiant than he will ever be. I would tell him that he is slated to become nothing more than a vessel of dishonor."

He reached for the sword as well as one of the scrolls. He walked over to Imani and gently tipped her chin. "I'm sorry, Imani. You deserved far better than me."

He kissed her gently on the forehead and then left the study.

Imani's legs felt as if they were giving out. She pulled out a chair from the table and sat down. The moment she did, a stifling pain shot up her back, forcing her to release a silent scream. She grabbed for anything that her hands could find while her body was under assault. When she opened her eyes, she found herself clutching the few loose scrolls and a book of old parchments that sat on Sahlin's desk.

Chapter 32

Searing embers popped from the fireplace as another piece of wood exploded under the immense heat of the flame. Although one of the sparks soared through the air and hit Akinidad in the leg, it failed to divert his attention from the report that he received.

"Then, it is confirmed?" the general asked Djabal.

"Yes, sir. Our operatives followed them from the Great Round House to the Gate of Sufra on the east side of the city. We believe that they will most likely proceed to a marshaling place from there, my lord."

Akinidad nodded at the commander, then turned to Naytal. "Generals from the southern armies are meeting with members of the Council. Any comments?"

"It's not totally unexpected," she said, diverting her eyes from his.

"But it's what you wished to avoid. If they join forces with the Geilian forces . . ."

"Yes, I know what will happen . . ."

"Such an accord on their part will nullify the approach of the northern armies." Akinidad shook his head. He wondered if the female mind was even capable of comprehending military principles. "You see, Your Highness, this is why you strike to kill without asking questions."

"My lord, if we hurry, we can still intercept them before they reach their encampments to the east. The cover of night will be a great asset," Djabal reported, anxious to atone for his earlier failure to kill the grand vizier.

Try as she could, Naytal could not mask the expression of unrest upon her face. In order for her plan to succeed, she needed the southern army generals to back her just as they were going to back Harmais against the Council and the Geilian forces. Now that seemed unlikely.

She was quickly running out of options. The only thing they seemed destined for at this point was a horrific bloodbath—something that Akinidad and the disillusioned northern madmen could not wait to commence.

". . . kill them all . . ." Akinidad was ordering Djabal. The commander spun around and proceeded to execute his grim mission.

"Wait!" Naytal called. Djabal came to a halt. "There still may be a way to prevent the southern armies from uniting with the Geilian regiments and prevent a massive battle."

Akinidad stared at her like a jilted lover.

"General, I'll need for you to go with him."

❧   ❧   ❧

The chilly night air whipped past Bakka's face and made him squint like an eagle as he tried to keep his horse steadied on the road leading away from the capital city. The light provided by the yellow moon burning in the black heavens was just enough to make the night ride possible albeit unwise. He clenched his teeth and coaxed his horse to pick up speed.

Sahlin prodded his horse to stay right behind Bakka. With his huge bodyguard directly in front of him, he could hardly make out any portion of the road. Sahlin's heart pumped feverishly as they sped through a desolate region just east of the city.

Though the excessive wind in his face made his eyes water, the condition of his emotions squeezed more than a few tears from his eyes during the ride. In typical Malae fashion, he simply tightened his lips and stiffened his neck. The die had been cast. There was nothing that he could do to alter the path of his destiny. Whatever fate awaited him, he would meet it with as much pride and honor as he could scrape from the bottom of his bankrupt heart.

The farther east they traveled, the lower the profile of the surrounding forest dropped. Bakka slowed and then banked left. From what Sahlin could gather, they were slowly working their way up an incline, avoiding trees and shrubbery all along the way. They didn't ride far before the incline flattened out, and the road began to widen.

They slowed down to a trot until they finally came to a clearing. A short distance away, Sahlin could make out a structure flanked by two obelisks rising silently into the night sky. As they drew closer, the moonlight revealed that the edifice was the crumbling remains of an ancient temple.

"We're here," Bakka announced in a subdued voice.

Sahlin's eyes strained as he surveyed the clearing. "We couldn't have possibly arrived here before them."

"No, they're here. This way."

Bakka led them around the old temple until they circled it once. When they arrived back at their original spot, four dark figures mounted on horses confronted them.

"Rogo," Sahlin called out.

"It is us," the minister replied, leading his party from the temple's shadow.

Sahlin could barely make out Tibo, Pot'non, and Kota in the hazy night light. "I don't see Makal," he voiced.

"We thought it best if one of us remained with the rest of the Council in order to stabilize the situation, if such intervention is needed," Tibo replied.

"And that was his idea?"

"It was his suggestion, but we all agreed to it, Grand Vizier Malae," Pot'non answered. "We must go. It is a long ride to the encampment from here."

As they rode, Sahlin was careful to track the movements of the moon and stars. By his calculations, they had been on the road for at least half an hour by the time they approached the edge of the forest. As the trees and brush thinned out into mere weeds and shrubbery, the terrain transformed into an grueling, barren country laden with hills, rocks, and boulders.

"Beyond those hills is the desert," Bakka yelled to Sahlin above the pounding of the horses. Strangely enough, something in Sahlin yearned for the security that would be provided by the desert's open expanse.

Like bats from a dark cave, they streaked from the shadows of the hills into the flatlands of the desert. Though Sahlin didn't know exactly where they were, he knew the southern army was encamped just beyond the desert's reach that extended maybe another fifteen miles. Their destination was in sight.

※   ※   ※

"We have to give her credit, my lord. She was right," Djabal remarked in utter amazement. "However did she find out they would use this pass?"

"She is as crafty as she is beautiful," Akinidad said, snapping his fingers.

"That makes her extremely dangerous," Djabal said as an archer hurried in front of them.

"Extremely dangerous, and extremely . . . alluring."

"As long as you remain the hunter and not the hunted." Djabal peered down into the dark desert below. From their vantage point, the moonlight gave them a sweeping view of the desert valley bathed in a hazy blue light.

The archer produced a single arrow and lit the tip of it on fire. He mounted the burning warhead and drew it back.

"Fire!" Akinidad ordered. The fiery arrow hissed from the archer's grip and arched across the sky, streaking in the wake of the men who had just emerged from the obscure pass in the hills. Though the arrow had no chance of striking any of the riders in the party, it did accomplish its mission during its fleeting flight.

Knowing that it would take them a while to negotiate down the hill, Akinidad and Djabal started down the path in a leisurely pace. The general was confident that nothing would go wrong.

Bakka sensed that there was something desperately wrong. When he started to turn around to inspect their wake, he snapped his head back again as an object whizzed past his head. He bit his lip and blinked.

Another projectile careened past him, then another, and then another. Finally, one of the missiles struck Rogo in the back, sending him flying from his horse. He hit the ground violently and was trampled by the remaining riders.

"We're being attacked!" Bakka managed to shout.

Sahlin glanced behind him to see scores of black figures descend upon them like demons. From sheer impulse, he veered to the left, away from his companions. His hand groped for his sword.

Though he never got a clear view of one, Bakka determined that the projectiles hurtled their way were miniature battle-axes, sharp enough to pierce pressed leather. His assumption was affirmed when General Kota fell to his death with an axe protruding from his back. Noticing that his counterpart had gone down, Pot'non slowed and drew his sword. Within moments, he was surrounded by dark fiends and hacked to pieces.

Bakka ducked and banked to his left. He had prepped Sahlin for such a scenario during their many contingency drills. He only hoped that the grand vizier remembered what to do next. As he rode away, he heard an agonized scream cut short by the cleaving sound of two or three blades. At that moment, he knew that Tibo had met death.

After banking through the darkness, Bakka peered around his immediate vicinity. He was shocked to see that no one had followed him. He remained still for a moment and tracked the foreboding sound of hoofbeats. However, none of them were approaching him. Then he heard a series of shouts that sounded like orders. He grimaced in anger and spurred his horse back toward the hills.

From what Sahlin could tell, he had evaded the initial band of attackers and was headed in the opposite direction of their last-known position. Though he had lost contact with Bakka, he knew enough to keep a low profile and to seek the refuge of the hills.

Sahlin tried to imagine who it was that had attacked them. Intuition told him it was a band of desert marauders. Such attacks were frequent outside of the capital city. Slave traders even crossed his mind, but he knew better than that.

He was about to explore another option when he heard several horsemen approach him from the rear. He snorted and urged his horse forward. He rode on for a few moments and then came to a complete halt. Dripping with sweat, he surveyed the area with his ears. From what he could make out, he was in a small canyon. Every sound that entered the cleft rattled from stone wall to stone wall.

He wiped the rolling sweat from his eyes and tried to find the contour of the hills against the dark horizon. As he did, he caught a brief glimpse of what appeared to be several men running along the edge of a ridge. He stiffened up and prompted his horse to move along. Aside from the occasional snorting of the horse, the canyon was completely silent.

He pulled his cloak back over his shoulders, wondering if he would ever again see the light of day. He took the moment and allowed himself to think about the words

Imani had spoken to him hours before. A flood of regret stormed through his heart. Even if he did survive through the evening, he would probably never get the opportunity to speak with *his* daughter, though he had no idea what he would say to her anyway. Everything that Imani had said was true—his career and family honor had taken precedence over everything in his life. Even if he had known his daughter, he most likely would have neglected her altogether.

Sahlin's ears perked up as he heard the harmless chirping of several playful birds somewhere in the darkness in front of him. Again, he dropped his head into his hands and rubbed his eyes. He looked into the sky for the moon's position, hoping that it would tell him the hour of the evening. As he studied the heavens, more bird chirping caught his ear. This time, it sounded as if the birds were over his shoulder. When he dropped his eyes to look in that direction, a large dark object struck him across the face, knocking him from the horse.

When he hit the ground, all he could see were stars. Some were those that sat in the black sky, while others were those that existed only in his head. He wasn't sure from where, but he sensed that he was bleeding. It really didn't matter to him because he could feel himself slipping away.

"Here he is, General," he heard a scratchy voice report.

"And he's the only one?"

"The bodyguard is still out there, but we'll secure him before the dawn breaks."

"Very well. The kandace will be pleased. Take him."

Chapter 33

Sahlin had been in many parts of the royal palace, but this was the first time he had ever traveled to the part of it hidden beneath the surface. Years ago, he heard that there was indeed a holding space for prisoners. He later discovered that was a myth. The dungeons were situated clear across the city next to the river. He speculated that the dank chambers were more likely used for storage of food and other goods.

The room was small and featureless. Sahlin sat on the floor and watched the dim lamp flame dance in place as it had for what he assumed to be hours. He had no idea if it was light outside or if even he was going to see the sun again.

He was exhausted and wanted desperately to sleep. He actually dozed off a few times only to be aroused by restless clanging noises just beyond the door. On each occasion, he prepared himself to meet the God that he called his own. But nothing happened. With every moment that passed, he found himself longing for the demise that would set him free from the wretched life his sense of family honor had carved out for him.

Prayer was his soul's only solace.

Lord God, my life is in utter ruin. Please end this. Whatever Your will is, I yield to it.

There was a clamor on the other side of the door.

Whatever Your will is, I yield to it.

The door opened wide enough for Sahlin to see Naytal standing in front of several soldiers that he assumed were from the north. He diverted his eyes and lowered his head.

Naytal stepped in alone and closed the door. She surveyed her beaten foe with an eye that reflected neither pleasure nor pity. "They didn't tell me that you were injured. I'll have someone look at those wounds."

Sahlin cocked an eyebrow and glared at her in disbelief. "Why would you do a thing like that? You managed to kill everyone else."

"If you are referring to your companions, that was not my doing."

"You had to have given the order."

Naytal sighed. "Sahlin, you misjudge me. "While it's true that I know who your attackers were, I wasn't the driving force behind the act. The men you rode with were considered renegades by the soldiers from the north."

"Renegades?"

"Wanted for war crimes against the northern provinces. From what was told to me, they committed some horrific atrocities . . ."

"Whatever, Naytal," he hissed, dropping his head

back against the wall. "What is it that you want with me? I'm rather anxious to die."

"Why do you say that?"

"Simply because I don't wish to live in a kingdom ruled by you."

Naytal traced the contour of her lip with one of her fingers. "You're still not convinced that I have the qualities of a monarch?"

"A Roman caesar, yes. A kandace of Meroë, never."

She stared at him from the corner of her eye and nodded. "We're alone, Sahlin. Why don't you simply attack me if you feel that way? End it all now."

"Because it wouldn't be the end that I want."

"Very well, how would you like to die?"

Sahlin followed the movements of her mouth as she spoke. Her gestures were slow and fluid and suggested that she was being exceedingly deliberate. "You betray yourself, Naytal. Nothing would please you more than to see me wallow in my own blood. So stop wasting my time and tell me what you want from me."

The comment irritated her enough to bring a brief sneer to her face. "I'd be more than happy to grant your death wish, Sahlin. However, it wouldn't look good."

"You are the kandace. Why would appearance matter to you?"

"I believe that you know why. We discussed this earlier. Within a fifty-mile radius of this city, there are three major armies preparing to do battle. I have sway over one of them, perhaps even over two. However, the third one—which happens to be the coalition that my brother built—is beyond my sphere of influence."

Sahlin shook is head in amusement and utter disgust. "I'm not even going to ask what you did to beguile the commanders of the Geilian regiments. The answer may disgust me."

"Control your imagination, Sahlin. It wasn't even *that* difficult. But, to answer your question of appearance, I have no desire to rule a nation that has been torn to shreds by a major civil conflict due to the mismanagement of my predecessors. See if you can follow me," she said, waiting for his eyes to meet hers before she continued. "If the southern armies attack, the Geilian and northern forces will respond in kind. As a result, the entire governmental structure of Meroë will cease to exist. I speculate that the Roman Empire will move in and establish their own brand of order, effectively bringing to an end over a thousand years of Nubian supremacy."

"Sounds like a problem for a queen," Sahlin said, dropping his head.

Naytal maintained her poise. "No, Sahlin. It's a problem for anyone who loves this nation. It's a problem for anyone whose family labored for centuries to forge it into what it is today. It's a problem for anyone who professes to be loyal and . . ."

"That's enough!"

"For anyone who professes to be loyal and has dedicated his life to the preservation of our great Kushite society."

"I said that's enough! You've manipulated everyone else, but you won't manipulate me. I know what kind of sick individual you are. Your inferior, diseased self-esteem will never provide you with enough security to guide a tribe, much less a kingdom . . ."

"You are wrong! Curse you; you are wrong!"

Sahlin shot to his feet. "No, Naytal! Curse you! Curse you!" The moment that the words left his mouth, the pit of his stomach became heavy and his legs weary. Something deep within him began to weep uncontrollably—so much that he fell back against the wall and slid slowly to the ground. Somehow, he knew he had grieved the Christ.

Naytal bit her lip as she watched him sink to the floor. Everything within her wanted to brandish that dagger hidden beneath her cloak and carve out his heart. She started to leave, fully prepared to give the guards outside the nod to extinguish his putrid life.

As she reached for the handle, she felt compelled to ask one last question. "If I spare your life, will you confirm me as the kandace? Your actions will preserve Meroë and spare the lives of tens of thousands of soldiers who will otherwise die senseless deaths." She tilted her head in his direction. "It is your choice."

"Yes," he gruffed almost inaudibly. "I will speak on your behalf."

A bitter moment of silence soured the stale air in the chamber.

Naytal opened the door and addressed the soldiers outside. "The delegation from the southern armies should be here in several hours. See to it that he is cleaned up and made presentable as a grand vizier should be."

Chapter 34

Tension filled the air in the capital city of Meroë. In accordance with the decree, noblemen and high-ranking officials made their way to the palace during the sixth hour of the day for an announcement from Naytal. Many presumed that the dictum had something to do with the armies converging on the city. Though the forces were not yet in plain sight, the inhabitants knew that they were there and were followed by a black war cloud preparing to consume them all.

The palace throne room was crowded and boisterous. Many of the men present openly scoffed when Naytal entered and took her position upon the throne. They quickly quieted when they saw the hawkish Nubian general and a dozen or so officers who strolled in behind her. Sarcasm soon gave way to anticipation.

Imani pressed her way through the crowd until she came to the edge. T'Sheba was right behind her. "I still don't understand what it is we're doing here," the young woman argued. "You are sick and need to be in bed."

"They said that this assembly was extremely important," Imani answered, choking back the screams of discomfort that her body issued.

"I'm sure that it's nothing to die over."

Imani gave her daughter a corrective glare and then turned to search the sea of faces in the crowd. The adjacent aisle was lined with dignitaries and noblemen from various provinces of the kingdom. There were viziers, peshtes, and even several junior members of the Council of Ministers. She counted herself fortunate that she had been able to call in a few favors to grant T'Sheba and herself access to the throne room for this most important decree. She continued to scan the crowd and eventually came across the ruddy face of young Kalibae. She perused the men in his immediate vicinity, disappointed to see that Sahlin was nowhere to be found. In fact, she couldn't find him anywhere in the throne room.

A herald stood at the entrance of the room and made several introductions.

"What's happening?" T'Sheba asked, trying to get a better view.

"I don't know," said Imani. "He just introduced several soldiers."

A tense silence descended upon the crowd as four massive soldiers approached Naytal's throne and opened a dialogue with her and the half dozen advisers standing at her side.

"Southern armies," Imani heard someone whisper. She shivered and found herself wondering if Sahlin were dead. Finally, she forced herself to listen to Naytal.

"I assure you, General Ta'Pol, that every effort is being

made to find Pot'non and Kota. However, I fear that nomads may have ambushed them."

"I respectfully submit to Her Highness that such a case is most unlikely." The general's words were laced with an unmistakably foreboding tone. Everyone in the hall knew that the general was ready to march his armies through Meroë to get at the armies that had traveled from the north. "I believe that it is more likely that someone else is responsible for their disappearances, perhaps even for the rash of untimely deaths that seem to plague the capital city as of late."

"Yes, the gods have frowned upon us. But I'm certain that their ire will not remain, if we only but repent."

Ta'Pol didn't even wait for Naytal to complete her sentence before he glanced back at his fellow officers. The slight was noticed by every breathing soul in the throne room. Despite the groaning that arose from a few of her advisers, Naytal held her peace.

"Your Highness, my officers and I would like to dispatch patrols to assist with the search," Ta'Pol suggested.

"Your offer is extremely gracious, but it will not be necessary . . ."

"And why not?"

"Because . . . because there was an eyewitness to the entire event." She nodded at one of her guards. "This man was traveling with the generals and can fill you in on the tragic events that befell the party last evening."

A soft rumble rose up from the crowd as a palace guard escorted Sahlin Malae into the throne room from a side entrance. He was dressed in fine linen but was still somewhat disheveled from his ordeal. Imani gasped at the vicious wound running along the backside of his head.

Naytal's smile was courtly. "This is . . ."

"Grand Vizier Malae," Ta'Pol said, saluting Sahlin.

"At ease, General," Sahlin ordered. Ta'Pol nodded as he relaxed slightly.

Naytal's blood boiled when she saw the measure of respect that Ta'Pol granted Sahlin. However, she was determined to conceal her rancor for the moment. "Grand Vizier Malae, will you please tell the representatives from the southern armies what happened last evening?"

Sahlin turned towards the soldiers but knew that Naytal wanted the explanation to be heard by the entire congregation. He glanced their way only briefly. There had to have been a hundred or more spectators in the crowd. He was certain that he knew all of them by name.

"We were riding out to the encampment last night when a band of nomads attacked us. I'm not sure how many there were. The generals fought bravely, but it was dark . . . it was very dark."

"How did you escape, my lord?" Ta'Pol asked.

"My bodyguard . . . he gave his life for me."

Imani's heart sank as she pictured Bakka fulfilling his vow to protect Sahlin to the death. She was certain that he went down swinging his massive sword.

"It's so unfortunate," Naytal chimed. "As if we haven't had enough tragedy as of late. Grand Vizier Malae, why was your group out so far at such an hour?"

Sahlin didn't even look at her. He knew what she wanted. He uttered a silent prayer requesting Jehovah's forgiveness. "It was an emergency trip. Not only were the generals with us, but two members of the Council of Ministers as well—Minister Rogo and Vizier Tibo. I can only assume that they are dead too."

The assembly gasped in astonishment. Ta'Pol's eyes narrowed on Sahlin.

Though he tried, Sahlin couldn't make eye contact with the general. "We were en route to inform you that we had decided to confirm the qar as the kandace of Meroë."

The congregation was abuzz with chatter. Imani's jaw lowered as she tried to reconcile the words that she had just heard Sahlin speak with those that he had uttered the night before.

"The man's finally done something worthy of honor and respect," T'Sheba croaked to her mother.

Sahlin felt ill. Every ounce of pride he once had possessed seeped through the cracks of the polished stone floors beneath his feet. "We were aware of the many stories and half-truths that had funneled out about Qar Naytal. We wanted to reach you with all haste and assure you that she has garnered our unconditional support."

Ta'Pol locked eyes with Sahlin, as if he were searching for some deeper message. "And this is your recommendation, my lord?"

"It is my recommendation, and it is my order."

Ta'Pol peered up at Naytal. "But what of the army advancing from the north?"

"A troop redeployment initiated by King Harmais for reasons known only to him," Naytal reported. Ta'Pol stared at her blankly. "I speculate that he was trying to reposition the troops in response to the civil unrest in the area, no doubt caused by rebels unhappy with their defeat at the hands of Sherakarer some time ago. The commanding officer of the northern army is General Akinidad from Kerma. He should be arriving sometime today. I will arrange for a meeting that will allow all of us the opportunity to sit and discuss the issue."

Ta'Pol started to nod in agreement but quickly raised an eyebrow. "And what of the forces from Gebel Geili?

Sources have informed me that they were preparing for battle."

"As the grand vizier will attest, they have been ordered to stand down." Ta'Pol's attention was drawn to a man clad in the usual black and white attire worn by the Council of Ministers. Sahlin blinked in disbelief as Makal emerged from behind several of Naytal's advisors. "They were simply surprised by the northern army's unexpected movement."

"I see," Ta'Pol said. He glanced at Sahlin who granted him a confirming nod. "I'm looking forward to speaking with General Akinidad and yourself, Kandace Naytal."

Naytal bowed graciously and granted them leave. After they left, she turned towards Makal. "Minister Makal, your assistance has been invaluable."

Sahlin's eyes snapped from the queen to Makal. A shadow of dread fell on him. Without warning, Pot'non's words from the night before rang through his head like a cymbal. *It was his suggestion, but we all agreed to it . . .*

"Well then, I suppose that there is cause for celebration," Naytal started to say. The crowd took Naytal's lead and started to mill about. Makal's voice curtailed their movements.

"Gracious queen, there is one matter that the gods have implored me to bring to your attention."

Sahlin's heart started to race.

"Yes, Minister Makal, please."

"I must first start by stating that the grand vizier is an honorable man from an extremely reputable house. Service to the kingdom by the Malae clan dates back centuries. Therefore, it is with great consternation and humility that I must report the following . . . improprieties to you that have been brought to my attention."

Sahlin wanted to refute him, but his mouth was sealed shut.

"Several months prior to his death, King Harmais installed a new chief treasurer. As you may recall, this was the post that Sahlin Malae held before he was promoted to the esteemed position of grand vizier. Recently, documents suggestive of clandestine accounts housing massive amounts of money came into the new treasurer's possession."

"That hardly sounds like a crime, Minister Makal. I'm certain that we all have some forms of hidden accounts," Naytal said.

"Yes, my queen, but there were certain notations attached to the records of these accounts. Notes that imply that Sahlin and King Harmais were at one time involved in a plot to finance the overthrowing of Kandace Amanitore and King Sherakarer."

The crowd was in an uproar. Naytal waved her hand for silence.

"Minister Makal, a court would demand that you produce proof to support your claims."

"Your Highness, there is ample documentation to back up the shameful charges brought against the grand vizier. Ample documentation and then some."

Naytal shifted upon her throne. "Sahlin, how do you respond to such allegations?"

As Sahlin gazed aimlessly at the queen, everything fell into place. Her baleful dark eyes silently declared that she was already aware of the charges brought against him as well as the fact that the allegations possessed just enough truth to shred what little dignity he had left. He also felt the full sting of betrayal, as Makal's deposition enabled him to reconcile how Naytal's henchmen were able to track them down so easily the night before. At any rate, he refused to provide Naytal with a spectacle.

"The minister's allegations are true. At one point, Harmais and I felt that the kingdom was headed in the wrong direction, and we siphoned away reserves in order to support a change in leadership."

Imani covered her mouth with her hand. Gasps and mumbles rumbled through the crowd.

"What a fool," T'Sheba said, her voice lost in the outcry around her.

Naytal rose to her feet and paced back and forth a few times. "By your own admission, you are guilty?"

Sahlin lowered his head, partly in shame and partly in defiance.

Naytal rolled her eyes, goading him into a confrontation. "My mother loved you like a son, Sahlin. And this is how you were going to repay her. You've committed treason against her memory and against our kingdom."

In the congregation, T'Sheba saw Imani's eyes start to well up with tears.

"What do you have to say for yourself?" Naytal demanded.

"I've committed no form of treason against the kingdom . . ."

"But there is proof that you had collaborated with Harmais to conceive a war against Sherakarer and my mother."

"Yes, that much is true, but . . ."

"But what?"

"I was simply following orders." The revelation jolted another round of astonished groans from the assembly. "Several years ago, Paqar Harmais ordered me to begin stashing money away for his own purposes. We were friends, and I disagreed with him at the time. However, he ordered me to do it, and I foolishly obeyed him. Make no mistake about it, Your Highness. I love Meroë, and I am loyal to her. And those funds . . . I believe that you would agree with me when I say they were eventually used for constructive purposes."

Naytal's right eye twitched at the statement. No one but Sahlin noticed it.

After holding her words for a long moment, she drew a deep breath to speak. "You say that you are loyal to Meroë? Then prove it."

Sahlin knew exactly what she was demanding that he do. It was the only thing left that he could do—the only thing left that she could rip from his possession. However, his knees were locked in position.

"Prove your loyalty and convince us that you are worthy of the house you represent."

Although Sahlin was prepared to die right there, he felt a pair of invisible hands settle upon his shoulders and gently press him down. Within seconds, he lowered his head and knelt before Naytal.

Tears flowed freely down Imani's cheeks as Naytal towered over Sahlin.

"The gods have dealt with Harmais for his treachery," Naytal declared. "It falls to me to deal with you for your part in it. It is clear that you have served Meroë with all of your heart. However, it is also clear that your service has not been with the singular devotion that accompanied the service furnished by your fathers. For this reason, I must punish you."

A hush blanketed the assembly of nobles and officials.

"For the sake of your years of hard work for the kingdom, your life will be spared. However, because of the guile that has covered your heart and the poison that has invaded your veins, I hereby strip away your title as grand vizier. Furthermore, because of your actions, let the name of Malae be spoken of with contempt. I strip from you the honor that was established by the men who came before you. This is the sentence that you must bear for the rest of your life."

The same pair of invisible hands that helped Sahlin to his knees brought him to his feet. He didn't even bother to look at Naytal. Instead, he turned to face his worst nightmare. Before he did, Naytal's voice snatched him back.

"However, we are not without mercy. I seem to recall that you are one who subscribes to the Jewish faith. Perhaps that is the black honey which has placed a bitter taste in your mouth. The gods have blessed you with an incredible number of gifts, Sahlin. I wish to offer you a chance to redeem yourself in their eyes.

"As part of your sentence, I'm sending you to Napata for rehabilitation. There, you will work in the Temple of Isis as a scribe. Hopefully, in time, the gods will have their way with you and set you on the right path . . . the path that leads to life."

Two palace guards hurried to Sahlin's side and escorted him down the center aisle. Stunned beyond feeling, Sahlin was bombarded with stares of disbelief, anger, shame, and confusion. On one side, he saw Kalibae, who promptly averted his eyes. On the other side, he saw Imani and T'Sheba, his daughter. The young woman sneered at him and rolled her eyes. Several junior council members and viziers turned their backs on him.

As they departed the throne room, Sahlin emitted a vexed sigh as he transferred from one nightmare to another.

Chapter 35

The late afternoon sun burned softly through a thin patch of haze that drifted over the city of Meroë. Imani was grateful to the gods for the reprieve from the scorching heat wave that had baked the city for the past several days.

She waited next to the carriage that would take her on the first leg of her voyage back to Alondia for good. Her fragile feelings were mixed as she surveyed the city one more time. Though she was frightened about her uncertain future, part of her was thankful that she would never see the gleaming temples and proud obelisks again. Like the new queen of Meroë, the temples were beautiful on the outside but were rancid and corrupt within. Imani found solace in the thought that someday soon her eyes would close forever and deny her the anguish of watching Naytal transform the kingdom into a mirror image of herself.

T'Sheba approached the carriage with a large colorful

purse overstuffed with soft goods. "Here are a few things that I picked up for you at the bazaar. I know you said that you didn't want anything, but I just had to buy them for you."

Imani sighed and shook her head. "Thank you."

"Are you sure that you don't want to stay? Alondia is so far away. And the physicians there . . ."

"Are no better than the ones who are here. I was going to ask you a similar question. I really wish that you would come back with me."

"Yes, I know, but . . . this is Meroë. Everything is here. My friends are here. We're popular among the affluent of the city, and Kandace Naytal is absolutely brilliant."

Imani grunted, looking away.

"I can't believe that you find fault with her. I think that she is going to be a fabulous ruler—perhaps even one of the greatest."

Imani grimaced as she cleared her throat. "I've known Naytal for many years, almost since childhood. She may be a very beautiful and dazzling person, but her heart is as cold as the river and as hard as a diamond."

"If those are the qualities that a strong Nubian woman must have, then I want to be just like her."

Imani stood disheartened. She watched her daughter back-pedal into a pit that would surely one day consume her mind, body, and soul.

T'Sheba looked away from her mother. "And that general from the north . . . Akinidad . . . he's so strong and gorgeous. I'm sure they'll get married soon. They look like such a perfect couple."

Imani shook her head. "I don't know about that. Naytal is probably absorbed with the fact that her son is now in the position to become the next king. I can't really see a happy union between the two of them."

"Mother, at least give them a blessing before you give them a curse."

After realizing how grim she probably looked, Imani cracked a slight smile and then gave her daughter a kiss and an extended hug good-bye. Secretly, she regretted that she had hidden the severity of her condition from T'Sheba. Had the young woman known that this would be the last time she would see her mother in this world, she perhaps would have made the journey to Alondia. However, Imani did not want to manipulate her into making a decision. She decided this was the best way for both of them to let go. Only one thing burned on her mind.

"T'Sheba, if you ever get a chance, go and see him."

"Mother, I've told you. I have no interest in speaking with him. Besides, outside of the coronation, we'll rarely go to Napata."

"I know, my love, but he is your father, and he now knows it. I always thought that perhaps the two of you could . . ."

"No," T'Sheba asserted, her eyes narrowing. "He made his choice. Now I'm making mine. Isis herself will have to change my heart about that man."

The barrier of bitterness painfully rebuffed Imani. It was clear to her that she would never live to see if the rift between T'Sheba and Sahlin would ever be bridged.

She kissed T'Sheba once more on the cheek and got into the carriage. She signaled the driver to go. She turned to T'Sheba and coerced a smile. "I love you, my dear," she said as the carriage pulled away.

"I love you too, Mother."

※　　※　　※

"We've lost everything! You've dishonored our family name!" Kassa scolded, slapping Sahlin vehemently across the face. "How could you have been so reckless? How could you have been so foolish? You've lost everything!"

Kassa shut her eyes. She could not bear to see the tapestries and portraits on the walls that would very shortly end up in the possession of complete strangers. Her heart bled over the knowledge that the decree from the queen had snatched away the very home which had been in their family for centuries.

Worse yet, she still had no solid reason for the cursed turn of events that had rendered her homeless. She glared at Sahlin who stood in the midst of the house stunned. "I don't understand you," she hissed, her eyes burning with hot tears of anguish.

A half dozen servants scurried about loading a carriage with the few personal effects that an officer of Naytal's royal court allowed them to take. After the eviction, the servants would be taken away and auctioned off.

"I'm sorry, Kassa."

"Sorry? What happened, Sahlin? What did you do to the queen? What did you do to the kingdom?"

"I saved the kingdom," he muttered in a low voice.

"You what?" Kassa demanded, far too angry to listen to any excuse that he generated. She turned away and studied the exquisite marble statues that their great-grandfather had imported from Egypt long before either one of them had been born. "What am I going to do?"

Sahlin's heart ached. He wanted to reach out and embrace his sister, but he knew her well enough to know that she wanted no such contact with him. Never did he imagine that the queen would exercise her ill will towards him against his flesh and blood. For once, he found himself grateful that he had no other close relatives for fear that they would incur Naytal's inexplicable hatred.

"How will I live?" Kassa moaned, tears flowing.

After fishing for a document, Sahlin drew close to her. "Kassa, take this," he said softly as he slipped the folded parchment into her hand. He placed his body in between her and the doorway to block the view of the palace guard who was supervising the eviction. "Follow these instructions. They weren't able to take everything."

She accepted the parchment and squinted curiously at her brother as if he were a rambling fool. Being the masterful accountant that he was, she was certain he had been able to spare a good portion of the family fortune. She shook her head despondently and started to move away.

"Where will you go?" Sahlin asked.

"Wad Medani. It's peaceful there."

Sahlin nodded dejectedly. Wad Medani was a small town in the southernmost tip of the Isle of Meroë. The area was rural, and the political structure faint. It was the perfect place to live a quiet, uneventful life. "If anyone else asks where you are going, tell them that you are relocating to Axum."

"Axum?" Kassa glared at him in disbelief. Why he would want people to believe that she was moving to Meroë's southern neighbor was beyond her. For the most part, she didn't care what others thought. Like him, all of her life she clung to the proud family heritage that had been passed down from generation to generation. Now, it had come to an abrupt and cryptic halt.

Somehow knowing her thoughts, Sahlin called to her

as she turned to leave the mansion. "Kassa, honor comes from within. They may be able to strip that which is on the outside, but never . . . never let them take what has been deposited in here." He pointed to the center of his chest.

The bitter taste of failure and shame spread through Sahlin's mouth as he made his way up to his study. He wept as he imagined what might become of the scores of scrolls and works of literature that he would not be able to take with him to Napata. He could almost hear the ghosts of his father and grandfather raging against the hideous injustice perpetrated against his family.

In the background, a servant feverishly raced down the hallway from his bed chamber with the items that he specified to be loaded. Another one stood by his side and silently awaited direction. Sahlin pointed out several sentimental ornaments for him to place in a duffel bag.

While the young man sadly stripped the shelves of the precious items, Sahlin mulled over a collection of parchments far more valuable to him than anything else in the house. He thumbed through his grandfather's journal and whispered an apology. Inwardly, he wanted nothing more in his life than to make his father and grandfather proud and to elevate the extraordinary tradition that had been bequeathed to him. The emptiness of his soul and the dryness of his spirit bemoaned his failure.

Suddenly, a lesson that his father once taught him surfaced in his mind.

There are no failures in life, only results from the choices that you make.

Sahlin sneered begrudgingly at one of the foundational lessons upon which he had built his life. Back in Nuri, Dikembul once told him that he had to choose which type of vessel he would be. He had made the honorable choice given the situation. However, the backlash of that decision drenched him with nothing but dishonor from a kingdom that he once served with all of his heart.

"Lord God, forgive me," he whispered. The only bright spot that even remotely glimmered near him was the agreeable fact that he would be closer to Dikembul and his daughter. In them, he found kindred spirits that were unassuming and pure. Just being around them made him feel likewise.

He neatly rolled up the scrolls that contained the works of the Hebrew prophets. There was little chance that the chief priests in Napata would allow him to bring the sacred writings near the temple. He feared that his reduction in status would surely strip away that cushion from the tyrannical influence that priests wielded against the common people.

"Lord Sahlin," a servant called. He looked up and saw the young man who had been loading personal items from his bedroom. "My lord, there is someone here who wishes to speak with you."

Sahlin placed the last of the scrolls into a dark leather carrying case and sealed it with a strap. "Who is it?"

"A man from the city, my lord. His name is . . ."

"If he's from the city, then he has to know that I don't have the time to talk casually." Sahlin wanted to give in to the frustrated temper that ate away at his soul.

"I'm sorry, my lord. I'll send him away . . ."

"No," Sahlin said, composing himself. "I'll go and speak with him myself. Please see to it that these items are brought down and loaded. And . . . thank you for everything." Knowing that he had most likely given the young man his last order, Sahlin offered him a courteous nod.

Sahlin strolled through the hallway and down the stairs one last time. With each step, he promised himself that he would never again think of the mansion in which he grew up. He relegated every attribute of the house to the scrap heap of lost dreams and forgotten hopes.

He reached the bottom of the stairs and marched into the living room. The person who awaited him was actually a very young man. "If you have any business here, you will have to get it over with very quickly."

The young man followed the sound of Sahlin's voice until they made eye contact. "Lord Sahlin Malae?"

"Yes, young man. What is your business here? As you can see, I'm in the process of vacating this house."

Slightly confused, the youth looked around. "You're leaving?"

"Yes, what does it look like?" Sahlin shook his head in annoyance. "I thought that the entire region would have known about it by now. My servant said that you were from the city. Who sent you?"

The young man stared blankly at Sahlin for a moment and then responded. "Oh . . . I'm not from Meroë. I mean, I was just there, but I'm not from there."

With his patience all but exhausted, Sahlin folded his arms and walked over to the young man. "Your dialect is odd. What province are you from?"

Again, a strange pause preceded the young man's response. "I . . . I think you're asking me what part of the country I am from. I grew up in Samaria."

Sahlin's eyes fixed on his light skin tone. "Well, now. Is this better?" Sahlin asked in Greek.

"Much better, sir. I did my best to learn the language, but I guess I didn't account for the variation between the northern and southern dialects and . . ."

"Yes, yes. Who are you?"

"My name is Aron, my lord, and . . ."

"Very well, Aron. You appear to be a long way from home. What do you want with me?"

Aron cleared his throat nervously. He had practiced this particular moment in his mind hundreds of times. However, part of him never believed that he would actually come face-to-face with the Ethiopian chamberlain. "I don't even know if you will be able to recall this man, but I was sent by Philip . . . and the elders of the church."

"Church? You must be mistaken. I don't know anyone named Phil . . . lip . . ." Sahlin drew a breath but couldn't exhale.

Aron tried to hide the expression of disappointment that overran his handsome young face. "I suppose it would have been close to two years ago that the two of you met on the desert road in Gaza. That is, of course, if you are the correct Sahlin Malae. I believe that you told him you were a court official of the kandace of Meroë. Perhaps I'm mistaken. For all I know, there could be a hundred Sahlin Malaes in the city of Meroë alone." He leaned against a table and lowered his head.

Back in Jerusalem, at least twenty men in a square block could possess several variations of the same name. Aron shuddered at the possibility of that scenario duplicating itself before him. After a long moment passed, he started to embrace the ugly reality that unfolded before him. "I'm sorry, sir. You must be the wrong person."

"No, wait," Sahlin called. "Please wait. You said that this Philip sent you? Why?"

"He said that he had a dream." Aron felt silly divulging the contents of another man's vision, but he pressed on. "He said that God told him to send someone to contact the

Ethiopian chamberlain. To tell him that he wasn't alone. To tell him that there are people praying for him."

Sahlin wanted to weep, but he was far too drained emotionally. He placed his hand upon Aron's shoulder and squeezed it to make sure that the young man was real. "I remember Philip. Like it was yesterday, I remember him. He told me about Jesus, the Christ. And, he baptized me in a lake . . . a lake in the desert."

Aron's face was gripped with astonishment. He opened his mouth to offer praise unto the Lord but was cut off.

"Malae! It's time to move now!" The head guard was right behind them. "Your servants have finished packing the carriage. Out of the house, now!"

Aron frowned as the hulking guard stormed outside. "What's happening?"

"God brought you at a very formidable time. I'm being forced to leave the city."

"Forced? But why?"

Sahlin grinned at the young man's innocent demeanor. "There isn't much time to talk here. I have a very long journey ahead of me." He tried to transfer the deeper meaning of his statement to the young black Samaritan.

"God has already brought me a long way. I'd be honored to accompany you . . . with your permission."

"The honor would be mine," Sahlin said, already smiling more than he had in the last week.

The two walked out of the mansion under the watchful eyes of the guards.

"Where are your things?" Sahlin asked.

"This is all that I have," Aron replied, gesturing at the sizable duffel bag strapped to his back. Sahlin relieved him of the load and planted it among the other items in the carriage.

Sahlin looked the young man in the face as they entered the carriage. Though he appeared uncertain and perplexed, Aron's countenance radiated a hope and joy that energized Sahlin's beleaguered spirit. "Actually, you arrived just in time. God's wisdom knows no bounds."

The driver mounted the top of the carriage and pulled on the reins. The vehicles started to pull away but then stopped abruptly. Sahlin poked his head out to investigate the commotion brewing off to the side. "I must speak with the grand vizier," he heard a familiar voice demand.

"Makal is now the grand vizier," the guard replied angrily. "Sahlin Malae is being sent to Napata. He is nothing now."

"I must speak with him," the voice pressed, pushing his way past the guard who obviously seemed powerless to stop him.

Just as Sahlin had imagined, the man who ignored a direct order from the royal guards had to be brazenly bold. For the second time in a few minutes, he found a broad smile sweep across his face.

"Bakka!"

"I apologize for losing track of you, my lord," the strapping warrior said, bowing his head deeply.

"Thank God you're alive, my old friend." Sahlin was overjoyed to see him, but the reality of the current situation eclipsed his jubilant feelings. "I'm afraid that much has changed since the last time we saw each other. I've been stripped of everything. I have no home, no name, and no honor."

Bakka sat erect on his dark brown horse, his eyes as sharp as iron spears. "A man chooses whether or not to have honor, my lord. No matter what your choice is, where you go, I will go."

Sahlin's heart fluttered as the old warrior kept pace with the carriage when it started to travel down the road. He was tempted to look back at the mansion once more but somehow found the power to resist. His path was set by an invisible yet benevolent force that seemed to orchestrate his every move despite what his flesh yearned for. Weary of denying the hand of the Lord, he leaned back and begged God to forge his thoughts and desires.

As he did, an ancient Hebrew Scripture echoed in his heart and brought with it a wave of peace and hope that purged the maniacal dark talons that had grappled with his soul for so long.

Let the words of my mouth and the meditation of my heart be acceptable in Your sight, O Lord, my rock and my Redeemer.

Sahlin Malae had never felt so at ease, so at peace, and so redeemed.

Glossary

Alondia—Southeastern province of the kingdom of Meroë

Amun—(Amen, Amon-Ra)—the chief of all gods in the Nubian religion believed to be the god of creation, the father of all the gods, the god of the sun, of fertility, and of the Nile Inundation (flooding)

Apedemack—Nubian deity of warfare resembling a man with the head of a lion and often depicted holding a bow or spear

Apis—Egyptian deity resembling a bull with a solar disk between its horns

Baiyuda—Southwestern province of the kingdom of Meroë

Cataract—one of six great waterfalls along the Nile that often served as landmarks and boundaries

Dufufa—Large, complex structures that served as the administrative and religious centers for Nubian cities and settlements; also often fortified and used as military outposts

Ephod—Decorative linen robe worn by priests and other high-ranking temple officials

Falasha—Term used to describe African Jews settled throughout Nubia and Ethiopia

Gebel—Nubian term used to describe a mountain or large land mass

Gladius—A short sword used by Roman legionnaires

Horus—Egyptian royal god represented by a falcon; denoted as the sky god, he was regarded as the son of Isis and considered the ruler of the day

Isis—Egyptian/Kushite deity regarded as queen of all gods, goddesses, and women

Isle of Meroë—Term used to describe to the mass of fertile land surrounded by the Blue Nile, the Nile, and the Atbarah rivers; served as Meroë's central province

Kandace—Official title for the queen of Meroë

Kerma—Western province of the kingdom of Meroë

Kizra—A flat tortilla-like bread made by the Nubians

Kush—Terminology used in antiquity to describe the lands south of Egypt and the Great Desert; people originating from those lands were termed *Kushites*

Masjid—a house of worship for the Falasha Jews similar in structure and order of a synagogue in traditional Judaism

Makoria—Northeastern province of Meroë

Nobatia—Northernmost province of Meroë which borders Roman Egypt

Nubia—"Land of Gold"; the term used to describe the land south of Egypt

Obelisk—Tall, decorative monuments generally carved out of stone

Osiris—Egyptian deity regarded as the dead king who watches over the netherworld and serves as the symbol of eternal life

Qar—Feminine version of the term *paqar;* the title given to a princess of the royal court

Qeren—Official title for the king of Meroë

Paqar—Administrative title given to a prominent court official, usually a royal prince; paqars were generally placed over provinces

Pelmes-adab—General of the land; administrator in a Nubian province who generally reported to the peshte and who was responsible for ensuring that the trade routes were secure

Pelmes-ate—General of the water; title of the administrative officer who generally reported to the peshte and who was responsible for conducting commerce and communications along the Nile River

Peshte—Leading officer in charge of administration who usually reported to the vizier of the city/region

Sacarri—Rogue bands of robbers that frequented the desert regions of Judea

Sanhedrin—the highest ruling body among the Jews in ancient time; the council was comprised of leading priests and distinguished aristocrats and met in Jerusalem

Sheol—The abode of the dead, the underworld where departed souls are believed to dwell

Tej—A form of honey wine fermented in the northern provinces in the kingdom of Ethiopia

Vizier—Official title given to magistrates and administrators in the kingdom of Meroë; the vizier often ruled as the governor over a province or state

Wadis—Dry path of a river; wadis were often formed during the dry seasons and channeled water to the Nile during the wet seasons

SINCE 1894, Moody Publishers has been dedicated to equip and motivate people to advance the cause of Christ by publishing evangelical Christian literature and other media for all ages around the world. Because we are a ministry of the Moody Bible Institute of Chicago, a portion of the proceeds from the sale of this book go to train the next generation of Christian leaders.

If we may serve you in any way in your spiritual journey toward understanding Christ and the Christian life, please contact us at www.moodypublishers.com.

"All Scripture is God-breathed and is useful for teaching, rebuking, correcting and training in righteousness, so that the man of God may be thoroughly equipped for every good work."
—2 TIMOTHY 3:16, 17

MOODY
PUBLISHERS

THE NAME YOU CAN TRUST®

More Than a Slave

The Life of Katherine Ferguson

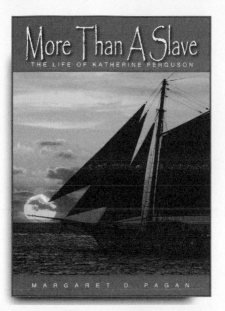

ISBN: 0-8024-3481-9

In 1772, freedom was little more than a pie-in-the-sky dream for first-generation slave Sowei, kidnapped from her Mende village and sold into slavery. For her daughter Hannah Williams, freedom was worth the risk of stowing away in the belly of a trading vessel . . . penniless, hungry, and ready to deliver her first child, Katherine.

But the struggle for freedom in the Revolutionary War era wouldn't come easily—or without great price. Only after nearly two decades of servitude in New York did Katherine Ferguson (born during that clandestine voyage), earn the privilege of living free—at least free by society's standards.

This is the fictionalized account of Katherine's courage, dedication, faith and vision, told by African American history scholar Margaret Pagan.

MOODY
PUBLISHERS

THE NAME YOU CAN TRUST.

1-800-678-6928 www.MoodyPublishers.com

VESSEL OF HONOR TEAM

ACQUIRING EDITOR:
Cynthia Ballenger

COPY EDITOR:
Diane Masters

BACK COVER COPY:
Lisa Ann Cockrel

COVER DESIGN:
Lydell Jackson

INTERIOR DESIGN:
Ragont Design

PRINTING AND BINDING:
Dickinson Press Inc.

The typeface for the text of this book is
Berkeley